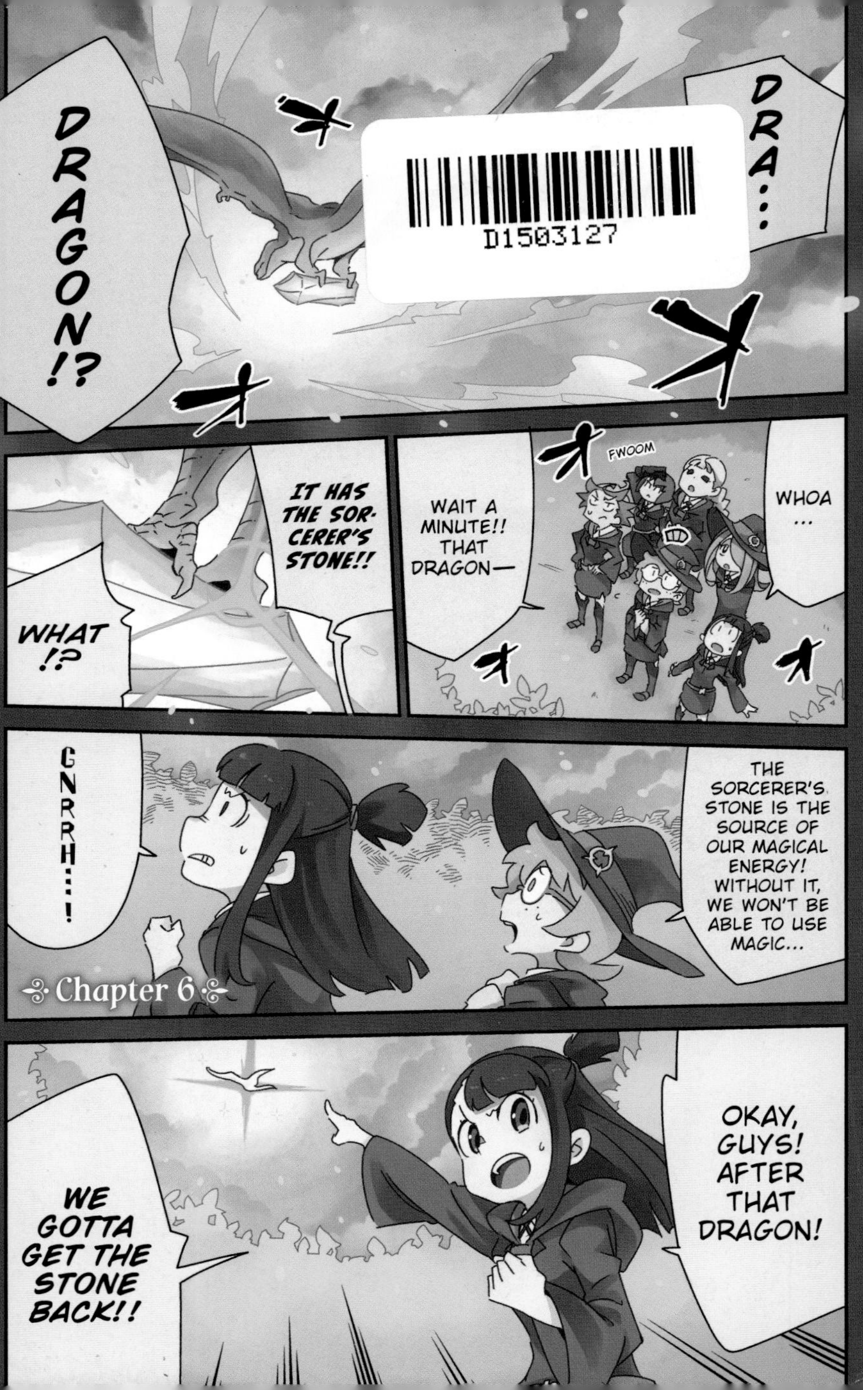
DRA...
DRAGON!?
WHOA ...
FWOOM
WAIT A MINUTE!! THAT DRAGON—
IT HAS THE SOR-CERER'S STONE!!
WHAT!?
THE SORCERER'S STONE IS THE SOURCE OF OUR MAGICAL ENERGY! WITHOUT IT, WE WON'T BE ABLE TO USE MAGIC...
GNRRH...!
Chapter 6
OKAY, GUYS! AFTER THAT DRAGON!
WE GOTTA GET THE STONE BACK!!

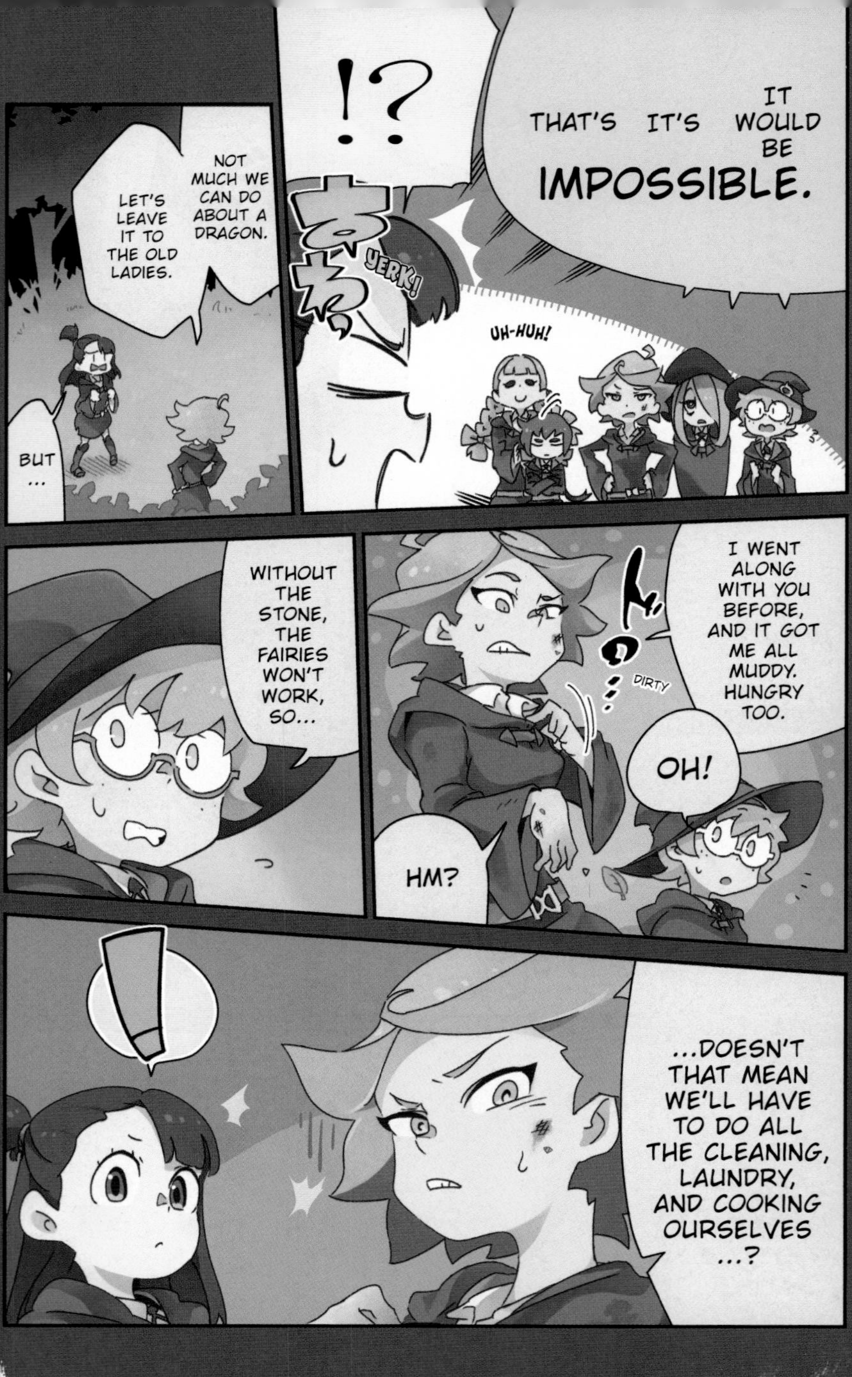
THAT'S IT'S IT WOULD BE IMPOSSIBLE.
!?
YERK!
UH-HUH!
NOT MUCH WE CAN DO ABOUT A DRAGON.
LET'S LEAVE IT TO THE OLD LADIES.
BUT...
I WENT ALONG WITH YOU BEFORE, AND IT GOT ME ALL MUDDY. HUNGRY TOO.
DIRTY
OH!
HM?
WITHOUT THE STONE, THE FAIRIES WON'T WORK, SO...
...DOESN'T THAT MEAN WE'LL HAVE TO DO ALL THE CLEANING, LAUNDRY, AND COOKING OURSELVES...?
!

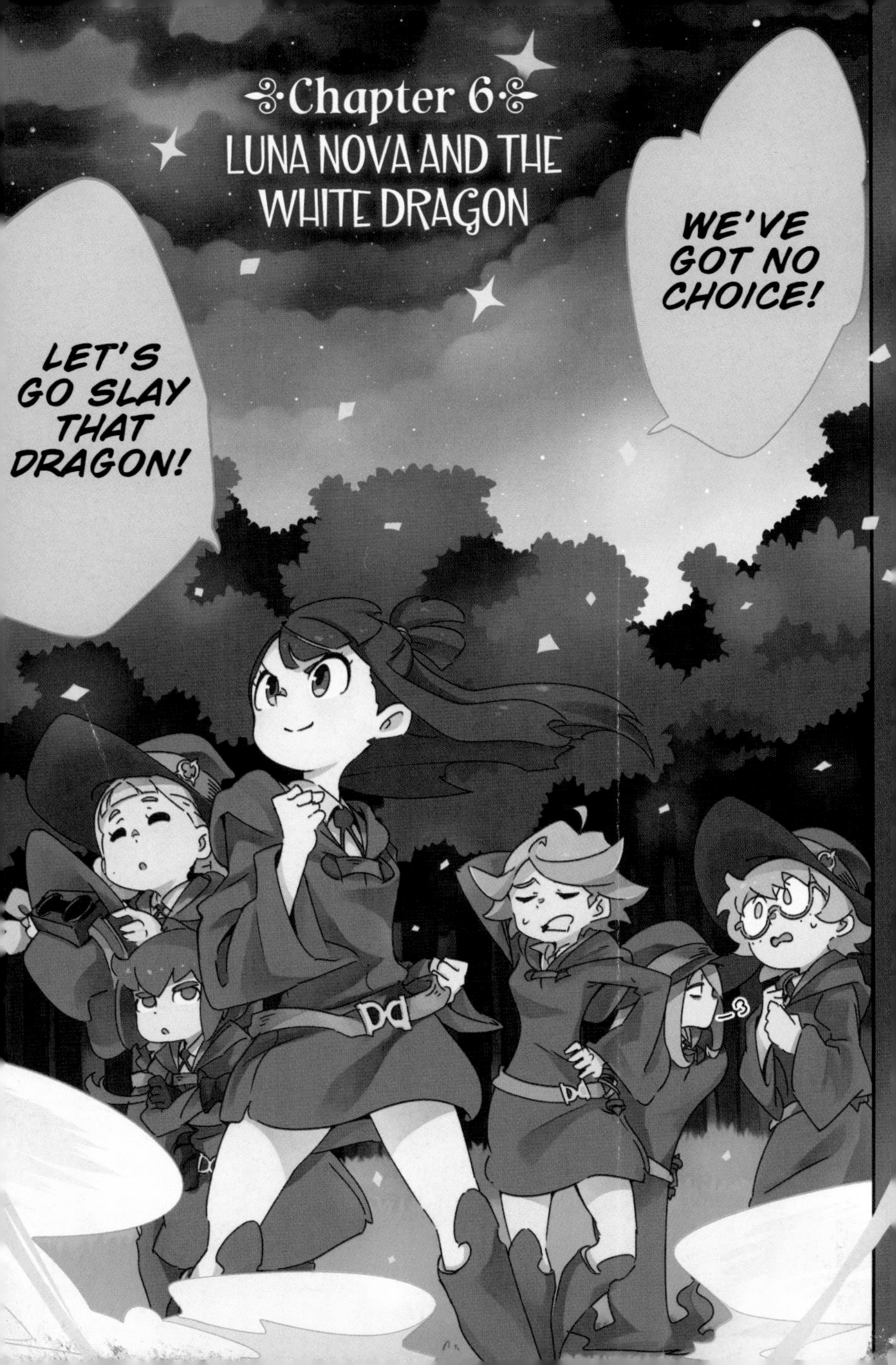
Chapter 6
LUNA NOVA AND THE WHITE DRAGON
WE'VE GOT NO CHOICE!
LET'S GO SLAY THAT DRAGON!

C o n t e n t s

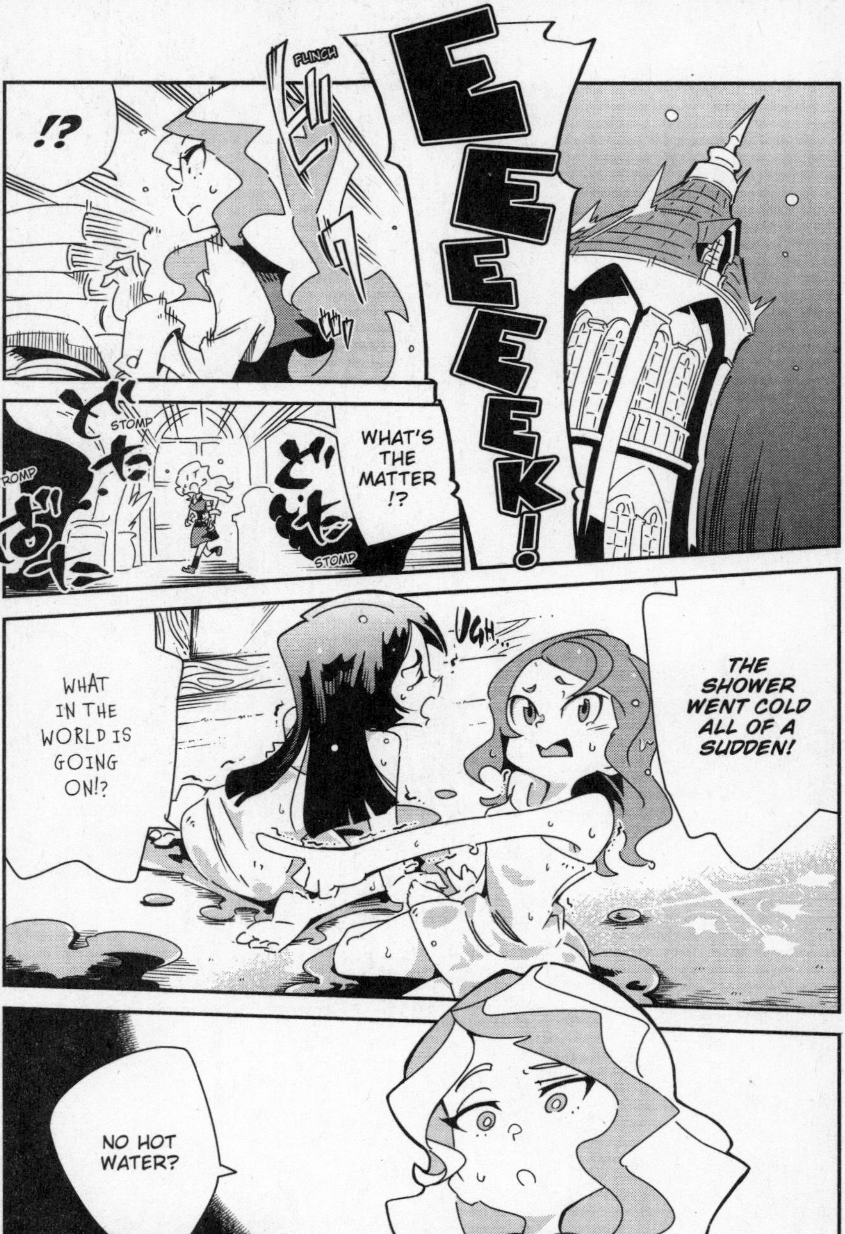
EEEEEEK!
FLINCH
!?
WHAT'S THE MATTER !?
STOMP
STOMP
TROMP
THE SHOWER WENT COLD ALL OF A SUDDEN!
UGH...
WHAT IN THE WORLD IS GOING ON!?
NO HOT WATER?

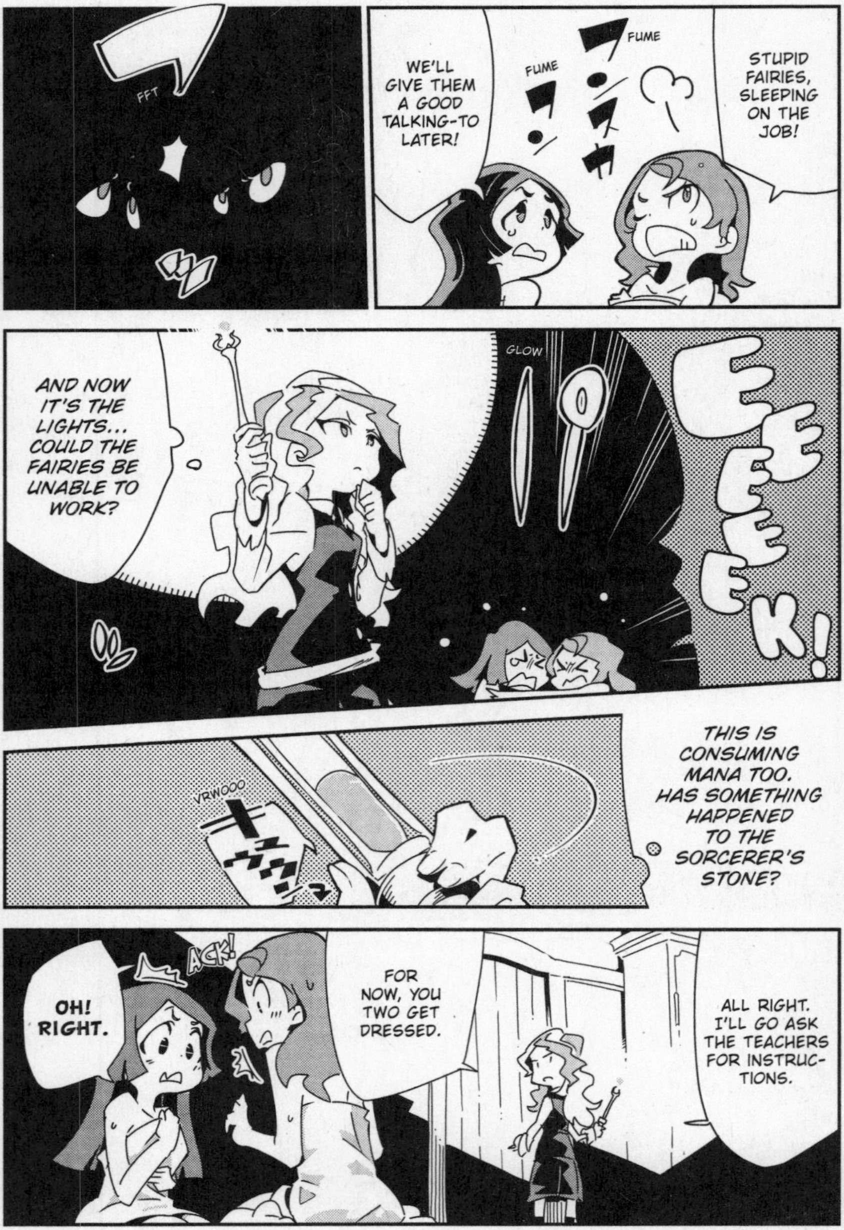
STUPID FAIRIES, SLEEPING ON THE JOB!
FUME
FUME
WE'LL GIVE THEM A GOOD TALKING-TO LATER!
FFT
EEEEEK!
GLOW
AND NOW IT'S THE LIGHTS... COULD THE FAIRIES BE UNABLE TO WORK?
THIS IS CONSUMING MANA TOO. HAS SOMETHING HAPPENED TO THE SORCERER'S STONE?
VRWOOO
ALL RIGHT. I'LL GO ASK THE TEACHERS FOR INSTRUCTIONS.
FOR NOW, YOU TWO GET DRESSED.
ACK!
OH! RIGHT.

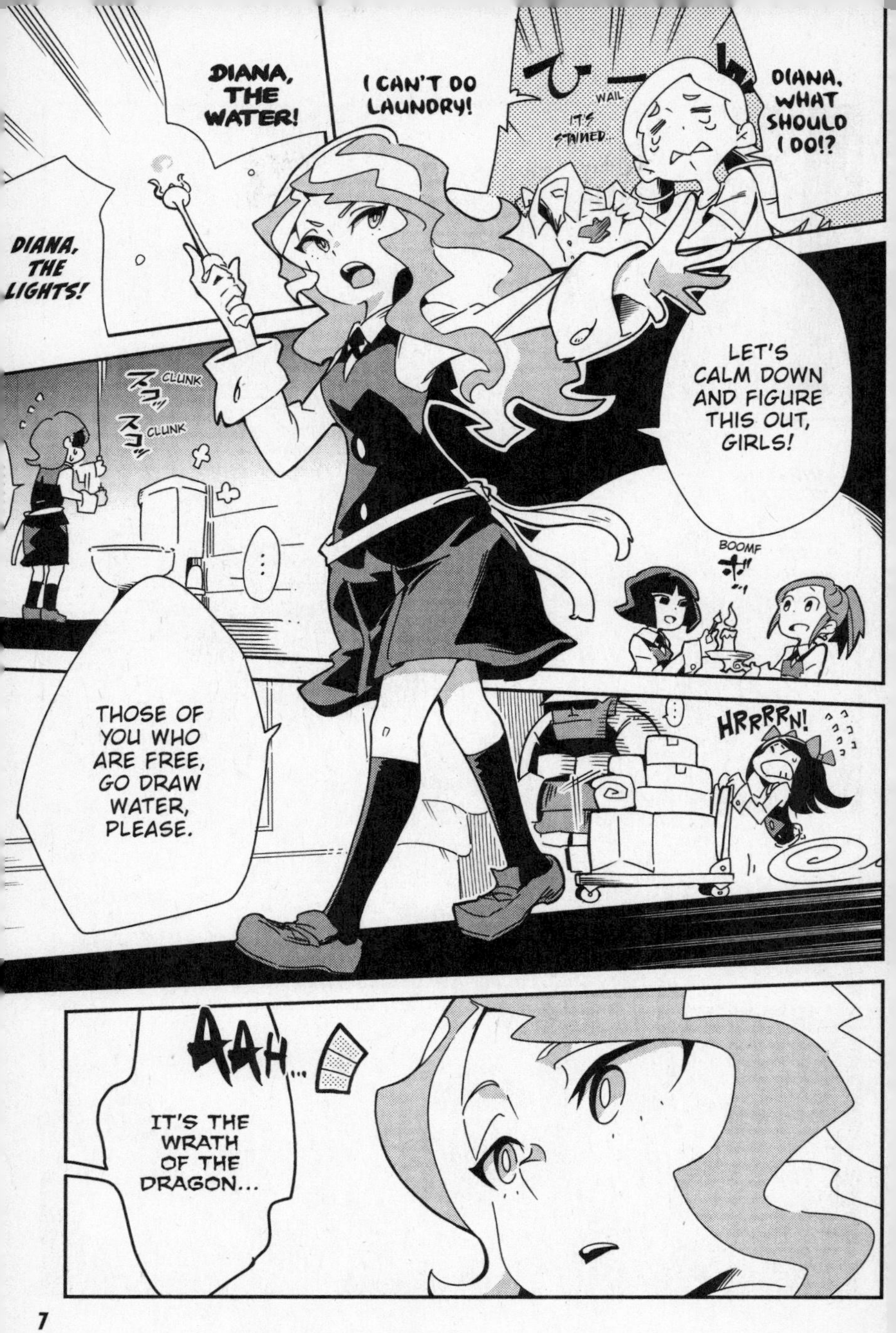
DIANA, WHAT SHOULD I DO!?
WAIL
IT'S STAINED...
I CAN'T DO LAUNDRY!
DIANA, THE WATER!
DIANA, THE LIGHTS!
LET'S CALM DOWN AND FIGURE THIS OUT, GIRLS!
BOOMF
CLUNK
CLUNK
...
HRRRRN!
...
THOSE OF YOU WHO ARE FREE, GO DRAW WATER, PLEASE.
AAH...
IT'S THE WRATH OF THE DRAGON...

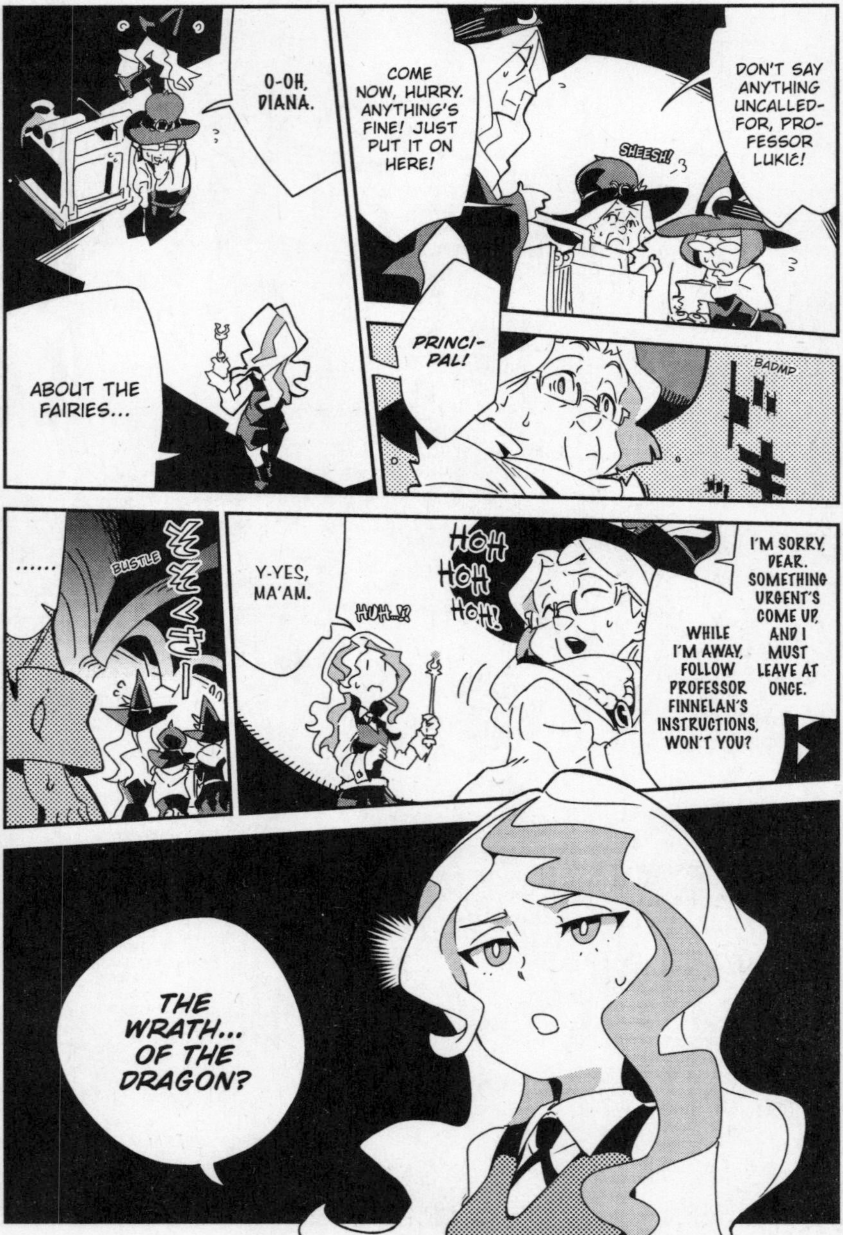
DON'T SAY ANYTHING UNCALLED-FOR, PROFESSOR LUKIĆ!
SHEESH!
COME NOW, HURRY. ANYTHING'S FINE! JUST PUT IT ON HERE!
PRINCIPAL!
BADMP
O-OH, DIANA.
ABOUT THE FAIRIES...
I'M SORRY, DEAR. SOMETHING URGENT'S COME UP, AND I MUST LEAVE AT ONCE.
WHILE I'M AWAY, FOLLOW PROFESSOR FINNELAN'S INSTRUCTIONS, WON'T YOU?
HOH HOH HOH!
Y-YES, MA'AM.
HUH...!?
......
BUSTLE
そそくさー
THE WRATH... OF THE DRAGON?

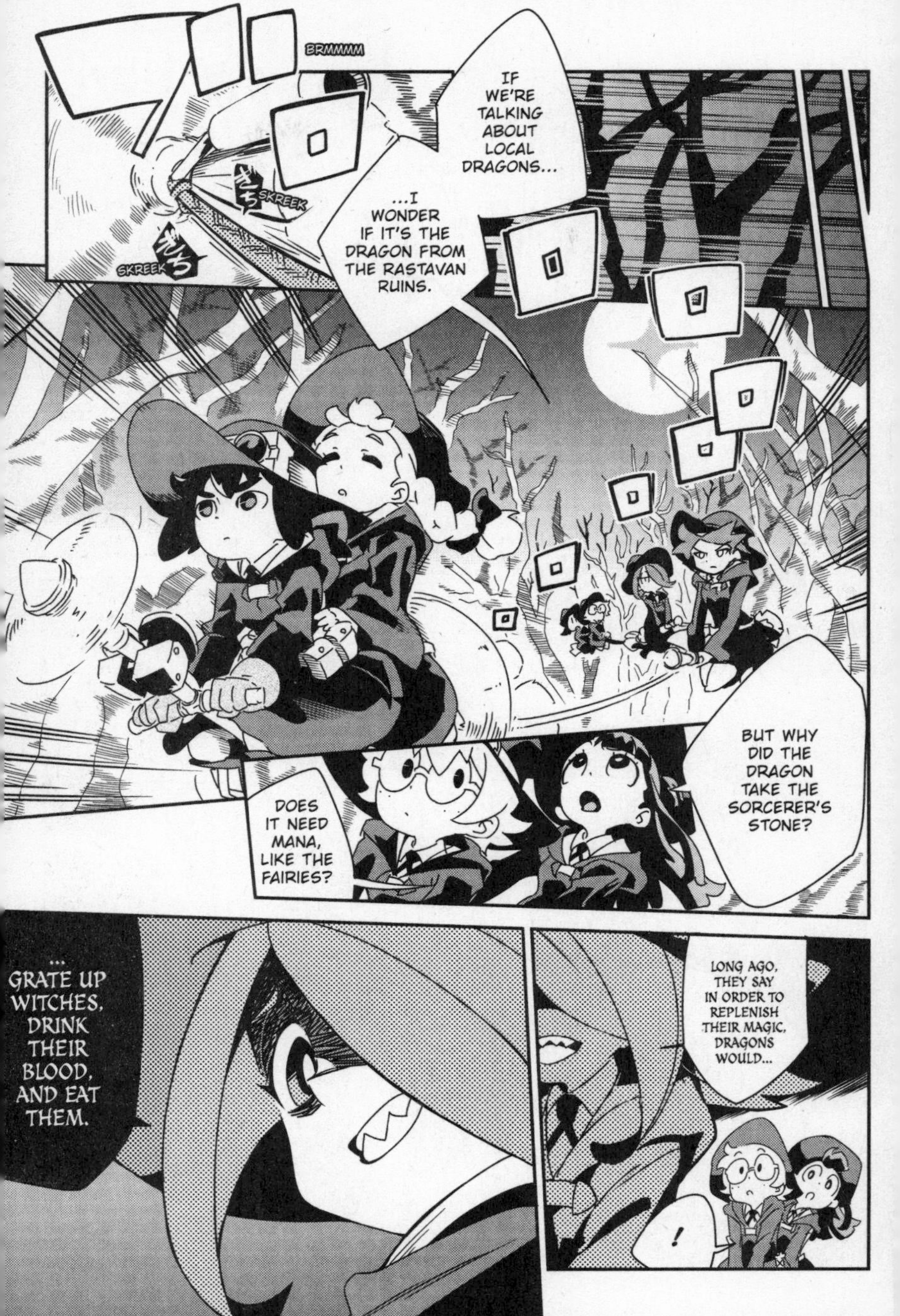
BRMMMM
IF WE'RE TALKING ABOUT LOCAL DRAGONS...
...I WONDER IF IT'S THE DRAGON FROM THE RASTAVAN RUINS.
SKREEK
SKREEK
BUT WHY DID THE DRAGON TAKE THE SORCERER'S STONE?
DOES IT NEED MANA, LIKE THE FAIRIES?
LONG AGO, THEY SAY IN ORDER TO REPLENISH THEIR MAGIC, DRAGONS WOULD...
!
... GRATE UP WITCHES, DRINK THEIR BLOOD, AND EAT THEM.

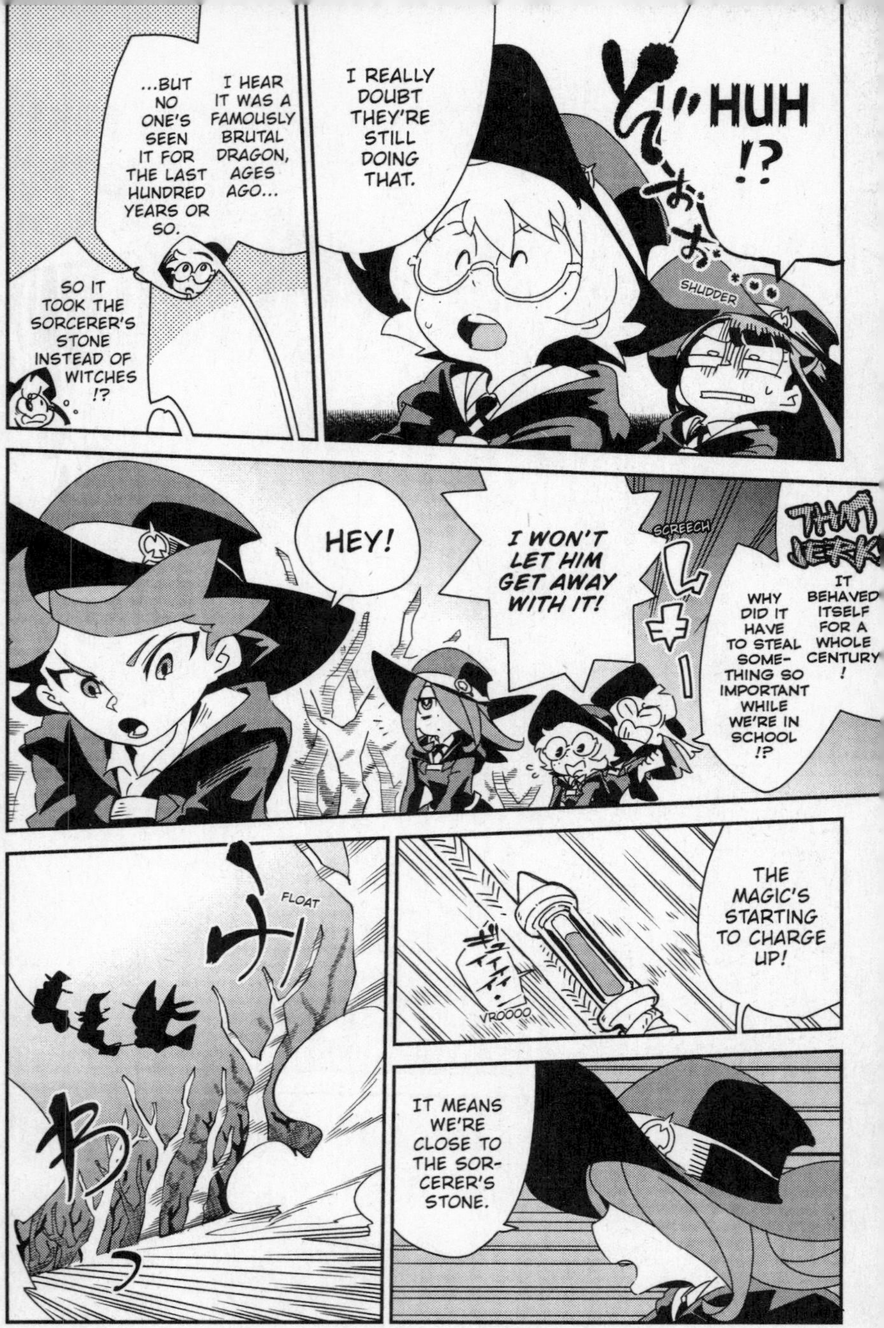
HUH!?
SHUDDER
I REALLY DOUBT THEY'RE STILL DOING THAT.
I HEAR IT WAS A FAMOUSLY BRUTAL DRAGON, AGES AGO...
...BUT NO ONE'S SEEN IT FOR THE LAST HUNDRED YEARS OR SO.
SO IT TOOK THE SORCERER'S STONE INSTEAD OF WITCHES!?
THAT JERK!
IT BEHAVED ITSELF FOR A WHOLE CENTURY!
WHY DID IT HAVE TO STEAL SOME-THING SO IMPORTANT WHILE WE'RE IN SCHOOL!?
SCREECH
I WON'T LET HIM GET AWAY WITH IT!
HEY!
THE MAGIC'S STARTING TO CHARGE UP!
VROOOO
IT MEANS WE'RE CLOSE TO THE SOR-CERER'S STONE.
FLOAT

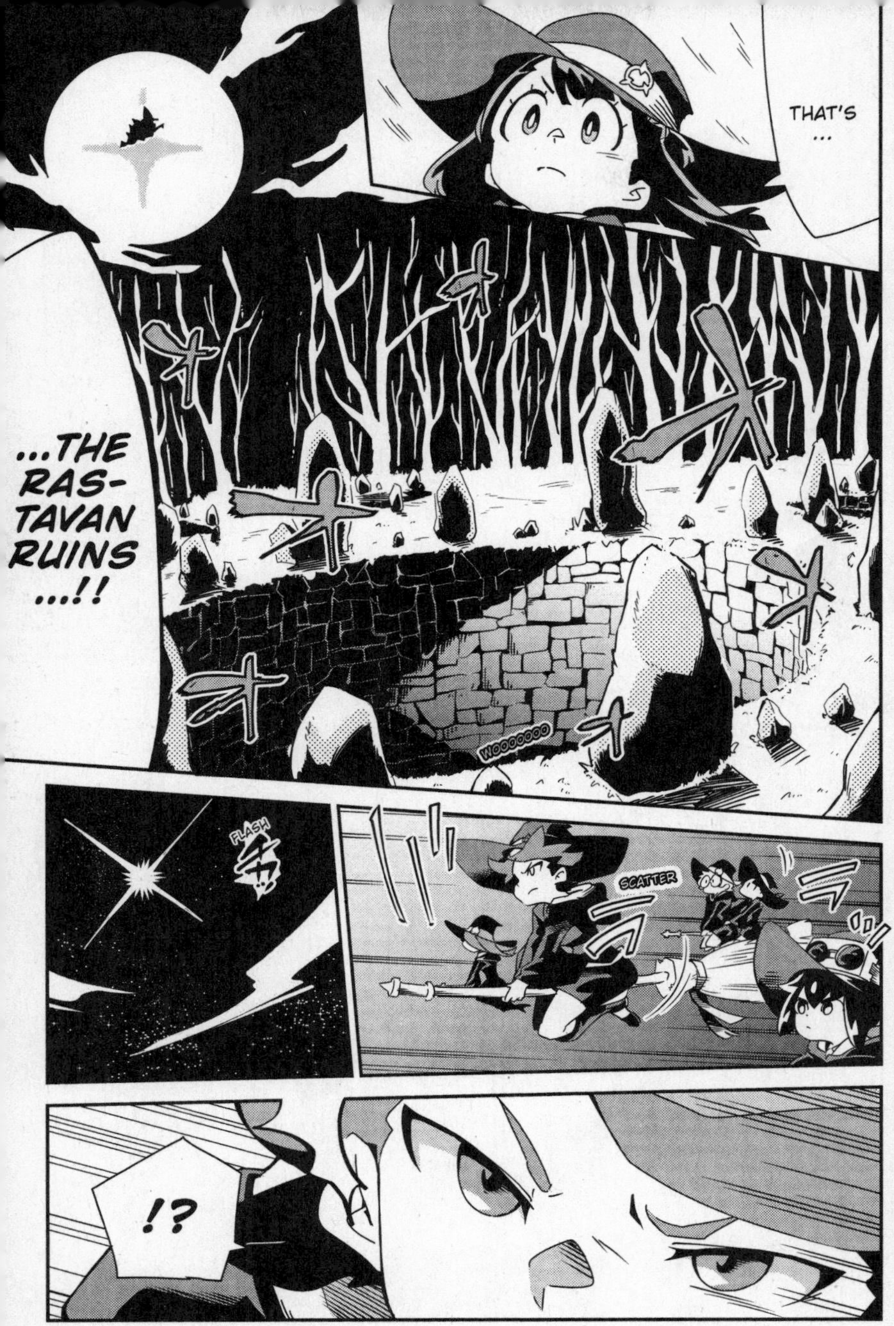
THAT'S ...
...THE RAS-TAVAN RUINS ...!!
WOOOOOOO
SCATTER
FLASH
!?

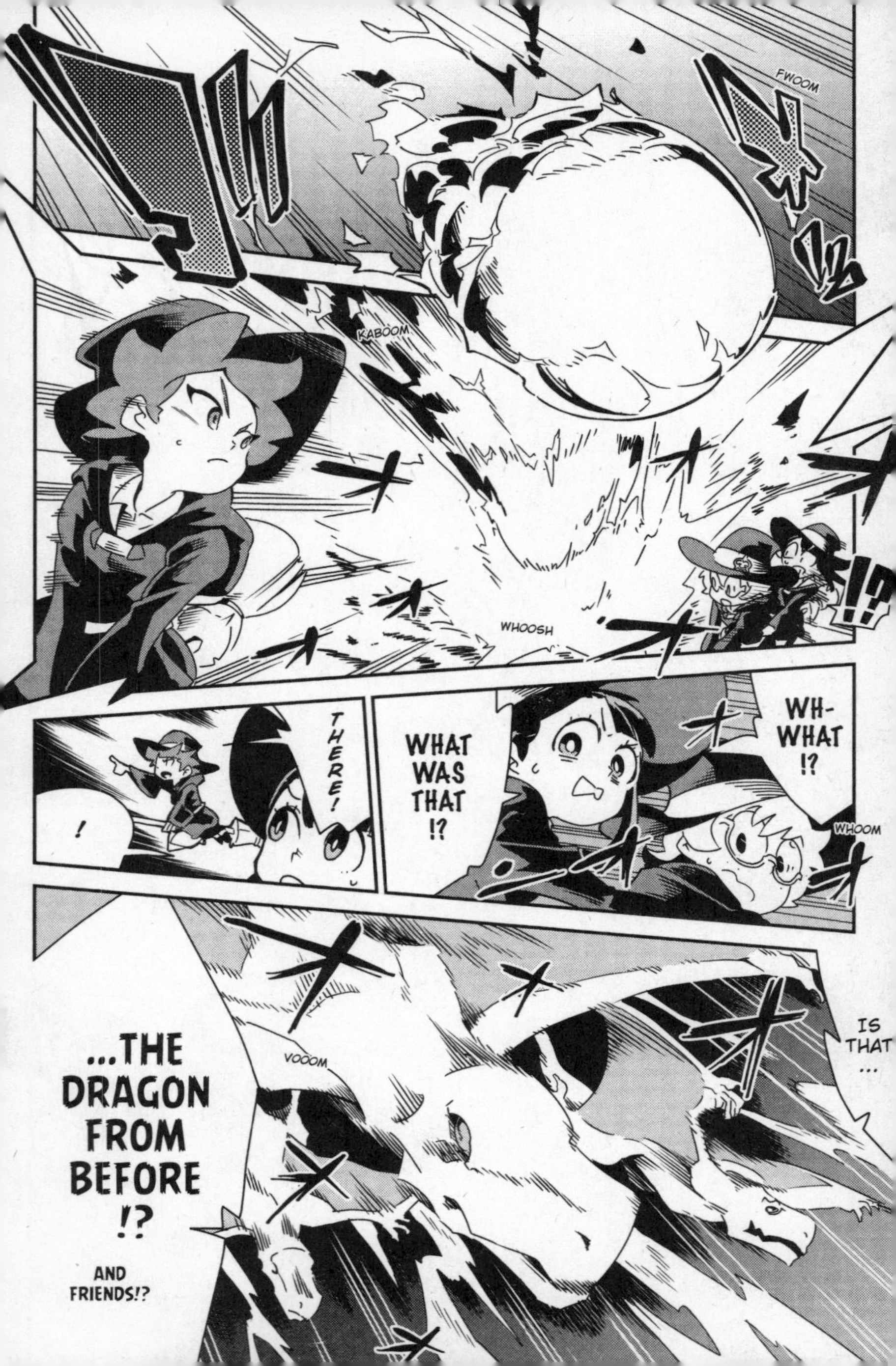
FWOOM
!?
KABOOM
!?
WHOOSH
WH-WHAT !?
WHOOM
WHAT WAS THAT !?
THERE!
!
IS THAT ...
...THE DRAGON FROM BEFORE !?
VOOOM
AND FRIENDS!?

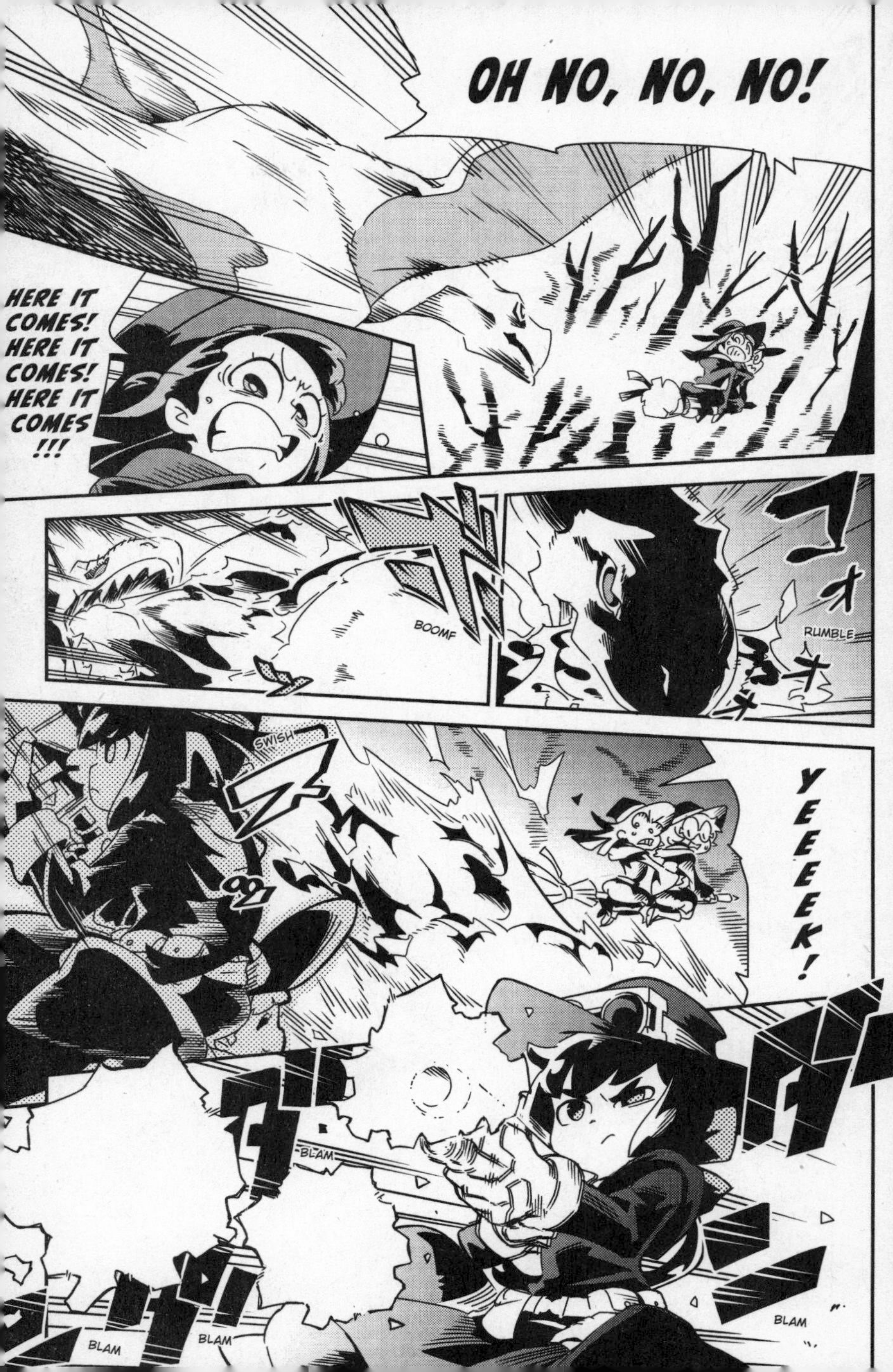
OH NO, NO, NO!
HERE IT COMES! HERE IT COMES! HERE IT COMES!!!
RUMBLE
BOOMF
YEEEEK!
SWISH
BLAM
BLAM
BLAM
BLAM

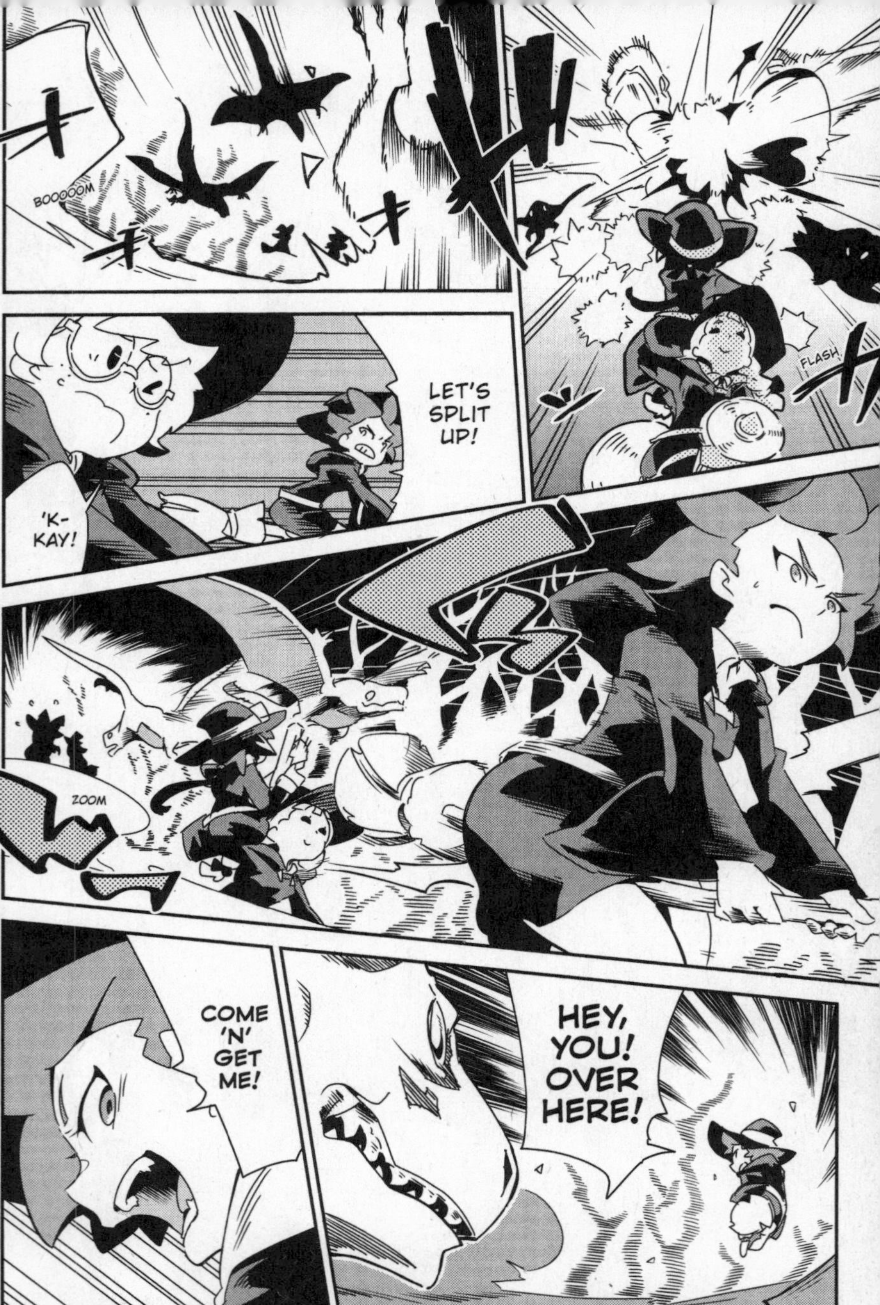
FLASH
BOOOOOM
LET'S SPLIT UP!
'K-KAY!
ZOOM
HEY, YOU! OVER HERE!
COME 'N' GET ME!

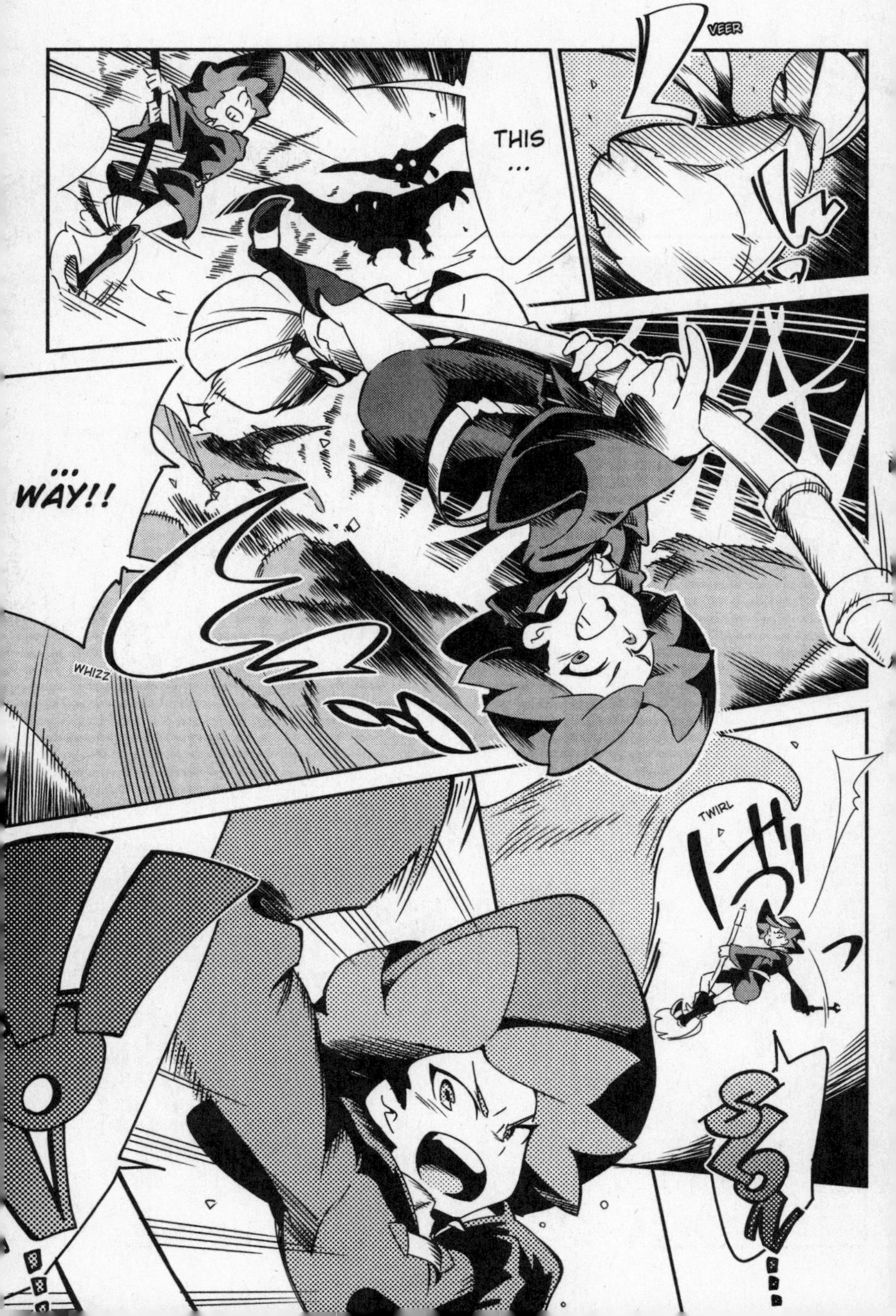
VEER
THIS ...
... WAY!!
WHIZZ
TWIRL

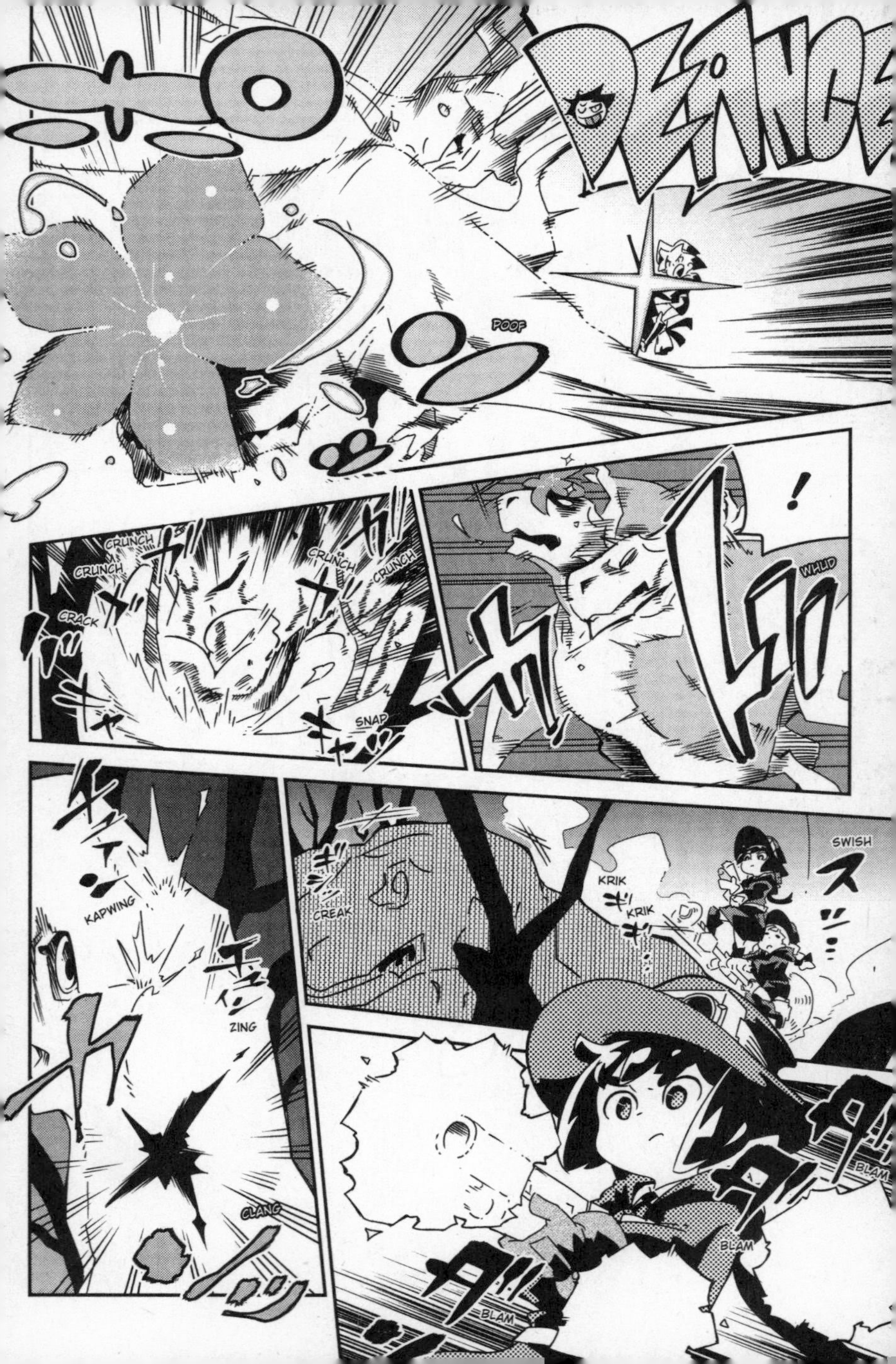
POOF
!
WHUD
CRUNCH
CRUNCH
CRACK
CRUNCH
CRUNCH
SNAP
SWISH
KRIK
KRIK
CREAK
BLAM
BLAM
BLAM
KAPWING
ZING
CLANG

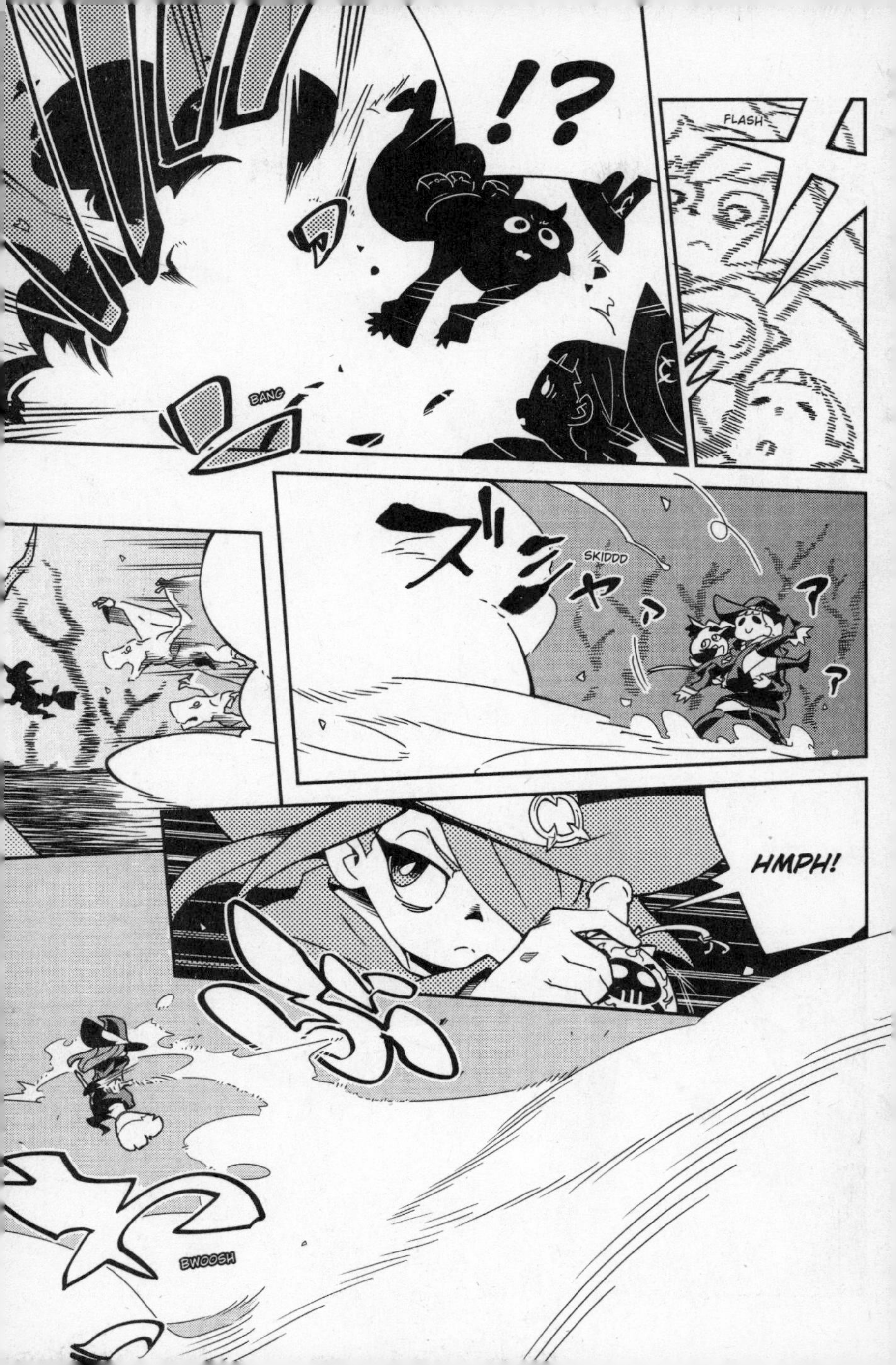
FLASH
!?
BANG
SKIDDD
HMPH!
BWOOSH

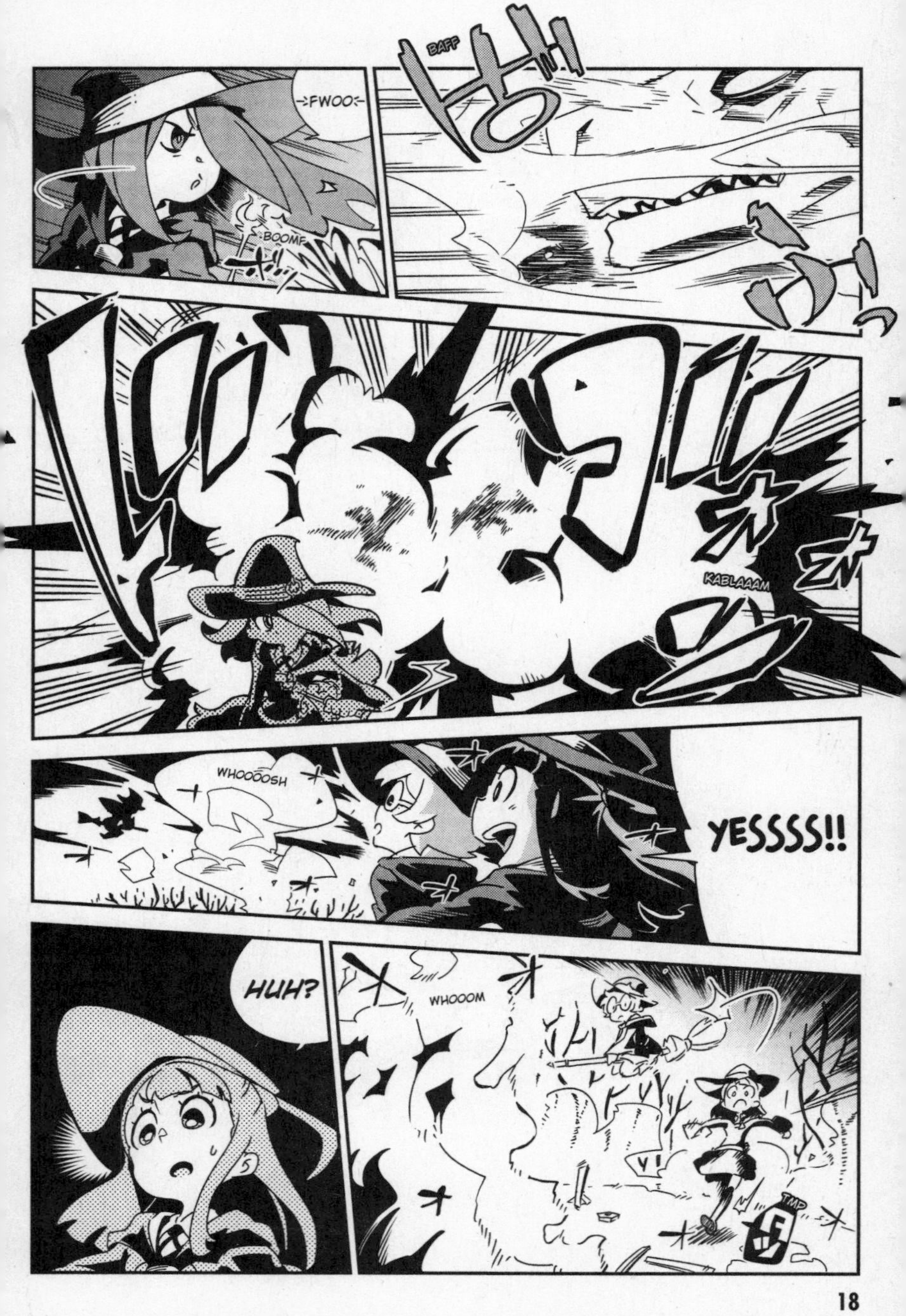
BAFF
FWOO
BOOMF
KABLAAAM
WHOOOOSH
YESSSS!!
WHOOOM
TMP
HUH?

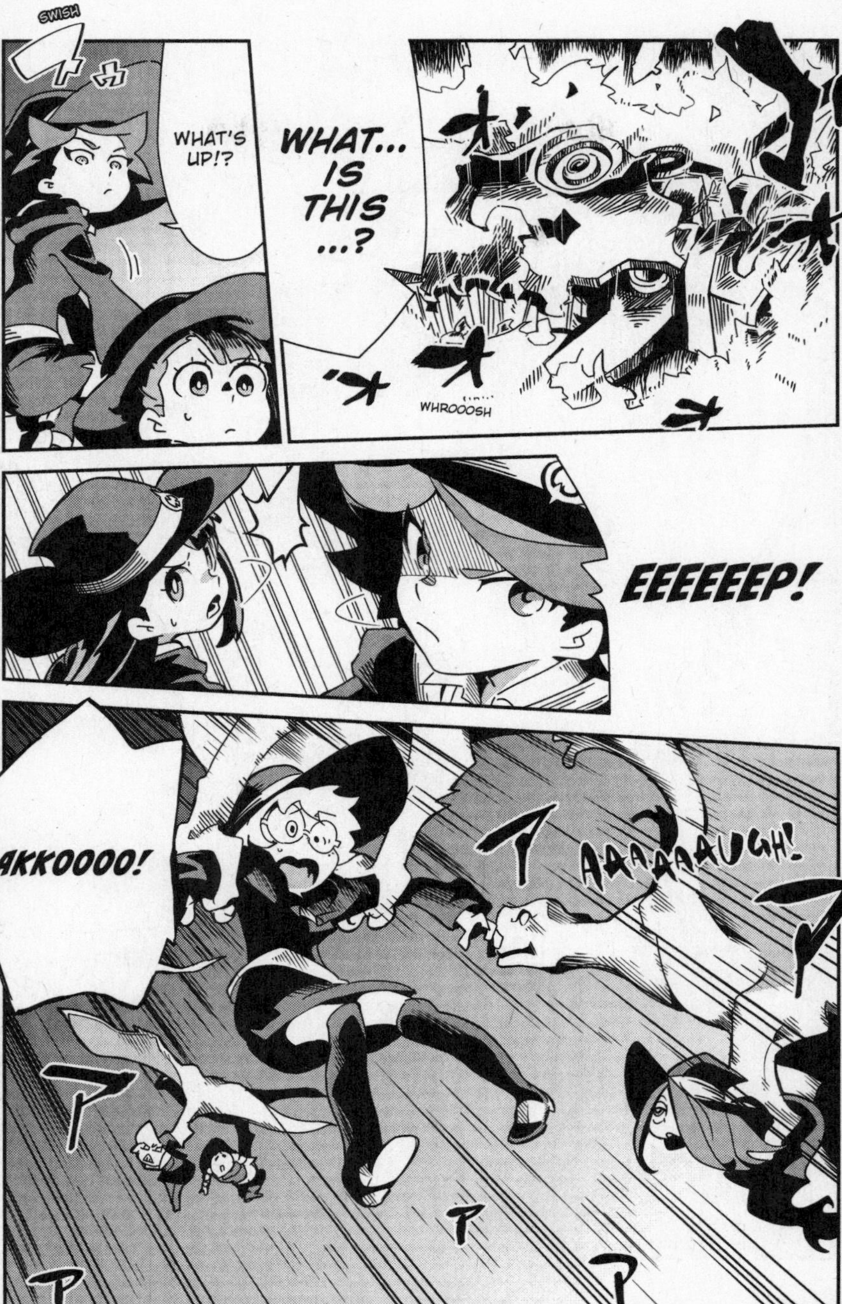

WHAT... IS THIS ...?
WHROOOSH
SWISH
WHAT'S UP!?
EEEEEEP!
AAAAAAUGH!
AKKOOOO!

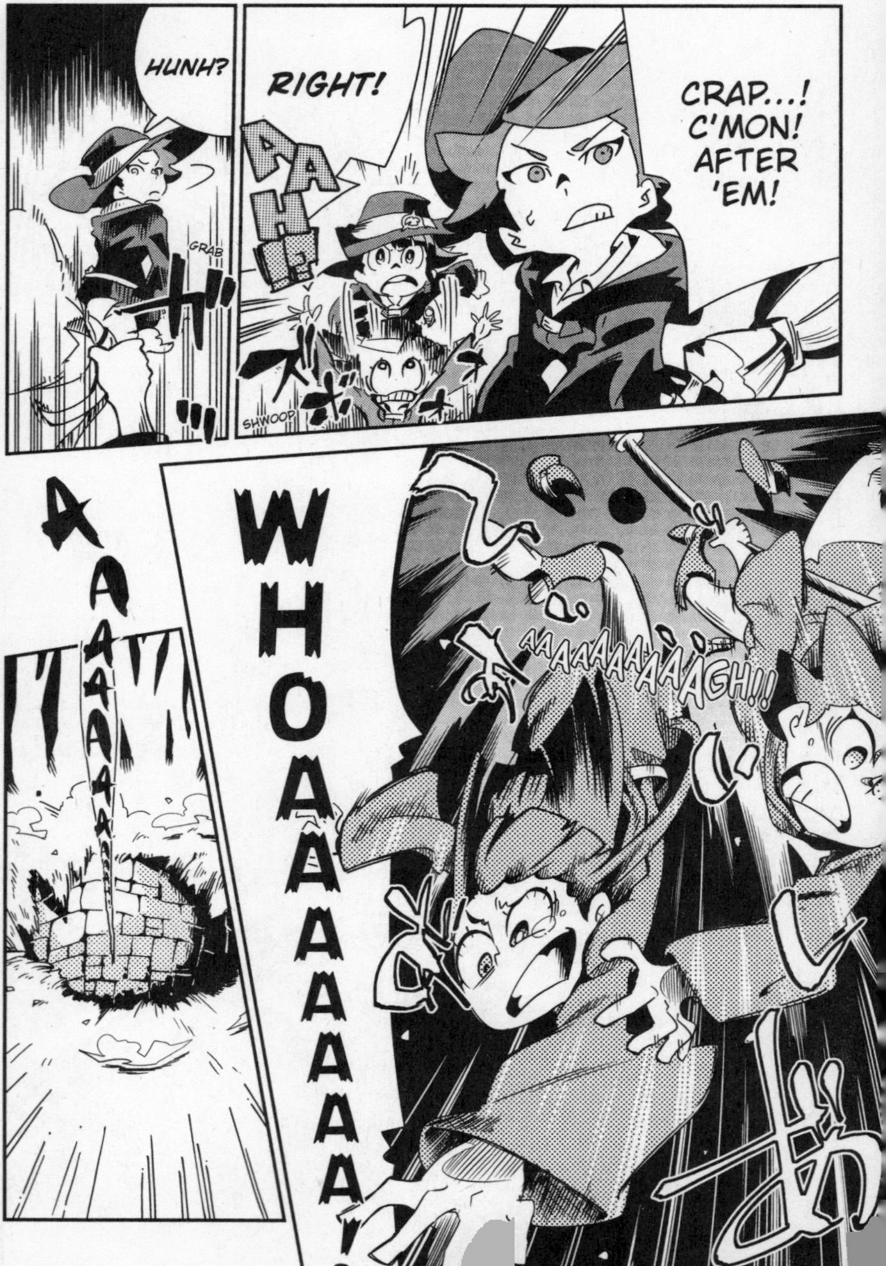
CRAP...! C'MON! AFTER 'EM!
RIGHT!
PAH!
SHWOOP
HUNH?
GRAB
AAAAAAAAAAAGH!!
WHOAAAAAAAA!
AAAAAAAAAA

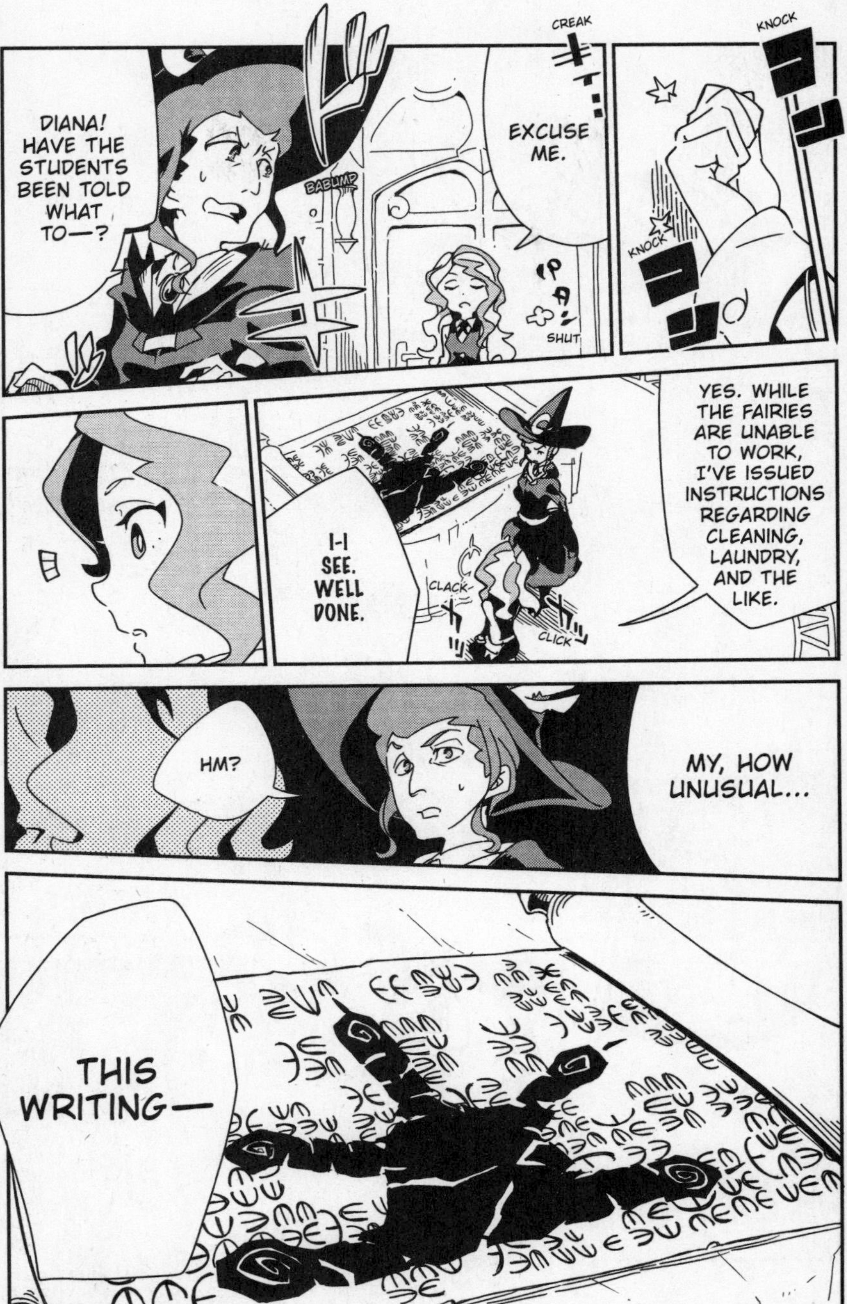
KNOCK
KNOCK
CREAK
EXCUSE ME.
SHUT
BABUMP
DIANA! HAVE THE STUDENTS BEEN TOLD WHAT TO—?
YES. WHILE THE FAIRIES ARE UNABLE TO WORK, I'VE ISSUED INSTRUCTIONS REGARDING CLEANING, LAUNDRY, AND THE LIKE.
CLACK
CLICK
I-I SEE. WELL DONE.
MY, HOW UNUSUAL...
HM?
THIS WRITING—

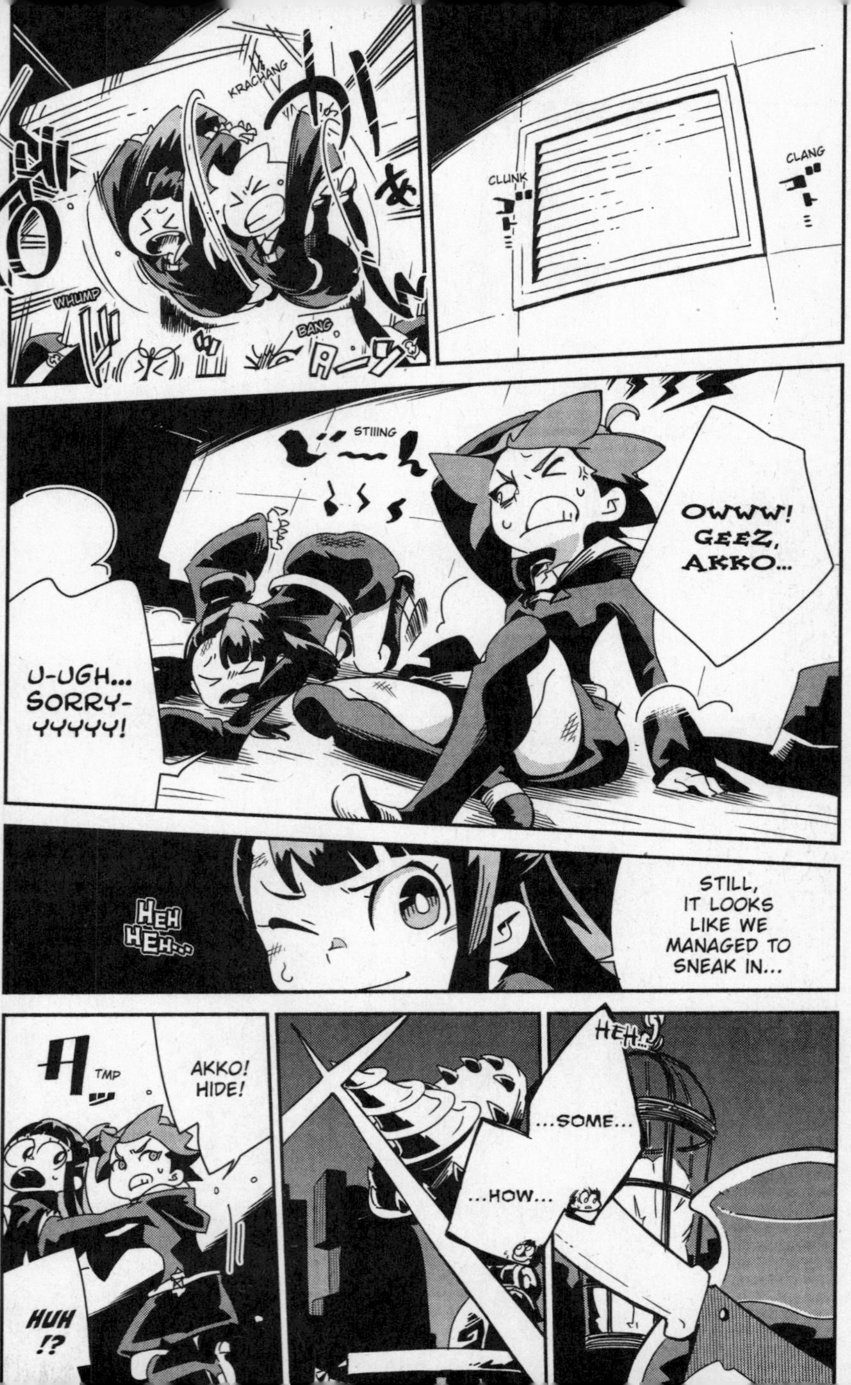
CLANG
CLUNK
KRACHANG
BANG
WHUMP
OWWW! GEEZ, AKKO...
STIIING
U-UGH... SORRY-YYYYY!
STILL, IT LOOKS LIKE WE MANAGED TO SNEAK IN...
HEH HEH...
HEH...
...SOME...
...HOW...
AKKO! HIDE!
TMP
HUH !?

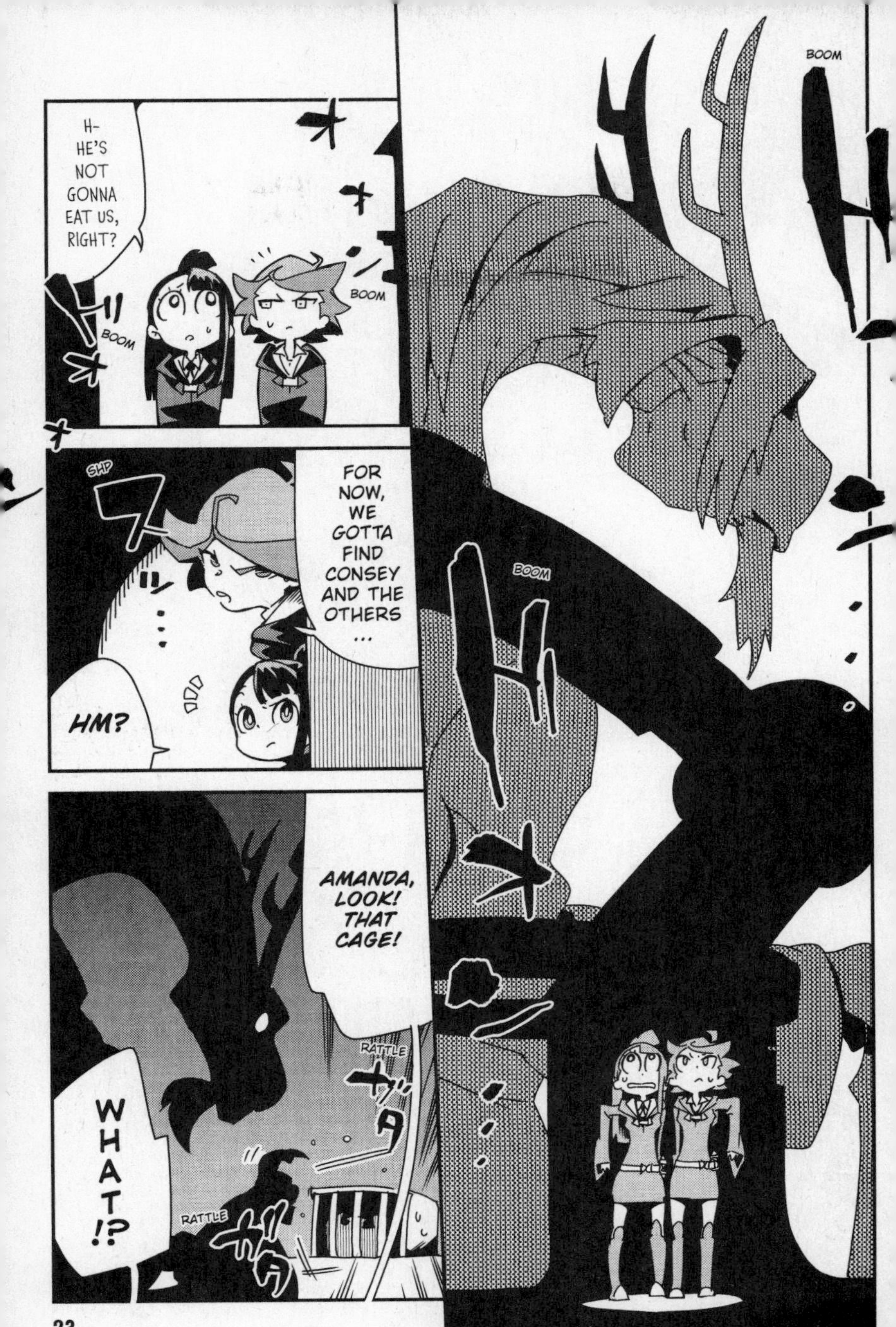
BOOM
BOOM
H-HE'S NOT GONNA EAT US, RIGHT?
BOOM
BOOM
FOR NOW, WE GOTTA FIND CONSEY AND THE OTHERS...
SHP
HM?
AMANDA, LOOK! THAT CAGE!
RATTLE
RATTLE
WHAT!?

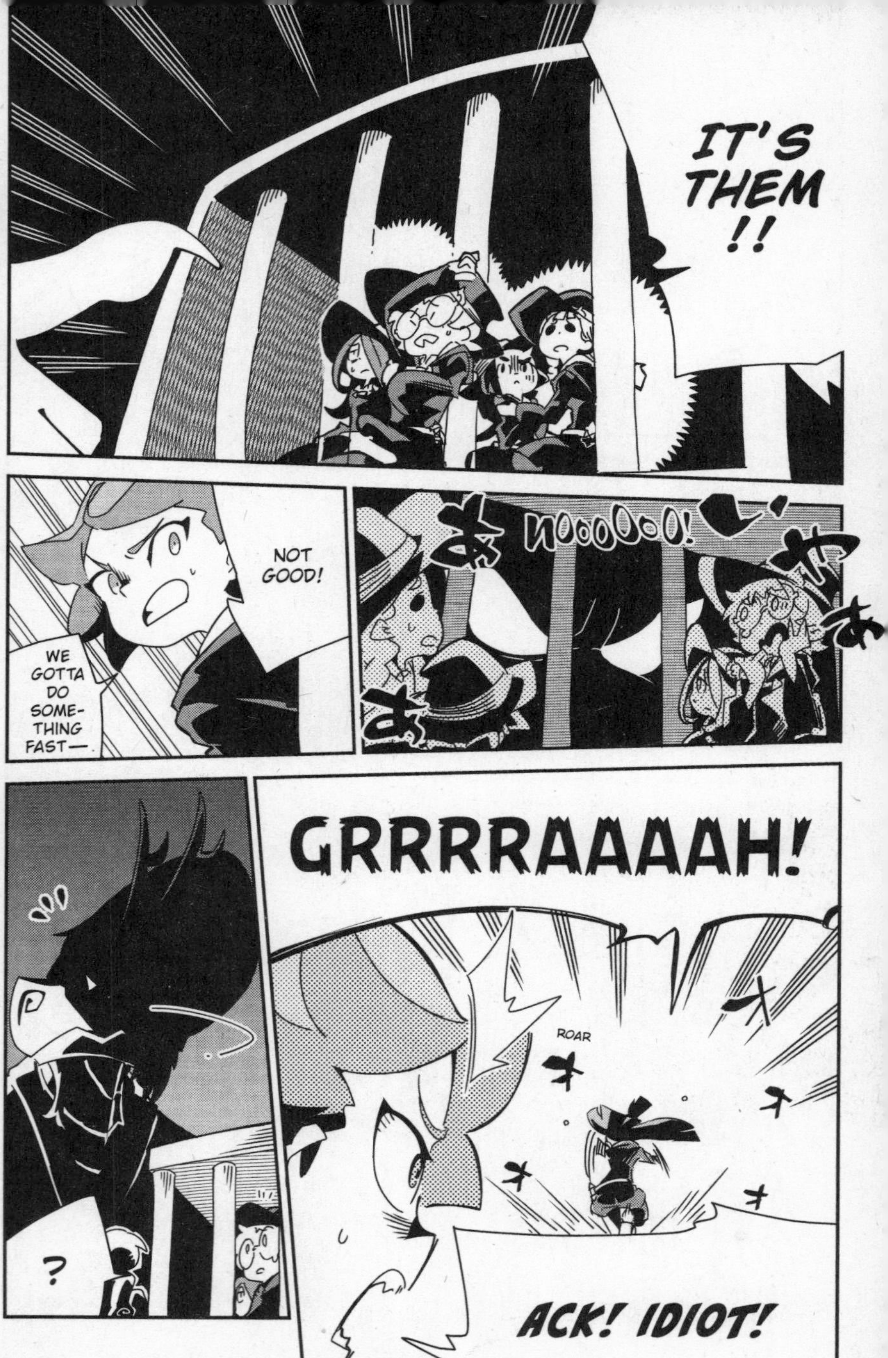
IT'S THEM!!
じゃあああ
NOOOOOO!
NOT GOOD!
WE GOTTA DO SOMETHING FAST—
GRRRRAAAAH!
ROAR
ACK! IDIOT!
?

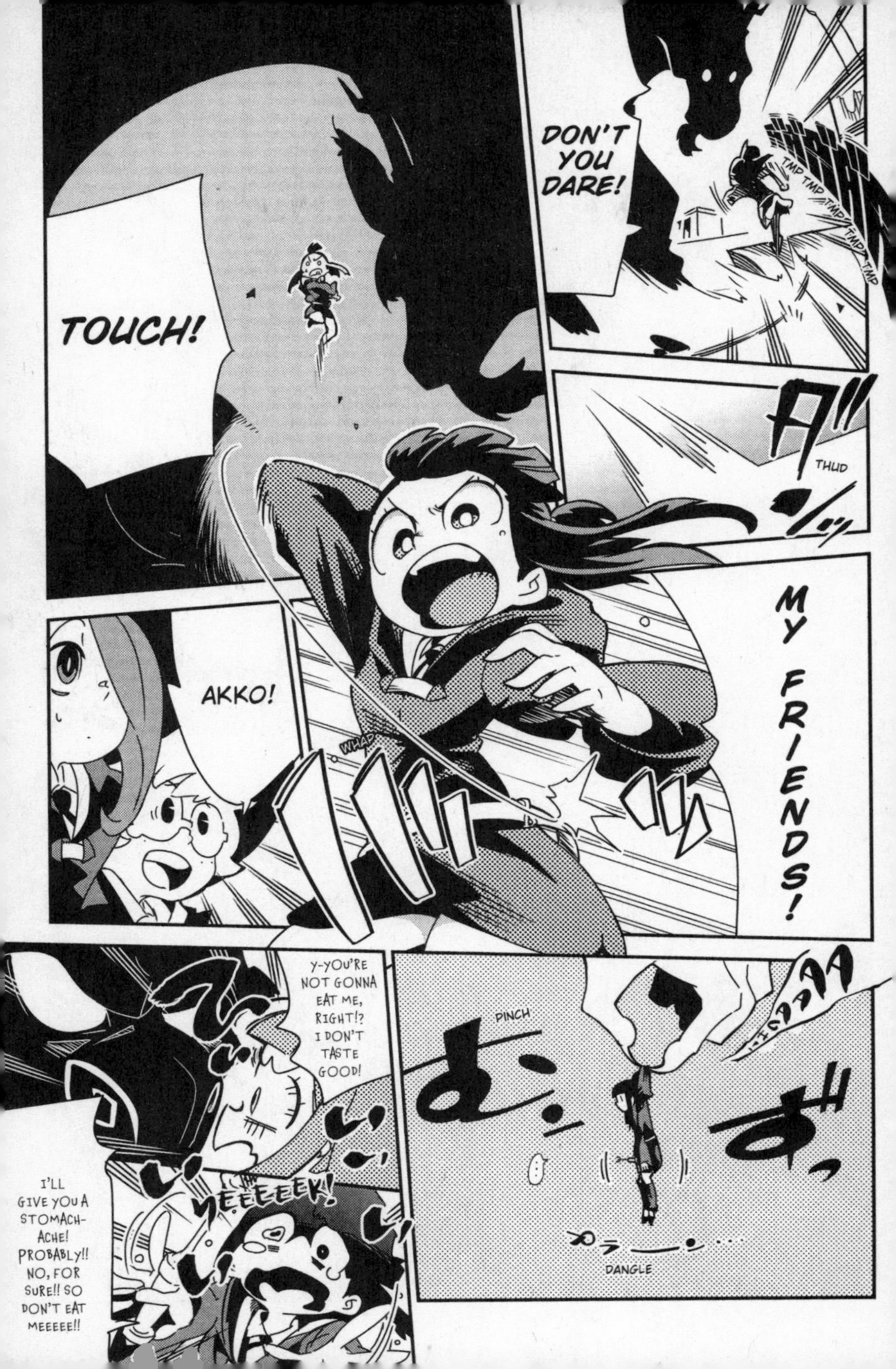

DON'T YOU DARE!
TMP TMP TMP TMP TMP TMP
THUD
TOUCH!
MY FRIENDS!
WHAP
AKKO!
PINCH
DANGLE
Y-YOU'RE NOT GONNA EAT ME, RIGHT!? I DON'T TASTE GOOD!
YEEEEEK!
I'LL GIVE YOU A STOMACH-ACHE! PROBABLY!! NO, FOR SURE!! SO DON'T EAT MEEEEE!!

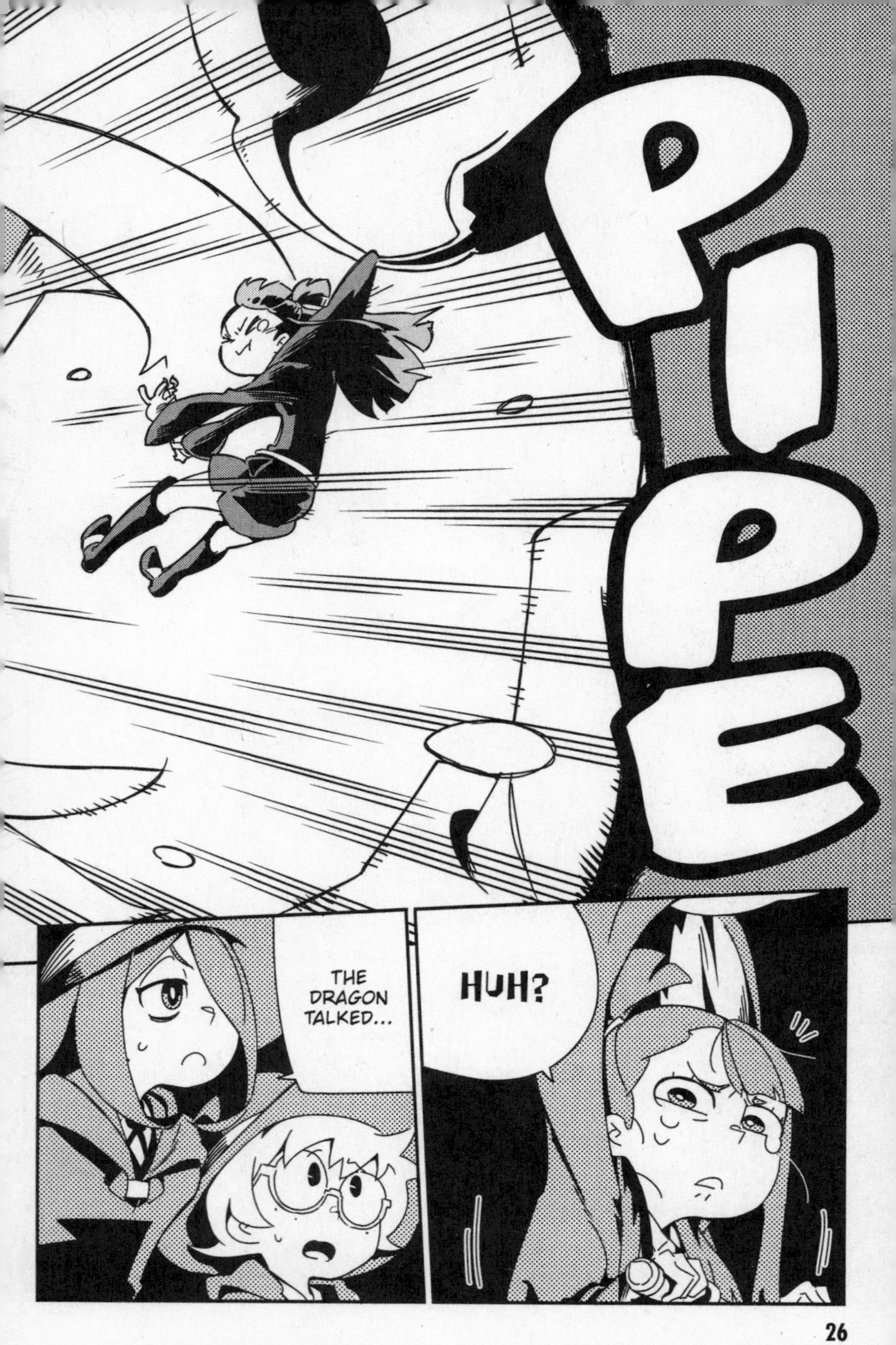
PIPE
HUH?
THE DRAGON TALKED...

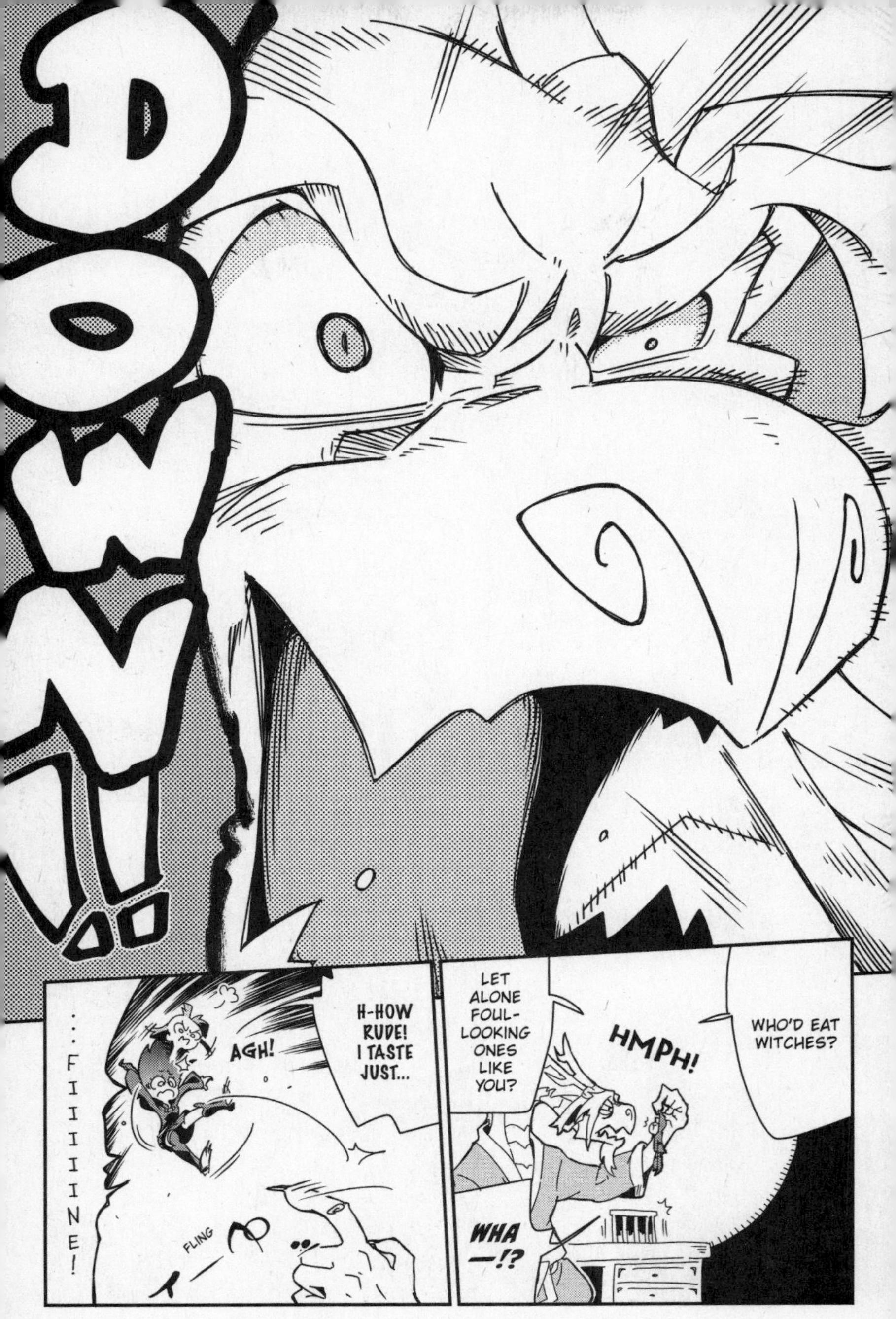
WHO'D EAT WITCHES?
HMPH!
LET ALONE FOUL-LOOKING ONES LIKE YOU?
WHA—!?
H-HOW RUDE! I TASTE JUST...
AGH!
FLING
...FIIIIINE!

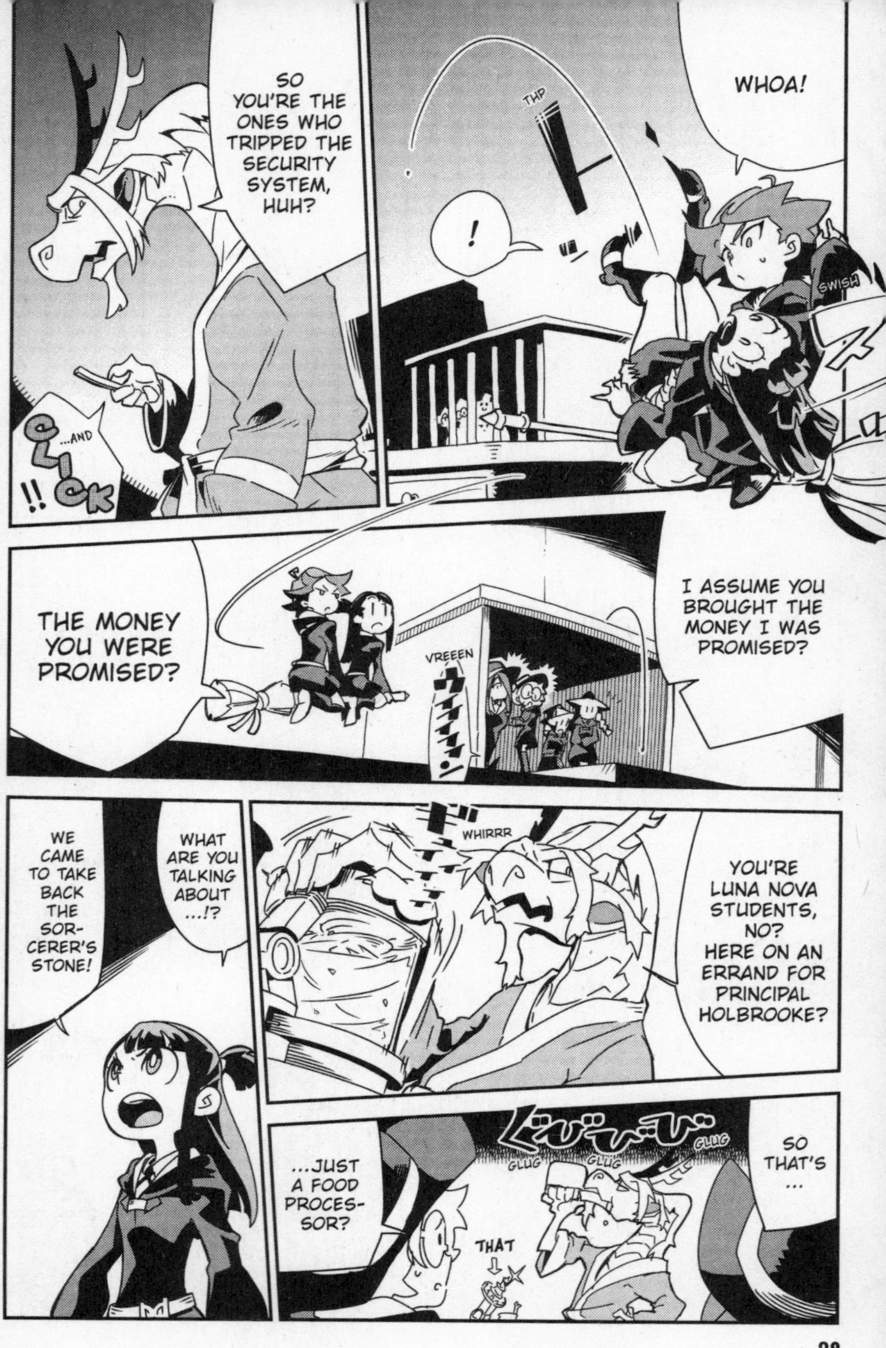
WHOA!
THP
!
SWISH
SO YOU'RE THE ONES WHO TRIPPED THE SECURITY SYSTEM, HUH?
...AND
CLICK
!!
I ASSUME YOU BROUGHT THE MONEY I WAS PROMISED?
VREEEN
THE MONEY YOU WERE PROMISED?
YOU'RE LUNA NOVA STUDENTS, NO? HERE ON AN ERRAND FOR PRINCIPAL HOLBROOKE?
WHIRRR
SO THAT'S ...
GLUG
GLUG
GLUG
...JUST A FOOD PROCES-SOR?
THAT
WHAT ARE YOU TALKING ABOUT ...!?
WE CAME TO TAKE BACK THE SOR-CERER'S STONE!

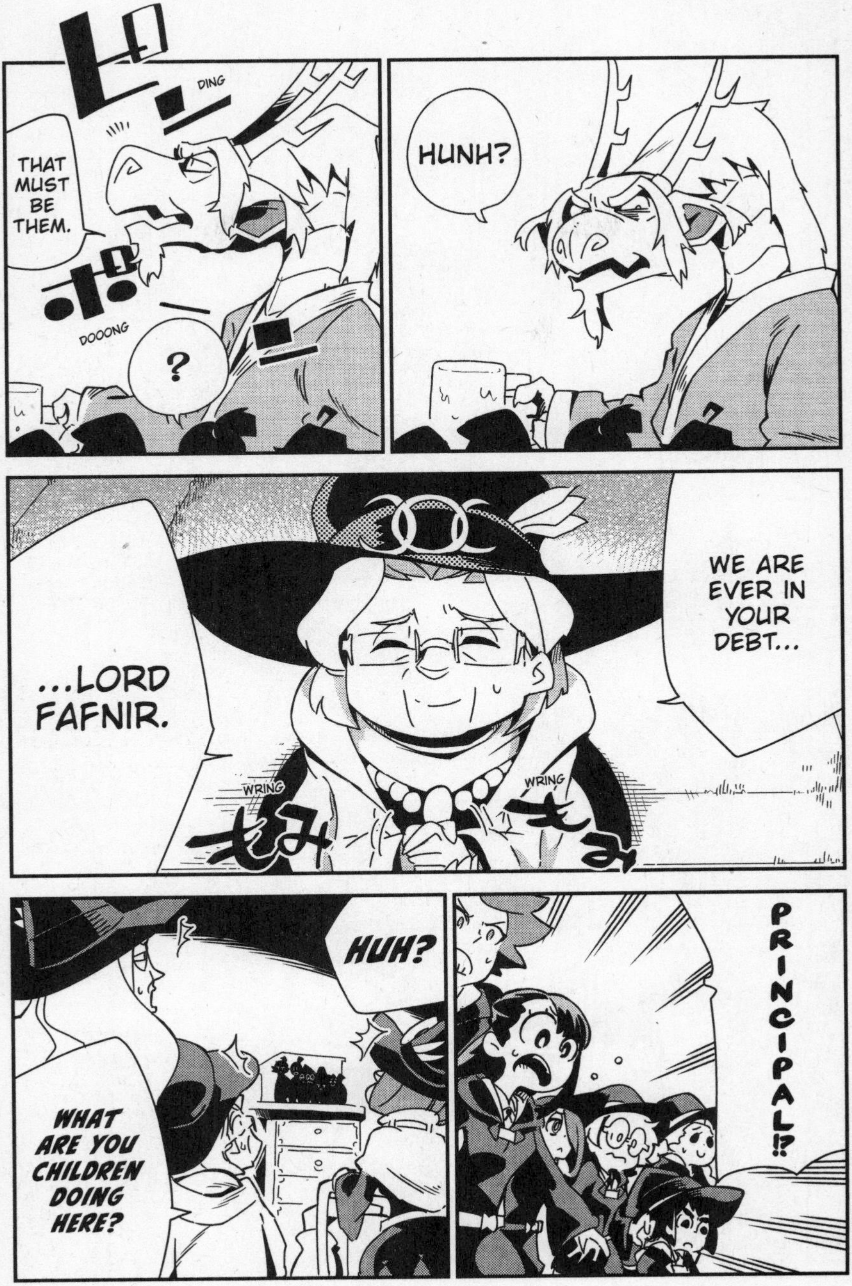
HUNH?
DING
THAT MUST BE THEM.
DOOONG
?
WE ARE EVER IN YOUR DEBT...
...LORD FAFNIR.
WRING
WRING
PRINCIPAL!?
HUH?
WHAT ARE YOU CHILDREN DOING HERE?

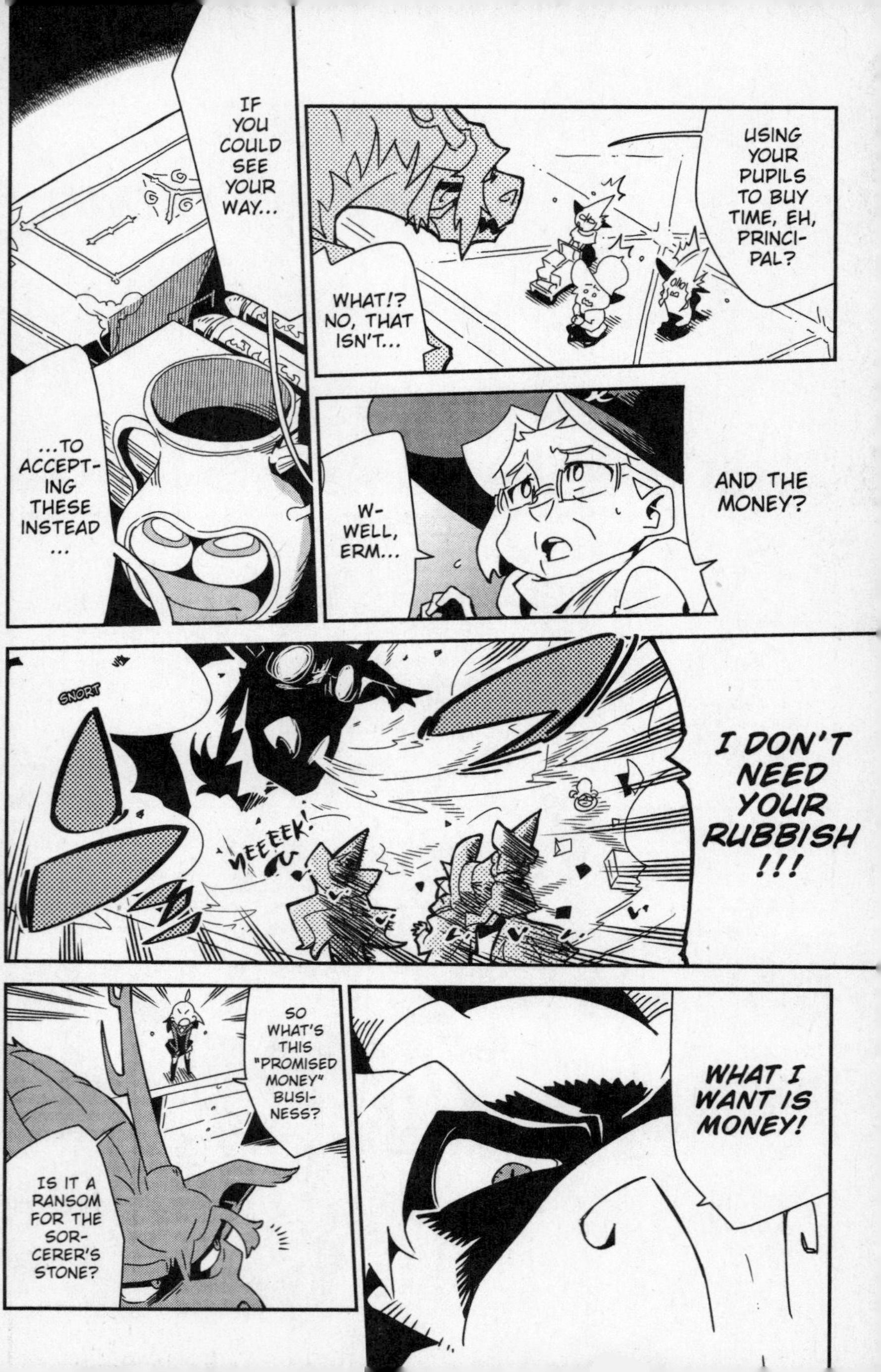
USING YOUR PUPILS TO BUY TIME, EH, PRINCIPAL?
WHAT!? NO, THAT ISN'T...
AND THE MONEY?
W-WELL, ERM...
IF YOU COULD SEE YOUR WAY...
...TO ACCEPTING THESE INSTEAD...
I DON'T NEED YOUR RUBBISH!!!
SNORT
NEEEEK!
WHAT I WANT IS MONEY!
SO WHAT'S THIS "PROMISED MONEY" BUSINESS?
IS IT A RANSOM FOR THE SORCERER'S STONE?

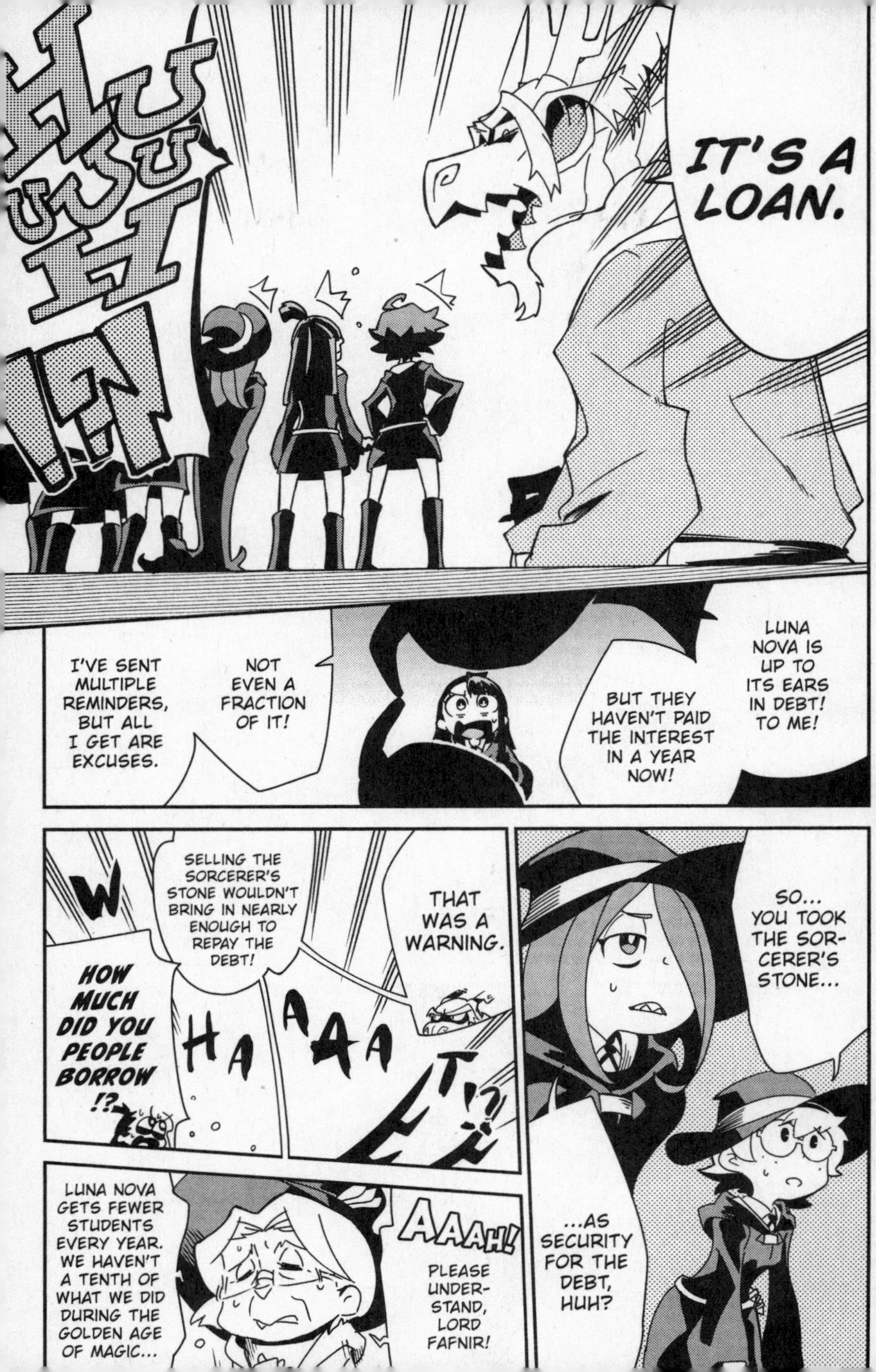
IT'S A LOAN.
LUNA NOVA IS UP TO ITS EARS IN DEBT! TO ME!
BUT THEY HAVEN'T PAID THE INTEREST IN A YEAR NOW!
NOT EVEN A FRACTION OF IT!
I'VE SENT MULTIPLE REMINDERS, BUT ALL I GET ARE EXCUSES.
SO... YOU TOOK THE SOR-CERER'S STONE...
...AS SECURITY FOR THE DEBT, HUH?
THAT WAS A WARNING.
SELLING THE SORCERER'S STONE WOULDN'T BRING IN NEARLY ENOUGH TO REPAY THE DEBT!
WHAAAAT!?
HOW MUCH DID YOU PEOPLE BORROW!?
AAAH!
PLEASE UNDER-STAND, LORD FAFNIR!
LUNA NOVA GETS FEWER STUDENTS EVERY YEAR. WE HAVEN'T A TENTH OF WHAT WE DID DURING THE GOLDEN AGE OF MAGIC...

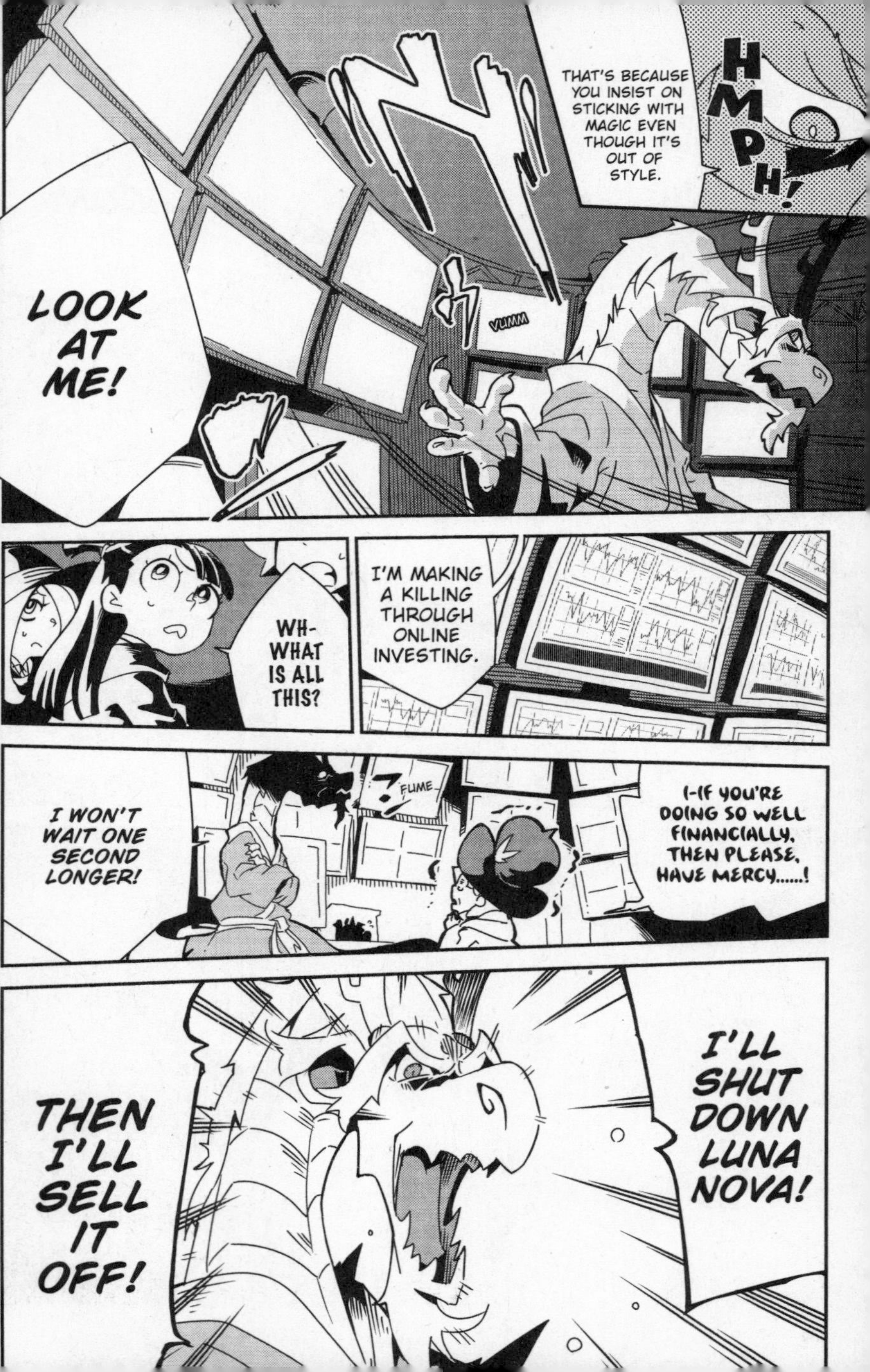
HMPH!
THAT'S BECAUSE YOU INSIST ON STICKING WITH MAGIC EVEN THOUGH IT'S OUT OF STYLE.
VUMM
LOOK AT ME!
I'M MAKING A KILLING THROUGH ONLINE INVESTING.
WH-WHAT IS ALL THIS?
I-IF YOU'RE DOING SO WELL FINANCIALLY, THEN PLEASE, HAVE MERCY......!
FUME
I WON'T WAIT ONE SECOND LONGER!
I'LL SHUT DOWN LUNA NOVA!
THEN I'LL SELL IT OFF!

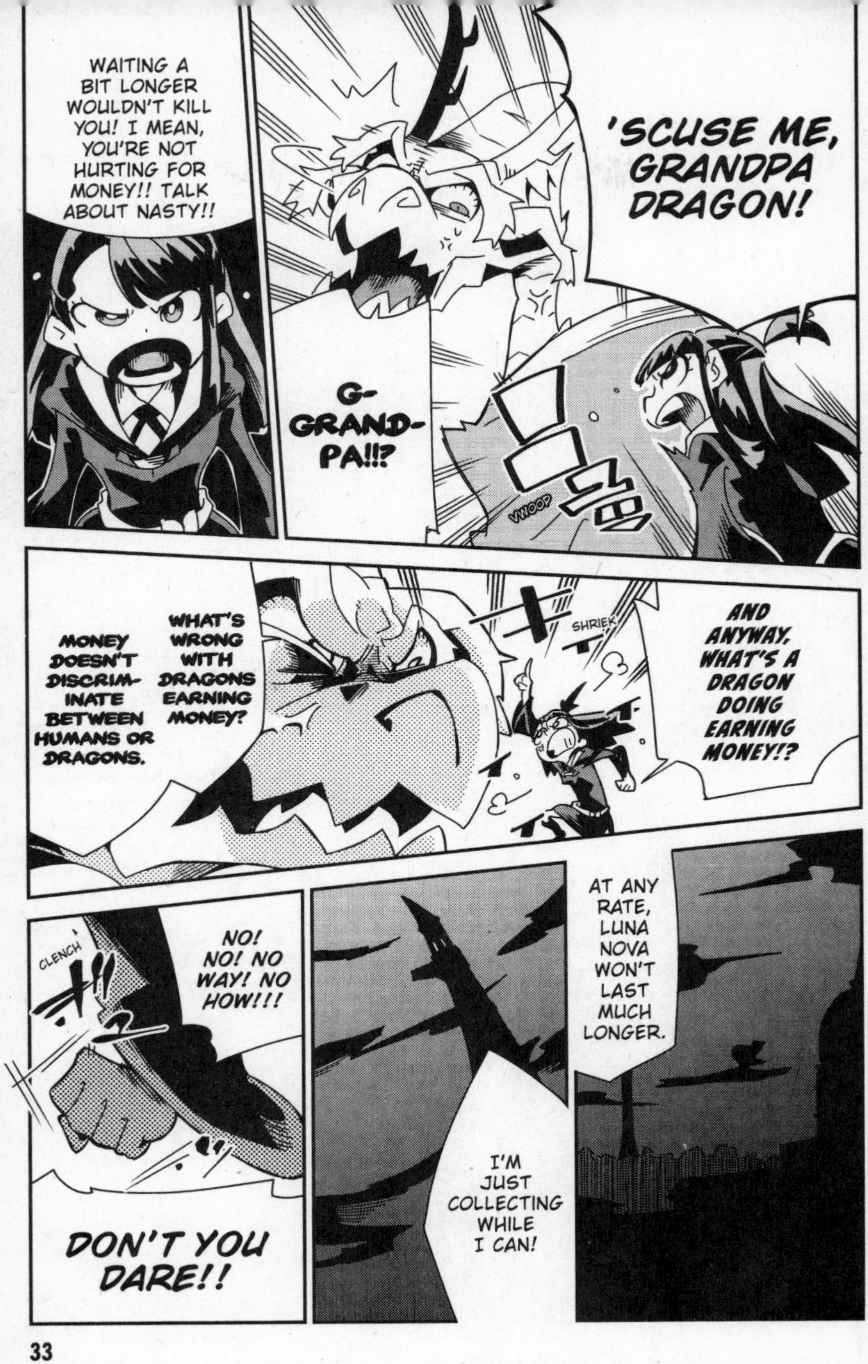
'SCUSE ME, GRANDPA DRAGON!
G-GRAND-PA!!?
VWOOP
WAITING A BIT LONGER WOULDN'T KILL YOU! I MEAN, YOU'RE NOT HURTING FOR MONEY!! TALK ABOUT NASTY!!
AND ANYWAY, WHAT'S A DRAGON DOING EARNING MONEY!?
SHRIEK
WHAT'S WRONG WITH DRAGONS EARNING MONEY?
MONEY DOESN'T DISCRIM-INATE BETWEEN HUMANS OR DRAGONS.
AT ANY RATE, LUNA NOVA WON'T LAST MUCH LONGER.
I'M JUST COLLECTING WHILE I CAN!
NO! NO! NO WAY! NO HOW!!!
CLENCH
DON'T YOU DARE!!

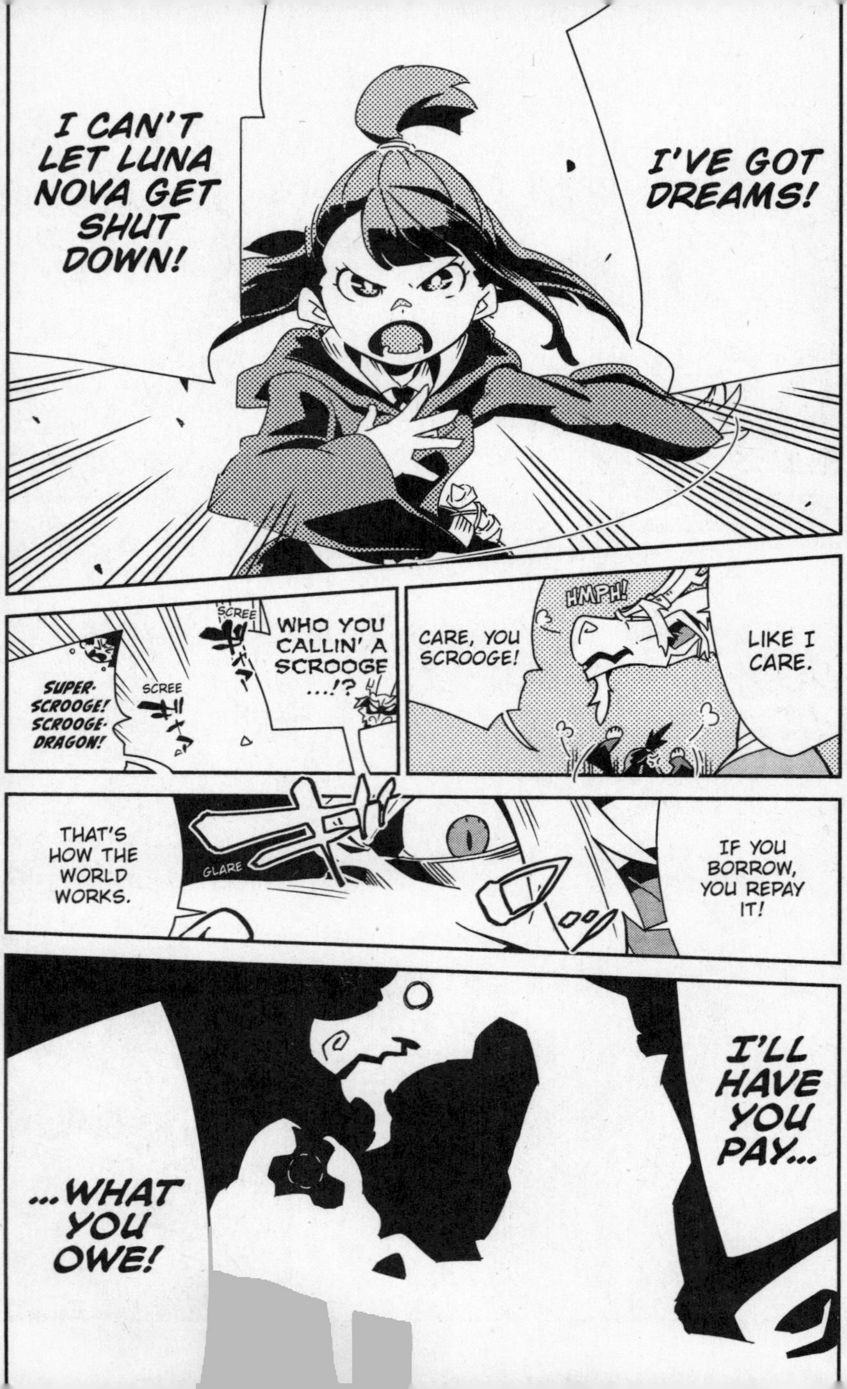
I'VE GOT DREAMS!
I CAN'T LET LUNA NOVA GET SHUT DOWN!
LIKE I CARE.
HMPH!
CARE, YOU SCROOGE!
WHO YOU CALLIN' A SCROOGE ...!?
SCREE
SCREE
SUPER-SCROOGE! SCROOGE-DRAGON!
IF YOU BORROW, YOU REPAY IT!
GLARE
THAT'S HOW THE WORLD WORKS.
I'LL HAVE YOU PAY...
...WHAT YOU OWE!

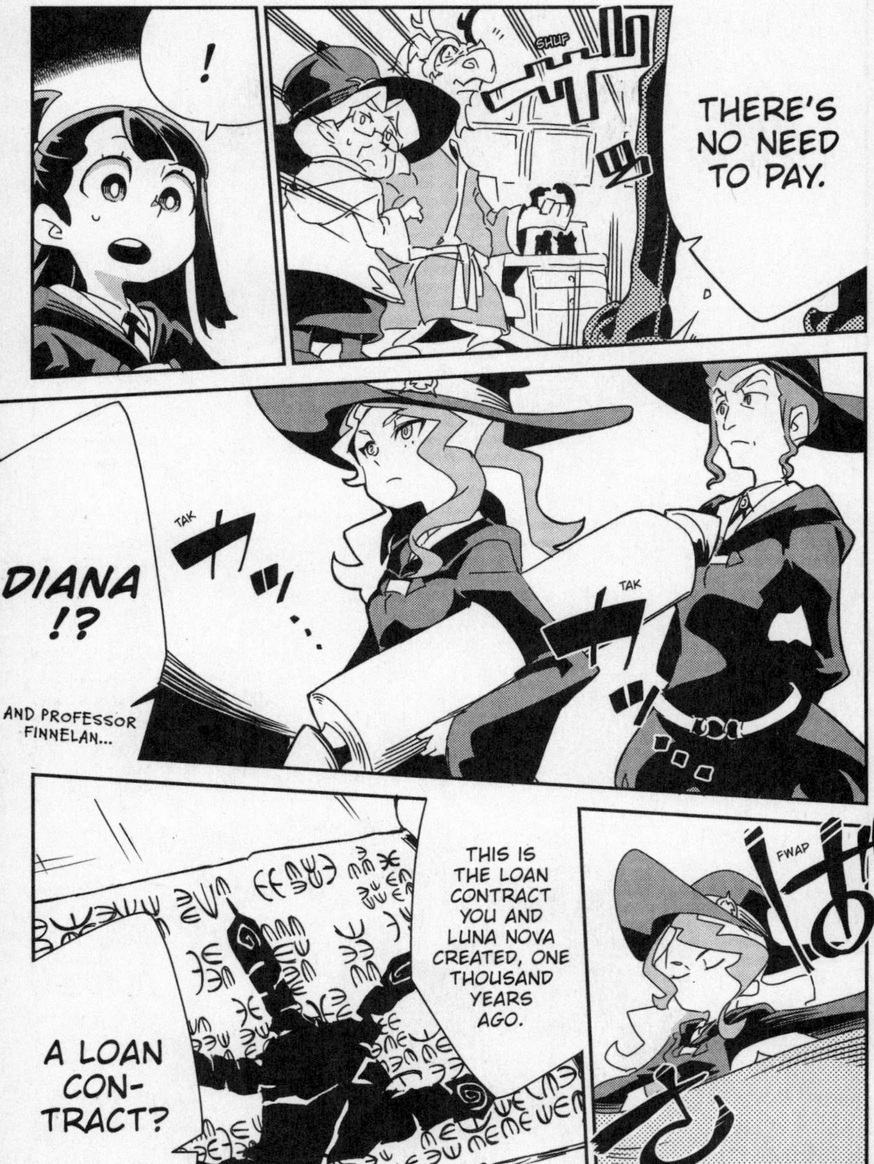
SHUF
THERE'S NO NEED TO PAY.
!
TAK
TAK
DIANA!?
AND PROFESSOR FINNELAN...
FWAP
THIS IS THE LOAN CONTRACT YOU AND LUNA NOVA CREATED, ONE THOUSAND YEARS AGO.
A LOAN CON-TRACT?

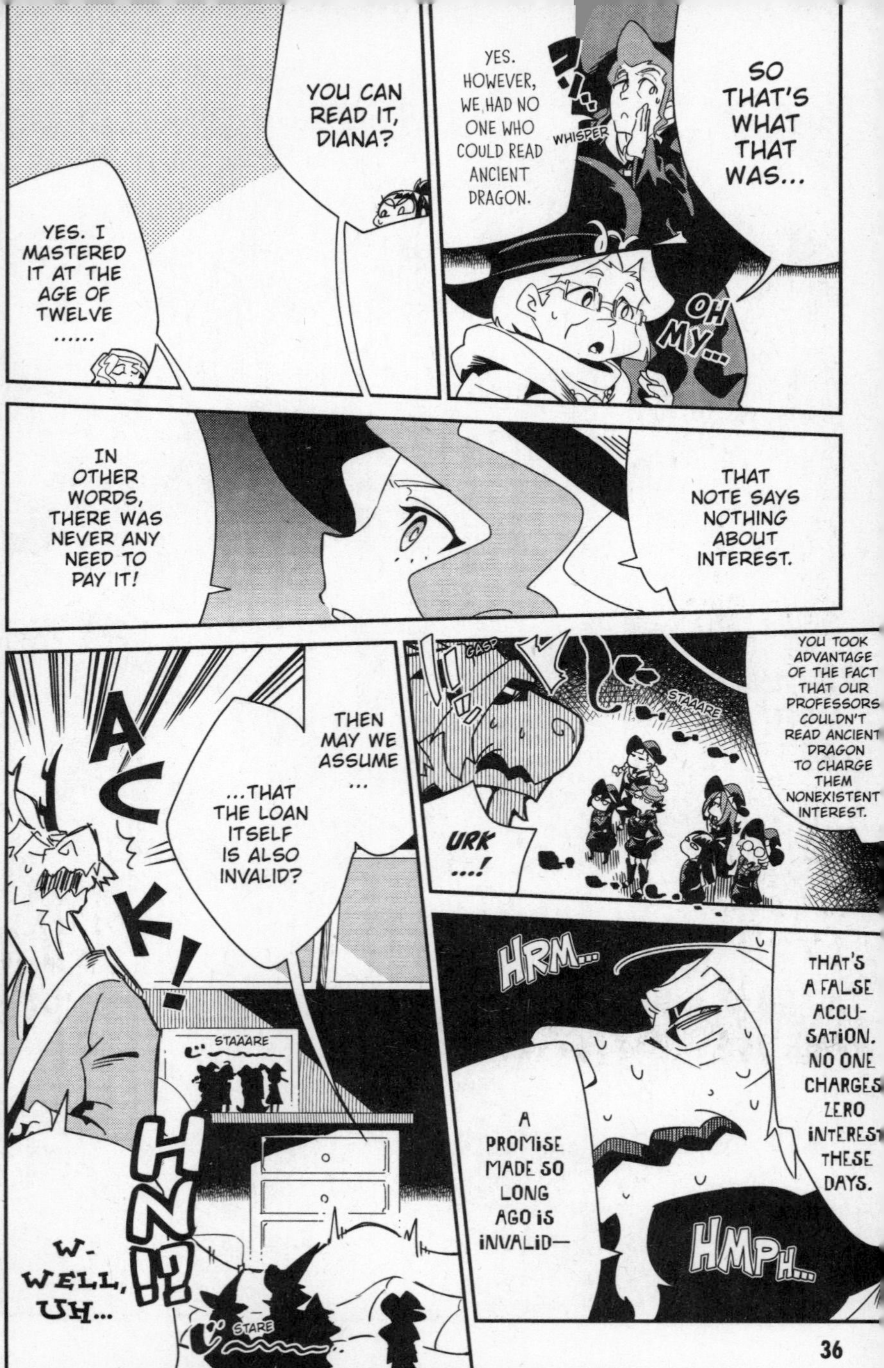
SO THAT'S WHAT THAT WAS...
YES. HOWEVER, WE HAD NO ONE WHO COULD READ ANCIENT DRAGON.
WHISPER
OH MY...
YOU CAN READ IT, DIANA?
YES. I MASTERED IT AT THE AGE OF TWELVE ......
THAT NOTE SAYS NOTHING ABOUT INTEREST.
IN OTHER WORDS, THERE WAS NEVER ANY NEED TO PAY IT!
YOU TOOK ADVANTAGE OF THE FACT THAT OUR PROFESSORS COULDN'T READ ANCIENT DRAGON TO CHARGE THEM NONEXISTENT INTEREST.
GASP
STAAARE
URK ...!
THAT'S A FALSE ACCU-SATION. NO ONE CHARGES ZERO INTEREST THESE DAYS.
HRM...
HMPH...
A PROMISE MADE SO LONG AGO IS INVALID—
THEN MAY WE ASSUME ...
...THAT THE LOAN ITSELF IS ALSO INVALID?
ACK!
STAAARE
HNN!?
W-WELL, UH...
STARE

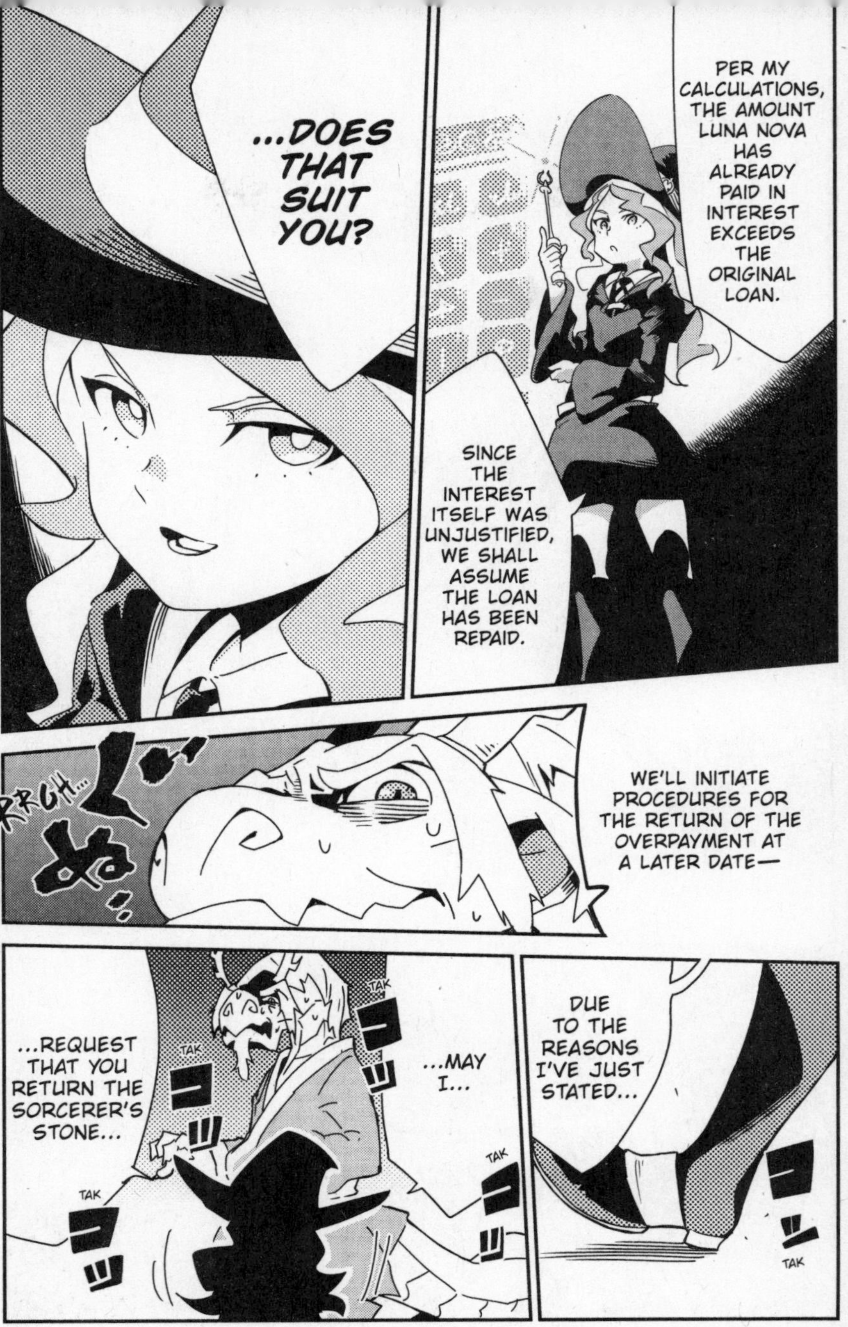
PER MY CALCULATIONS, THE AMOUNT LUNA NOVA HAS ALREADY PAID IN INTEREST EXCEEDS THE ORIGINAL LOAN.
SINCE THE INTEREST ITSELF WAS UNJUSTIFIED, WE SHALL ASSUME THE LOAN HAS BEEN REPAID.
...DOES THAT SUIT YOU?
WE'LL INITIATE PROCEDURES FOR THE RETURN OF THE OVERPAYMENT AT A LATER DATE—
RRGH... ぐぬ
DUE TO THE REASONS I'VE JUST STATED...
TAK
...MAY I...
TAK
TAK
...REQUEST THAT YOU RETURN THE SORCERER'S STONE...
TAK

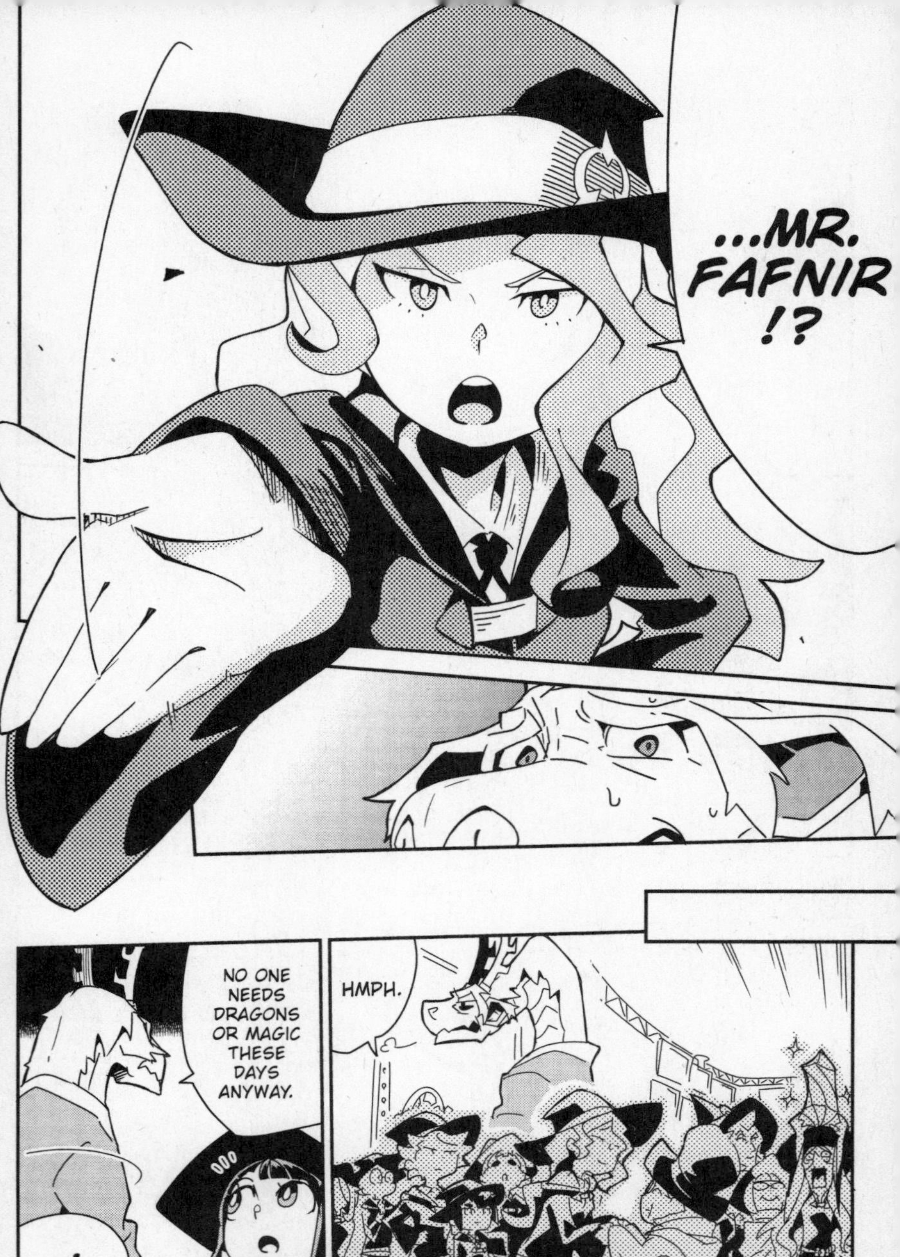
...MR. FAFNIR !?
HMPH.
NO ONE NEEDS DRAGONS OR MAGIC THESE DAYS ANYWAY.
!

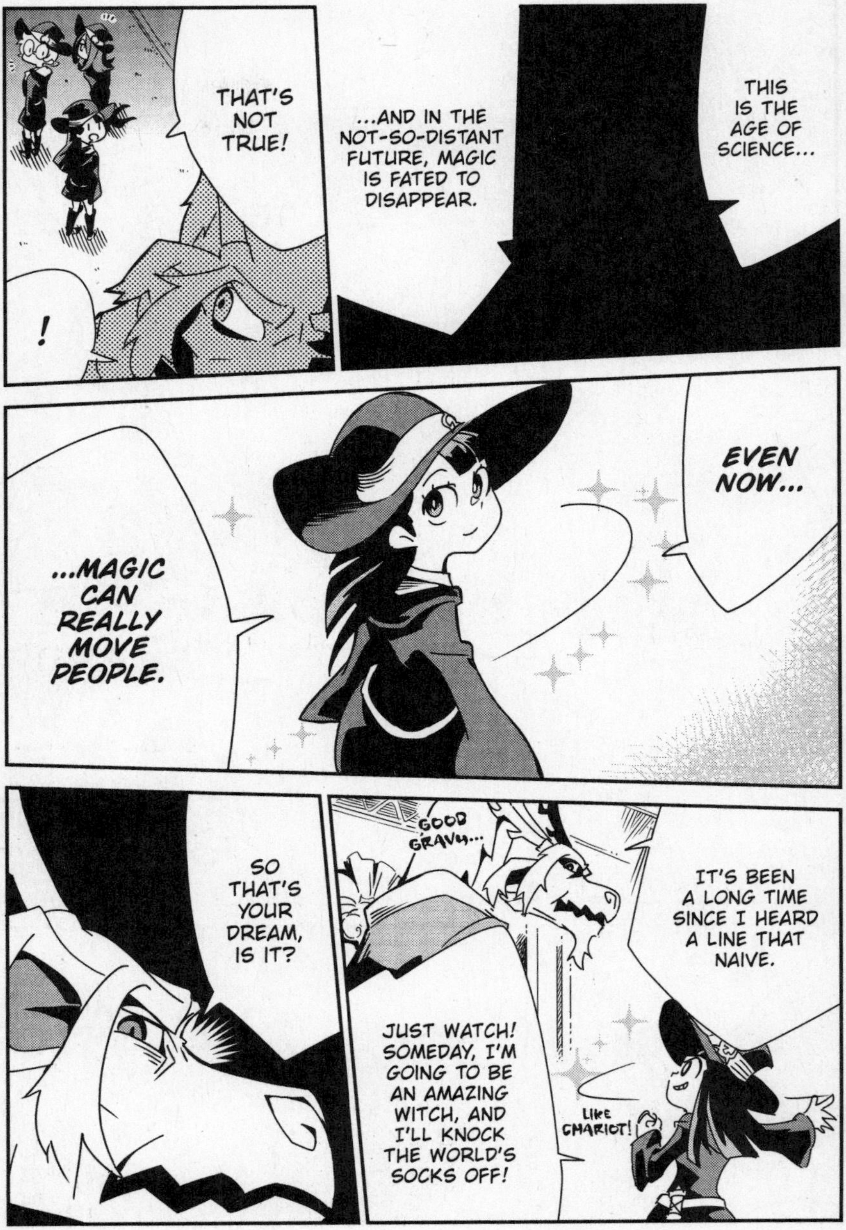
THIS IS THE AGE OF SCIENCE...
...AND IN THE NOT-SO-DISTANT FUTURE, MAGIC IS FATED TO DISAPPEAR.
THAT'S NOT TRUE!
!
EVEN NOW...
...MAGIC CAN REALLY MOVE PEOPLE.
IT'S BEEN A LONG TIME SINCE I HEARD A LINE THAT NAIVE.
GOOD GRAVY...
JUST WATCH! SOMEDAY, I'M GOING TO BE AN AMAZING WITCH, AND I'LL KNOCK THE WORLD'S SOCKS OFF!
LIKE CHARIOT!
SO THAT'S YOUR DREAM, IS IT?

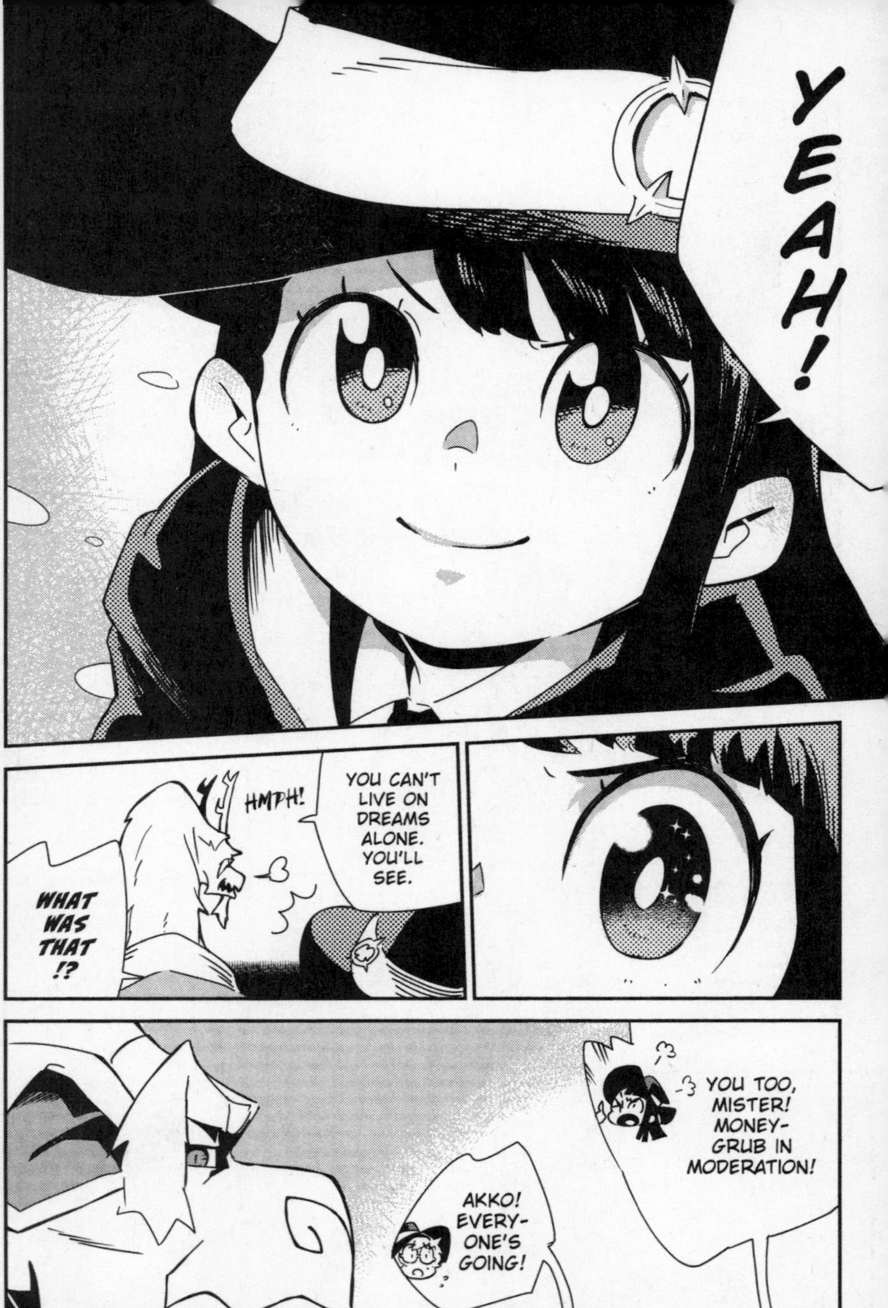
YEAH!
YOU CAN'T LIVE ON DREAMS ALONE. YOU'LL SEE.
HMPH!
WHAT WAS THAT!?
YOU TOO, MISTER! MONEY-GRUB IN MODERATION!
AKKO! EVERY-ONE'S GOING!

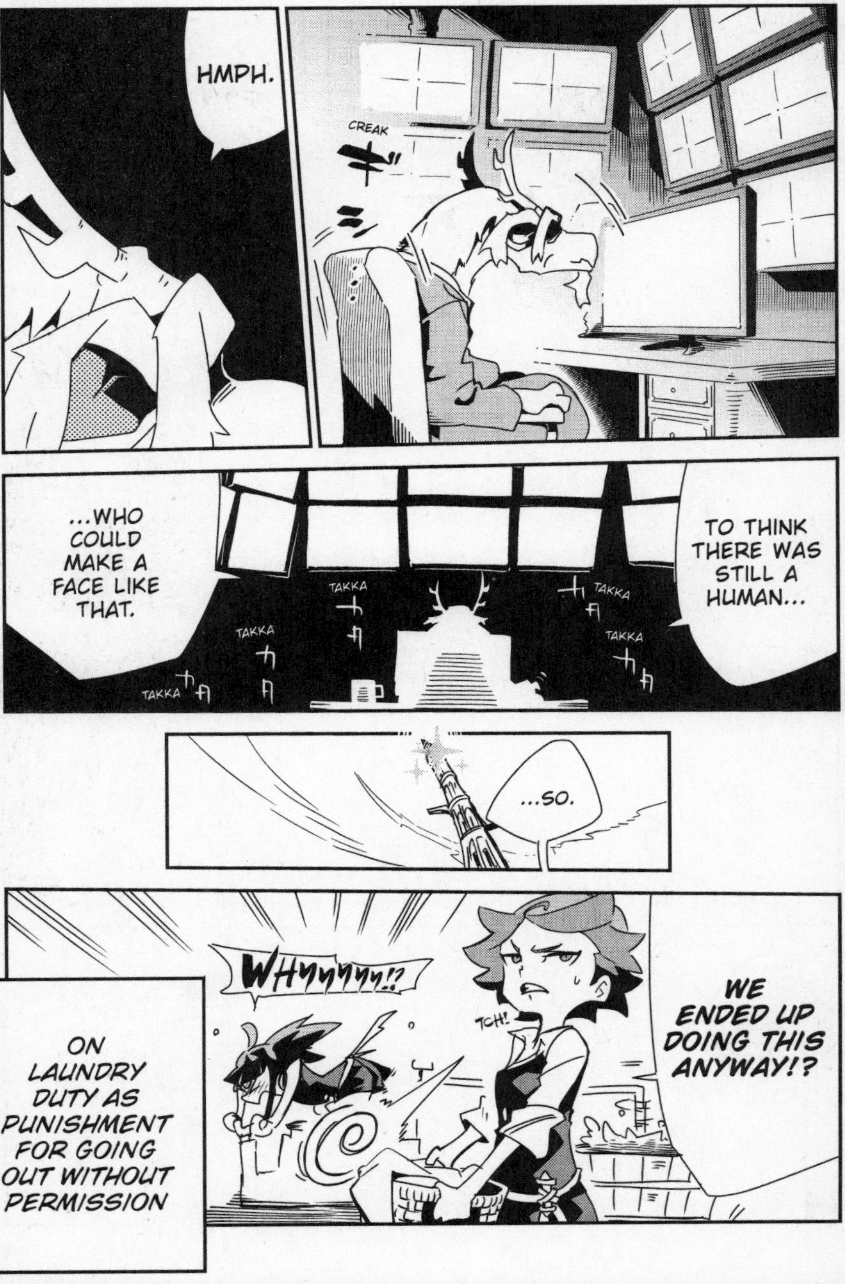

CREAK
HMPH.
TO THINK THERE WAS STILL A HUMAN...
...WHO COULD MAKE A FACE LIKE THAT.
TAKKA
TAKKA
TAKKA
TAKKA
TAKKA
...SO.
WE ENDED UP DOING THIS ANYWAY!?
WHYYYYYY!?
TCH!
ON LAUNDRY DUTY AS PUNISHMENT FOR GOING OUT WITHOUT PERMISSION

DIANA CAVENDISH

Akko's classmate. She comes from a family of distinguished British witches. Her keen mind and strong sense of justice sometimes bring her into conflict with Akko...

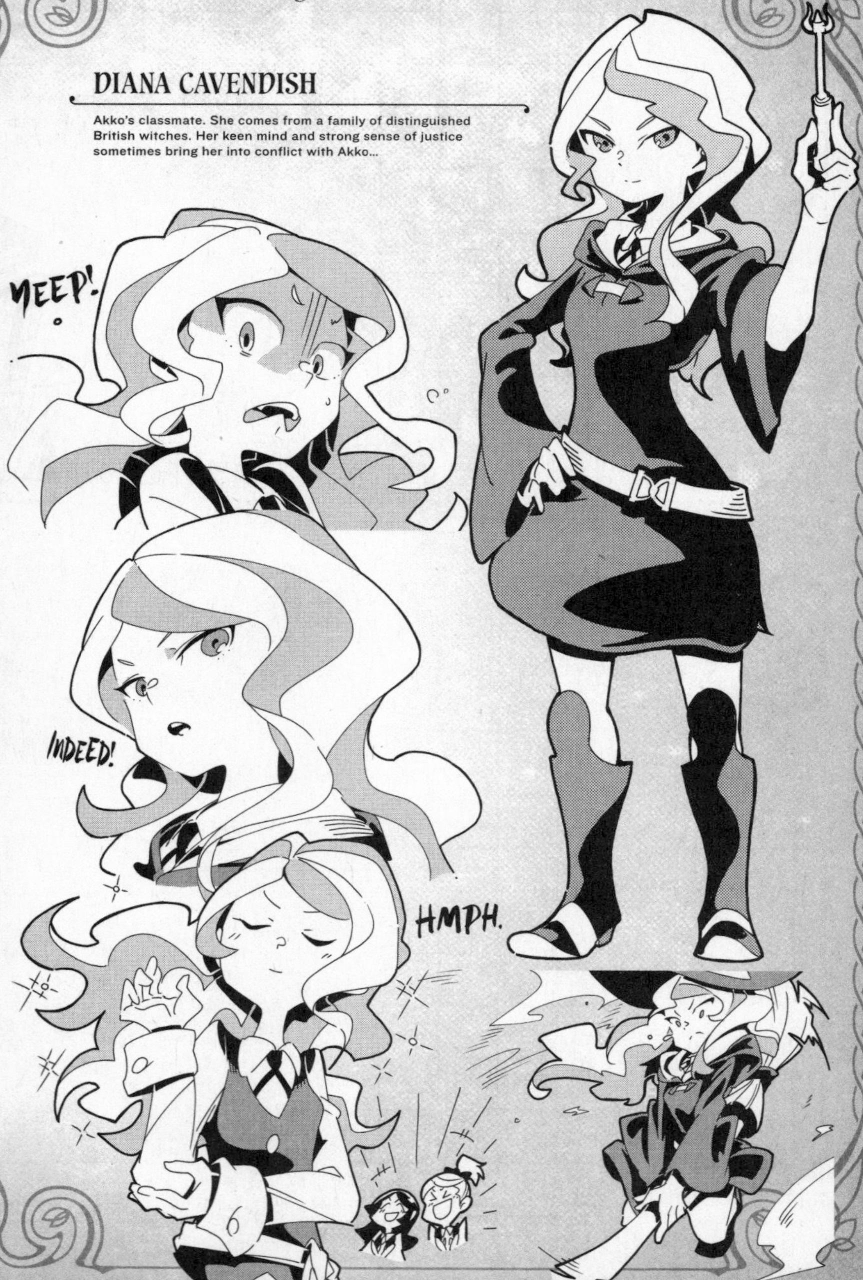
YEEP!
INDEED!
HMPH.

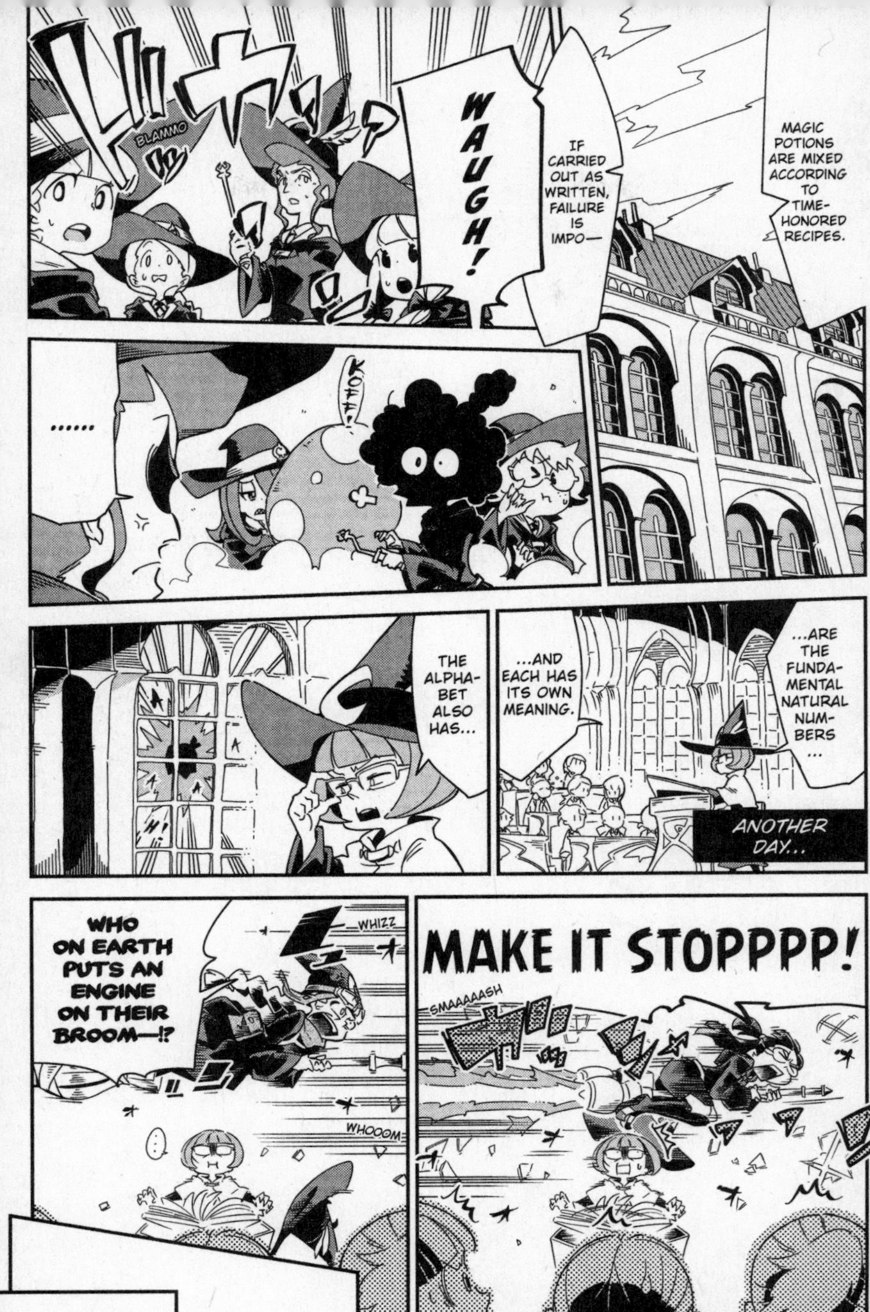
MAGIC POTIONS ARE MIXED ACCORDING TO TIME-HONORED RECIPES.
IF CARRIED OUT AS WRITTEN, FAILURE IS IMPO—
WAUGH!
BLAMMO
......
KOFF!
ANOTHER DAY...
...ARE THE FUNDAMENTAL NATURAL NUMBERS...
...AND EACH HAS ITS OWN MEANING.
THE ALPHABET ALSO HAS...
MAKE IT STOPPPP!
SMAAAAASH
WHO ON EARTH PUTS AN ENGINE ON THEIR BROOM—!?
WHIZZ
WHOOOM
...

Chapter 7

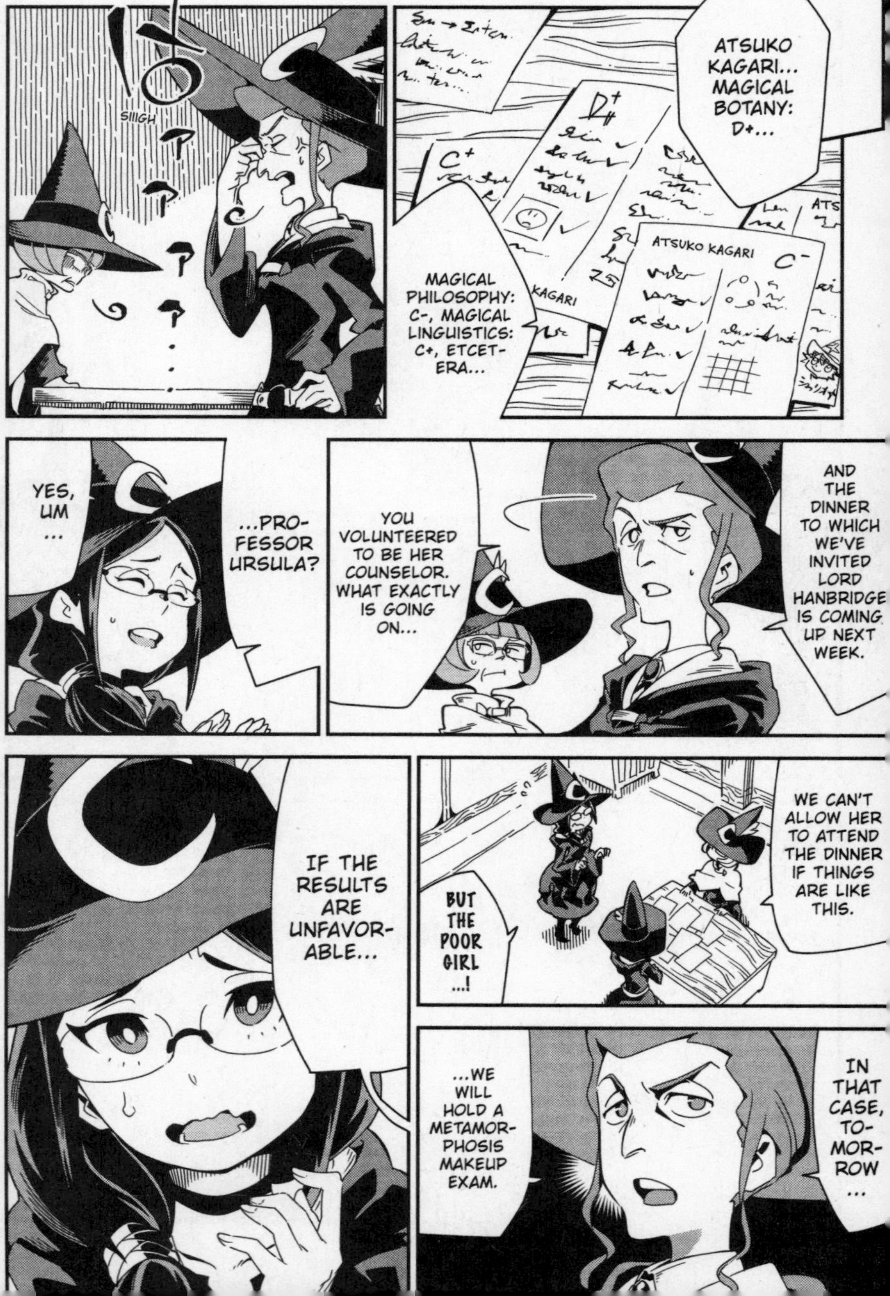
ATSUKO KAGARI... MAGICAL BOTANY: D+...
ATSUKO KAGARI
MAGICAL PHILOSOPHY: C-, MAGICAL LINGUISTICS: C+, ETCETERA...
SIIIGH
AND THE DINNER TO WHICH WE'VE INVITED LORD HANBRIDGE IS COMING UP NEXT WEEK.
YOU VOLUNTEERED TO BE HER COUNSELOR. WHAT EXACTLY IS GOING ON...
...PROFESSOR URSULA?
YES, UM...
WE CAN'T ALLOW HER TO ATTEND THE DINNER IF THINGS ARE LIKE THIS.
BUT THE POOR GIRL...!
IN THAT CASE, TOMORROW...
...WE WILL HOLD A METAMORPHOSIS MAKEUP EXAM.
IF THE RESULTS ARE UNFAVORABLE...

Chapter 7

AKKO'S ADVENTURE

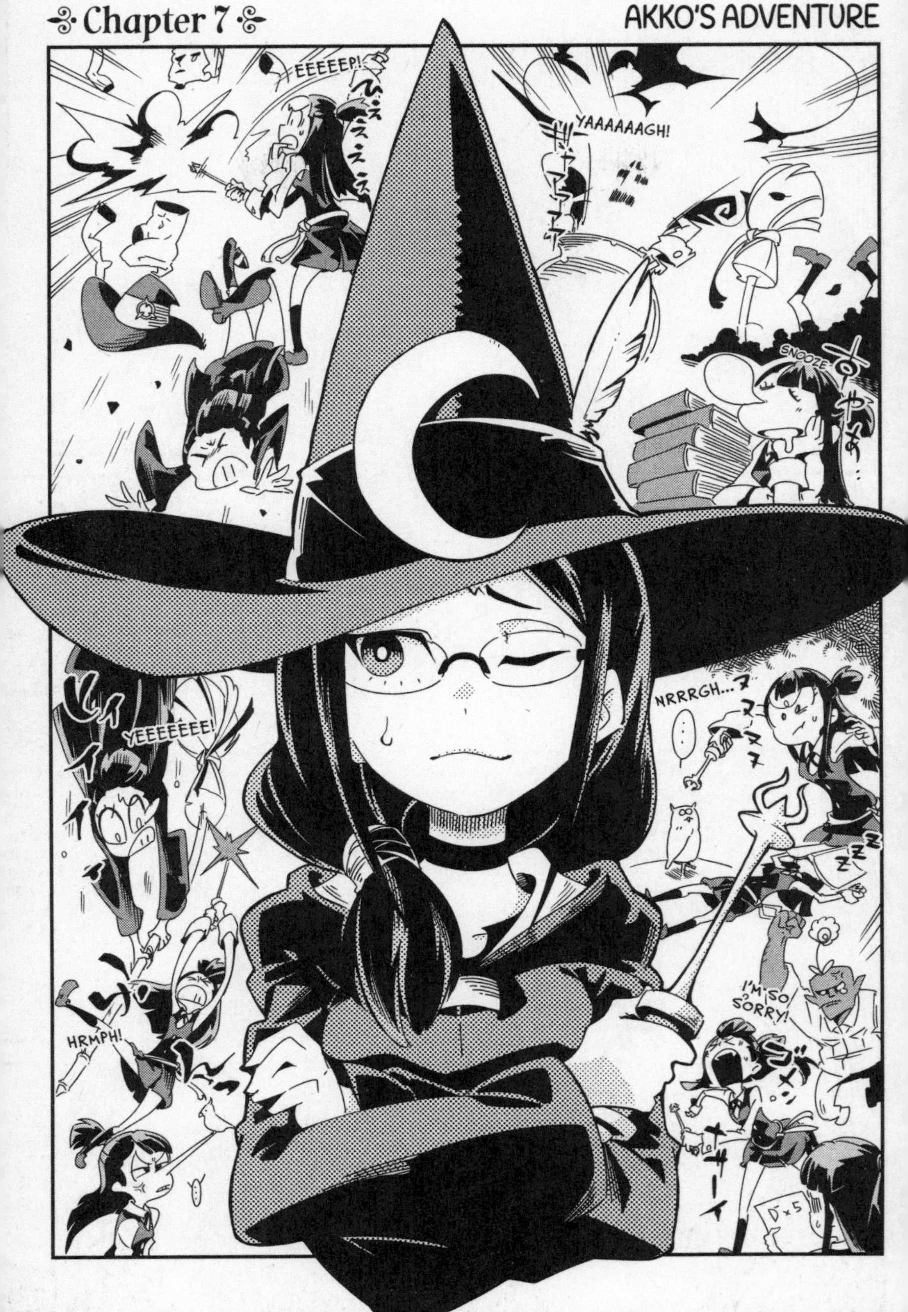
YAAAAAAGH!
EEEEEP!
SNOOZE
NRRRGH...
YEEEEEEE!
I'M SO SORRY!
HRMPH!

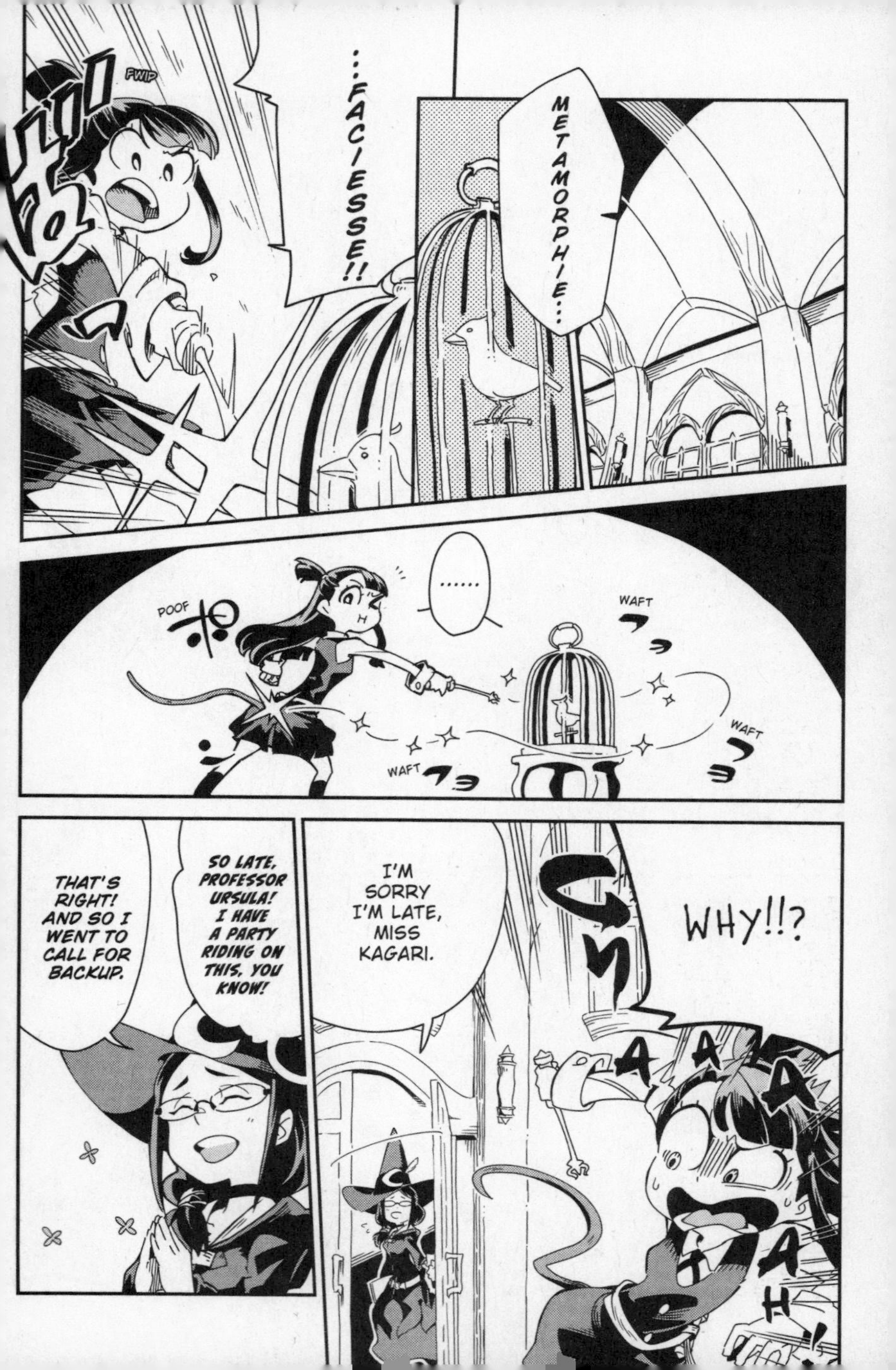
METAMORPHIE...
...FACIESSE!!
FWIP
POOF
......
WAFT
WAFT
WAFT
WHY!!?
I'M SORRY I'M LATE, MISS KAGARI.
AAAAAH!
SO LATE, PROFESSOR URSULA! I HAVE A PARTY RIDING ON THIS, YOU KNOW!
THAT'S RIGHT! AND SO I WENT TO CALL FOR BACKUP.

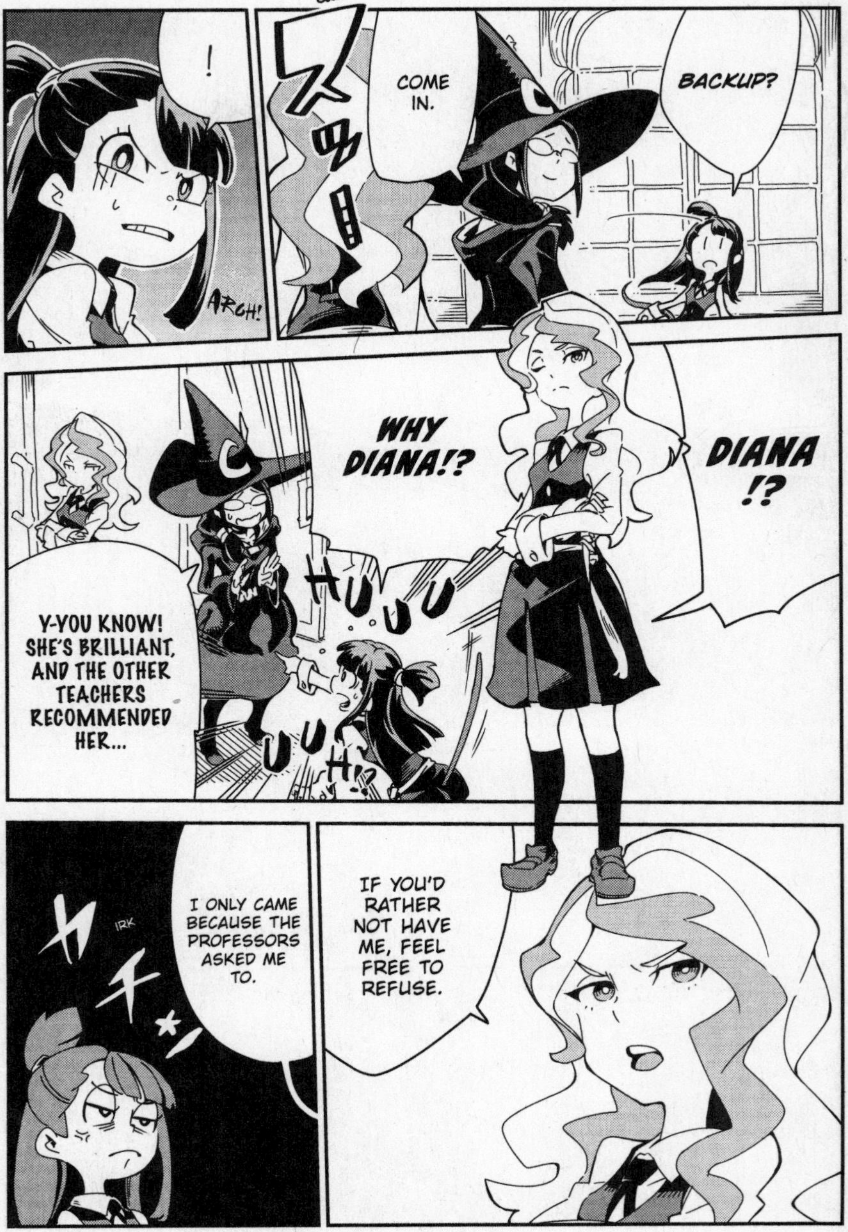
BACKUP?
SHUF
COME IN.
!
ARGH!
DIANA!?
WHY DIANA!?
HUUUUUH!?
Y-YOU KNOW! SHE'S BRILLIANT, AND THE OTHER TEACHERS RECOMMENDED HER...
IF YOU'D RATHER NOT HAVE ME, FEEL FREE TO REFUSE.
I ONLY CAME BECAUSE THE PROFESSORS ASKED ME TO.
IRK

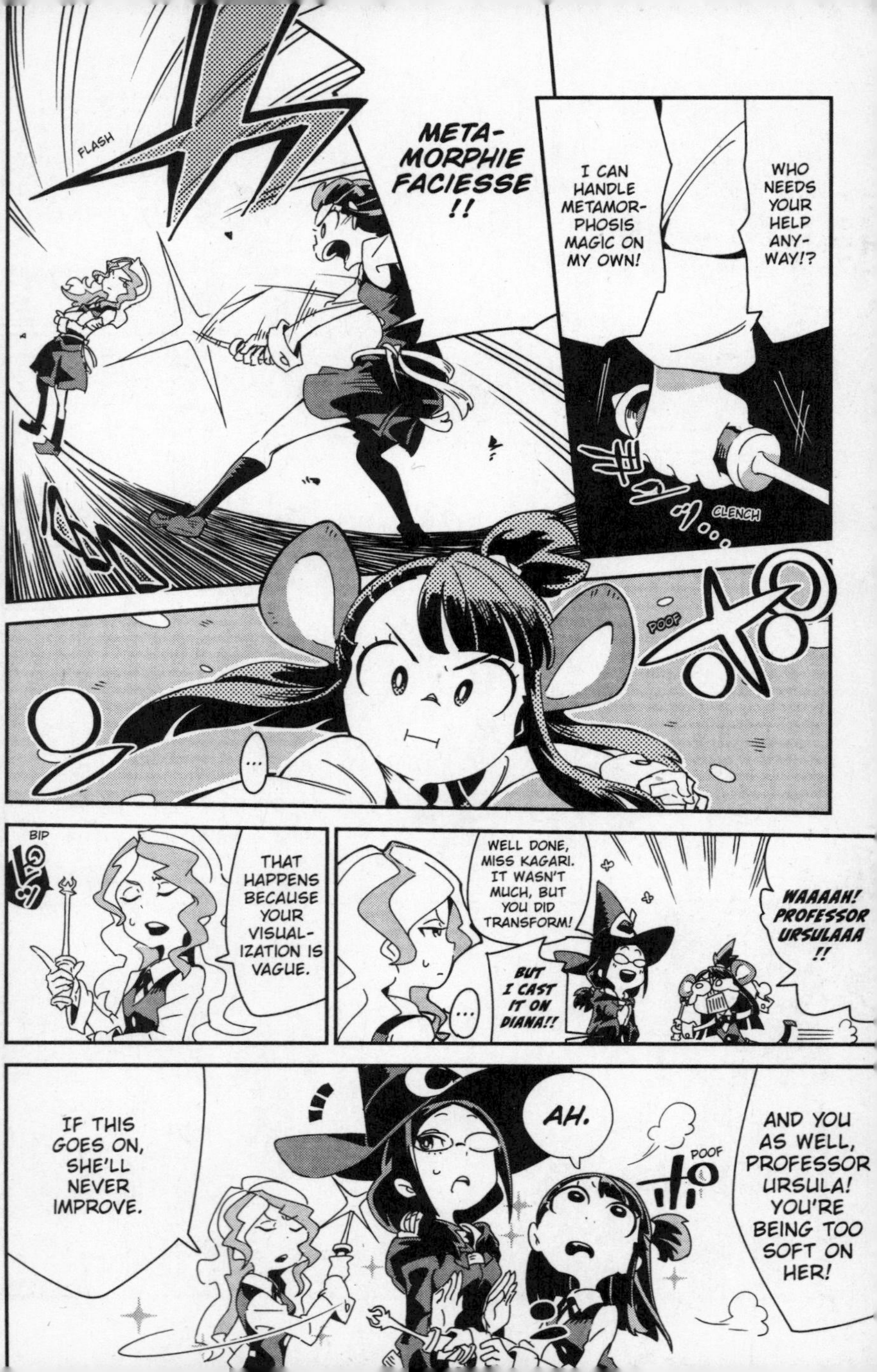
WHO NEEDS YOUR HELP ANYWAY!?
I CAN HANDLE METAMORPHOSIS MAGIC ON MY OWN!
CLENCH
META-MORPHIE FACIESSE !!
FLASH
POOF
...
WAAAAH! PROFESSOR URSULAAA !!
WELL DONE, MISS KAGARI. IT WASN'T MUCH, BUT YOU DID TRANSFORM!
BUT I CAST IT ON DIANA!!
...
THAT HAPPENS BECAUSE YOUR VISUAL-IZATION IS VAGUE.
BIP
AND YOU AS WELL, PROFESSOR URSULA! YOU'RE BEING TOO SOFT ON HER!
POOF
AH.
IF THIS GOES ON, SHE'LL NEVER IMPROVE.

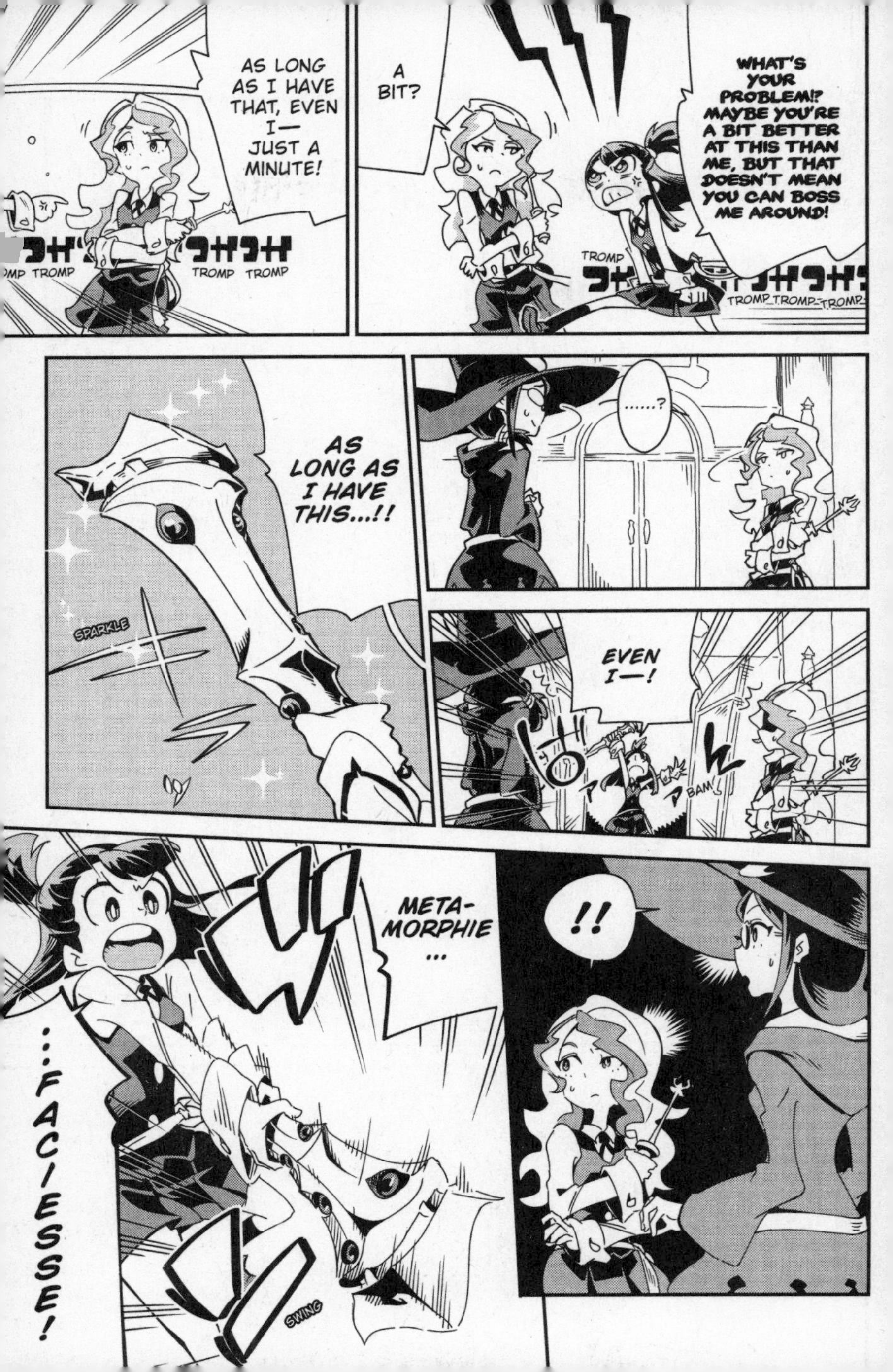
WHAT'S YOUR PROBLEM!? MAYBE YOU'RE A BIT BETTER AT THIS THAN ME, BUT THAT DOESN'T MEAN YOU CAN BOSS ME AROUND!
A BIT?
TROMP
TROMP TROMP TROMP
AS LONG AS I HAVE THAT, EVEN I— JUST A MINUTE!
TROMP TROMP
OMP TROMP
......?
EVEN I—!
BAM
AS LONG AS I HAVE THIS...!!
SPARKLE
!!
META-MORPHIE ...
...FACIESSE!
SWING

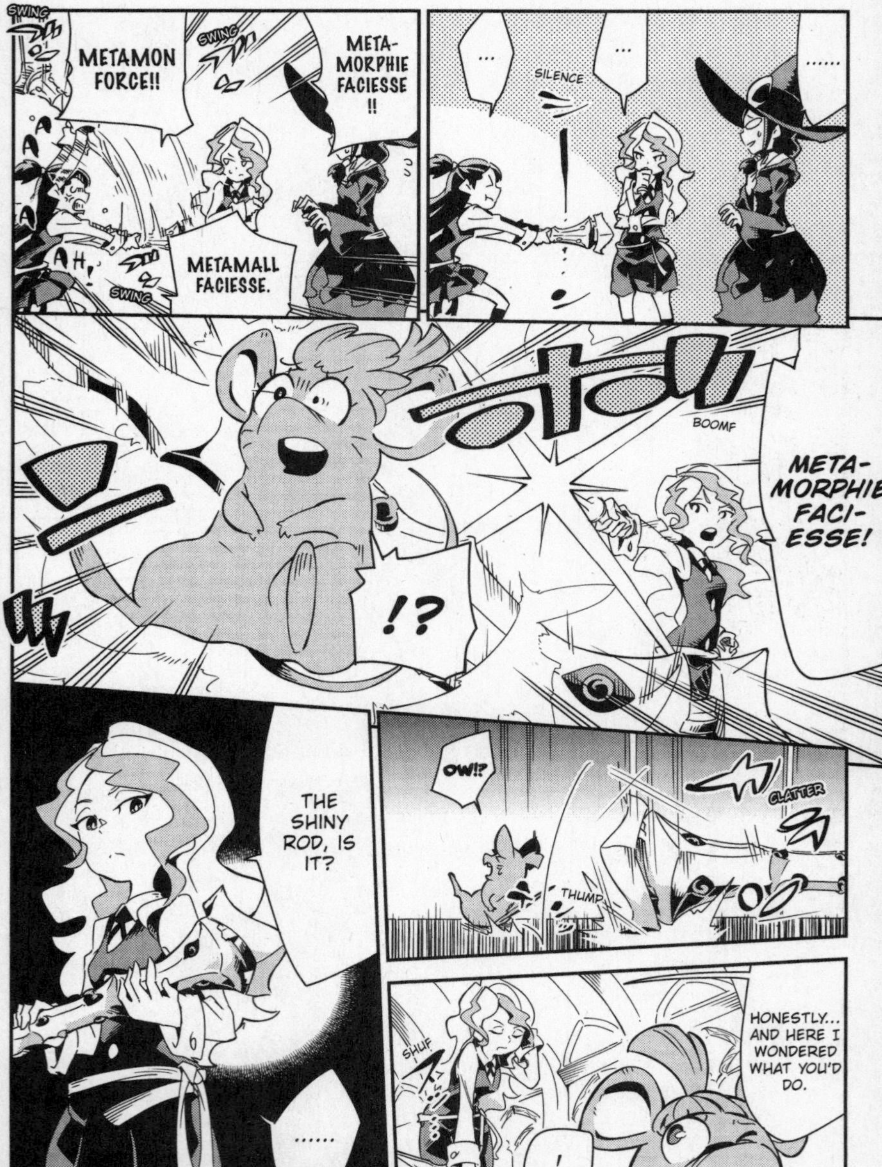
...
...
SILENCE
......
META-MORPHIE FACIESSE !!
SWING
SWING
METAMON FORCE!!
AH!
METAMALL FACIESSE.
SWING
META-MORPHIE FACI-ESSE!
BOOMF
!?
OW!?
CLATTER
THUMP
HONESTLY... AND HERE I WONDERED WHAT YOU'D DO.
!
SHUF
THE SHINY ROD, IS IT?
......

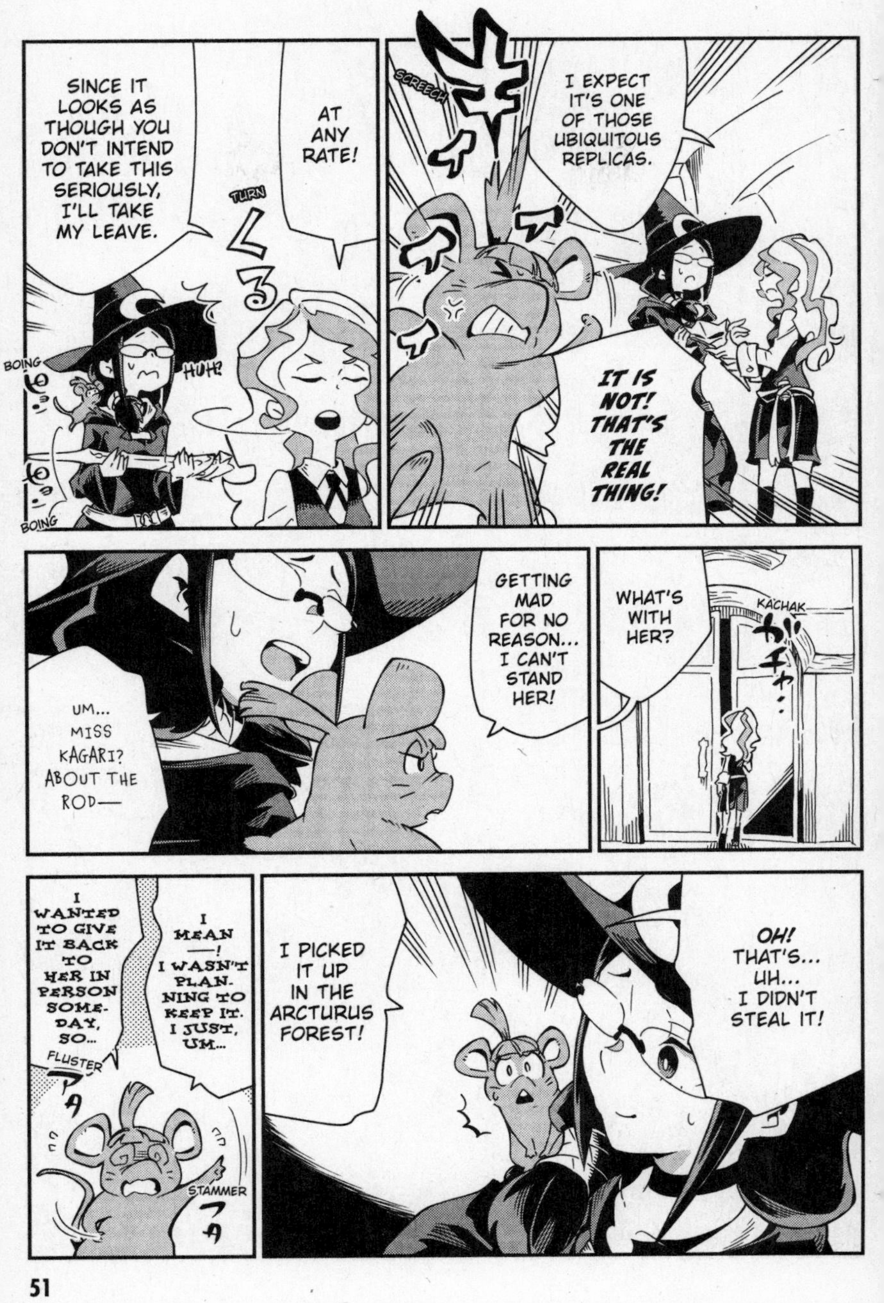
SCREECH
I EXPECT IT'S ONE OF THOSE UBIQUITOUS REPLICAS.
IT IS NOT! THAT'S THE REAL THING!
AT ANY RATE!
SINCE IT LOOKS AS THOUGH YOU DON'T INTEND TO TAKE THIS SERIOUSLY, I'LL TAKE MY LEAVE.
TURN
HUH?
BOING
BOING
WHAT'S WITH HER?
KACHAK
GETTING MAD FOR NO REASON... I CAN'T STAND HER!
UM... MISS KAGARI? ABOUT THE ROD—
OH! THAT'S... UH... I DIDN'T STEAL IT!
I PICKED IT UP IN THE ARCTURUS FOREST!
I MEAN—! I WASN'T PLAN-NING TO KEEP IT. I JUST, UM...
I WANTED TO GIVE IT BACK TO HER IN PERSON SOME-DAY, SO...
FLUSTER
STAMMER

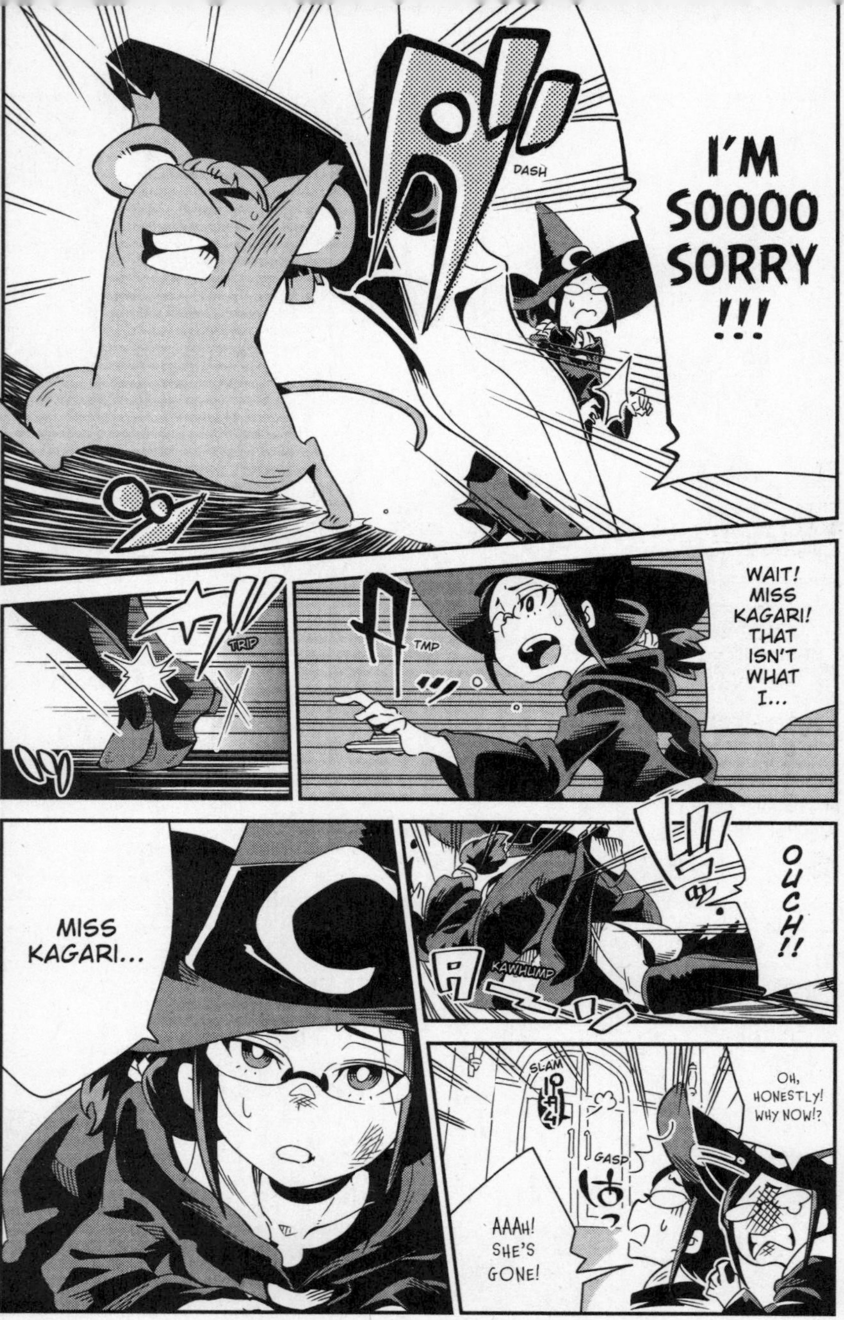
DASH
I'M SOOOO SORRY!!!
WAIT! MISS KAGARI! THAT ISN'T WHAT I...
TMP
TRIP
OUCH!!
KAWHUMP
OH, HONESTLY! WHY NOW!?
SLAM
GASP
AAAH! SHE'S GONE!
MISS KAGARI...

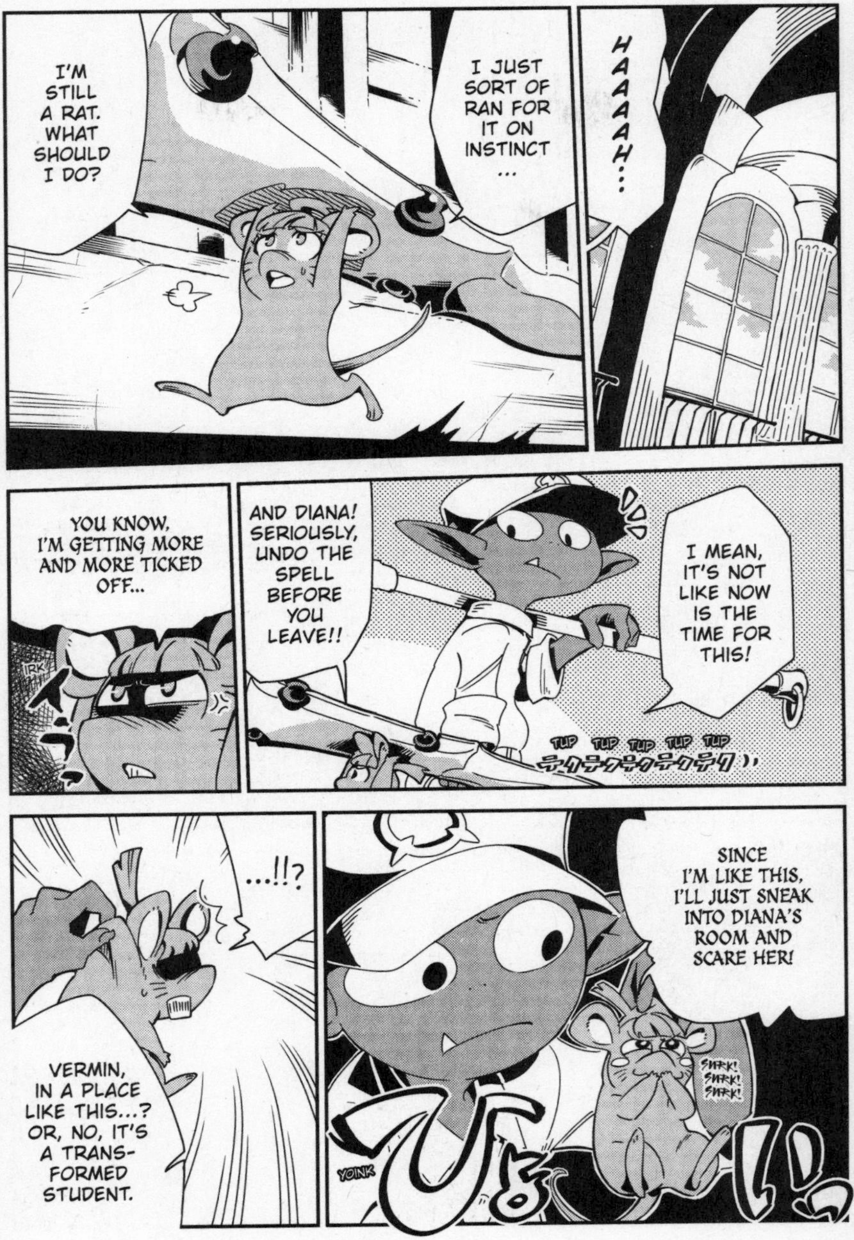
HAAAAAH...
I JUST SORT OF RAN FOR IT ON INSTINCT ...
I'M STILL A RAT. WHAT SHOULD I DO?
I MEAN, IT'S NOT LIKE NOW IS THE TIME FOR THIS!
AND DIANA! SERIOUSLY, UNDO THE SPELL BEFORE YOU LEAVE!!
TUP TUP TUP TUP TUP
YOU KNOW, I'M GETTING MORE AND MORE TICKED OFF...
IRK
SINCE I'M LIKE THIS, I'LL JUST SNEAK INTO DIANA'S ROOM AND SCARE HER!
SNRK! SNRK! SNRK!
YOINK
...!!?
VERMIN, IN A PLACE LIKE THIS...? OR, NO, IT'S A TRANSFORMED STUDENT.

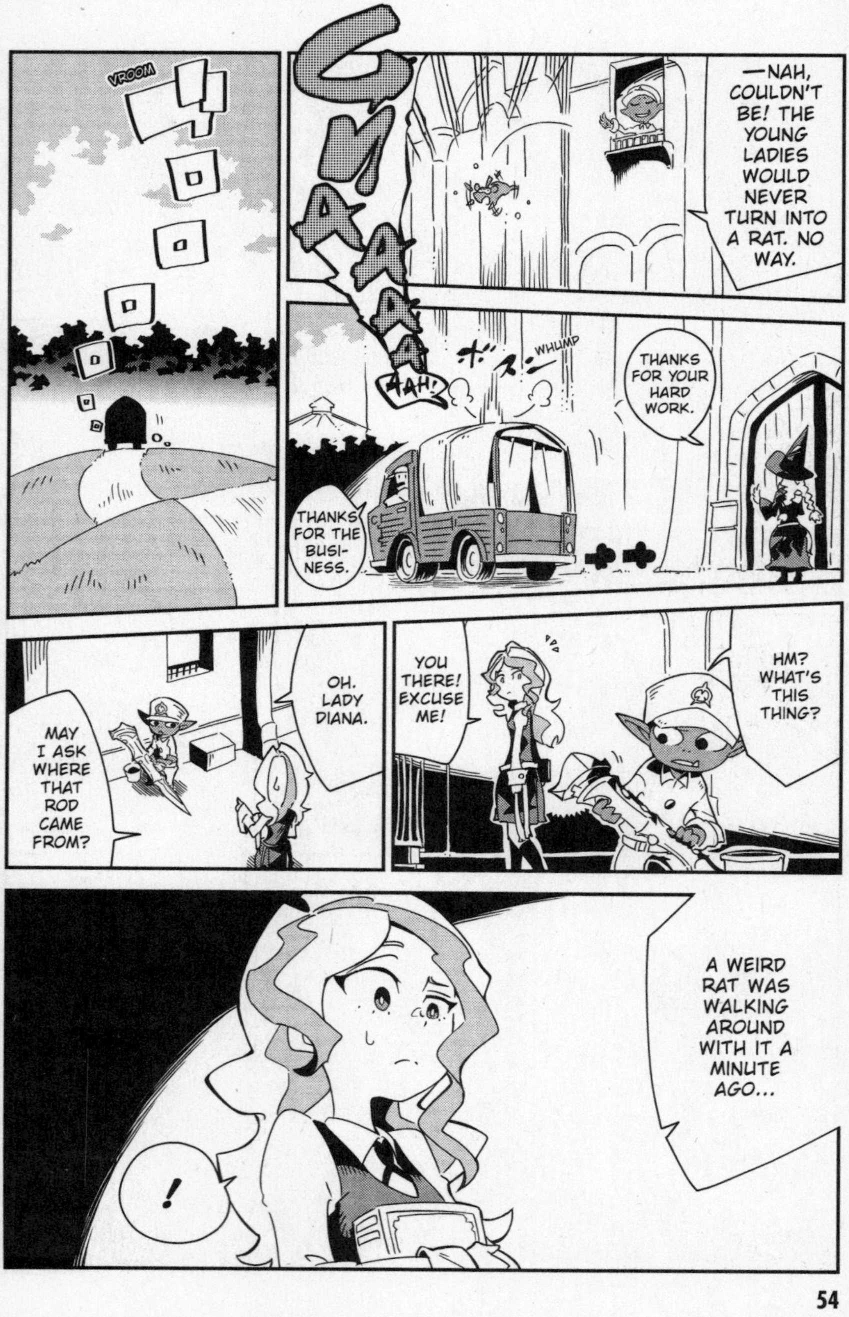

—NAH, COULDN'T BE! THE YOUNG LADIES WOULD NEVER TURN INTO A RAT. NO WAY.
AAH!
WHUMP
THANKS FOR YOUR HARD WORK.
THANKS FOR THE BUSI-NESS.
VROOM
HM? WHAT'S THIS THING?
YOU THERE! EXCUSE ME!
OH. LADY DIANA.
MAY I ASK WHERE THAT ROD CAME FROM?
A WEIRD RAT WAS WALKING AROUND WITH IT A MINUTE AGO...
!

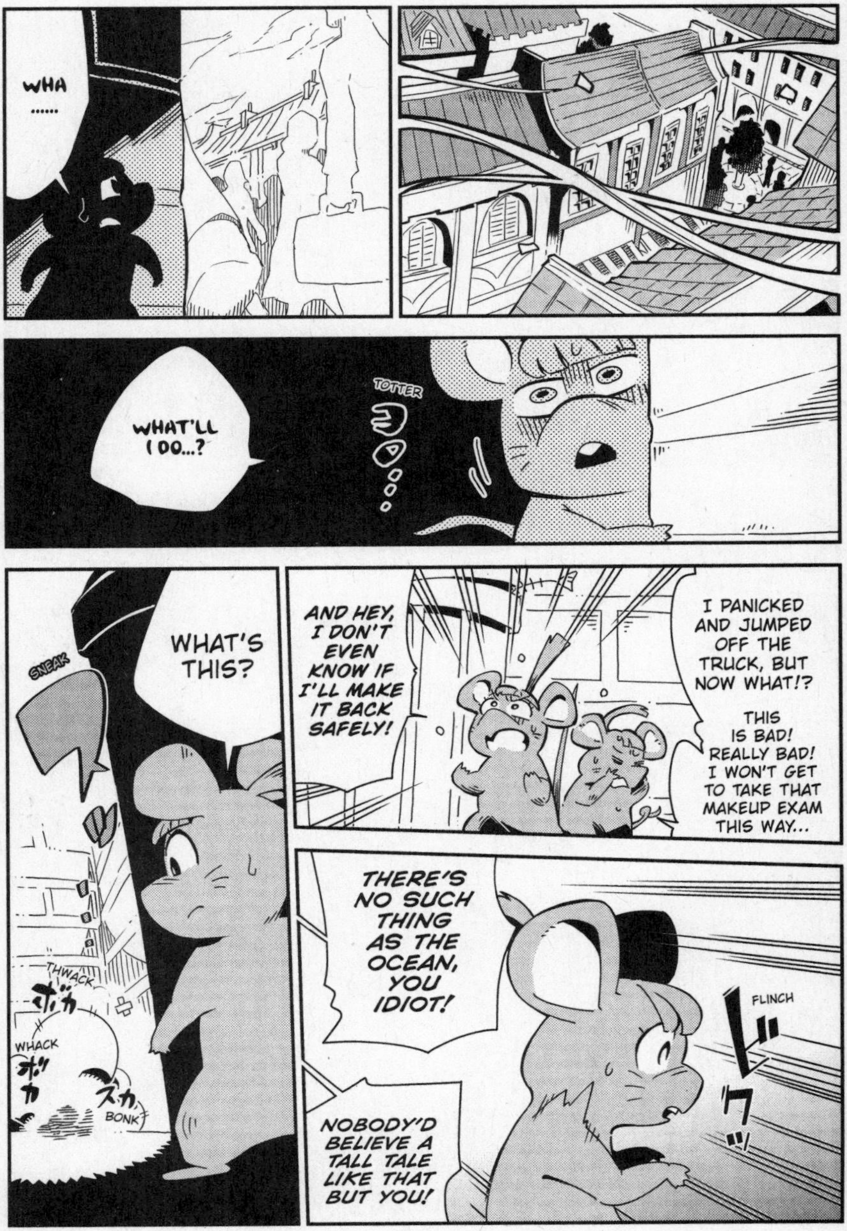
WHA ......
TOTTER
WHAT'LL I DO...?
I PANICKED AND JUMPED OFF THE TRUCK, BUT NOW WHAT!?
THIS IS BAD! REALLY BAD! I WON'T GET TO TAKE THAT MAKEUP EXAM THIS WAY...
AND HEY, I DON'T EVEN KNOW IF I'LL MAKE IT BACK SAFELY!
FLINCH
THERE'S NO SUCH THING AS THE OCEAN, YOU IDIOT!
NOBODY'D BELIEVE A TALL TALE LIKE THAT BUT YOU!
WHAT'S THIS?
SNEAK
THWACK
WHACK
BONK

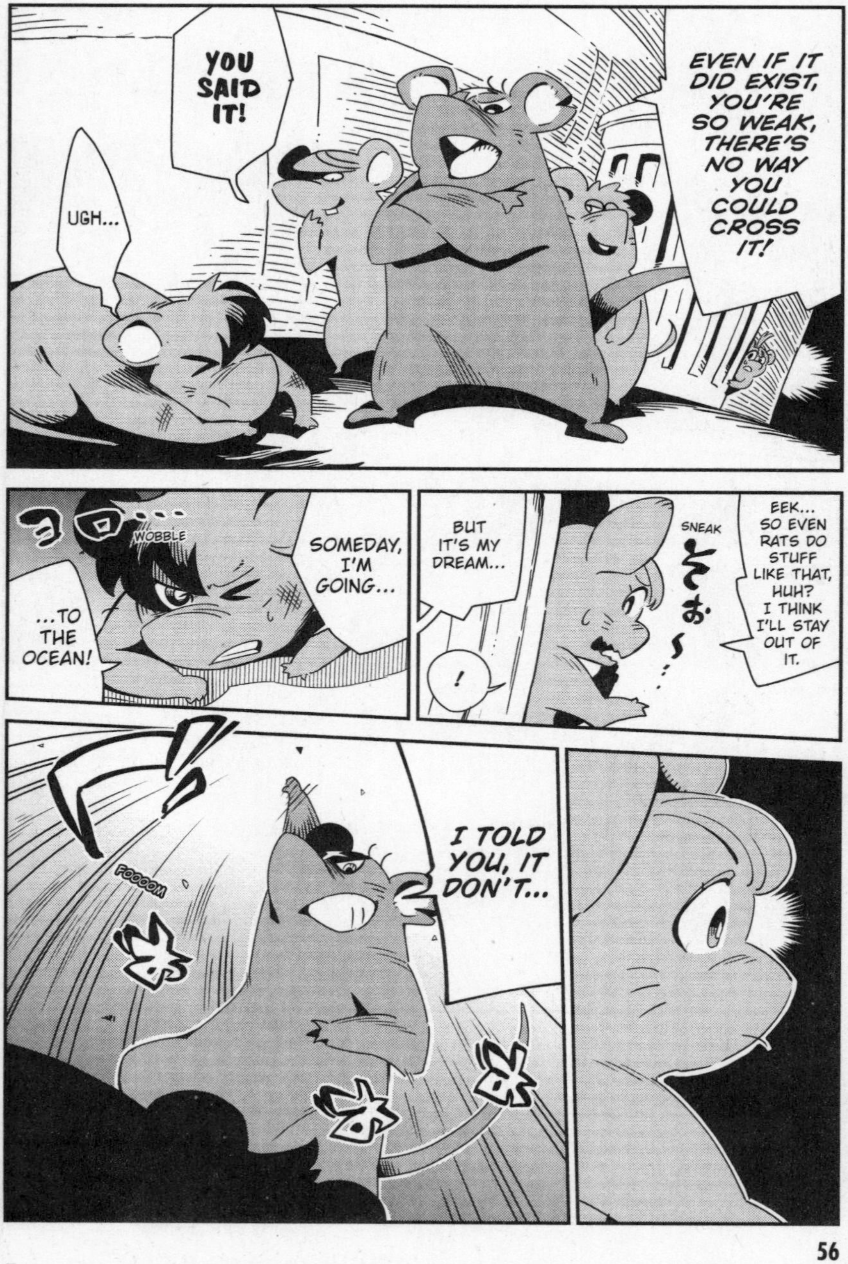
EVEN IF IT DID EXIST, YOU'RE SO WEAK, THERE'S NO WAY YOU COULD CROSS IT!
YOU SAID IT!
UGH...
EEK... SO EVEN RATS DO STUFF LIKE THAT, HUH? I THINK I'LL STAY OUT OF IT.
SNEAK
BUT IT'S MY DREAM...
!
SOMEDAY, I'M GOING...
WOBBLE
...TO THE OCEAN!
I TOLD YOU, IT DON'T...
FOOOOM

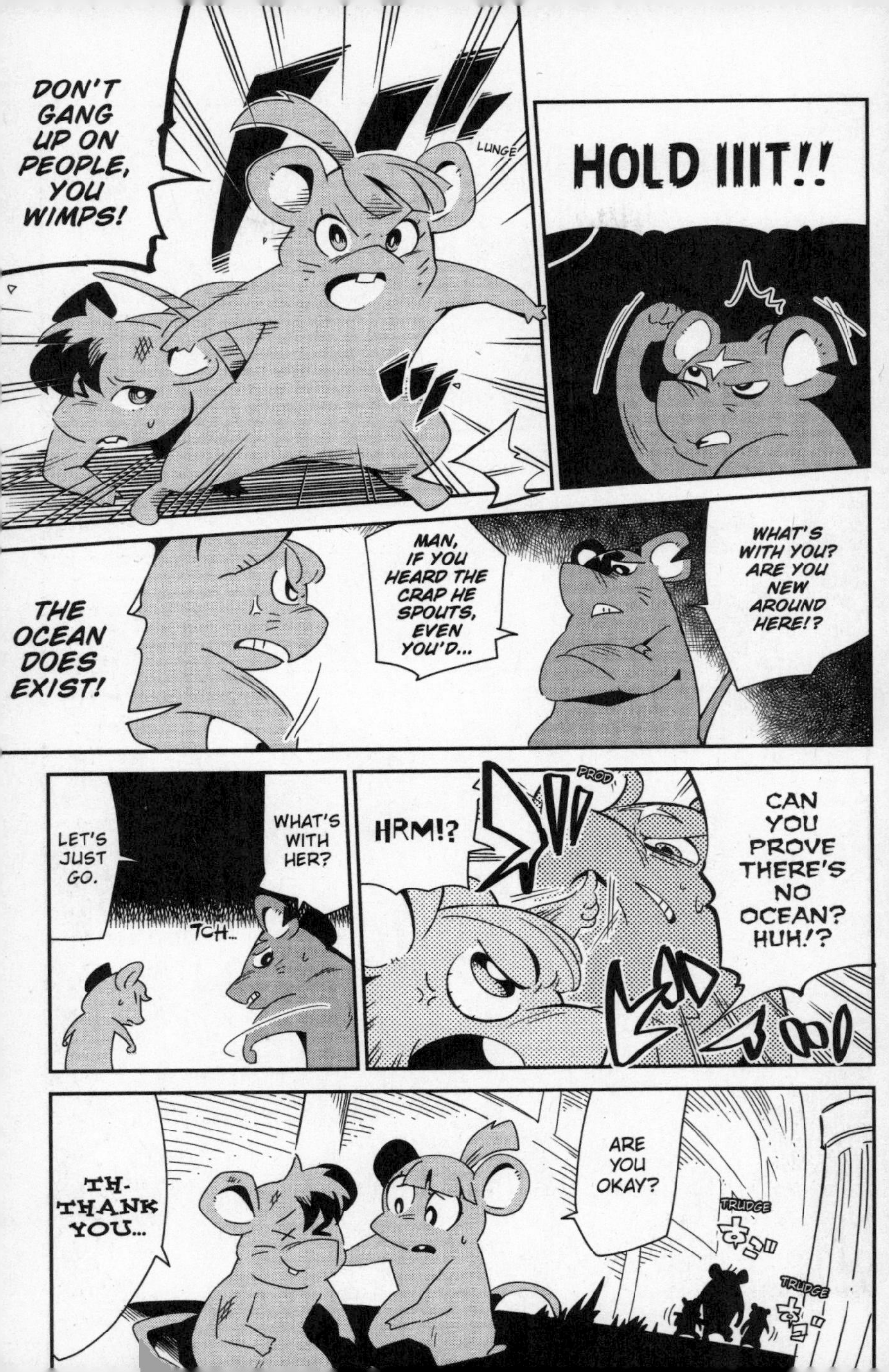
HOLD IIIT!!
LUNGE
DON'T GANG UP ON PEOPLE, YOU WIMPS!
WHAT'S WITH YOU? ARE YOU NEW AROUND HERE!?
MAN, IF YOU HEARD THE CRAP HE SPOUTS, EVEN YOU'D...
THE OCEAN DOES EXIST!
PROD
CAN YOU PROVE THERE'S NO OCEAN? HUH!?
HRM!?
WHAT'S WITH HER?
LET'S JUST GO.
TCH...
ARE YOU OKAY?
TRUDGE
TRUDGE
TH-THANK YOU...

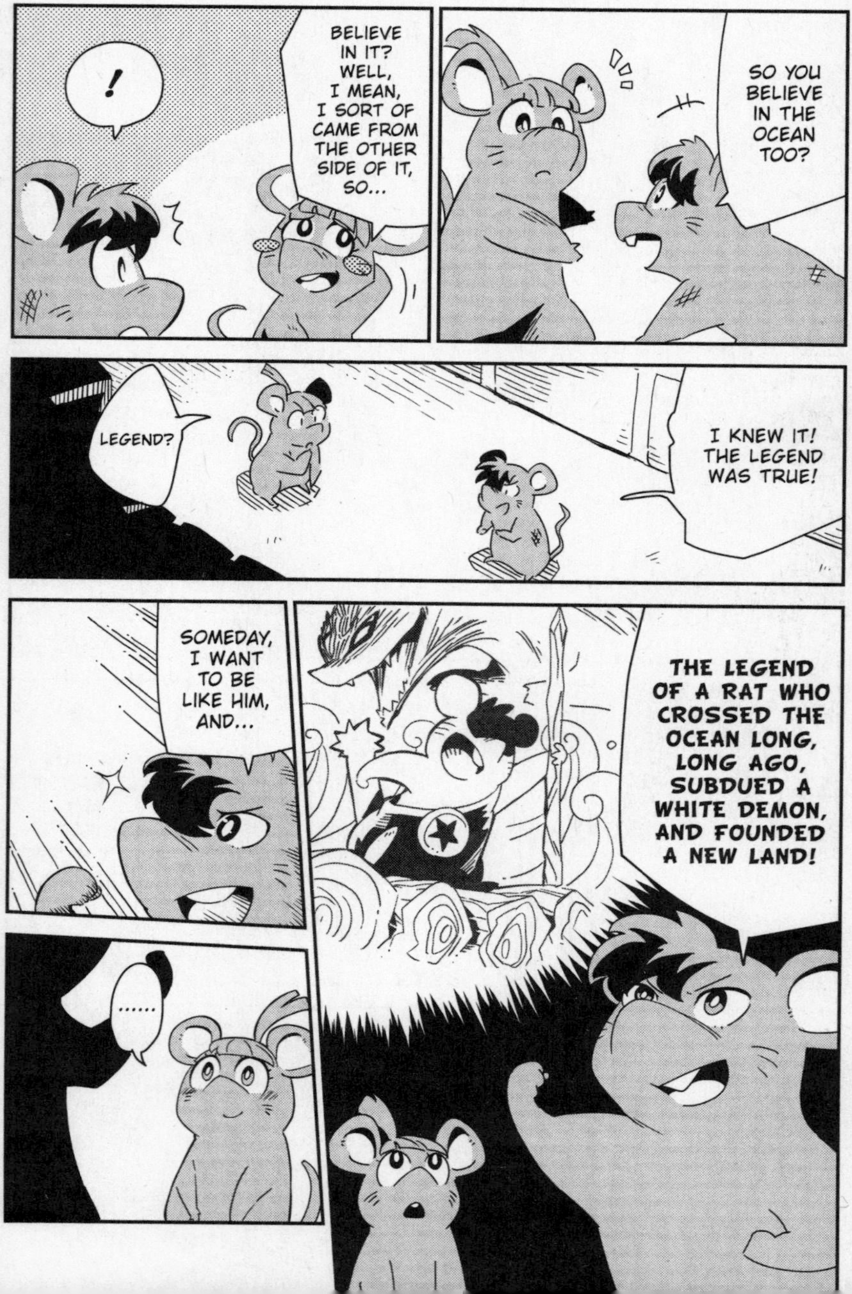
SO YOU BELIEVE IN THE OCEAN TOO?
BELIEVE IN IT? WELL, I MEAN, I SORT OF CAME FROM THE OTHER SIDE OF IT, SO...
!
I KNEW IT! THE LEGEND WAS TRUE!
LEGEND?
THE LEGEND OF A RAT WHO CROSSED THE OCEAN LONG, LONG AGO, SUBDUED A WHITE DEMON, AND FOUNDED A NEW LAND!
SOMEDAY, I WANT TO BE LIKE HIM, AND...
......

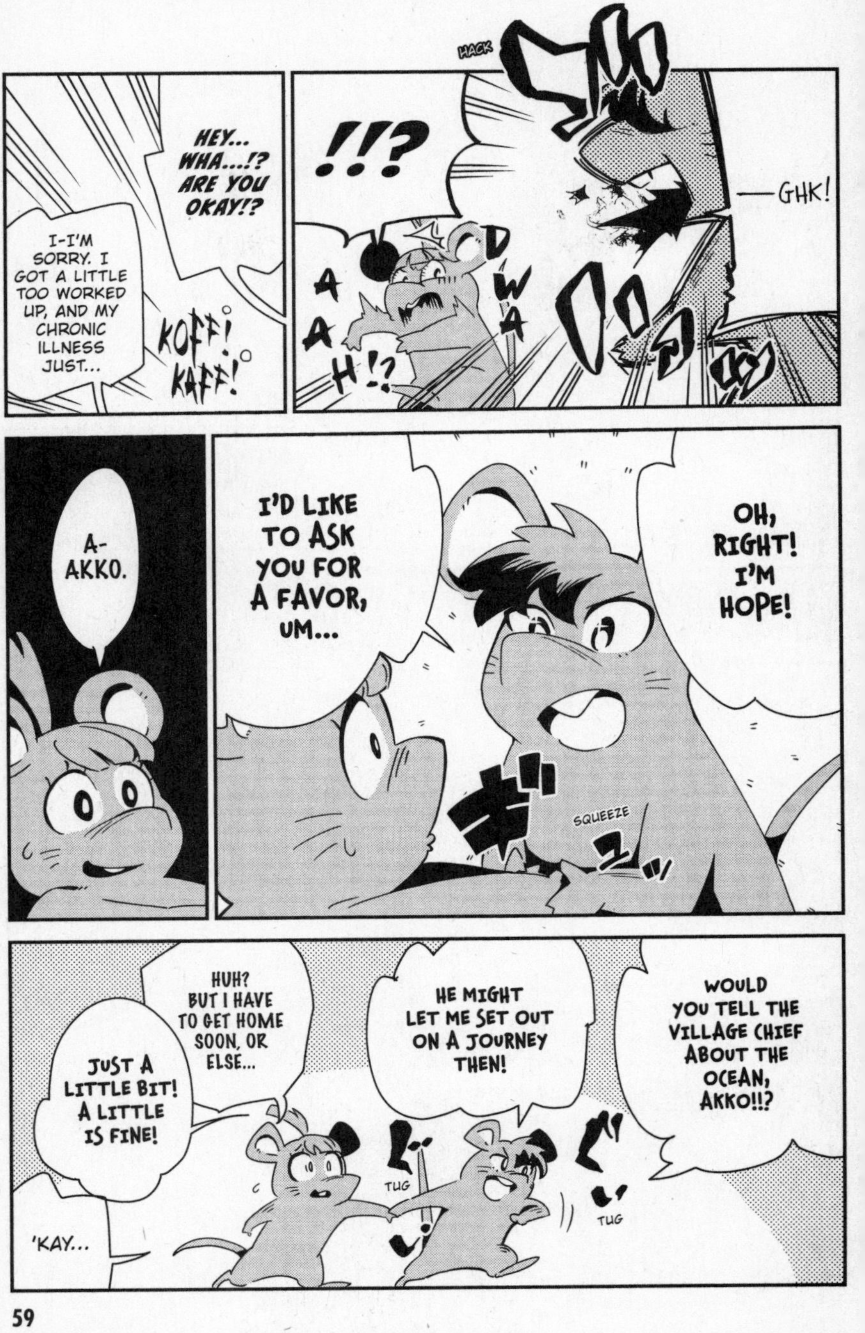
HACK
!!?
—GHK!
DWA
AAH!?
HEY... WHA...!? ARE YOU OKAY!?
I-I'M SORRY. I GOT A LITTLE TOO WORKED UP, AND MY CHRONIC ILLNESS JUST...
KOFF! KAFF!
OH, RIGHT! I'M HOPE!
I'D LIKE TO ASK YOU FOR A FAVOR, UM...
SQUEEZE
A- AKKO.
WOULD YOU TELL THE VILLAGE CHIEF ABOUT THE OCEAN, AKKO!!?
HE MIGHT LET ME SET OUT ON A JOURNEY THEN!
TUG
TUG
HUH? BUT I HAVE TO GET HOME SOON, OR ELSE...
JUST A LITTLE BIT! A LITTLE IS FINE!
'KAY...

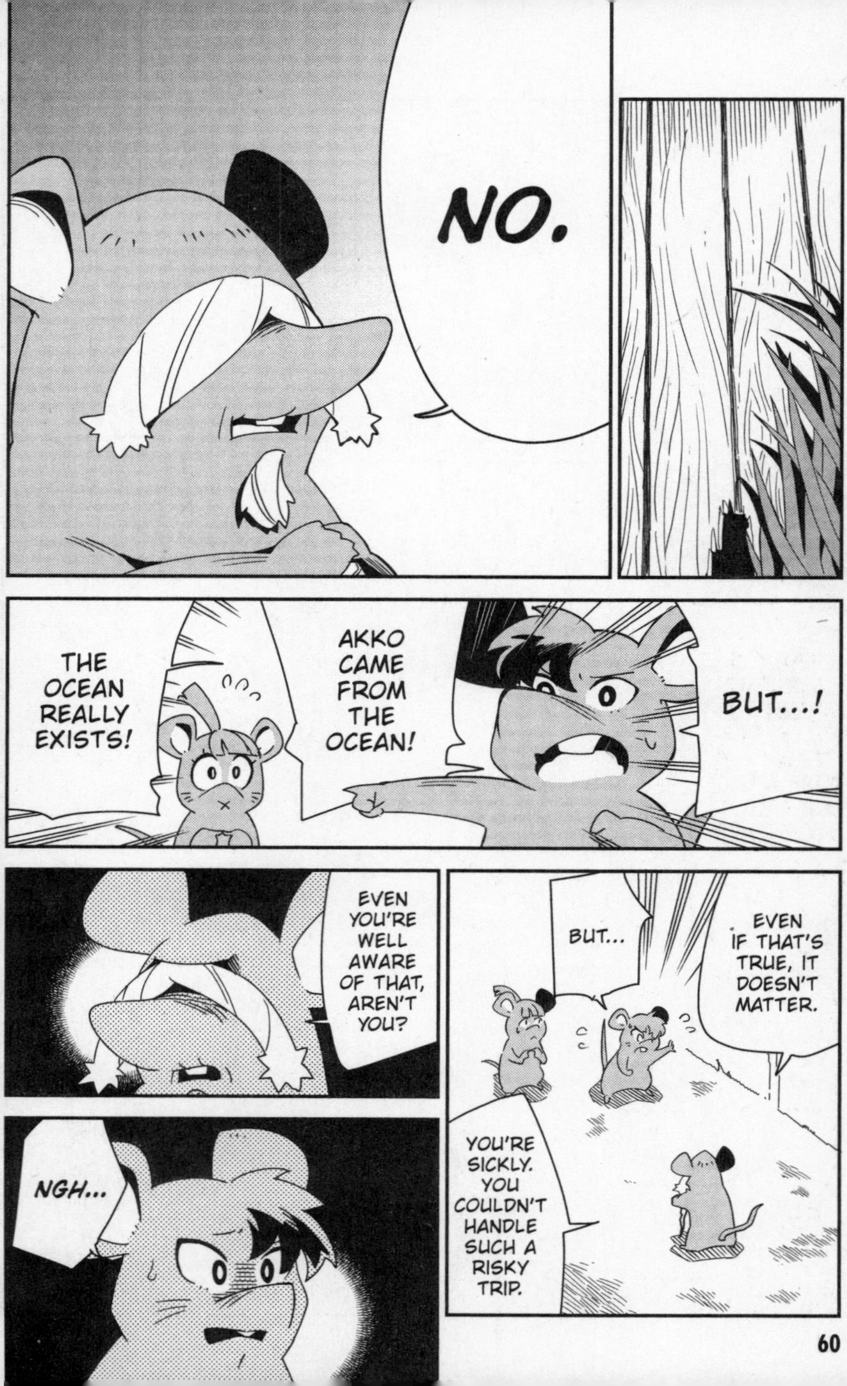
NO.
BUT...!
AKKO CAME FROM THE OCEAN!
THE OCEAN REALLY EXISTS!
EVEN IF THAT'S TRUE, IT DOESN'T MATTER.
BUT...
YOU'RE SICKLY. YOU COULDN'T HANDLE SUCH A RISKY TRIP.
EVEN YOU'RE WELL AWARE OF THAT, AREN'T YOU?
NGH...

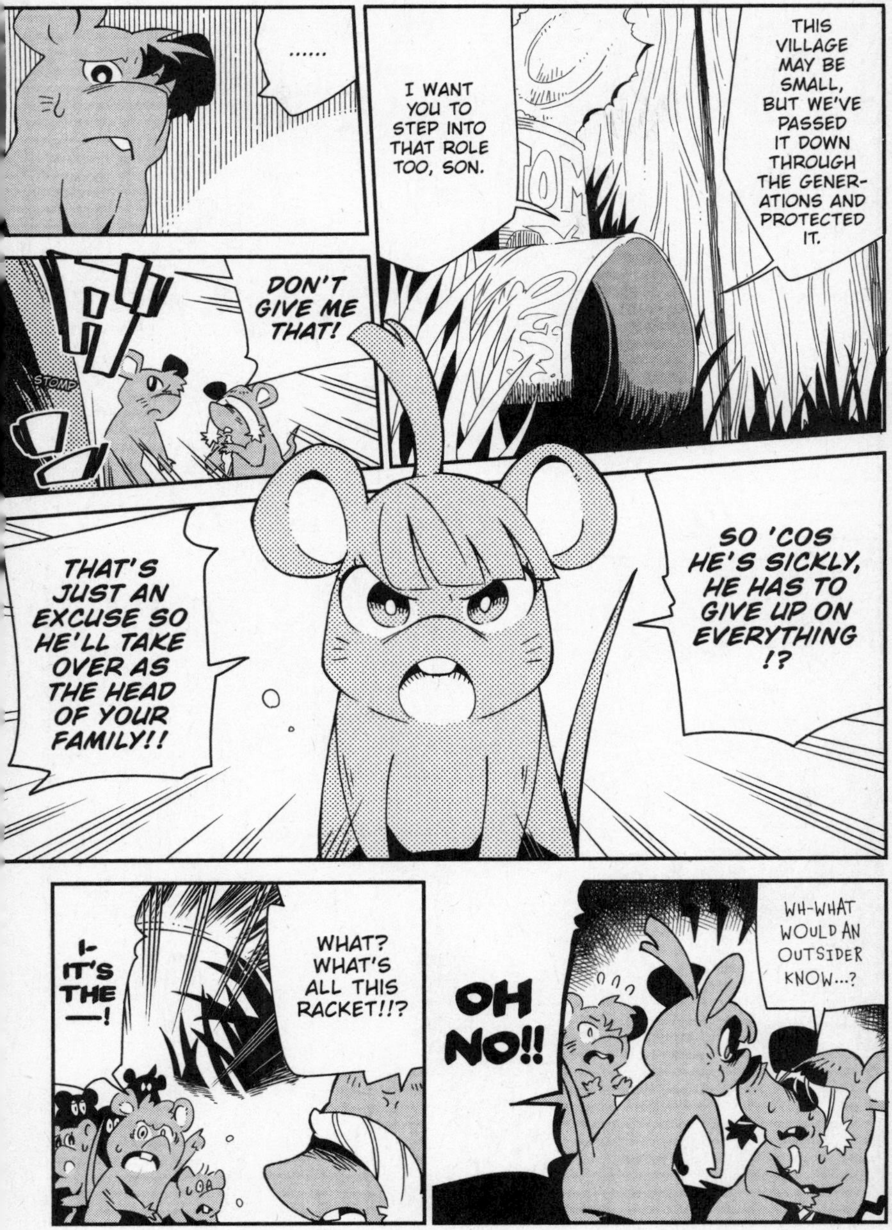
THIS VILLAGE MAY BE SMALL, BUT WE'VE PASSED IT DOWN THROUGH THE GENERATIONS AND PROTECTED IT.
I WANT YOU TO STEP INTO THAT ROLE TOO, SON.
......
DON'T GIVE ME THAT!
STOMP
SO 'COS HE'S SICKLY, HE HAS TO GIVE UP ON EVERYTHING !?
THAT'S JUST AN EXCUSE SO HE'LL TAKE OVER AS THE HEAD OF YOUR FAMILY!!
WH-WHAT WOULD AN OUTSIDER KNOW...?
OH NO!!
WHAT? WHAT'S ALL THIS RACKET!!?
I- IT'S THE—!

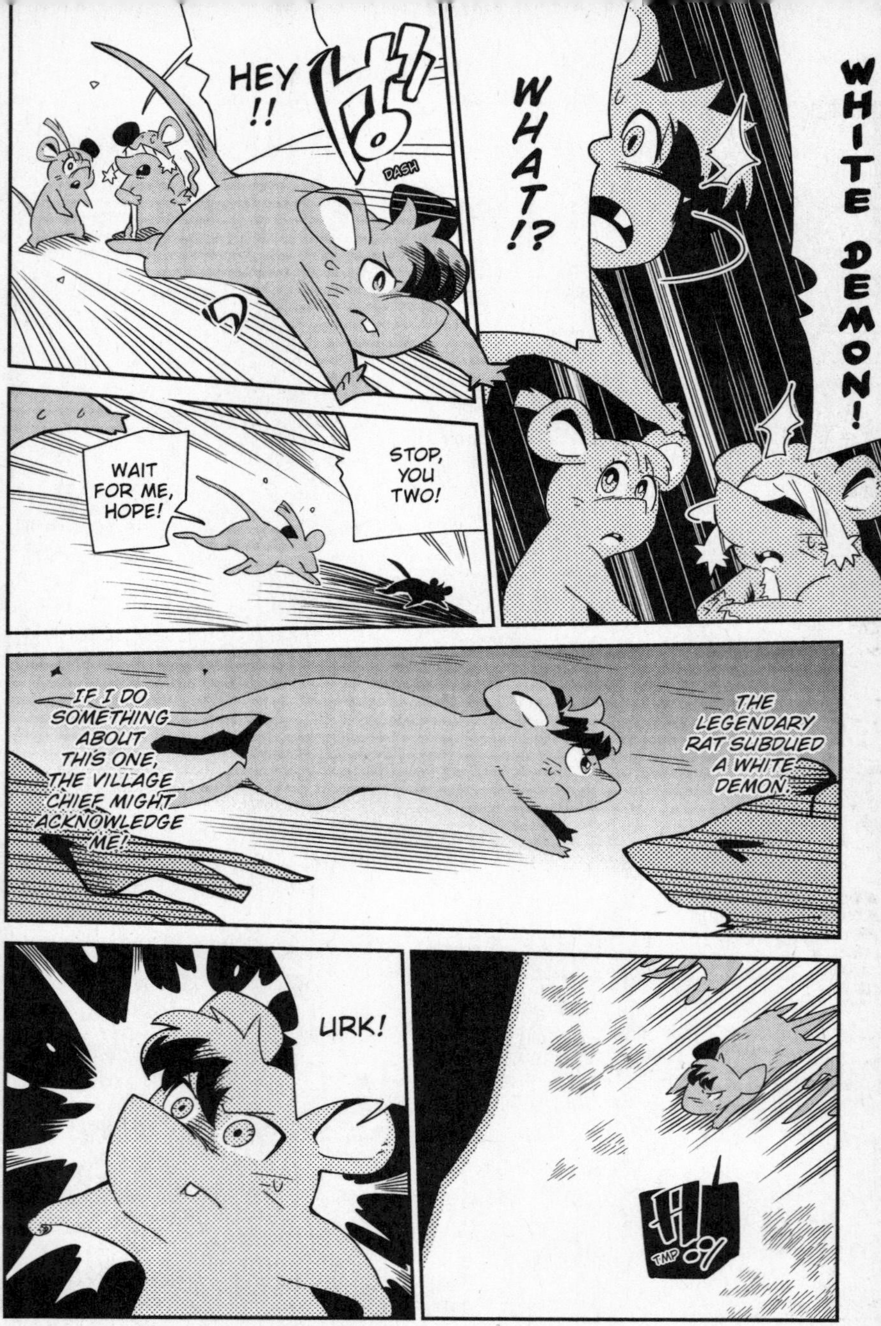
WHITE DEMON!
WHAT!?
HEY!!
DASH
STOP, YOU TWO!
WAIT FOR ME, HOPE!
THE LEGENDARY RAT SUBDUED A WHITE DEMON.
IF I DO SOMETHING ABOUT THIS ONE, THE VILLAGE CHIEF MIGHT ACKNOWLEDGE ME!
TMP
URK!

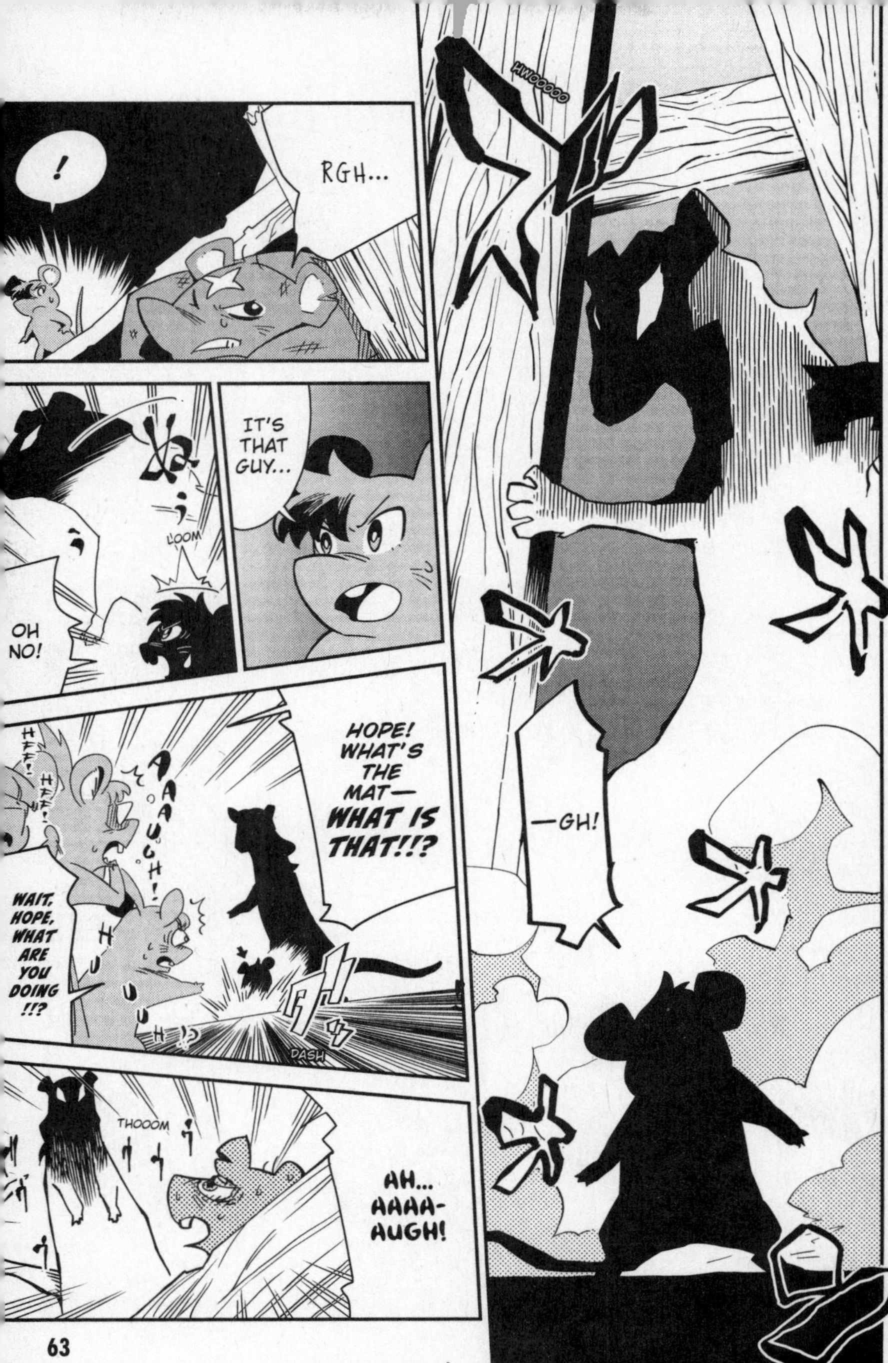
HWOOOOO
—GH!
RGH...
!
IT'S THAT GUY...
LOOM
OH NO!
HOPE! WHAT'S THE MAT— WHAT IS THAT!!?
AAAAUGH!
HFF! HFF!
WAIT, HOPE, WHAT ARE YOU DOING!!?
HUUUH!?
DASH
AH... AAAA-AUGH!
THOOOM

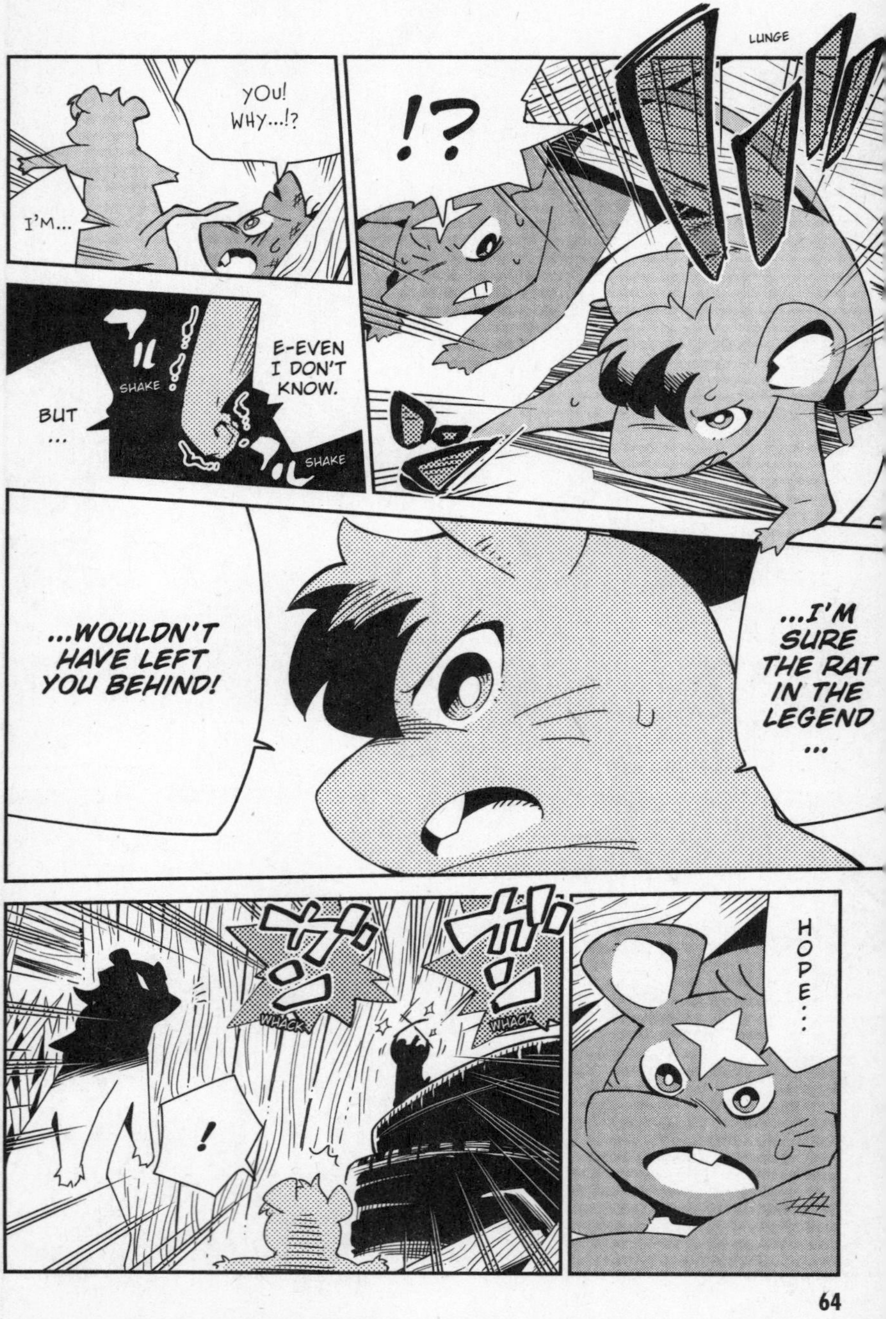
LUNGE
!?
YOU! WHY...!?
I'M...
E-EVEN I DON'T KNOW.
SHAKE
BUT ...
SHAKE
...I'M SURE THE RAT IN THE LEGEND ...
...WOULDN'T HAVE LEFT YOU BEHIND!
HOPE...
WHACK
WHACK
!

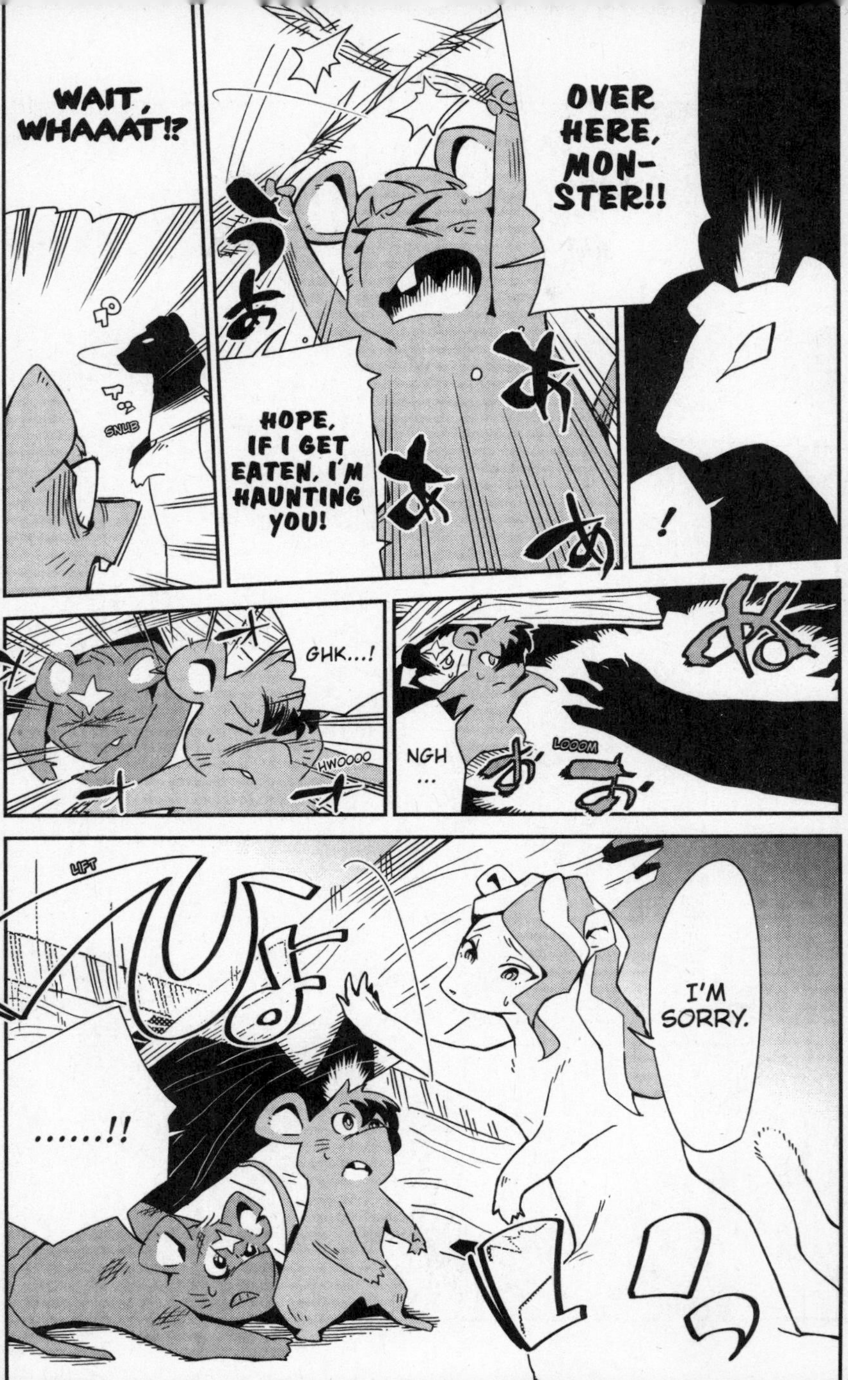
OVER HERE, MONSTER!!
!
HOPE, IF I GET EATEN, I'M HAUNTING YOU!
WAIT, WHAAAT!?
SNUB
LOOOM
NGH ...
GHK...!
HWOOOO
I'M SORRY.
LIFT
......!!

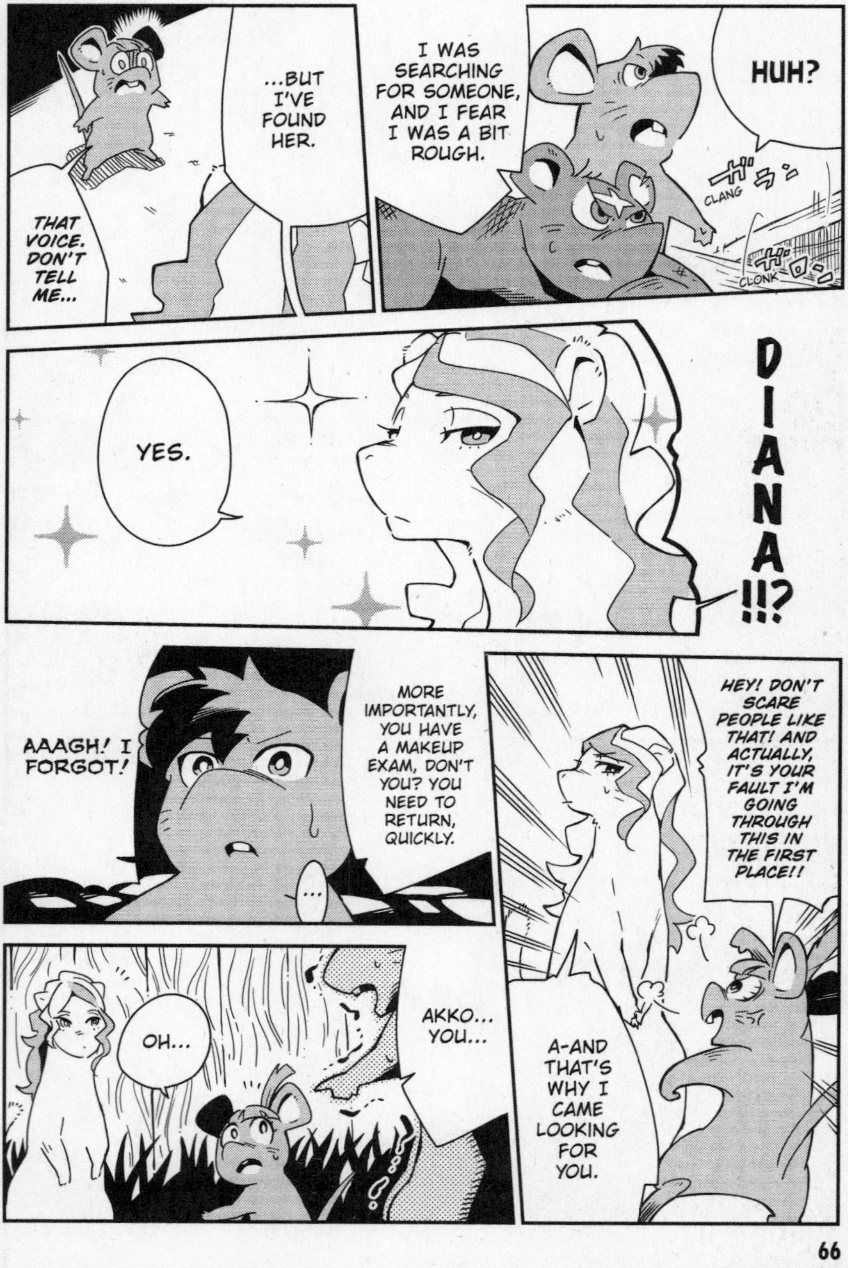
HUH?
CLANG
CLONK
I WAS SEARCHING FOR SOMEONE, AND I FEAR I WAS A BIT ROUGH.
...BUT I'VE FOUND HER.
THAT VOICE. DON'T TELL ME...
DIANA!!?
YES.
HEY! DON'T SCARE PEOPLE LIKE THAT! AND ACTUALLY, IT'S YOUR FAULT I'M GOING THROUGH THIS IN THE FIRST PLACE!!
A-AND THAT'S WHY I CAME LOOKING FOR YOU.
MORE IMPORTANTLY, YOU HAVE A MAKEUP EXAM, DON'T YOU? YOU NEED TO RETURN, QUICKLY.
AAAGH! I FORGOT!
...
AKKO... YOU...
OH...

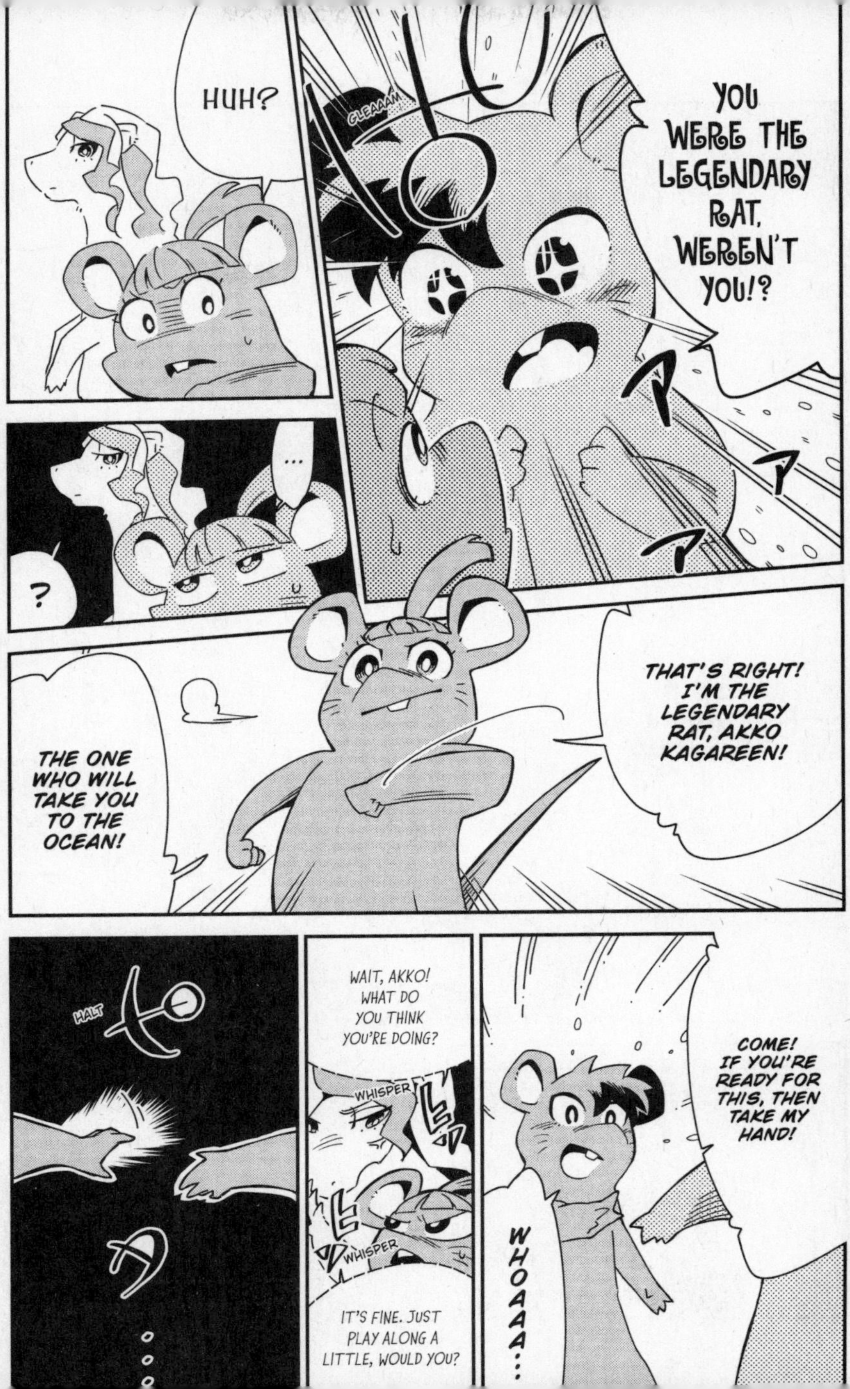
GLEAAAM
YOU WERE THE LEGENDARY RAT, WEREN'T YOU!?
HUH?
...
?
THAT'S RIGHT! I'M THE LEGENDARY RAT, AKKO KAGAREEN!
THE ONE WHO WILL TAKE YOU TO THE OCEAN!
COME! IF YOU'RE READY FOR THIS, THEN TAKE MY HAND!
WHOAAAA...
WAIT, AKKO! WHAT DO YOU THINK YOU'RE DOING?
WHISPER
WHISPER
IT'S FINE. JUST PLAY ALONG A LITTLE, WOULD YOU?
HALT

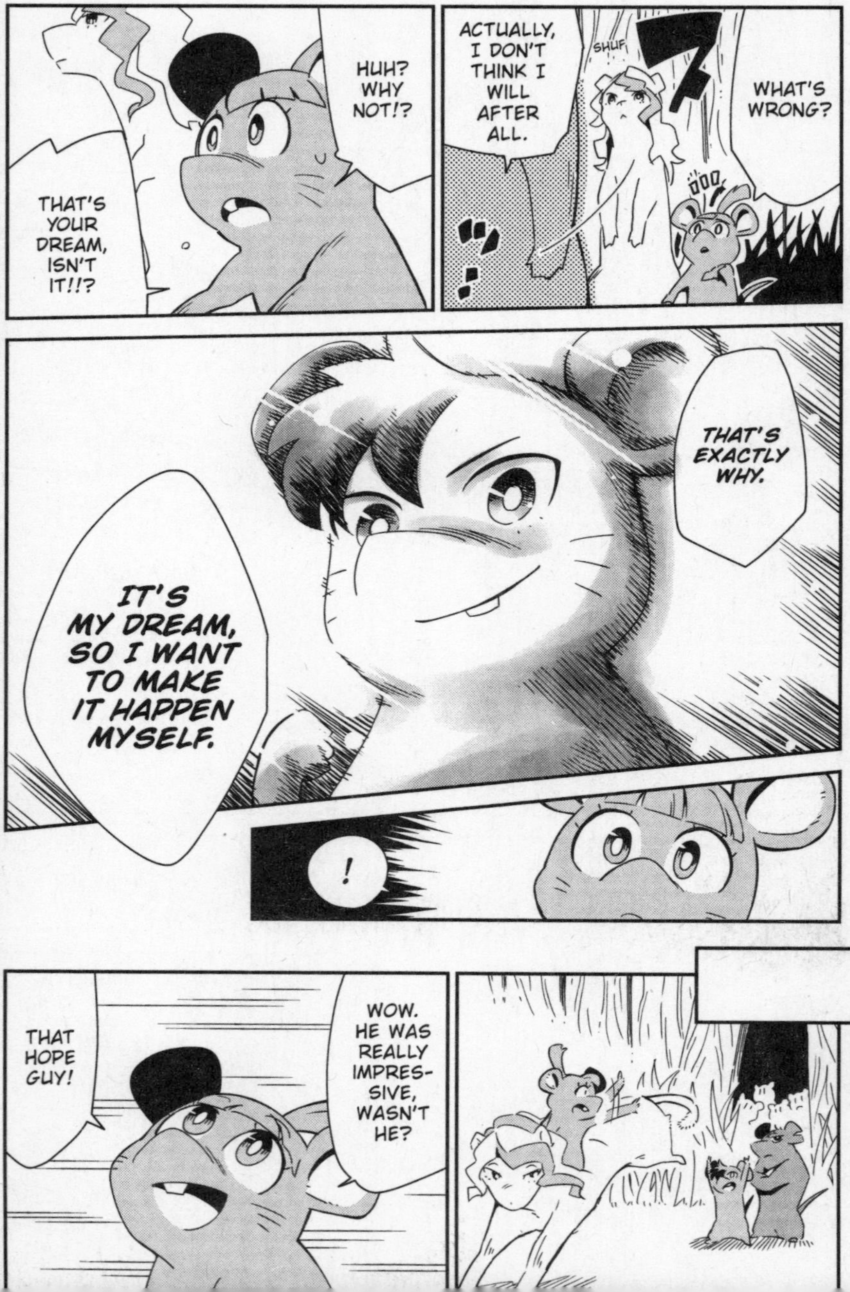
WHAT'S WRONG?
SHUF
ACTUALLY, I DON'T THINK I WILL AFTER ALL.
HUH? WHY NOT!?
THAT'S YOUR DREAM, ISN'T IT!!?
THAT'S EXACTLY WHY.
IT'S MY DREAM, SO I WANT TO MAKE IT HAPPEN MYSELF.
!
WOW. HE WAS REALLY IMPRES-SIVE, WASN'T HE?
THAT HOPE GUY!

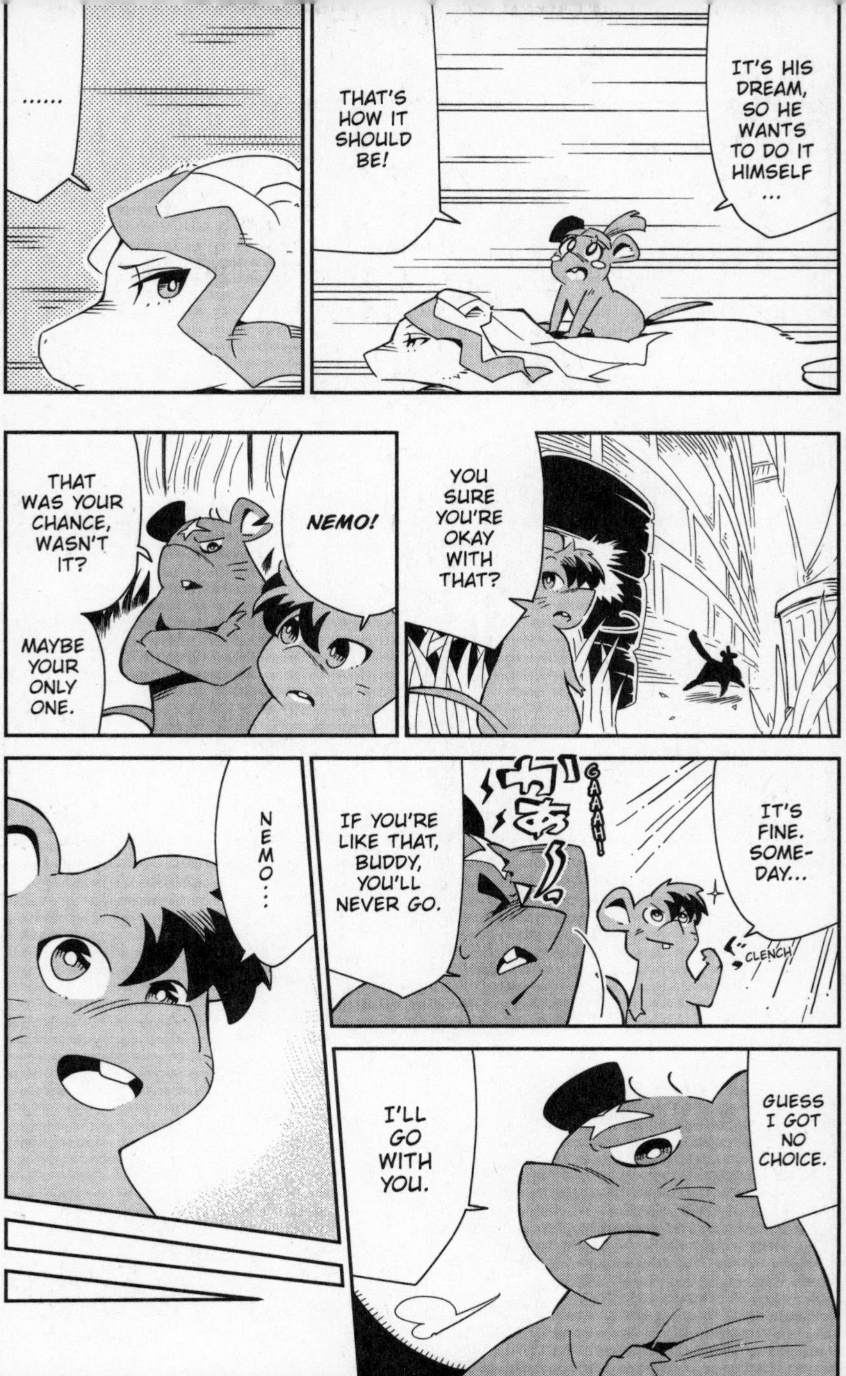
IT'S HIS DREAM, SO HE WANTS TO DO IT HIMSELF ...
THAT'S HOW IT SHOULD BE!
......
YOU SURE YOU'RE OKAY WITH THAT?
NEMO!
THAT WAS YOUR CHANCE, WASN'T IT?
MAYBE YOUR ONLY ONE.
IT'S FINE. SOME-DAY...
CLENCH
GAAAH!
IF YOU'RE LIKE THAT, BUDDY, YOU'LL NEVER GO.
GUESS I GOT NO CHOICE.
I'LL GO WITH YOU.
NEMO...

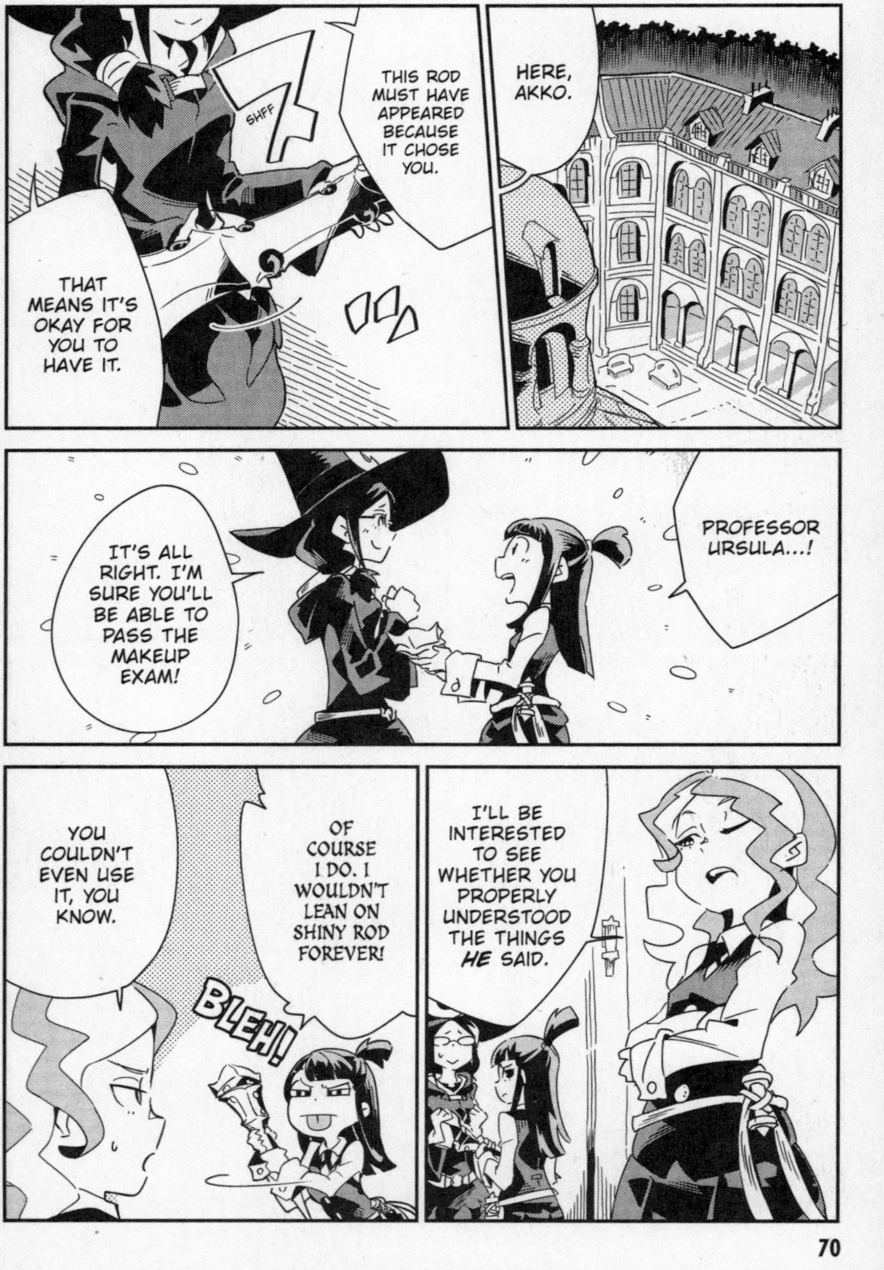
HERE, AKKO.
THIS ROD MUST HAVE APPEARED BECAUSE IT CHOSE YOU.
SHFF
THAT MEANS IT'S OKAY FOR YOU TO HAVE IT.
PROFESSOR URSULA...!
IT'S ALL RIGHT. I'M SURE YOU'LL BE ABLE TO PASS THE MAKEUP EXAM!
I'LL BE INTERESTED TO SEE WHETHER YOU PROPERLY UNDERSTOOD THE THINGS *HE* SAID.
OF COURSE I DO. I WOULDN'T LEAN ON SHINY ROD FOREVER!
YOU COULDN'T EVEN USE IT, YOU KNOW.
BLEH!

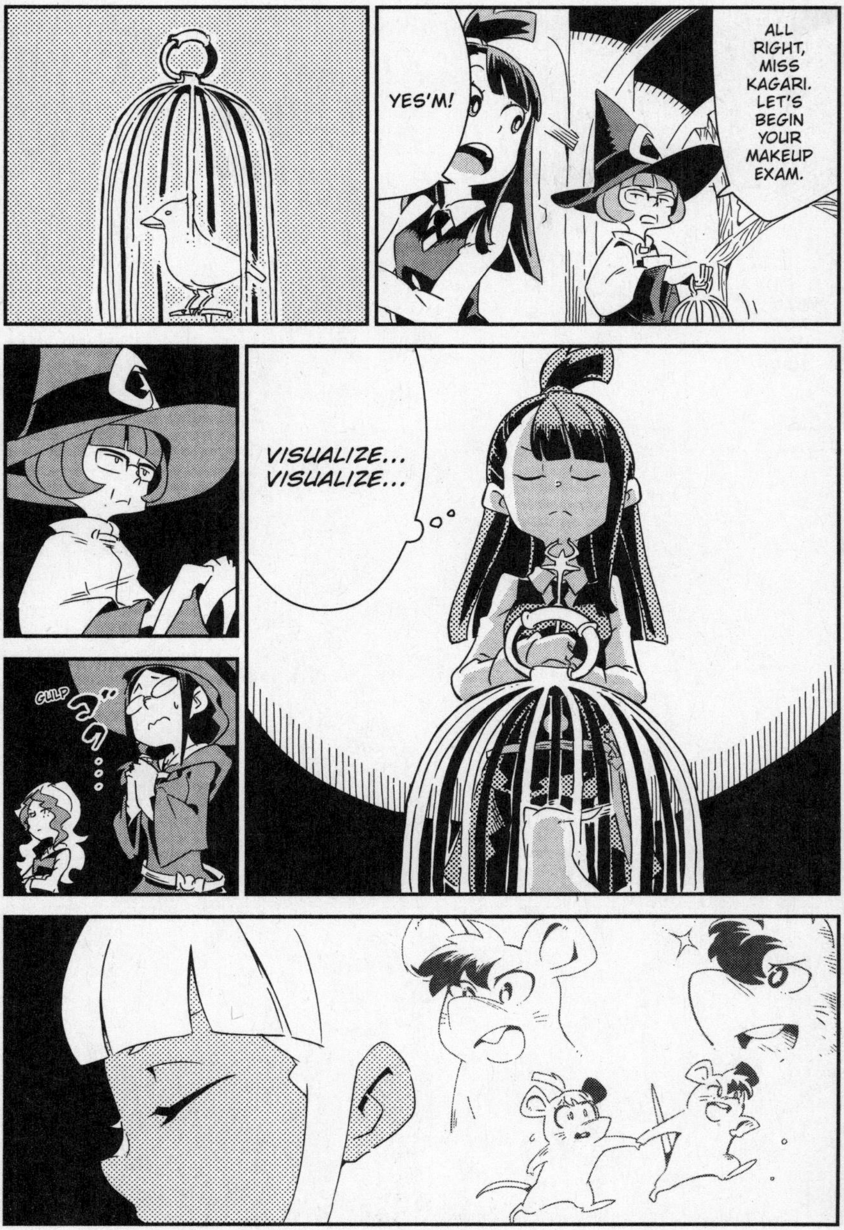

ALL RIGHT, MISS KAGARI. LET'S BEGIN YOUR MAKEUP EXAM.
YES'M!
VISUALIZE... VISUALIZE...
GULP

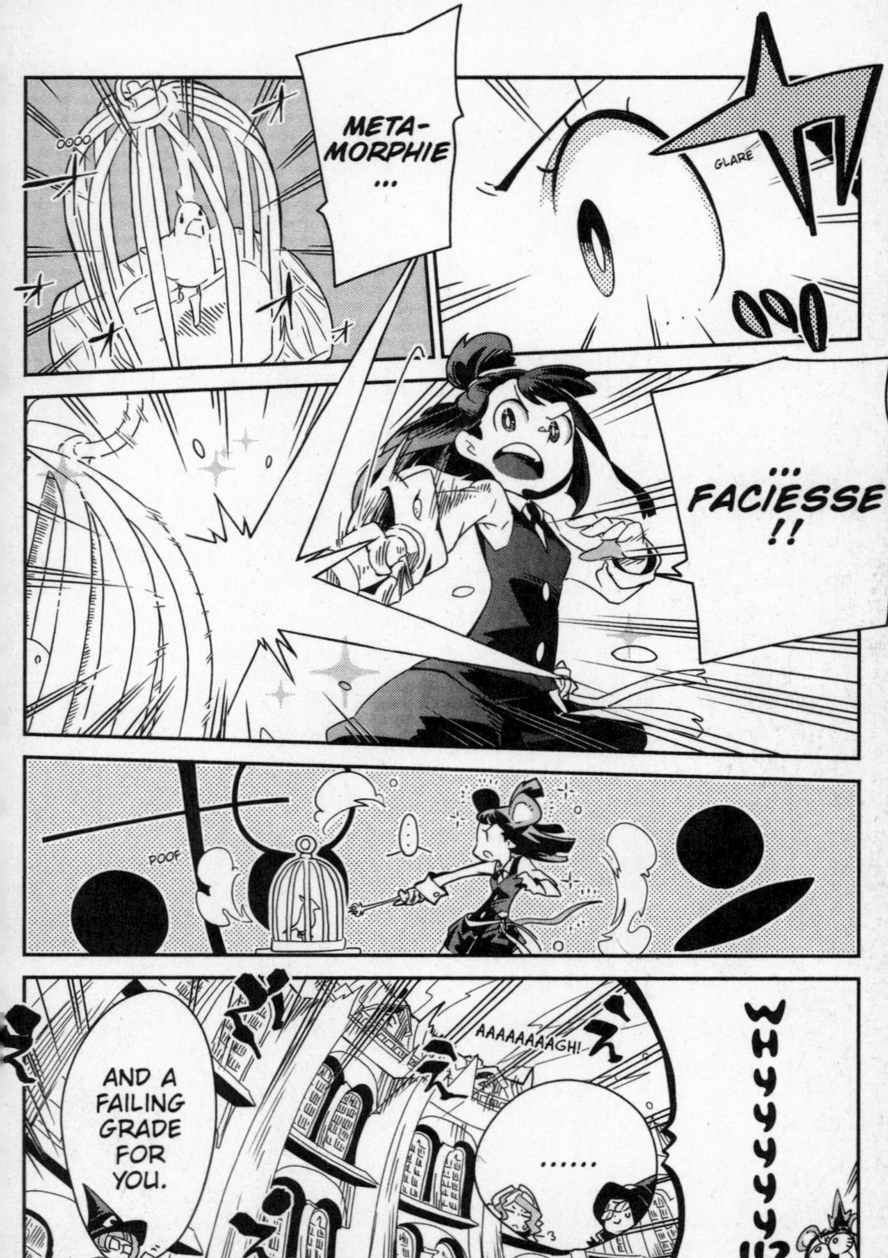
GLARE
META-MORPHIE ...
... FACIESSE !!
POOF
WHYYYYYY !!?
AAAAAAAAGH!
......
AND A FAILING GRADE FOR YOU.

Little Witch Academia

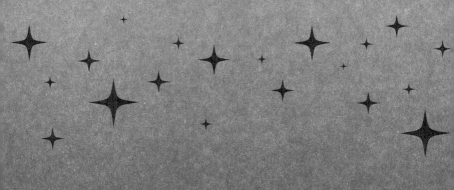

AMANDA O'NEILL

A delinquent American girl. She has sticky fingers, which she uses to mess with the school storehouses and security.

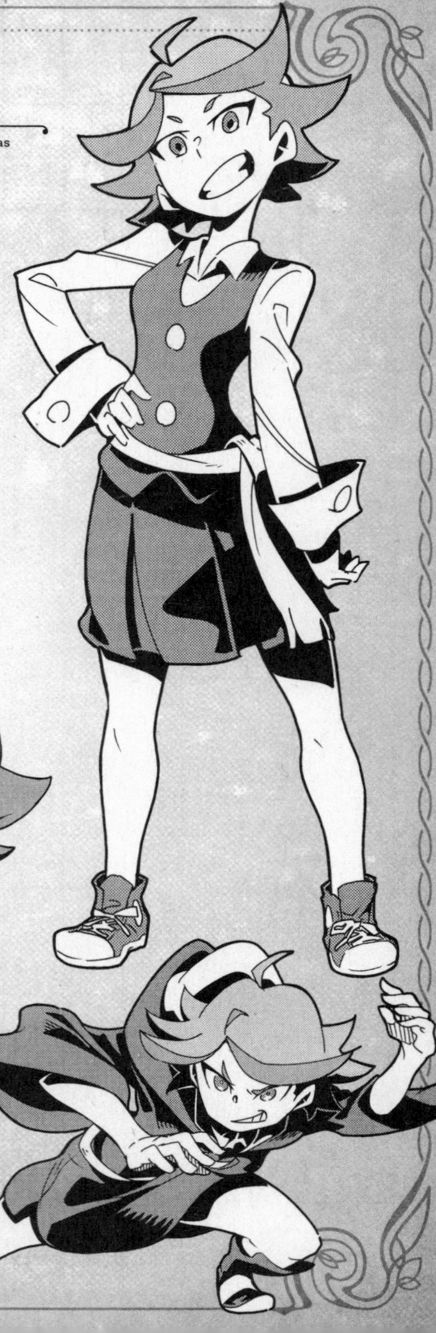

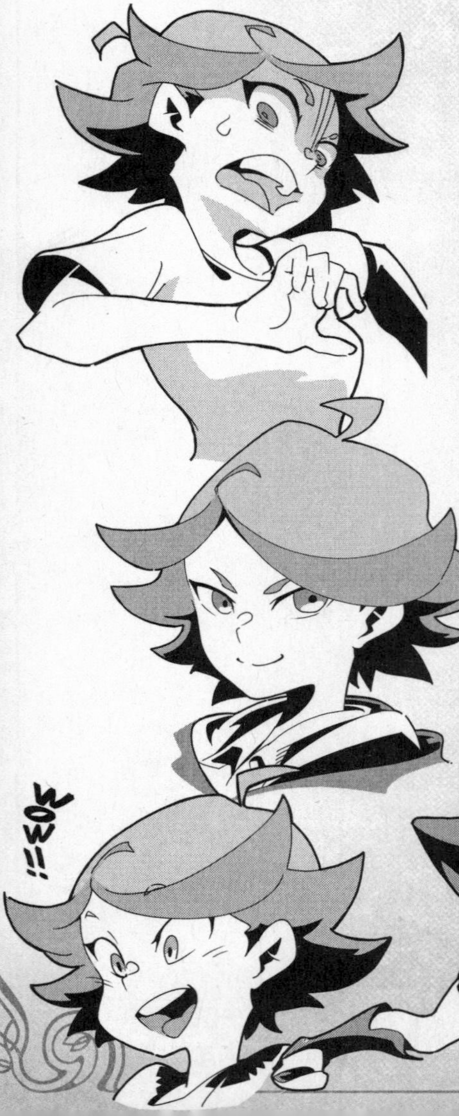
WOW!!

Chapter 8

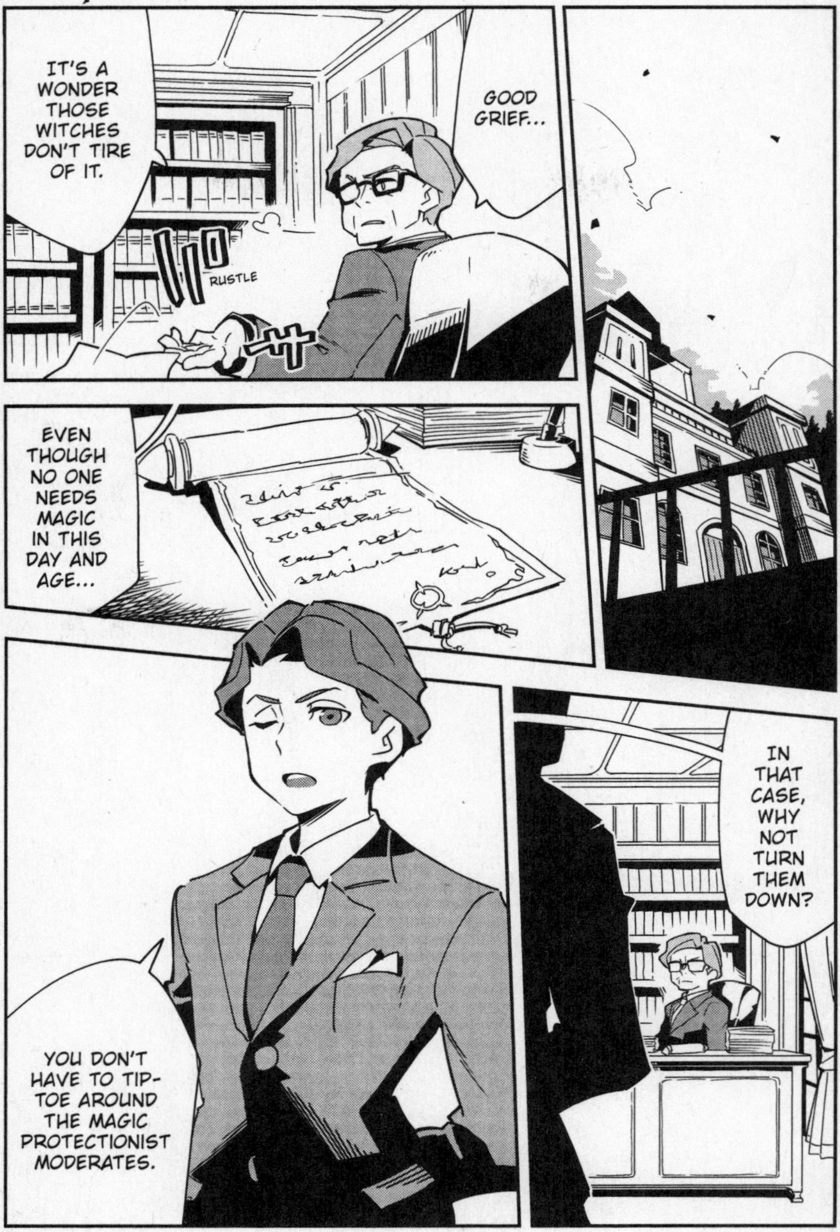

GOOD GRIEF...
IT'S A WONDER THOSE WITCHES DON'T TIRE OF IT.
RUSTLE
EVEN THOUGH NO ONE NEEDS MAGIC IN THIS DAY AND AGE...
IN THAT CASE, WHY NOT TURN THEM DOWN?
YOU DON'T HAVE TO TIP-TOE AROUND THE MAGIC PROTECTIONIST MODERATES.

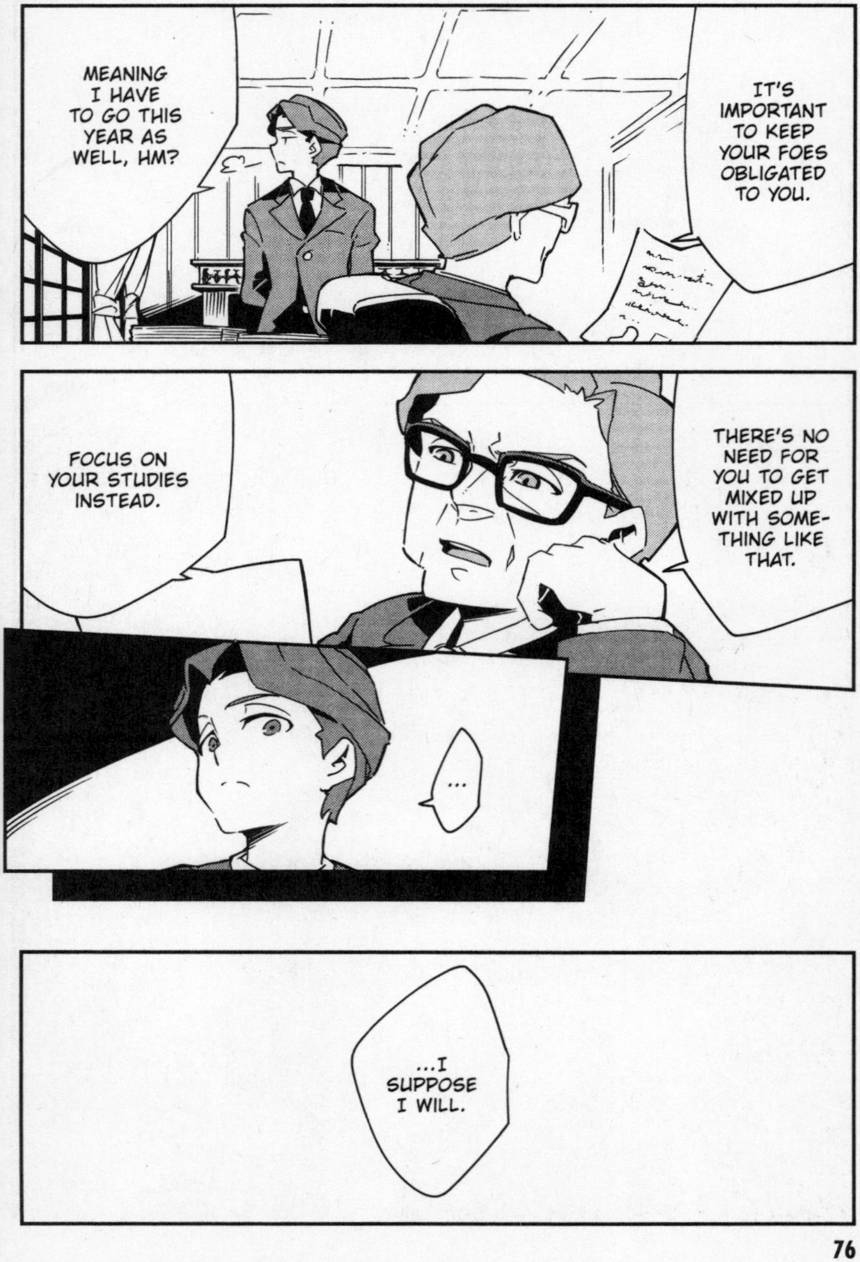
IT'S IMPORTANT TO KEEP YOUR FOES OBLIGATED TO YOU.
MEANING I HAVE TO GO THIS YEAR AS WELL, HM?
THERE'S NO NEED FOR YOU TO GET MIXED UP WITH SOME-THING LIKE THAT.
FOCUS ON YOUR STUDIES INSTEAD.
...
...I SUPPOSE I WILL.

Chapter 8 GENTLEMANLY CRITICISM

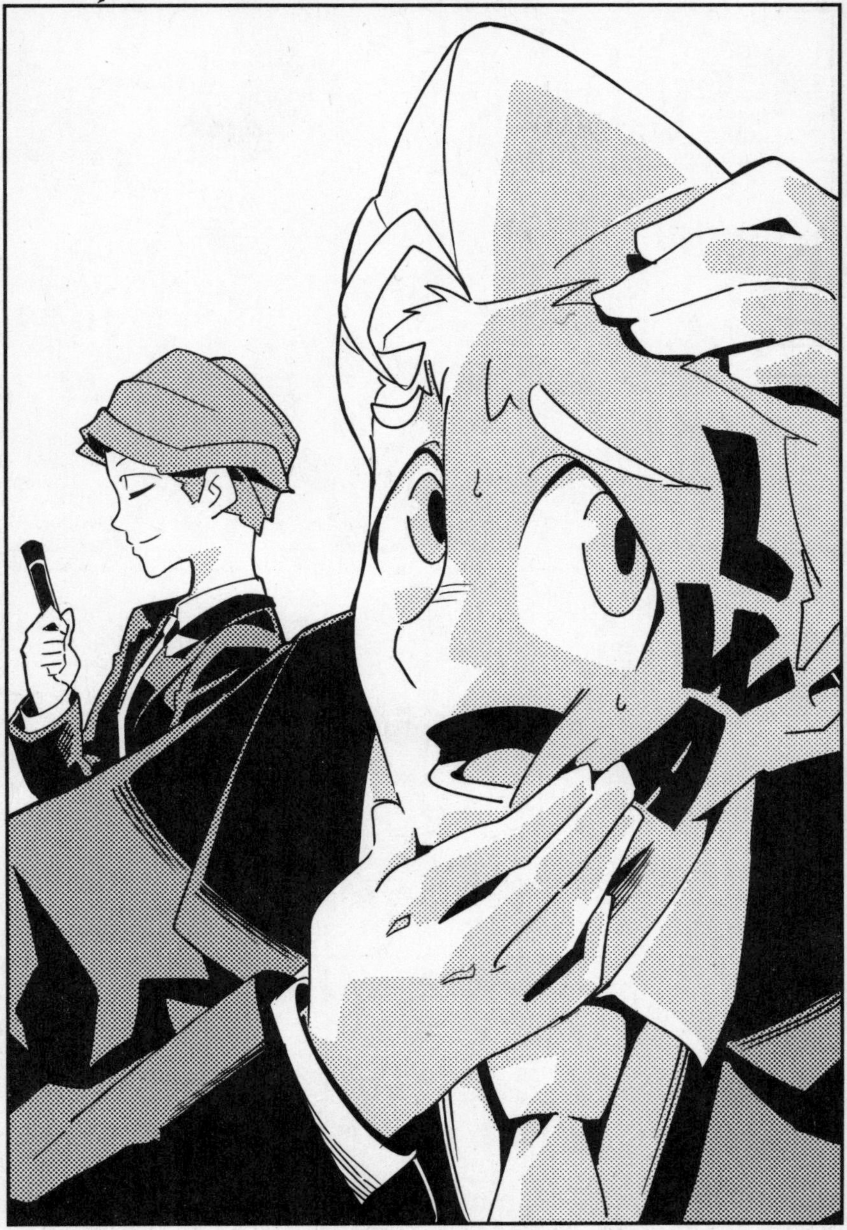

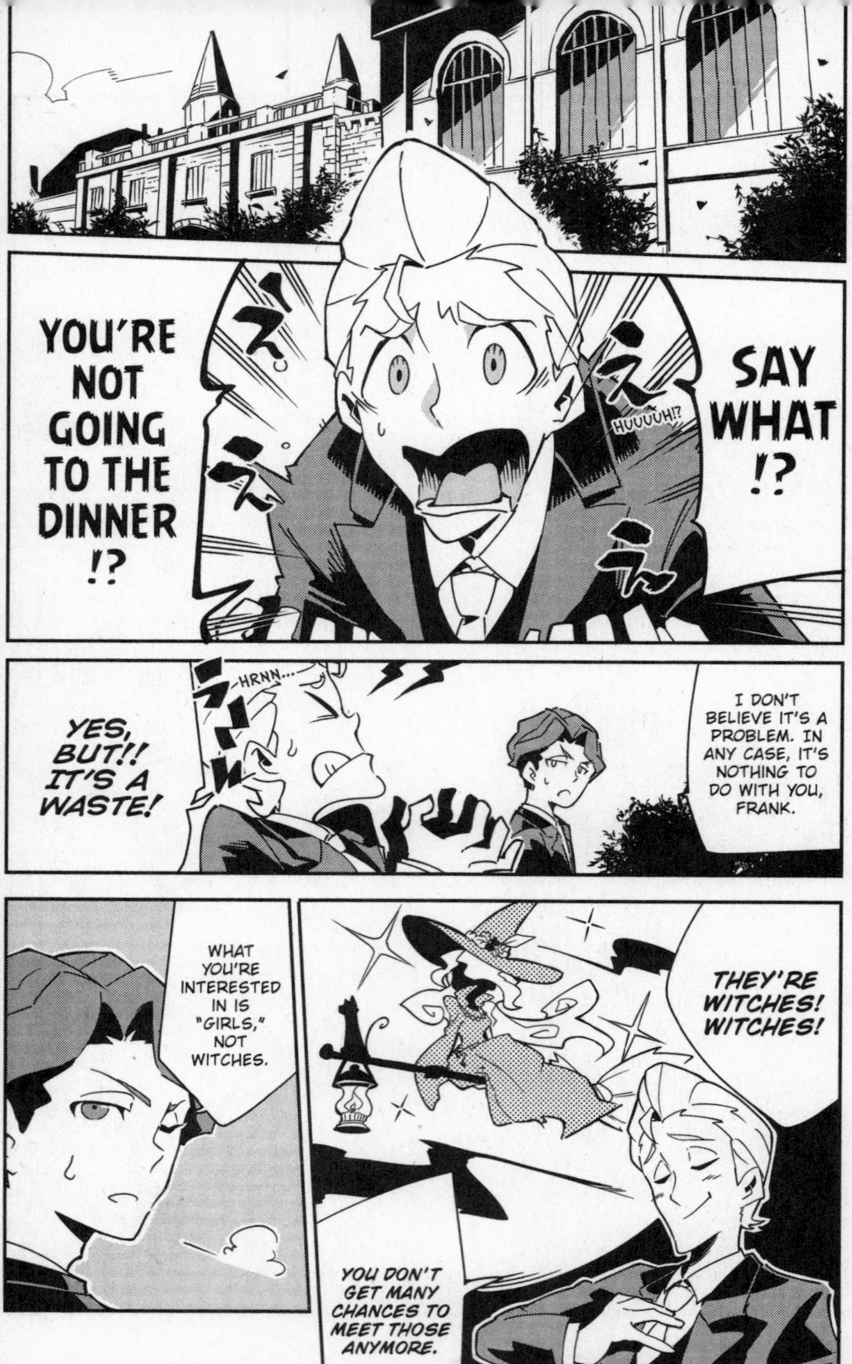
SAY WHAT!?
HUUUUH!?
YOU'RE NOT GOING TO THE DINNER!?
I DON'T BELIEVE IT'S A PROBLEM. IN ANY CASE, IT'S NOTHING TO DO WITH YOU, FRANK.
HRNN...
YES, BUT!! IT'S A WASTE!
THEY'RE WITCHES! WITCHES!
YOU DON'T GET MANY CHANCES TO MEET THOSE ANYMORE.
WHAT YOU'RE INTERESTED IN IS "GIRLS," NOT WITCHES.

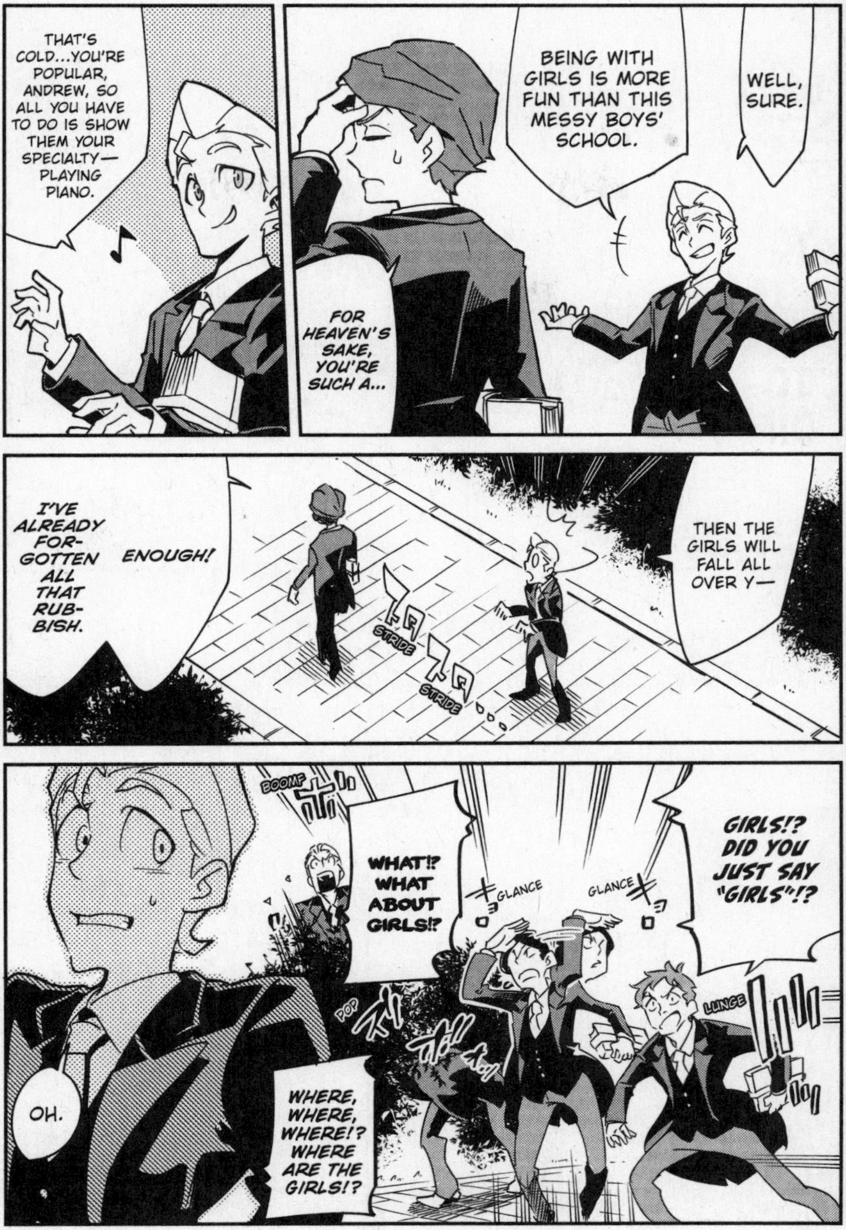
WELL, SURE.
BEING WITH GIRLS IS MORE FUN THAN THIS MESSY BOYS' SCHOOL.
FOR HEAVEN'S SAKE, YOU'RE SUCH A...
THAT'S COLD...YOU'RE POPULAR, ANDREW, SO ALL YOU HAVE TO DO IS SHOW THEM YOUR SPECIALTY—PLAYING PIANO.
THEN THE GIRLS WILL FALL ALL OVER Y—
ENOUGH!
I'VE ALREADY FOR-GOTTEN ALL THAT RUB-BISH.
STRIDE
STRIDE
GIRLS!? DID YOU JUST SAY "GIRLS"!?
LUNGE
GLANCE
GLANCE
WHAT!? WHAT ABOUT GIRLS!?
BOOMF
POP
WHERE, WHERE, WHERE!? WHERE ARE THE GIRLS!?
OH.

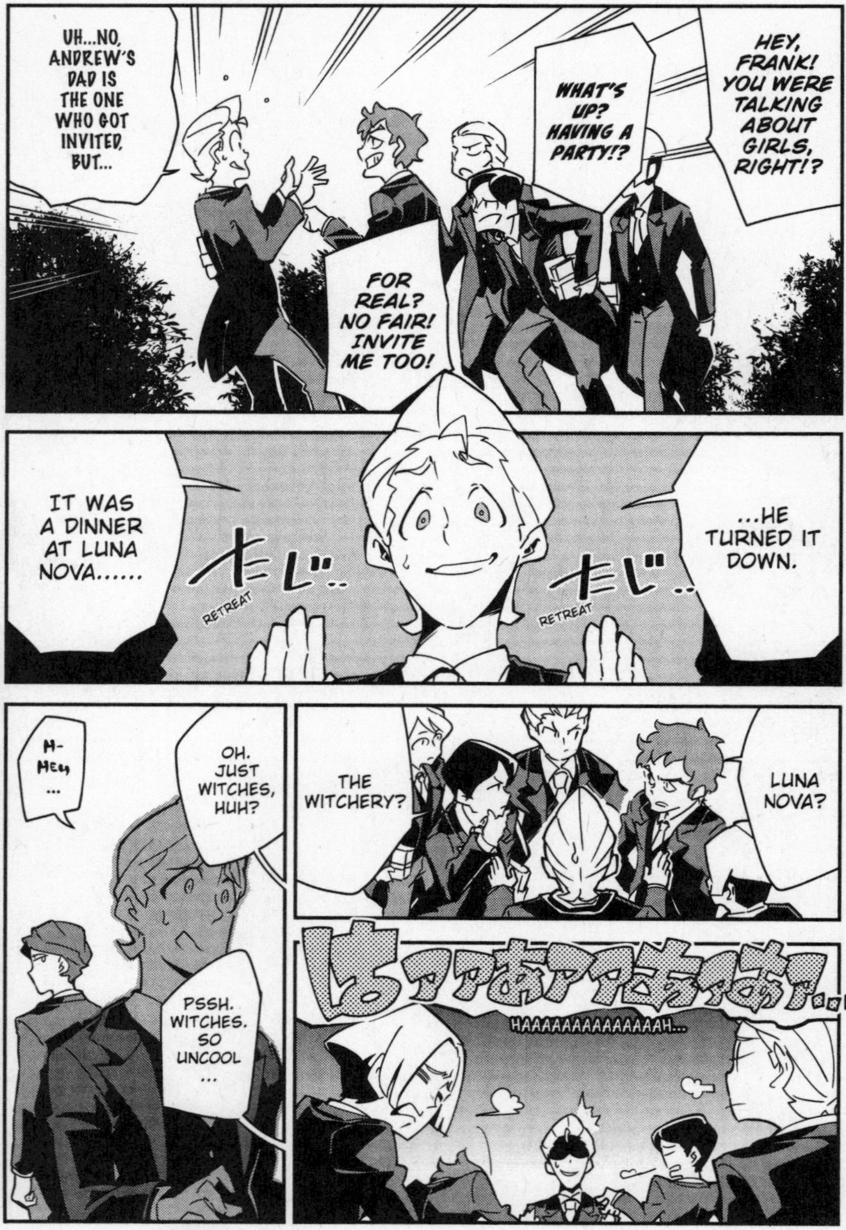

HEY, FRANK! YOU WERE TALKING ABOUT GIRLS, RIGHT!?
WHAT'S UP? HAVING A PARTY!?
FOR REAL? NO FAIR! INVITE ME TOO!
UH...NO, ANDREW'S DAD IS THE ONE WHO GOT INVITED, BUT...
...HE TURNED IT DOWN.
RETREAT
RETREAT
IT WAS A DINNER AT LUNA NOVA......
LUNA NOVA?
THE WITCHERY?
HAAAAAAAAAAAAAAAH...
OH. JUST WITCHES, HUH?
M-MEH...
PSSH. WITCHES. SO UNCOOL...

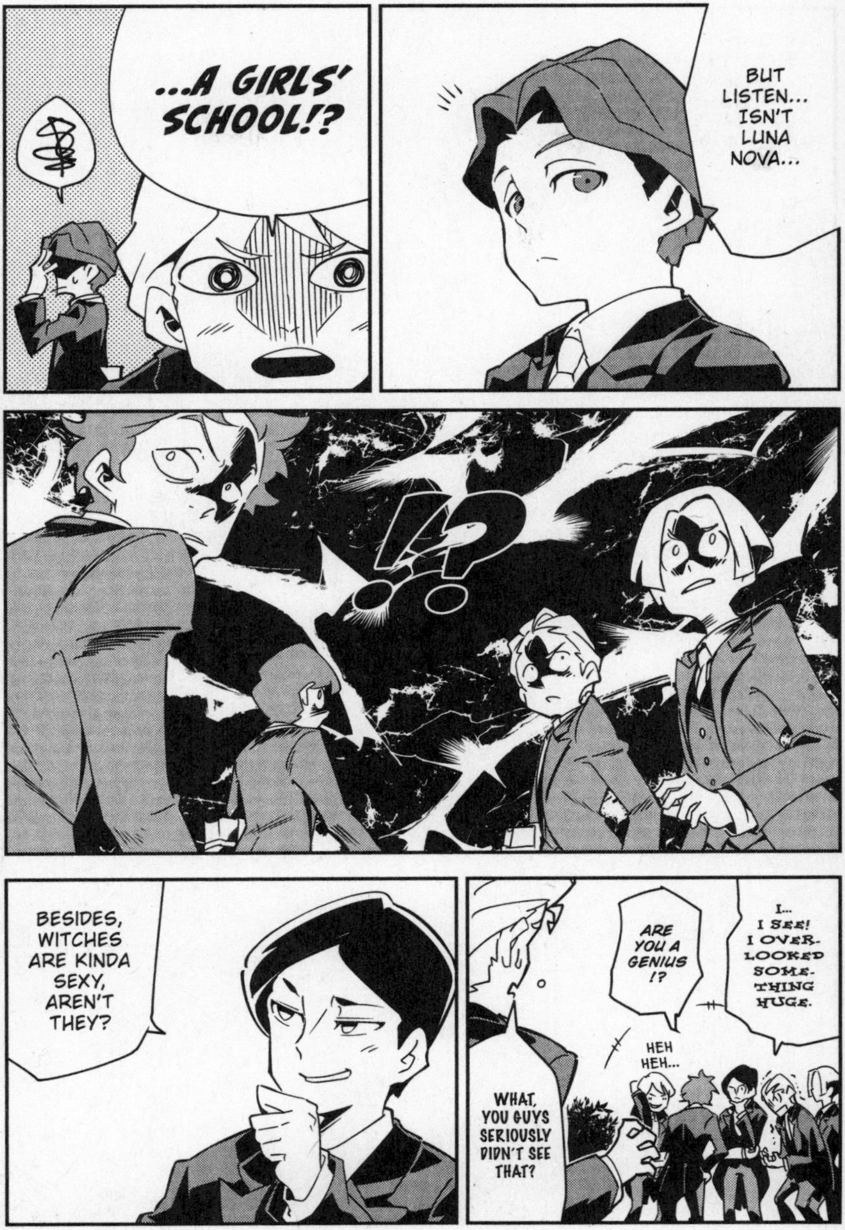
BUT LISTEN... ISN'T LUNA NOVA...
...A GIRLS' SCHOOL!?
!?
I... I SEE! I OVER-LOOKED SOME-THING HUGE.
ARE YOU A GENIUS !?
HEH HEH...
WHAT, YOU GUYS SERIOUSLY DIDN'T SEE THAT?
BESIDES, WITCHES ARE KINDA SEXY, AREN'T THEY?

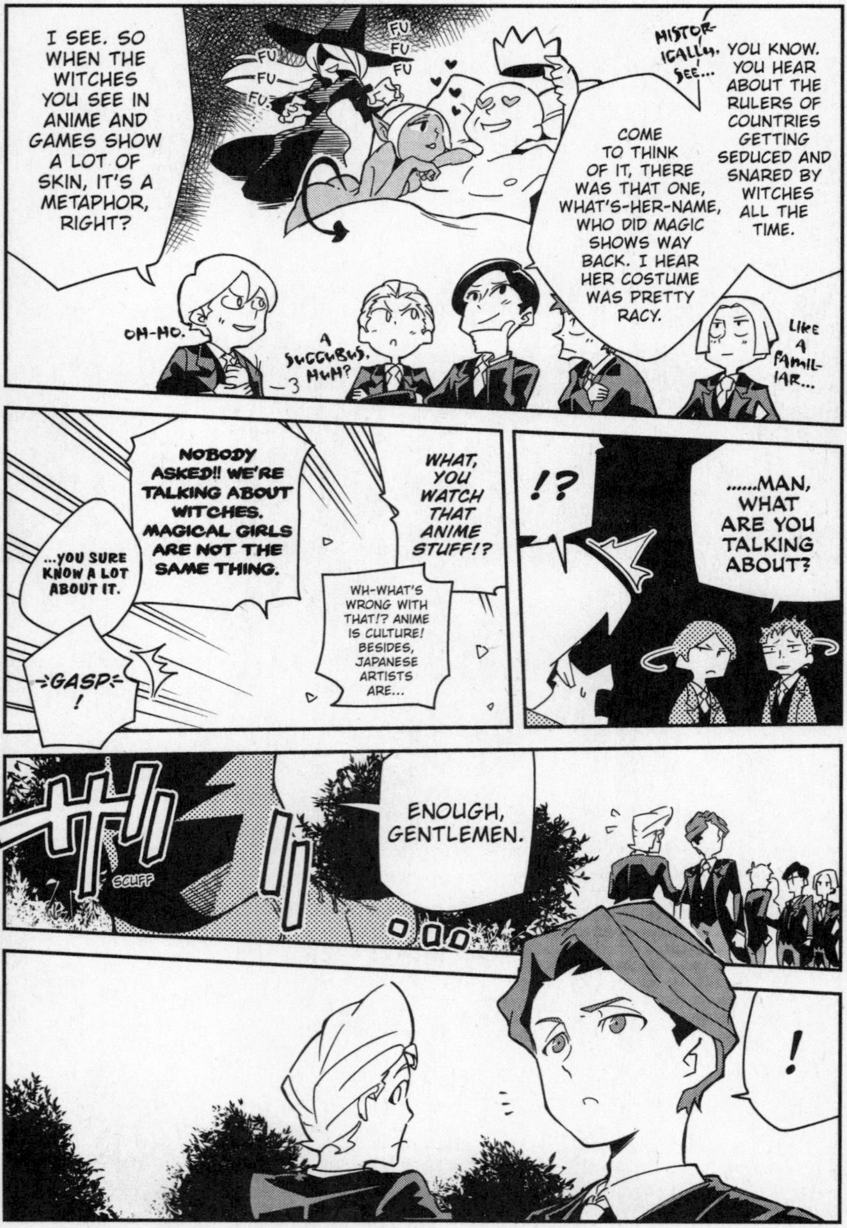
YOU KNOW. YOU HEAR ABOUT THE RULERS OF COUNTRIES GETTING SEDUCED AND SNARED BY WITCHES ALL THE TIME.
HISTOR-ICALLY, I SEE...
COME TO THINK OF IT, THERE WAS THAT ONE, WHAT'S-HER-NAME, WHO DID MAGIC SHOWS WAY BACK. I HEAR HER COSTUME WAS PRETTY RACY.
FU FU FU
FU FU FU
I SEE. SO WHEN THE WITCHES YOU SEE IN ANIME AND GAMES SHOW A LOT OF SKIN, IT'S A METAPHOR, RIGHT?
LIKE A FAMIL-IAR...
A SUCCUBUS, HUH?
OH-HO.
......MAN, WHAT ARE YOU TALKING ABOUT?
!?
WHAT, YOU WATCH THAT ANIME STUFF!?
WH-WHAT'S WRONG WITH THAT!? ANIME IS CULTURE! BESIDES, JAPANESE ARTISTS ARE...
NOBODY ASKED!! WE'RE TALKING ABOUT WITCHES. MAGICAL GIRLS ARE NOT THE SAME THING.
...YOU SURE KNOW A LOT ABOUT IT.
GASP !
ENOUGH, GENTLEMEN.
SCUFF
!

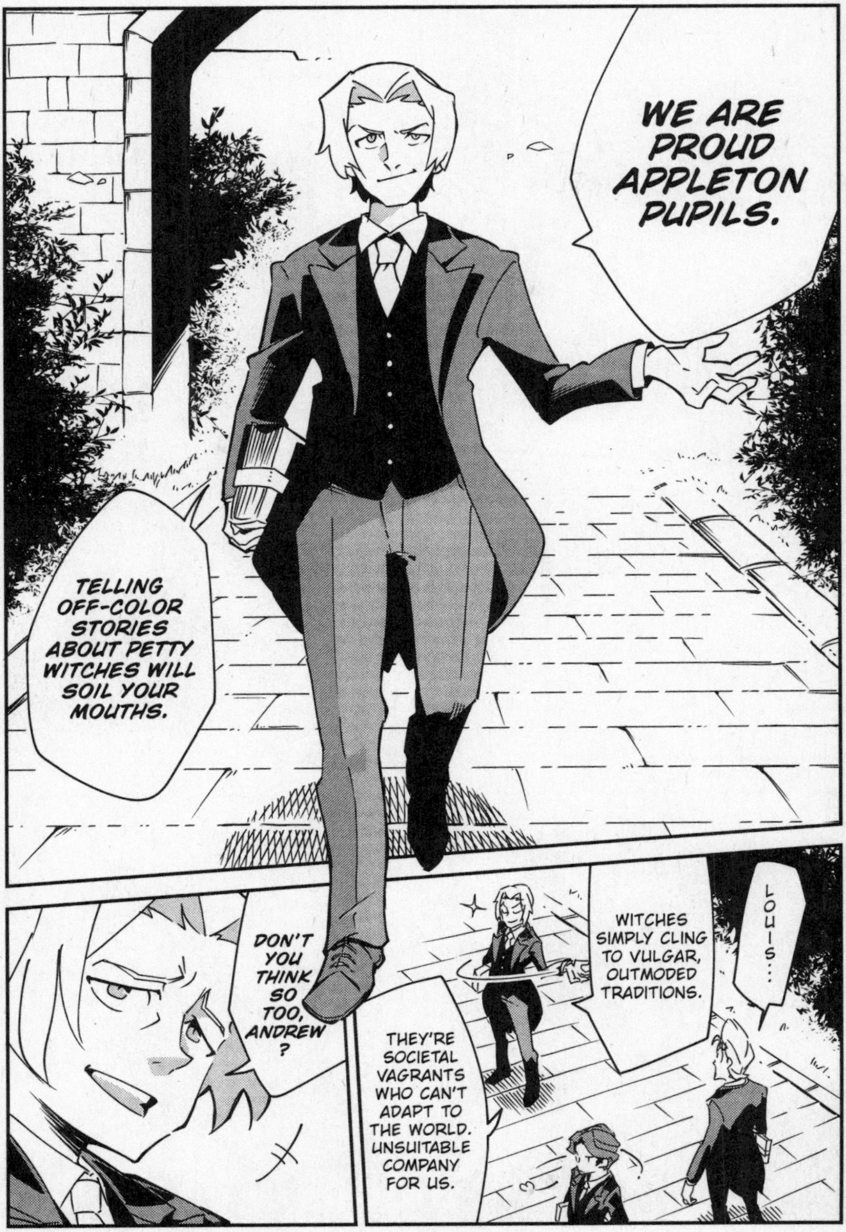
WE ARE PROUD APPLETON PUPILS.
TELLING OFF-COLOR STORIES ABOUT PETTY WITCHES WILL SOIL YOUR MOUTHS.
LOUIS...
WITCHES SIMPLY CLING TO VULGAR, OUTMODED TRADITIONS.
THEY'RE SOCIETAL VAGRANTS WHO CAN'T ADAPT TO THE WORLD. UNSUITABLE COMPANY FOR US.
DON'T YOU THINK SO TOO, ANDREW?

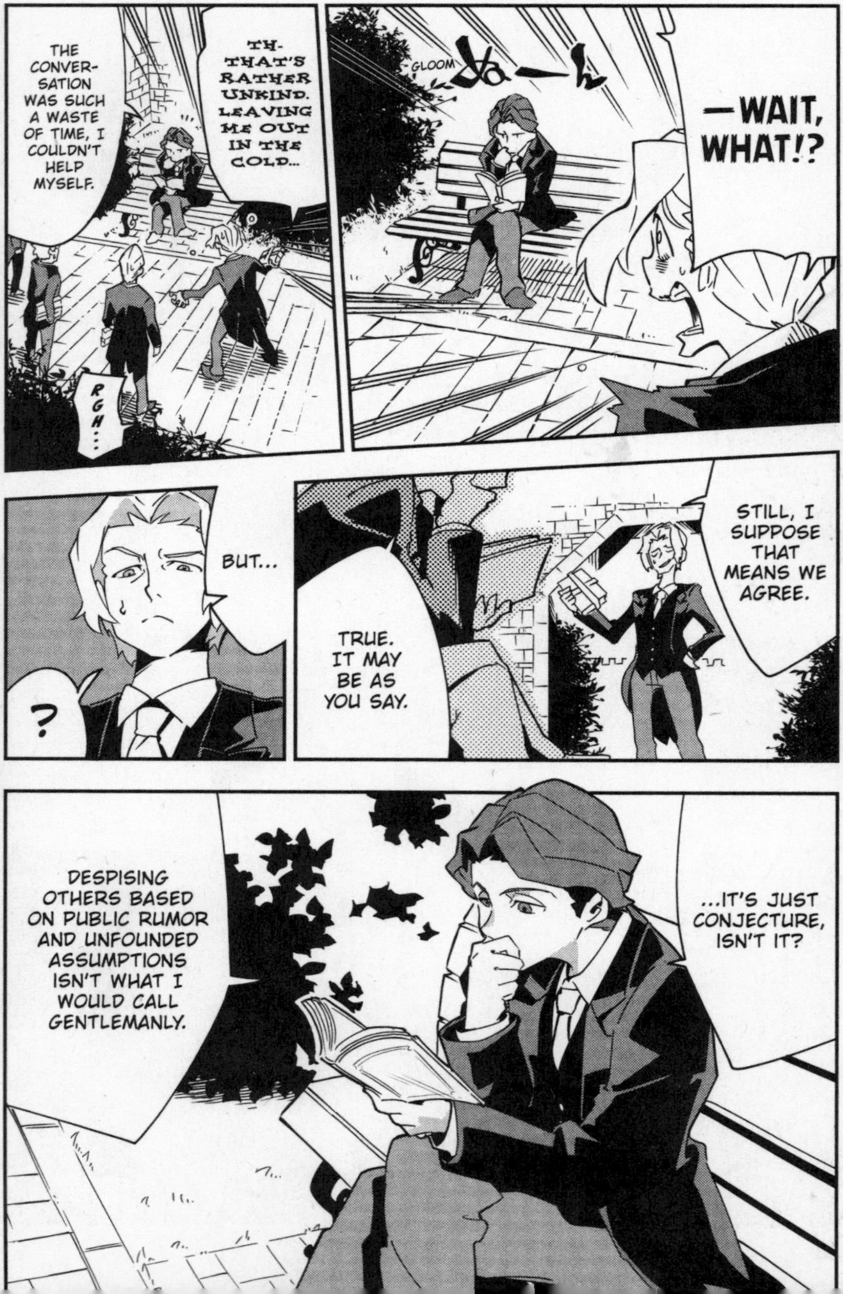
GLOOM
—WAIT, WHAT!?
TH-THAT'S RATHER UNKIND. LEAVING ME OUT IN THE COLD...
THE CONVERSATION WAS SUCH A WASTE OF TIME, I COULDN'T HELP MYSELF.
RGH...
STILL, I SUPPOSE THAT MEANS WE AGREE.
TRUE. IT MAY BE AS YOU SAY.
BUT...
?
...IT'S JUST CONJECTURE, ISN'T IT?
DESPISING OTHERS BASED ON PUBLIC RUMOR AND UNFOUNDED ASSUMPTIONS ISN'T WHAT I WOULD CALL GENTLEMANLY.

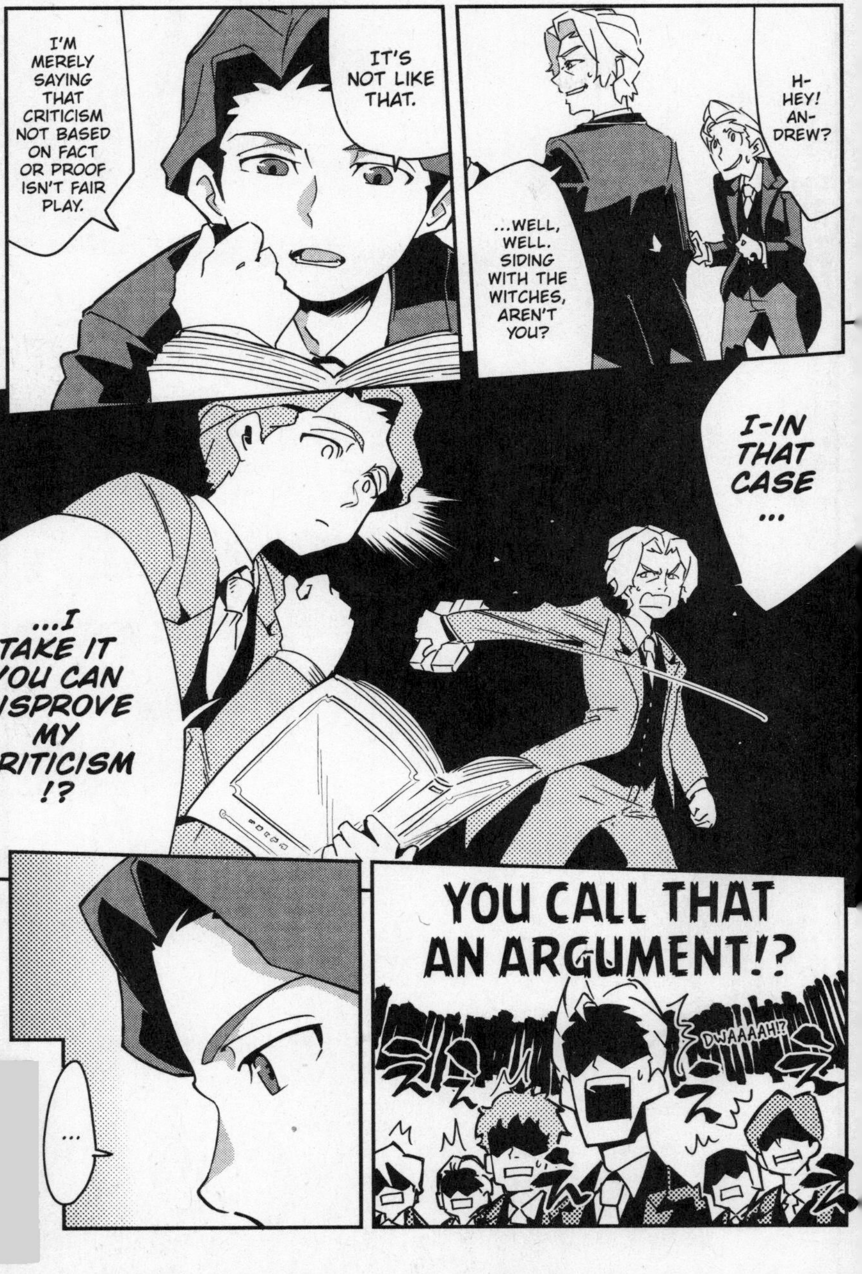
H-HEY! AN-DREW?
...WELL, WELL. SIDING WITH THE WITCHES, AREN'T YOU?
IT'S NOT LIKE THAT.
I'M MERELY SAYING THAT CRITICISM NOT BASED ON FACT OR PROOF ISN'T FAIR PLAY.
I-IN THAT CASE ...
...I TAKE IT YOU CAN DISPROVE MY CRITICISM!?
YOU CALL THAT AN ARGUMENT!?
DWAAAAH!?
...

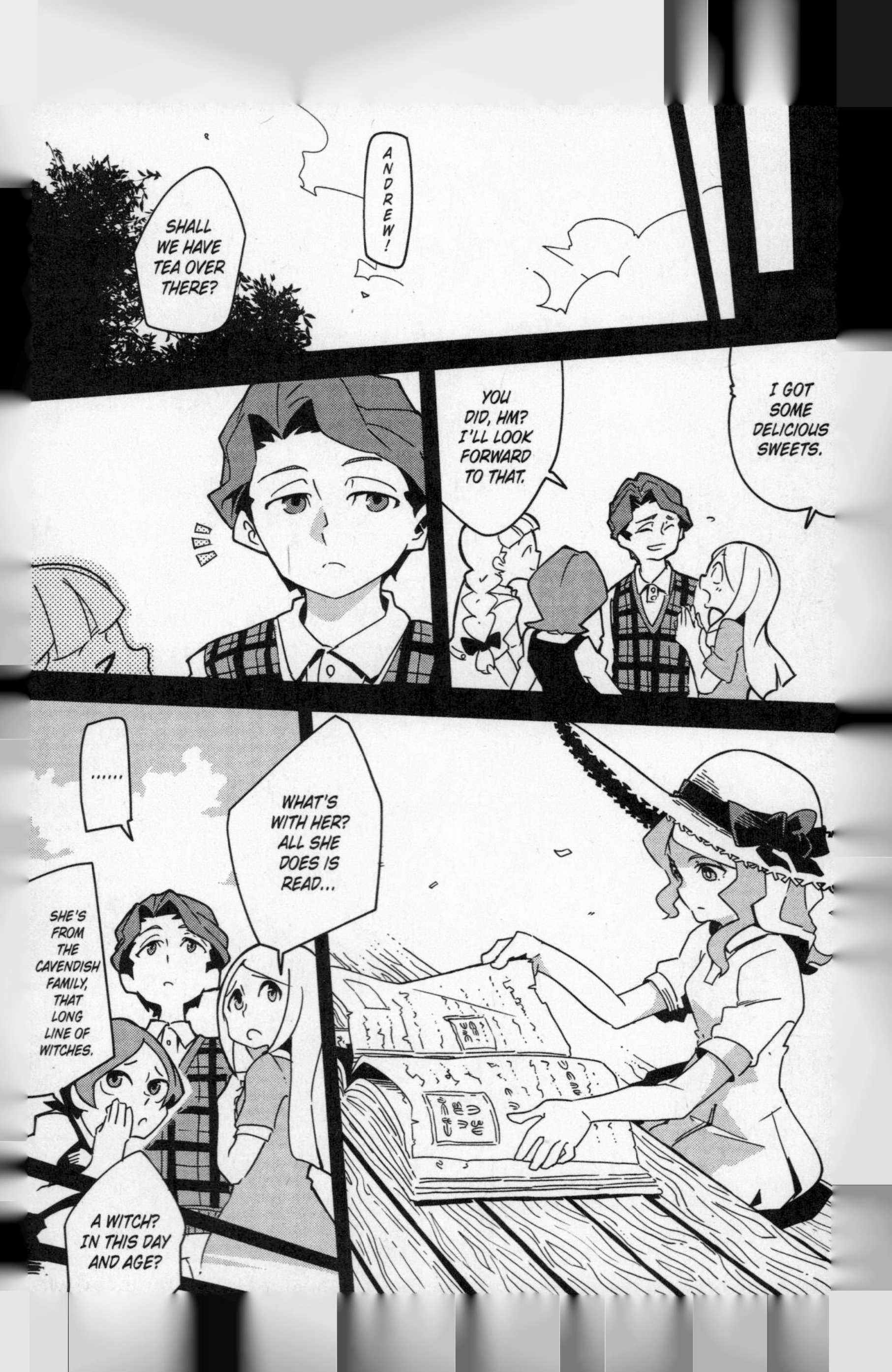
ANDREW!
SHALL WE HAVE TEA OVER THERE?
I GOT SOME DELICIOUS SWEETS.
YOU DID, HM? I'LL LOOK FORWARD TO THAT.
......
WHAT'S WITH HER? ALL SHE DOES IS READ...
SHE'S FROM THE CAVENDISH FAMILY, THAT LONG LINE OF WITCHES.
A WITCH? IN THIS DAY AND AGE?

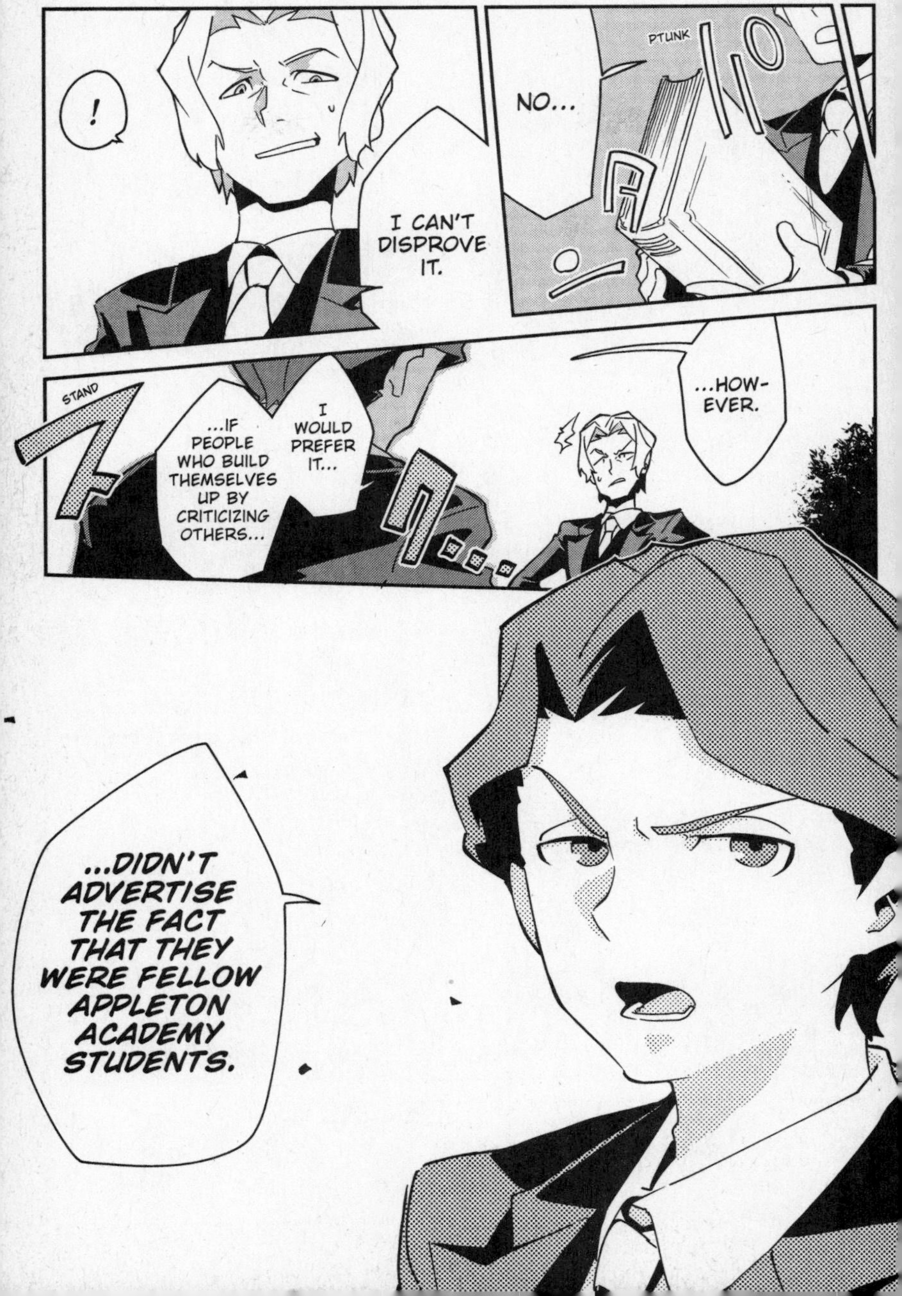
PTUNK
NO...
!
I CAN'T DISPROVE IT.
...HOW-EVER.
I WOULD PREFER IT...
...IF PEOPLE WHO BUILD THEMSELVES UP BY CRITICIZING OTHERS...
STAND
...DIDN'T ADVERTISE THE FACT THAT THEY WERE FELLOW APPLETON ACADEMY STUDENTS.

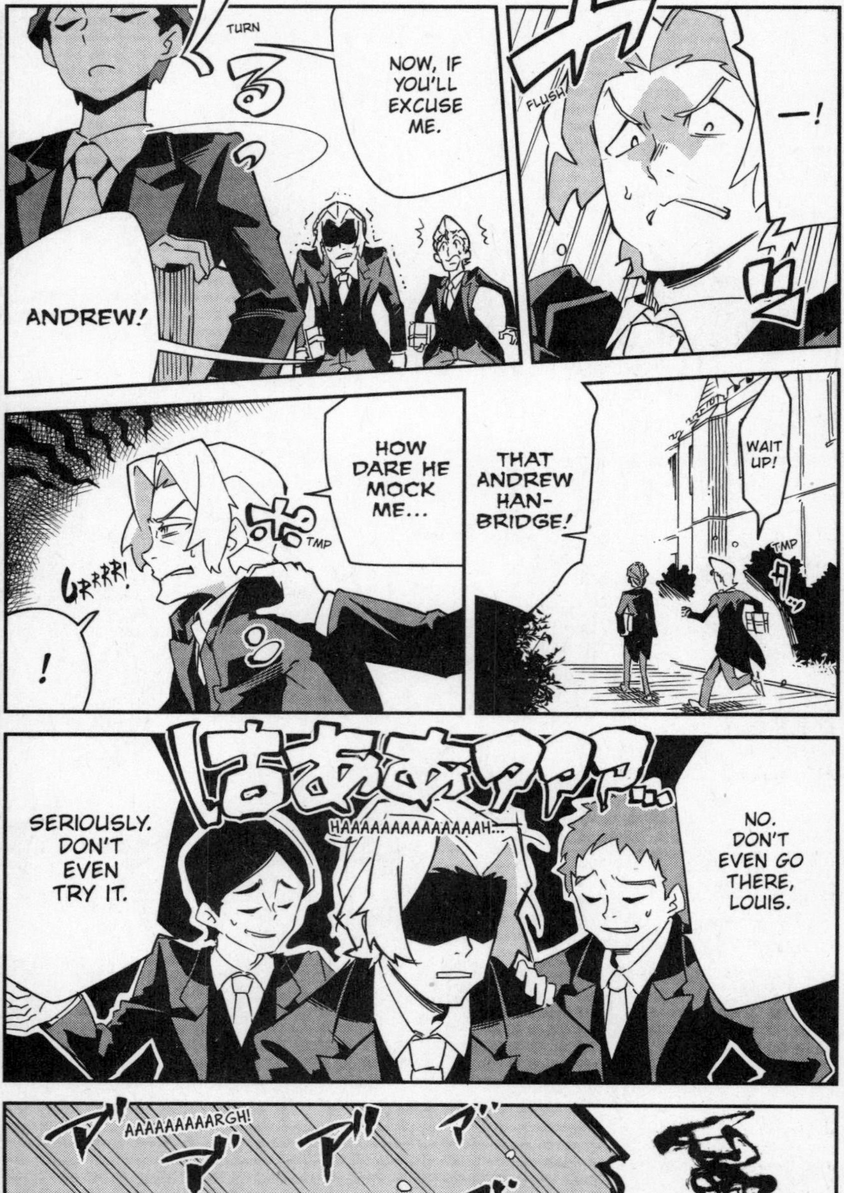
FLUSH
—!
NOW, IF YOU'LL EXCUSE ME.
TURN
ANDREW!
WAIT UP!
TMP
THAT ANDREW HAN-BRIDGE!
HOW DARE HE MOCK ME...
TMP
GRRRR!
!
HAAAAAAAAAAAAAAH...
NO. DON'T EVEN GO THERE, LOUIS.
SERIOUSLY. DON'T EVEN TRY IT.
AAAAAAAAARGH!

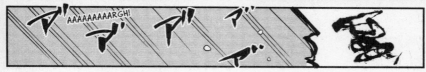

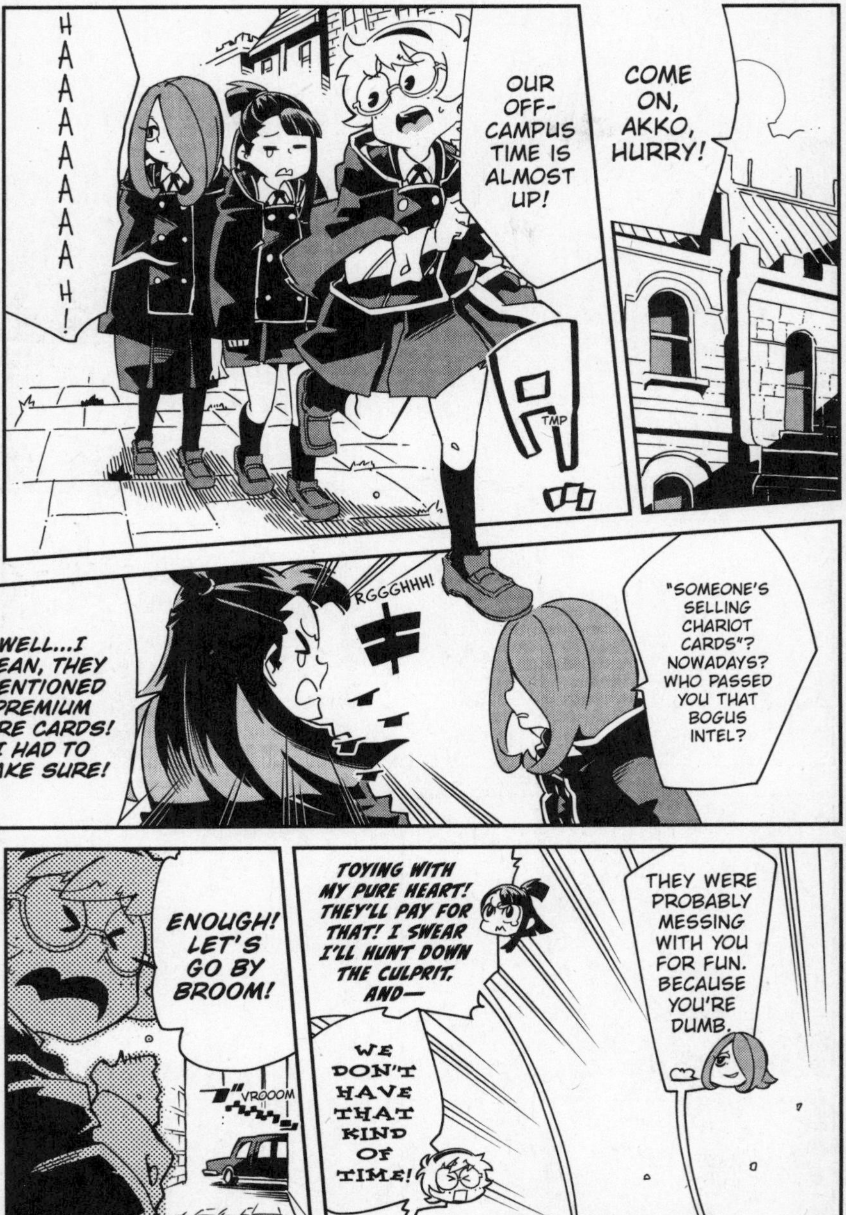

COME ON, AKKO, HURRY!
OUR OFF-CAMPUS TIME IS ALMOST UP!
TMP
HAAAAAAAAH!
"SOMEONE'S SELLING CHARIOT CARDS"? NOWADAYS? WHO PASSED YOU THAT BOGUS INTEL?
RGGGHHH!
WELL...I MEAN, THEY MENTIONED PREMIUM RARE CARDS! I HAD TO MAKE SURE!
THEY WERE PROBABLY MESSING WITH YOU FOR FUN. BECAUSE YOU'RE DUMB.
TOYING WITH MY PURE HEART! THEY'LL PAY FOR THAT! I SWEAR I'LL HUNT DOWN THE CULPRIT, AND—
WE DON'T HAVE THAT KIND OF TIME!
ENOUGH! LET'S GO BY BROOM!
VROOOM

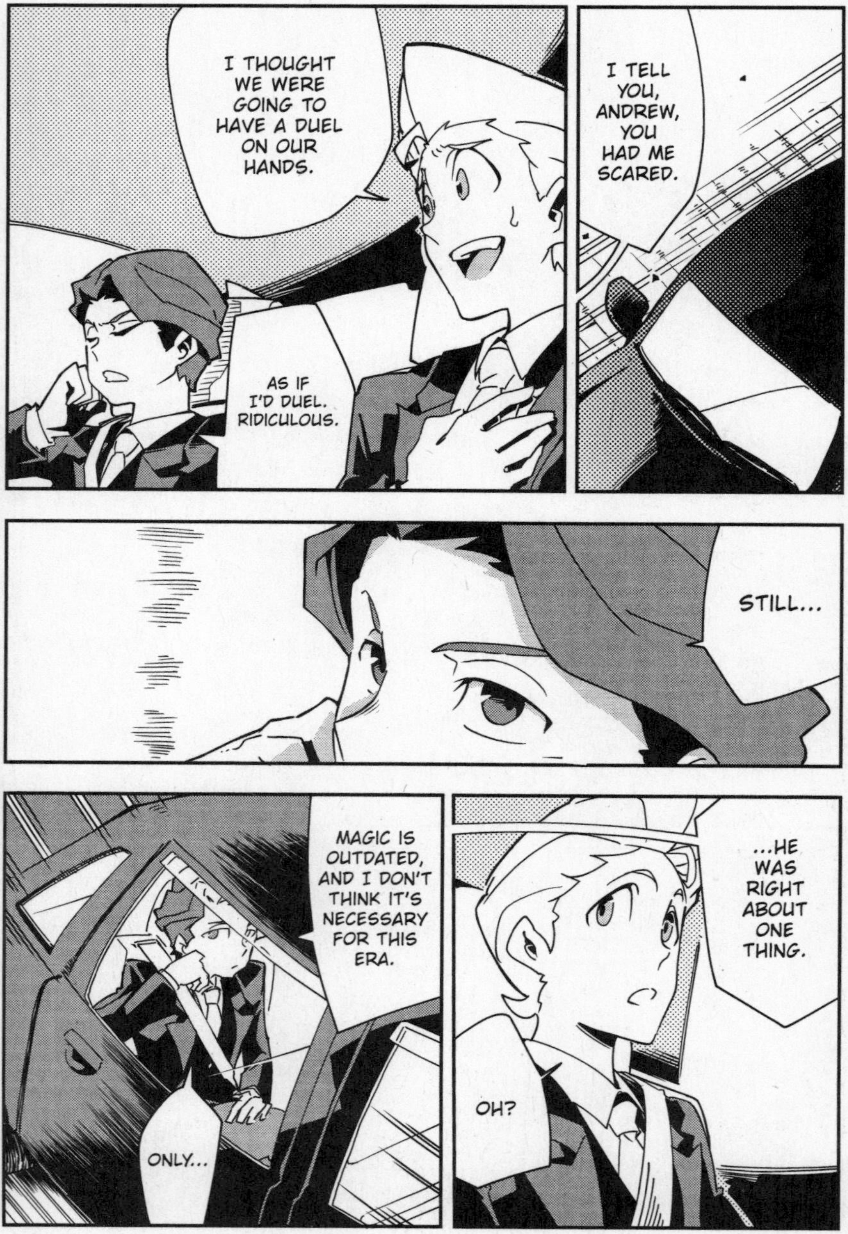
I TELL YOU, ANDREW, YOU HAD ME SCARED.
I THOUGHT WE WERE GOING TO HAVE A DUEL ON OUR HANDS.
AS IF I'D DUEL. RIDICULOUS.
STILL...
...HE WAS RIGHT ABOUT ONE THING.
OH?
MAGIC IS OUTDATED, AND I DON'T THINK IT'S NECESSARY FOR THIS ERA.
ONLY...

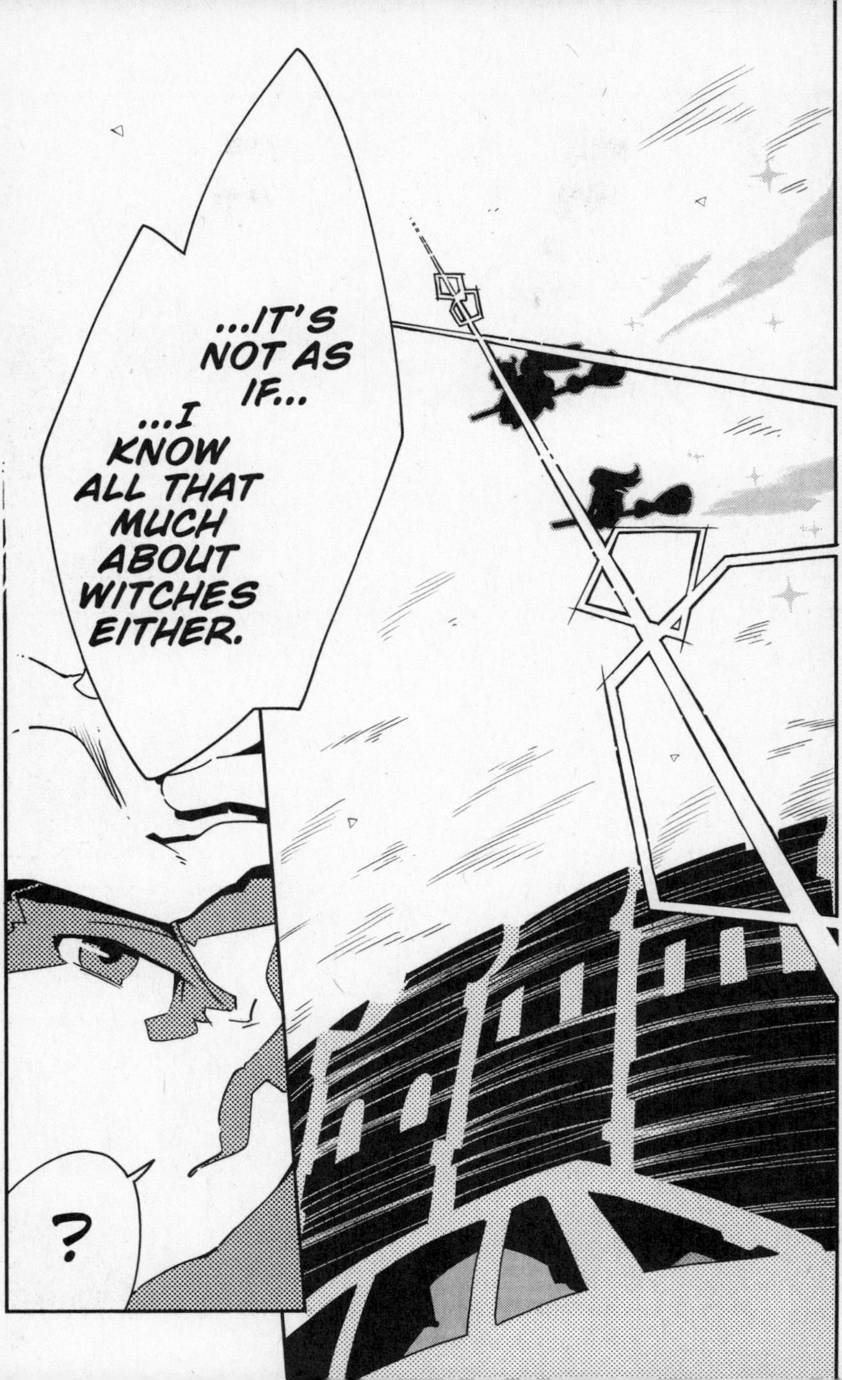
...IT'S NOT AS IF... ...I KNOW ALL THAT MUCH ABOUT WITCHES EITHER.
?

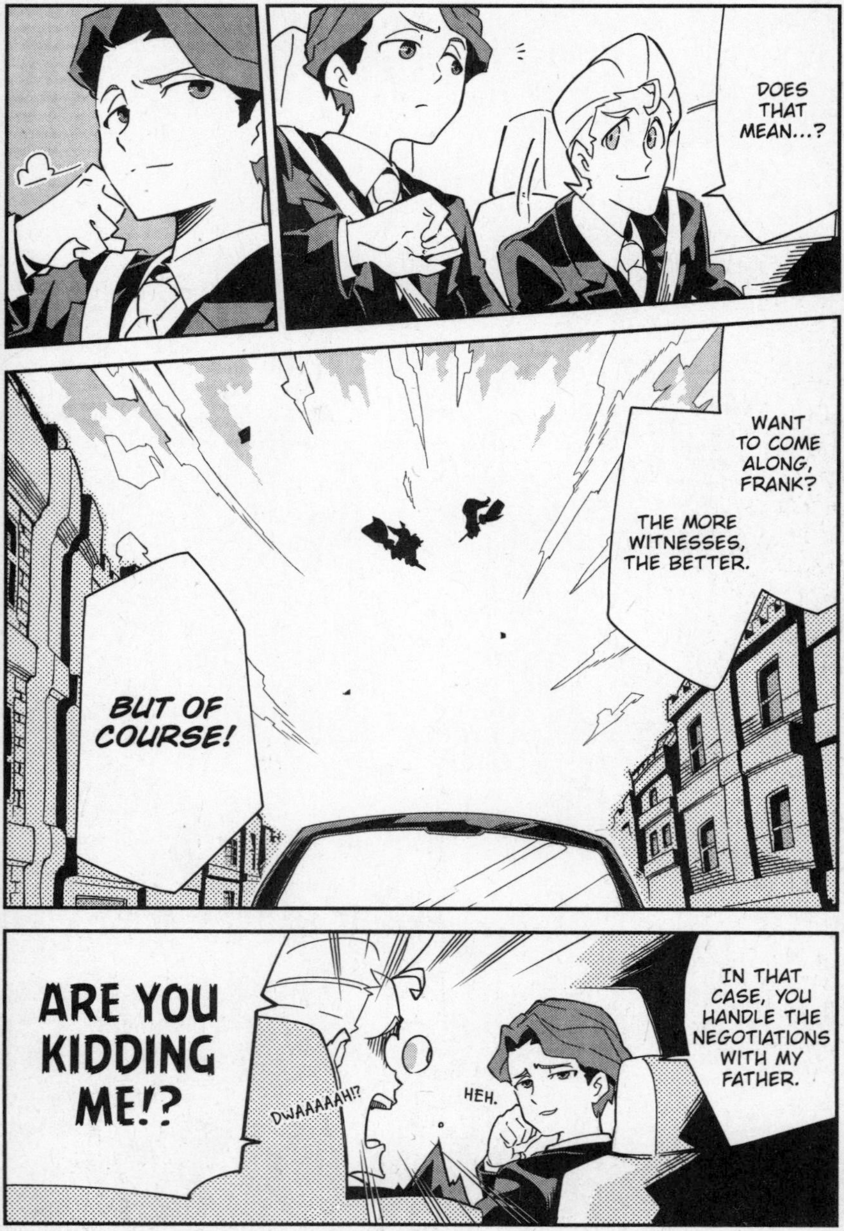
DOES THAT MEAN...?
WANT TO COME ALONG, FRANK?
THE MORE WITNESSES, THE BETTER.
BUT OF COURSE!
IN THAT CASE, YOU HANDLE THE NEGOTIATIONS WITH MY FATHER.
HEH.
DWAAAAAH!?
ARE YOU KIDDING ME!?

Little
Witch
Academia

CONSTANZE AMALIE VON BRAUNSCHBANK-ALBRECHTSBERGER

A mecha fiend from Germany. She brings in high-tech equipment that's against school rules, then sells it to students on the sly.

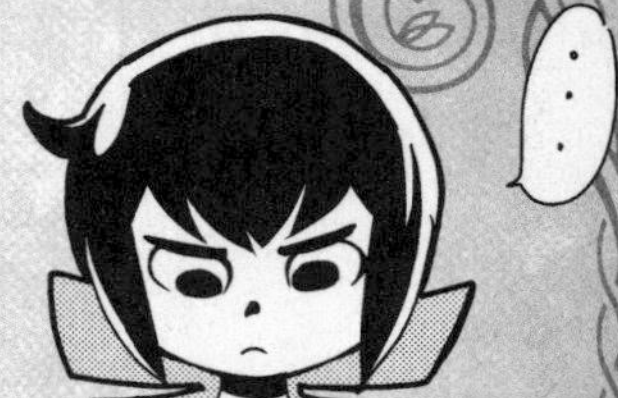

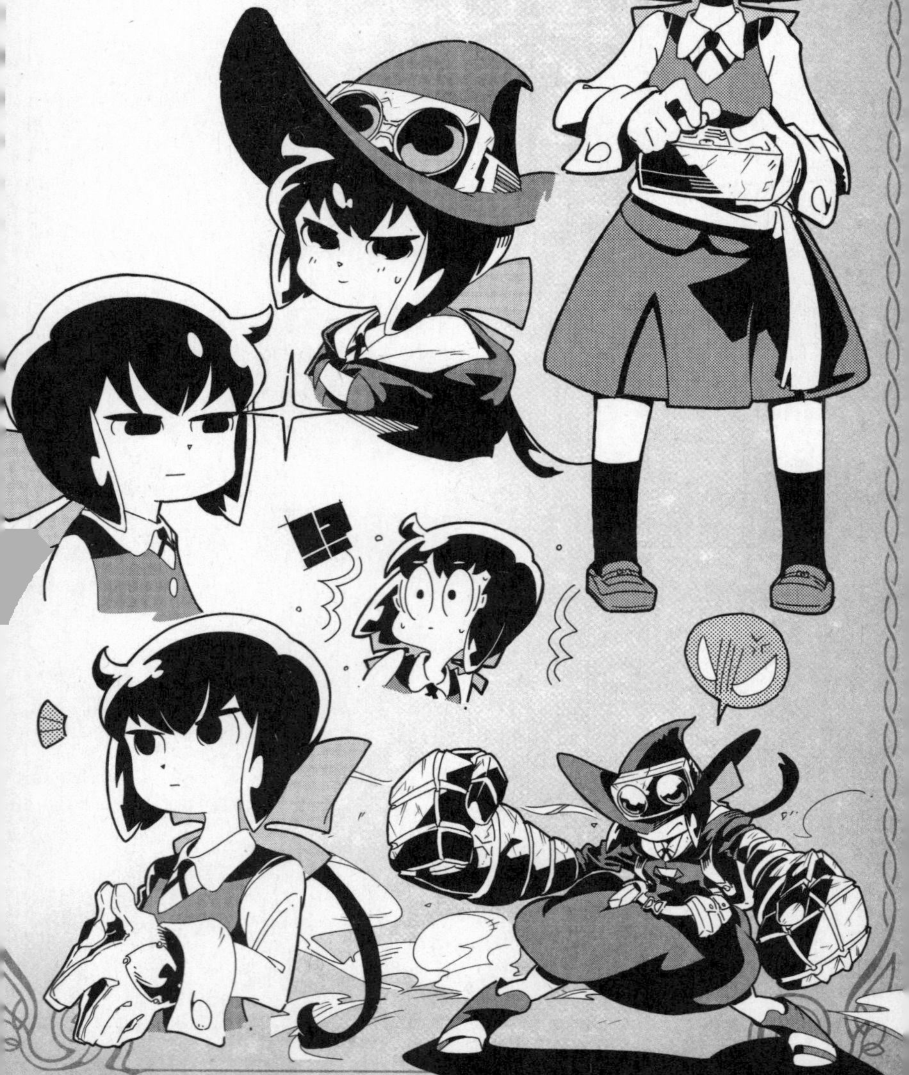

Chapter 9

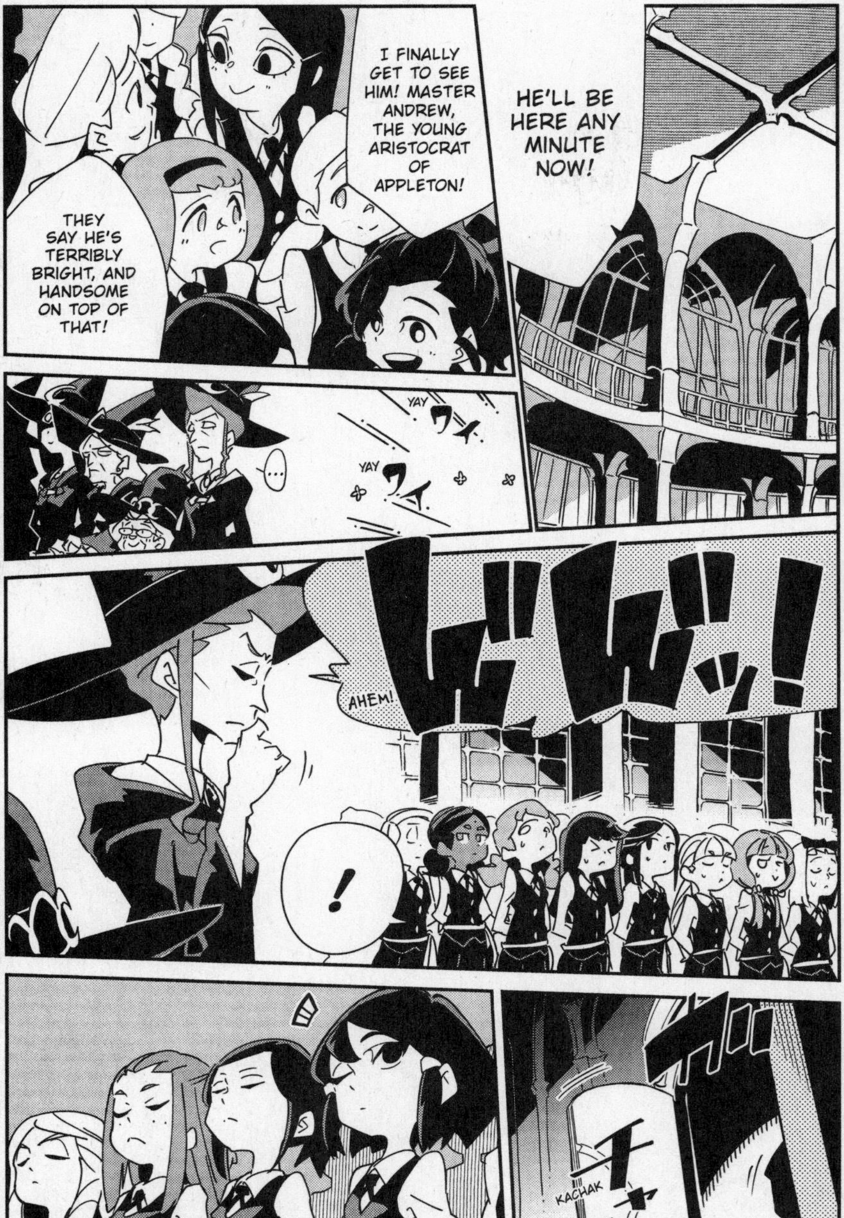

HE'LL BE HERE ANY MINUTE NOW!
I FINALLY GET TO SEE HIM! MASTER ANDREW, THE YOUNG ARISTOCRAT OF APPLETON!
THEY SAY HE'S TERRIBLY BRIGHT, AND HANDSOME ON TOP OF THAT!
YAY
YAY
...
AHEM!
!
KACHAK

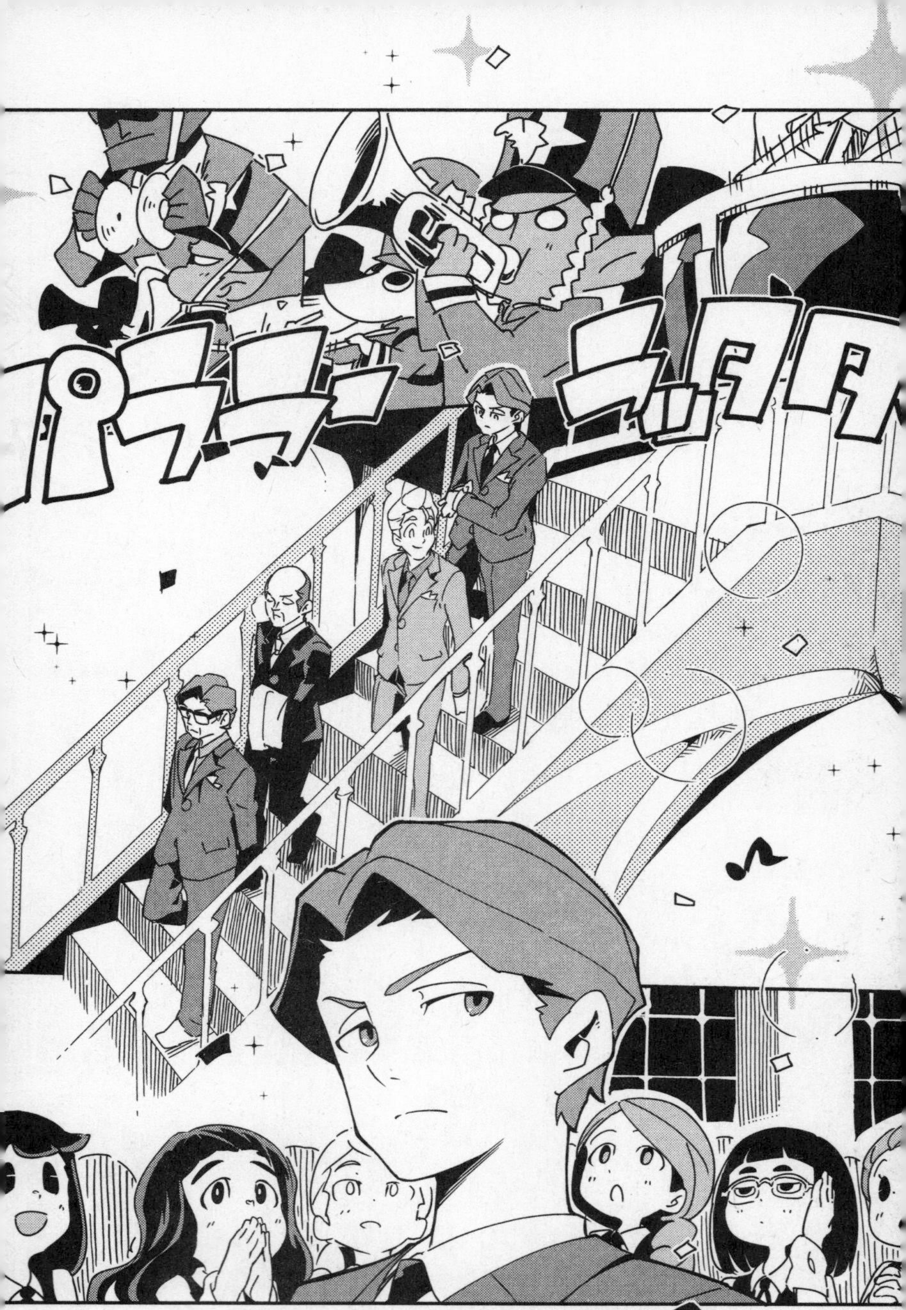

Chapter 9 THE FOUNTAIN OF POLARIS ~THE LATENT WITCH~

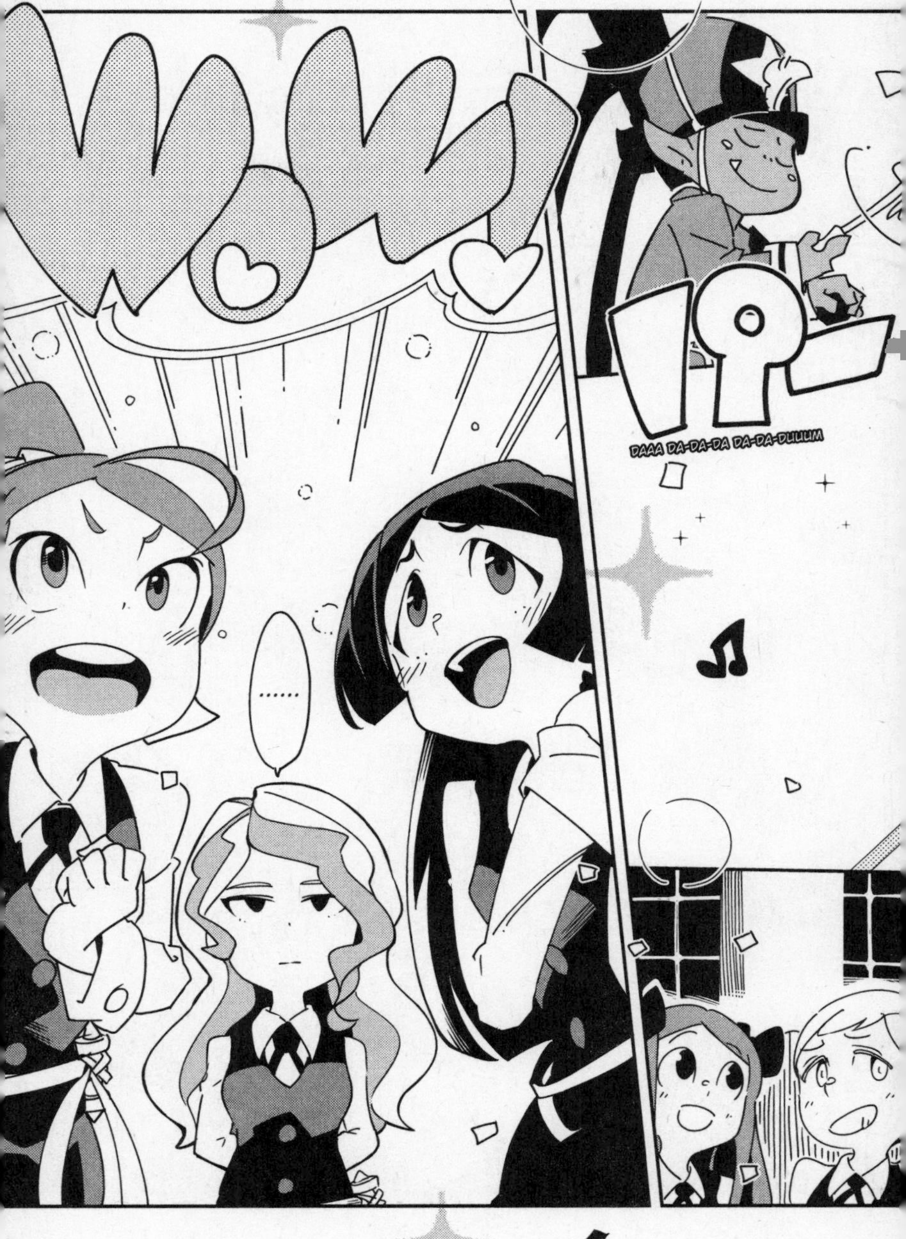
DAAA DA-DA-DA DA-DA-DUUUM
WOW
......

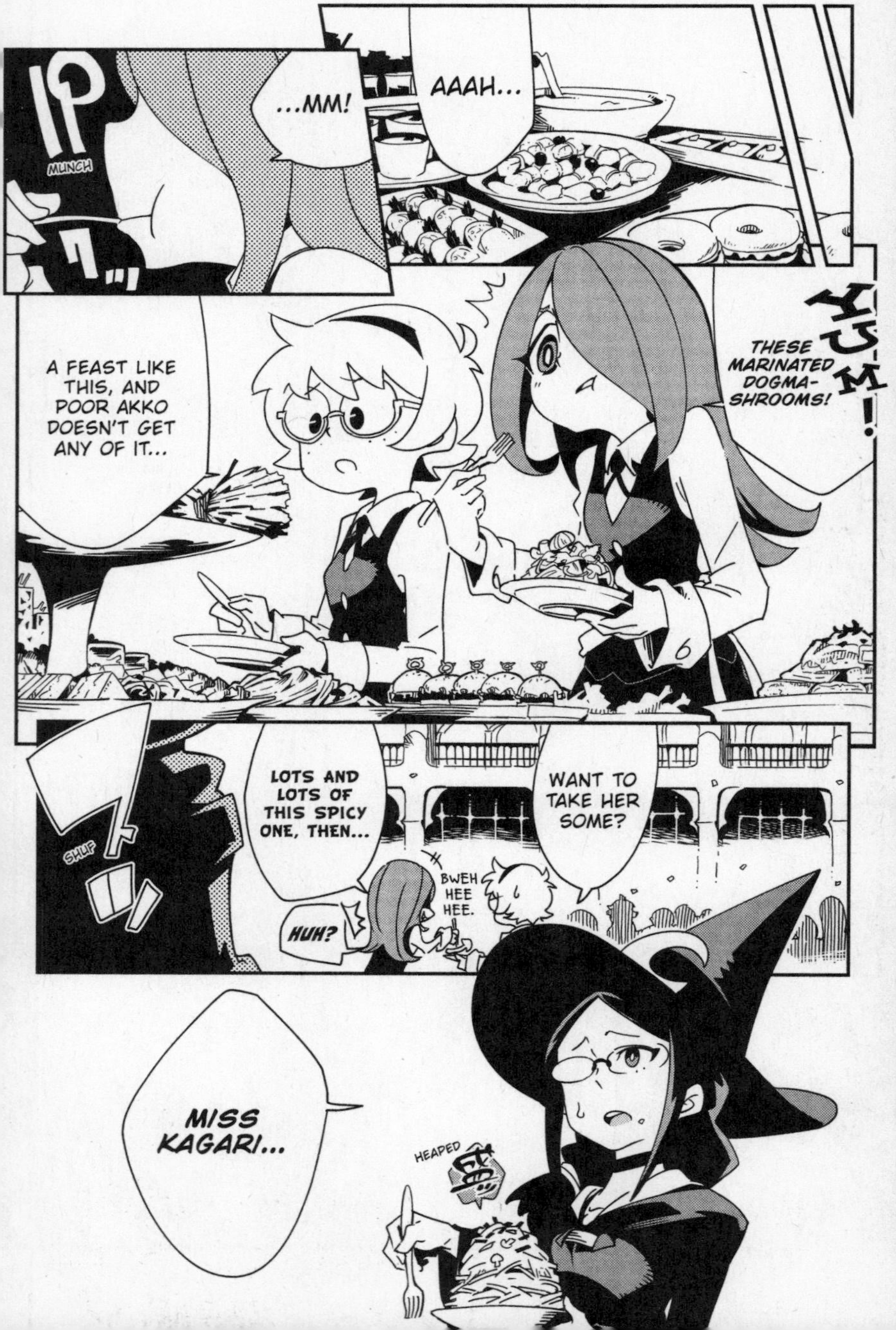
AAAH...
...MM!
MUNCH
YUM!
THESE MARINATED DOGMA-SHROOMS!
A FEAST LIKE THIS, AND POOR AKKO DOESN'T GET ANY OF IT...
WANT TO TAKE HER SOME?
LOTS AND LOTS OF THIS SPICY ONE, THEN...
BWEH HEE HEE.
HUH?
SHUF
HEAPED
MISS KAGARI...

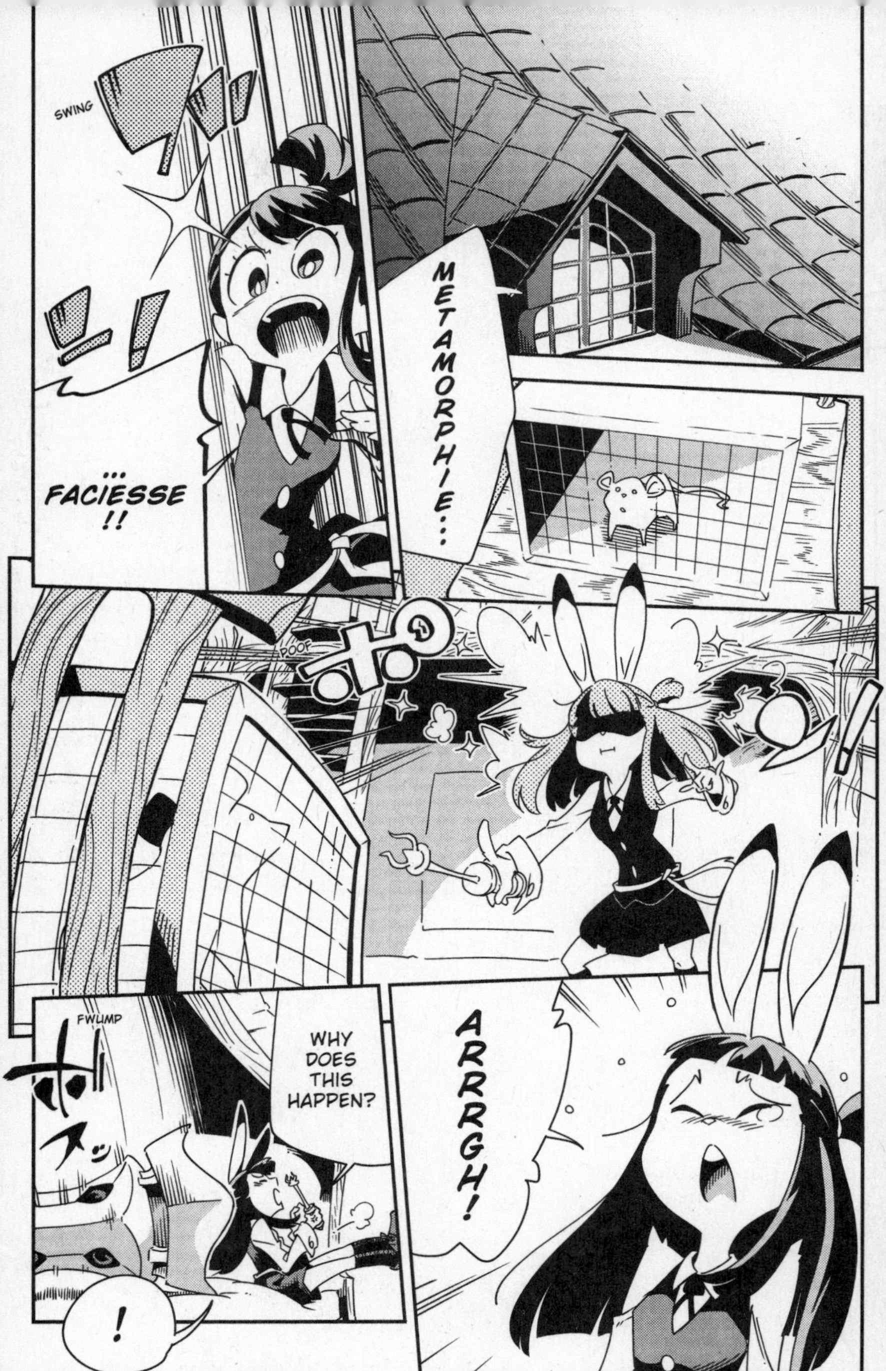
METAMORPHIE...
SWING
...FACIESSE!!
POOF
ARRRGH!
FWUMP
WHY DOES THIS HAPPEN?
!

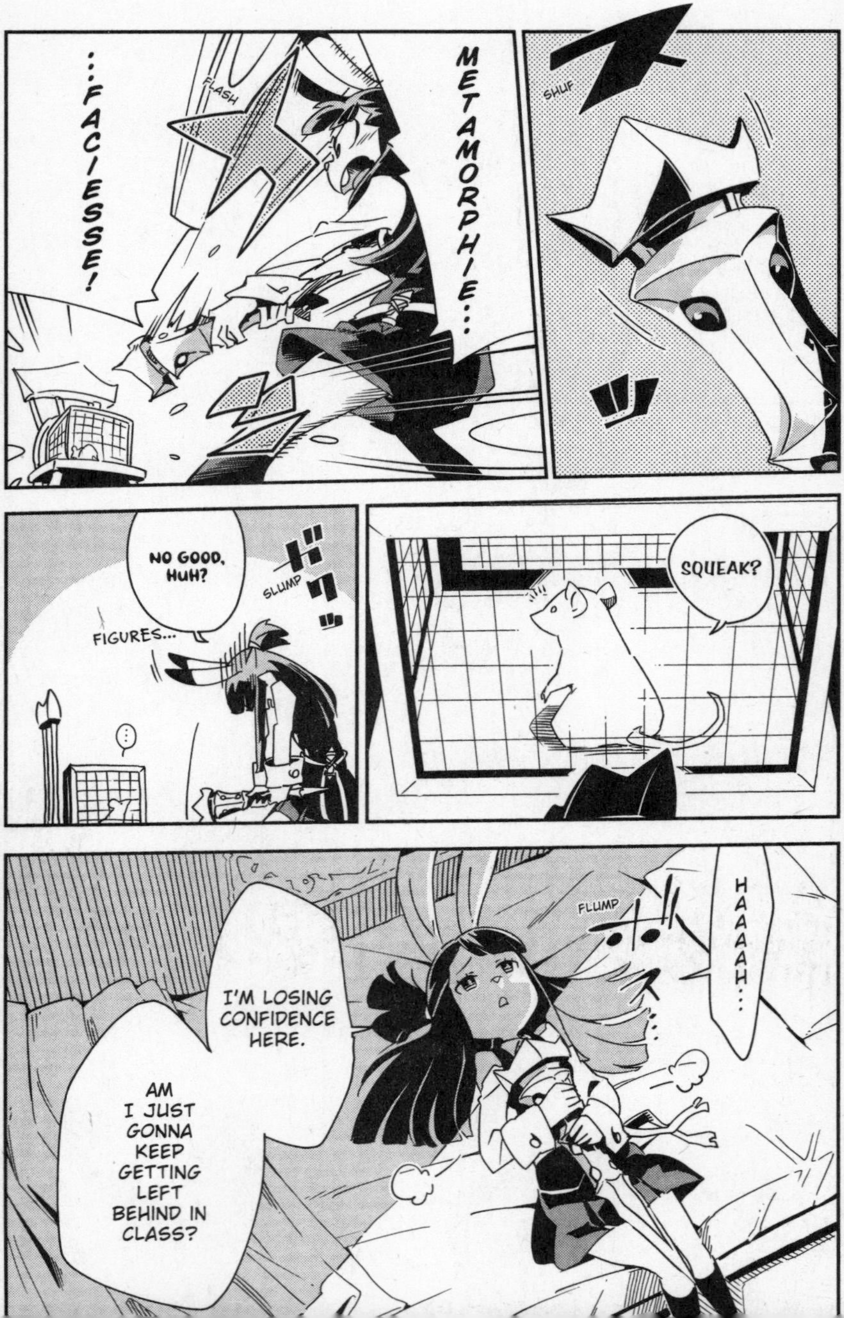
SHUF
METAMORPHIE...
FLASH
...FACIESSE!
SQUEAK?
NO GOOD, HUH?
SLUMP
FIGURES...
...
HAAAAH...
FLUMP
I'M LOSING CONFIDENCE HERE.
AM I JUST GONNA KEEP GETTING LEFT BEHIND IN CLASS?

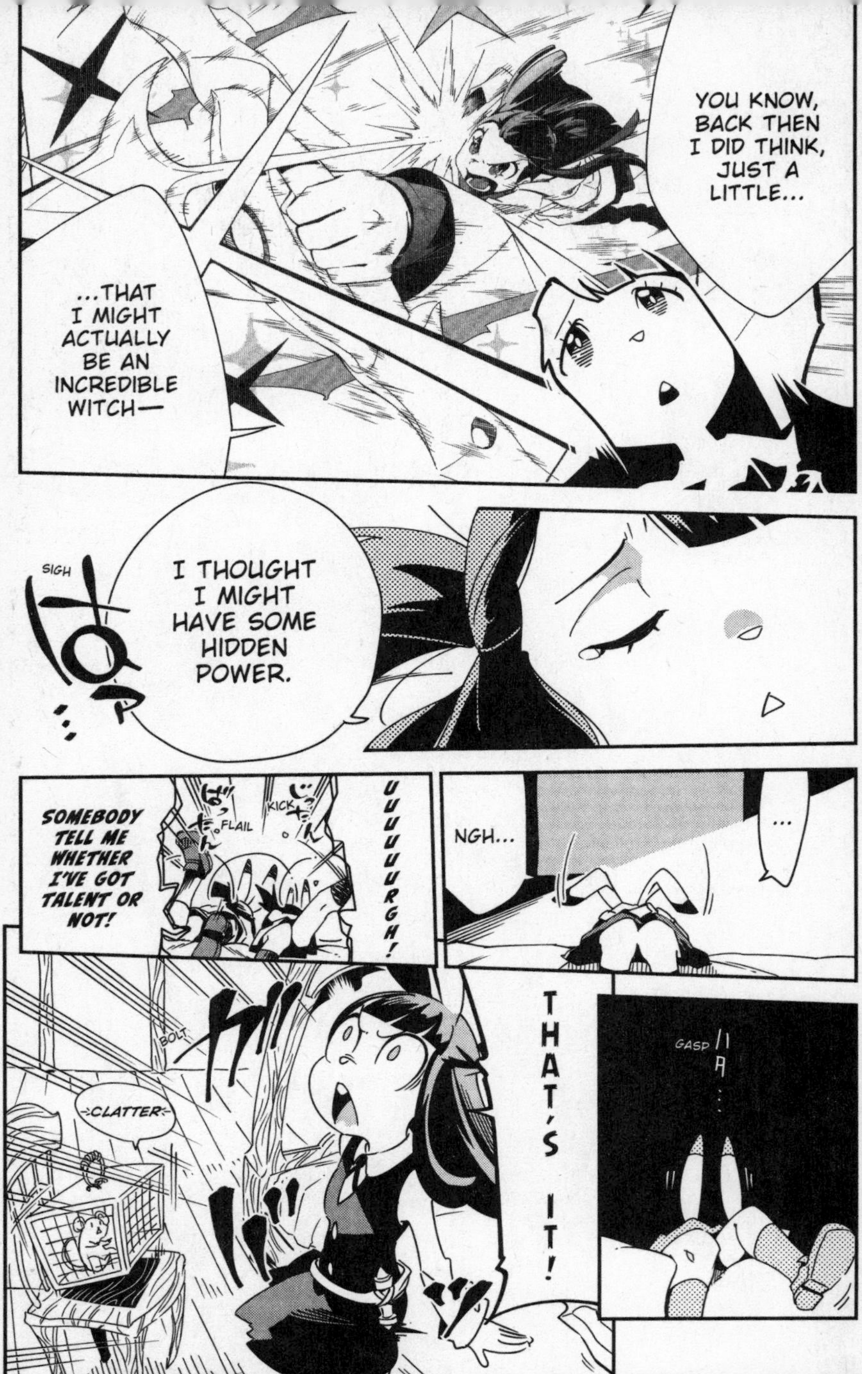

YOU KNOW, BACK THEN I DID THINK, JUST A LITTLE...
...THAT I MIGHT ACTUALLY BE AN INCREDIBLE WITCH—
I THOUGHT I MIGHT HAVE SOME HIDDEN POWER.
SIGH
...
NGH...
UUUUUUURGH!
KICK
FLAIL
SOMEBODY TELL ME WHETHER I'VE GOT TALENT OR NOT!
GASP
THAT'S IT!
BOLT
CLATTER

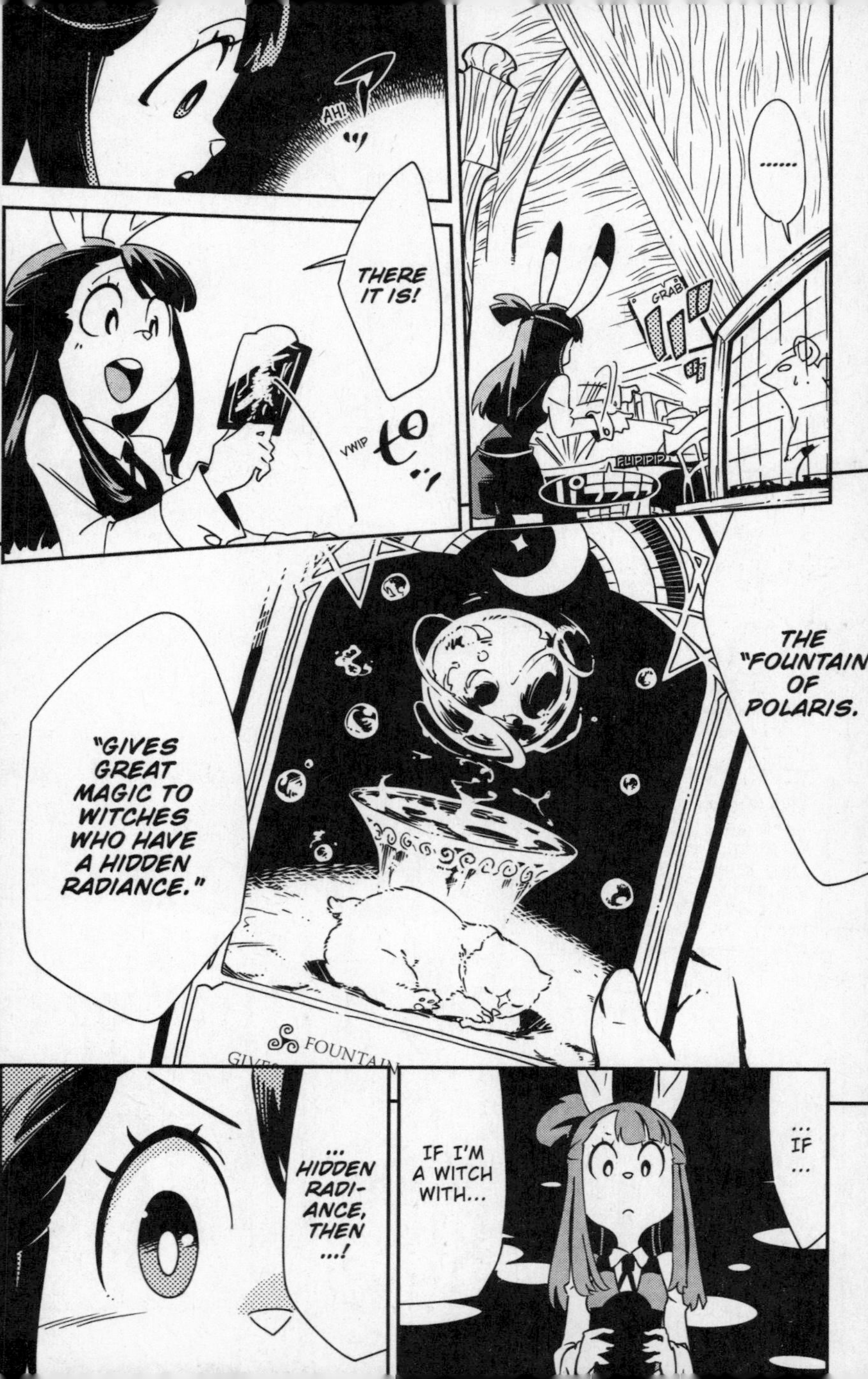
......
GRAB
FLIPIPIP
AH!
THERE IT IS!
VWIP
THE "FOUNTAIN OF POLARIS.
"GIVES GREAT MAGIC TO WITCHES WHO HAVE A HIDDEN RADIANCE."
FOUNTAIN
... IF ...
IF I'M A WITCH WITH...
... HIDDEN RADI-ANCE, THEN ...!

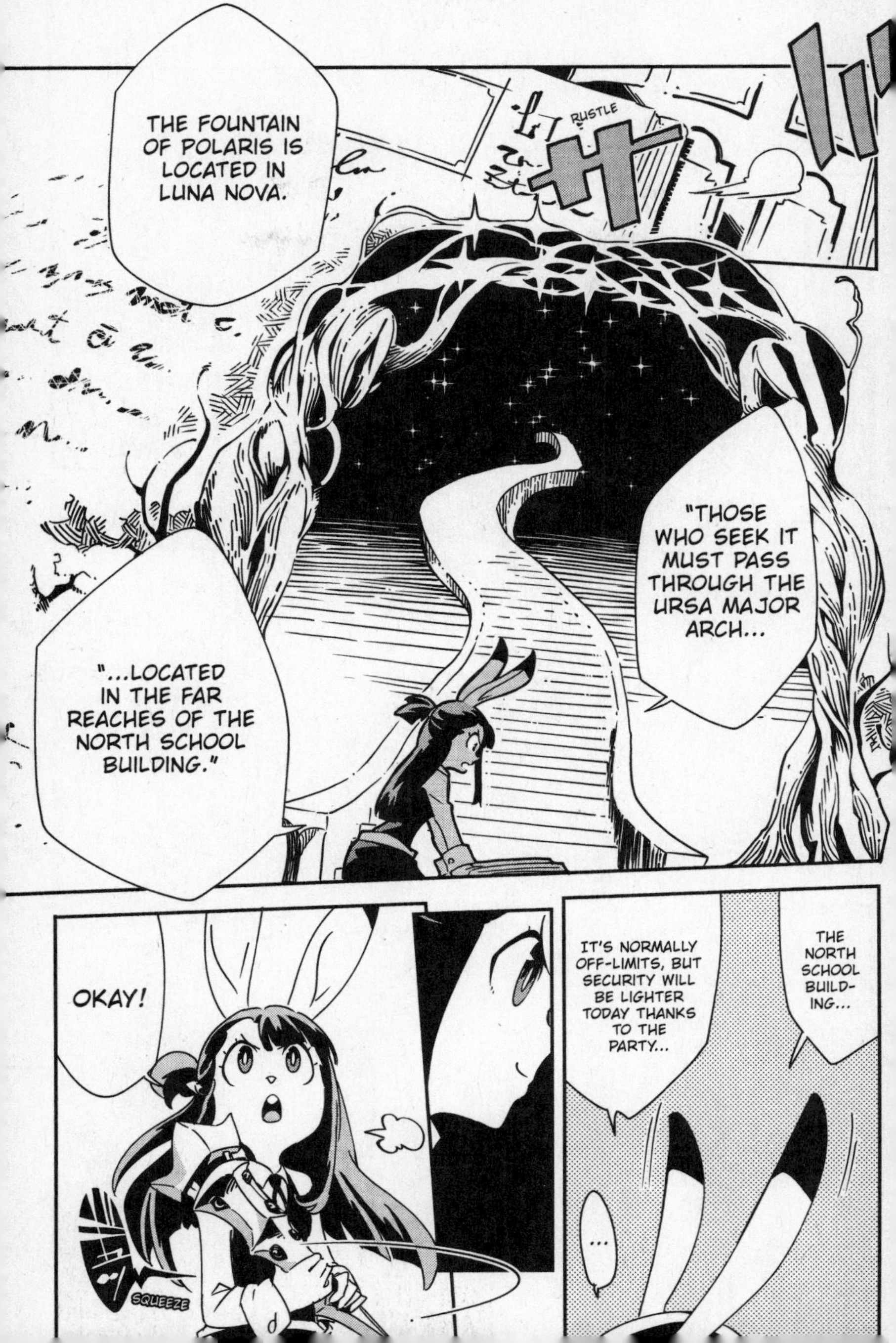
RUSTLE
THE FOUNTAIN OF POLARIS IS LOCATED IN LUNA NOVA.
"THOSE WHO SEEK IT MUST PASS THROUGH THE URSA MAJOR ARCH...
"...LOCATED IN THE FAR REACHES OF THE NORTH SCHOOL BUILDING."
THE NORTH SCHOOL BUILD-ING...
IT'S NORMALLY OFF-LIMITS, BUT SECURITY WILL BE LIGHTER TODAY THANKS TO THE PARTY...
...
OKAY!
SQUEEZE

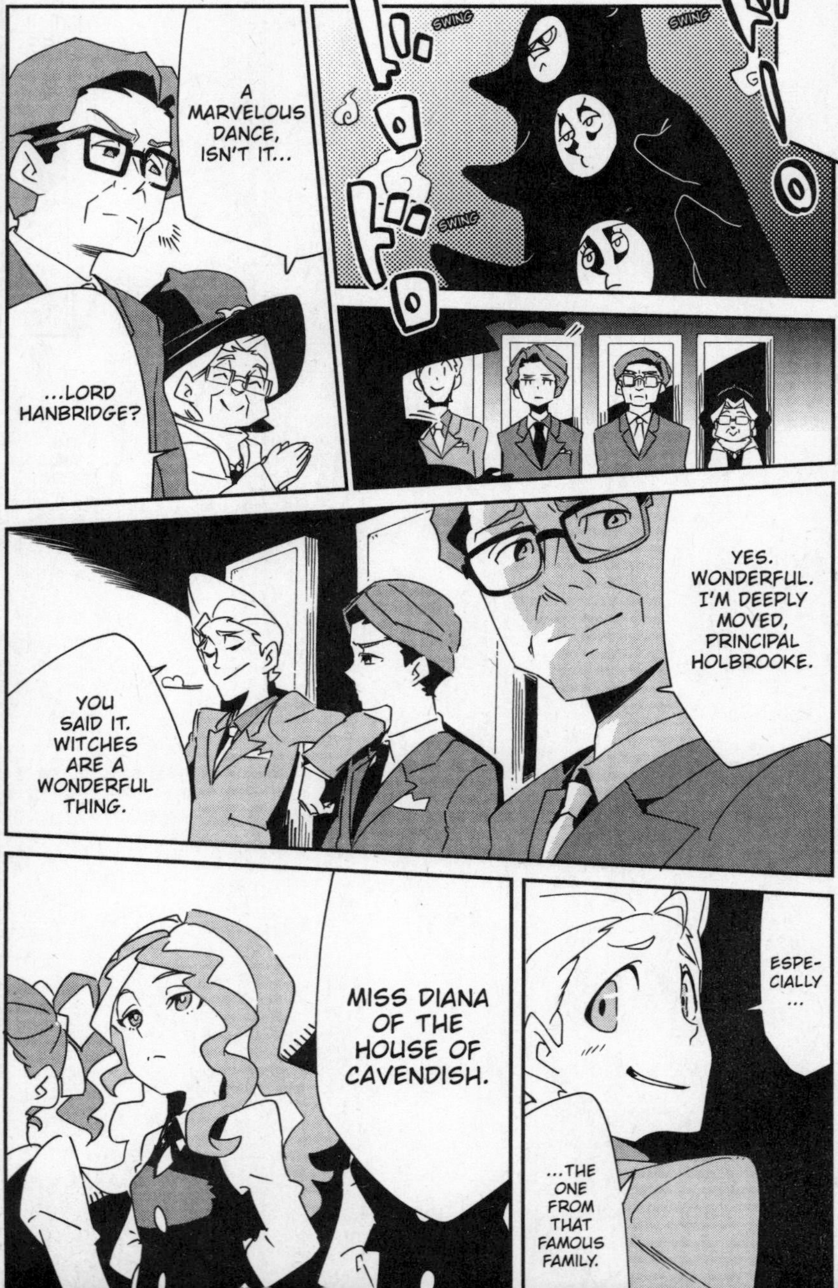
SWING
SWING
SWING
A MARVELOUS DANCE, ISN'T IT...
...LORD HANBRIDGE?
YES. WONDERFUL. I'M DEEPLY MOVED, PRINCIPAL HOLBROOKE.
YOU SAID IT. WITCHES ARE A WONDERFUL THING.
ESPE-CIALLY...
...THE ONE FROM THAT FAMOUS FAMILY.
MISS DIANA OF THE HOUSE OF CAVENDISH.

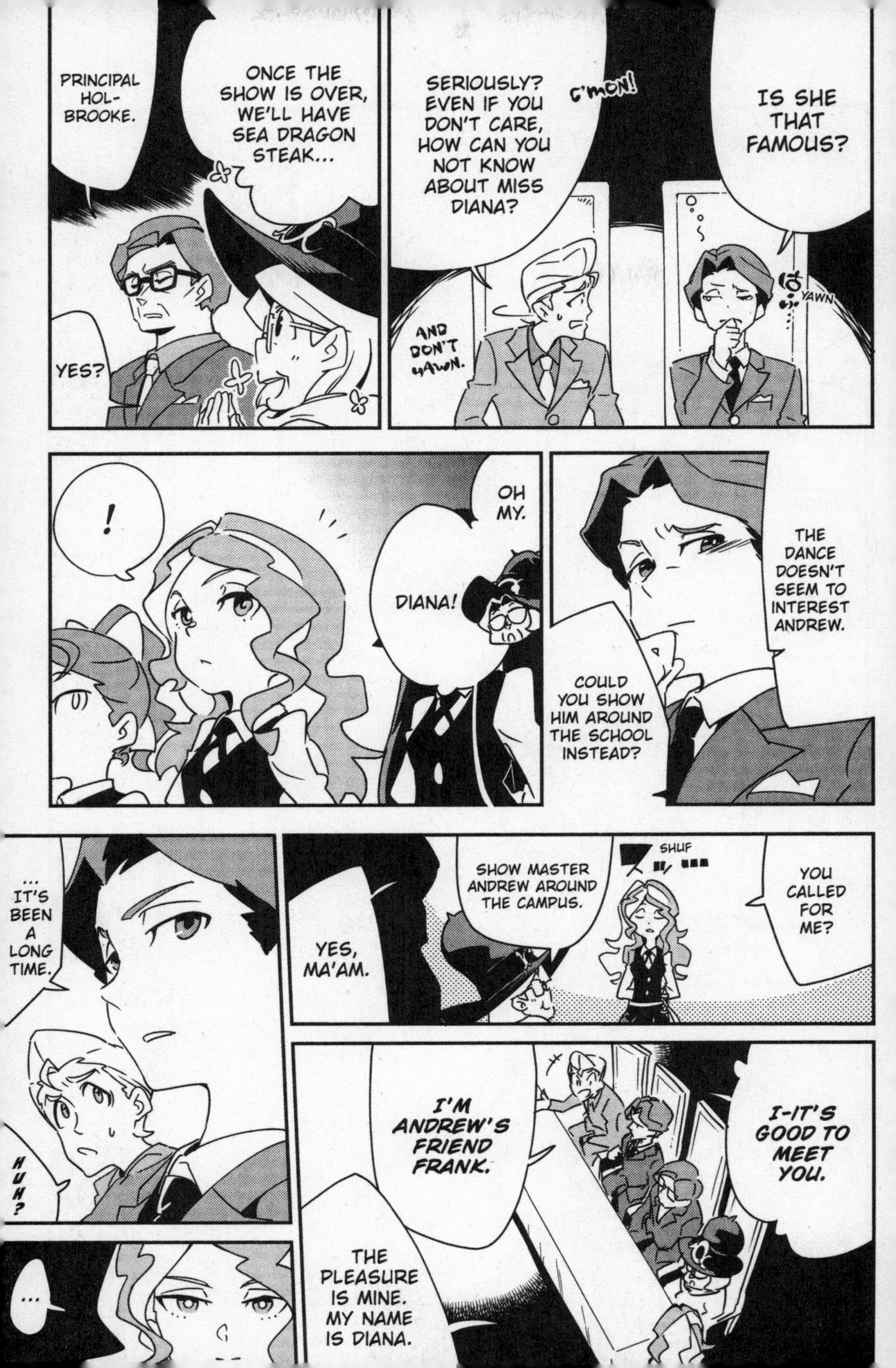
IS SHE THAT FAMOUS?
C'MON!
SERIOUSLY? EVEN IF YOU DON'T CARE, HOW CAN YOU NOT KNOW ABOUT MISS DIANA?
YAWN
AND DON'T YAWN.
ONCE THE SHOW IS OVER, WE'LL HAVE SEA DRAGON STEAK...
PRINCIPAL HOL-BROOKE.
YES?
THE DANCE DOESN'T SEEM TO INTEREST ANDREW.
COULD YOU SHOW HIM AROUND THE SCHOOL INSTEAD?
OH MY.
DIANA!
!
YOU CALLED FOR ME?
SHUF
SHOW MASTER ANDREW AROUND THE CAMPUS.
YES, MA'AM.
I-IT'S GOOD TO MEET YOU.
I'M ANDREW'S FRIEND FRANK.
THE PLEASURE IS MINE. MY NAME IS DIANA.
... IT'S BEEN A LONG TIME.
HUH?
...

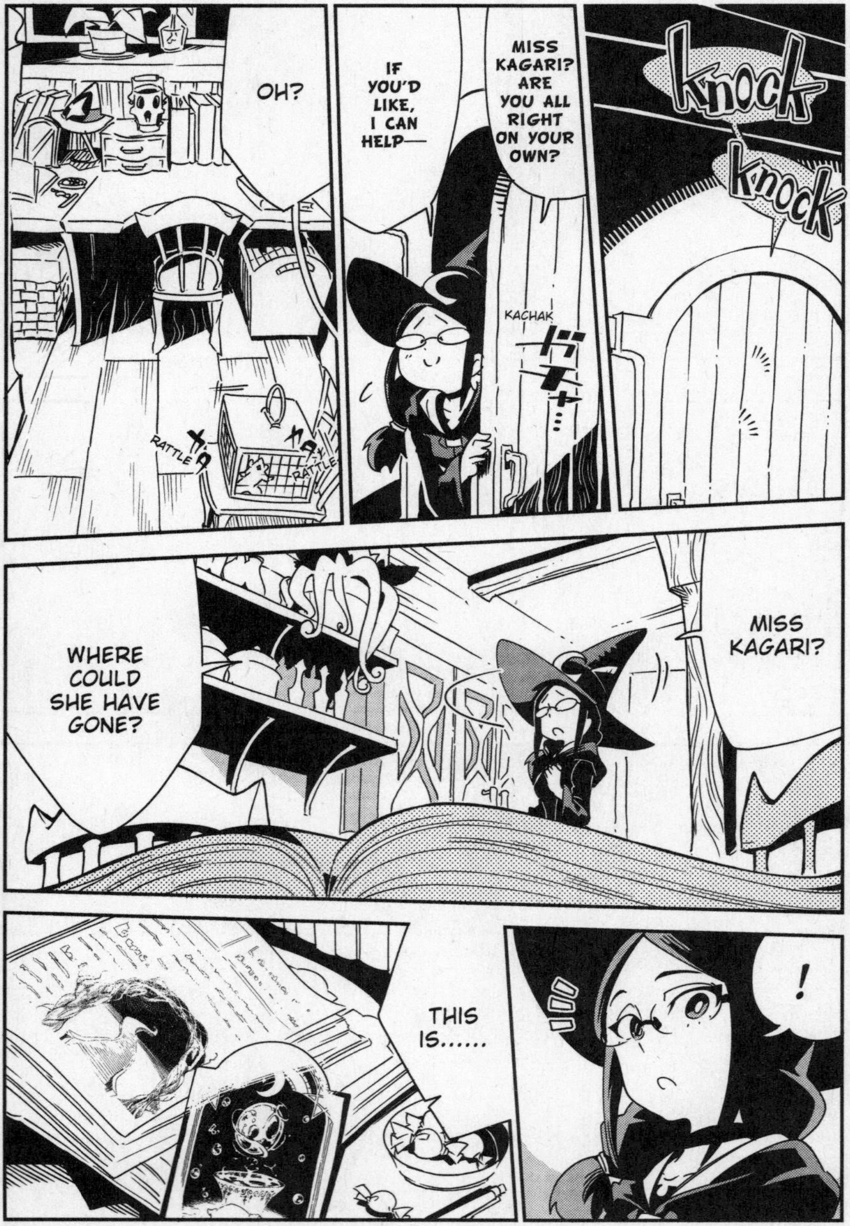

knock
knock
MISS KAGARI? ARE YOU ALL RIGHT ON YOUR OWN?
IF YOU'D LIKE, I CAN HELP—
KACHAK
OH?
RATTLE
RATTLE
MISS KAGARI?
WHERE COULD SHE HAVE GONE?
!
THIS IS......

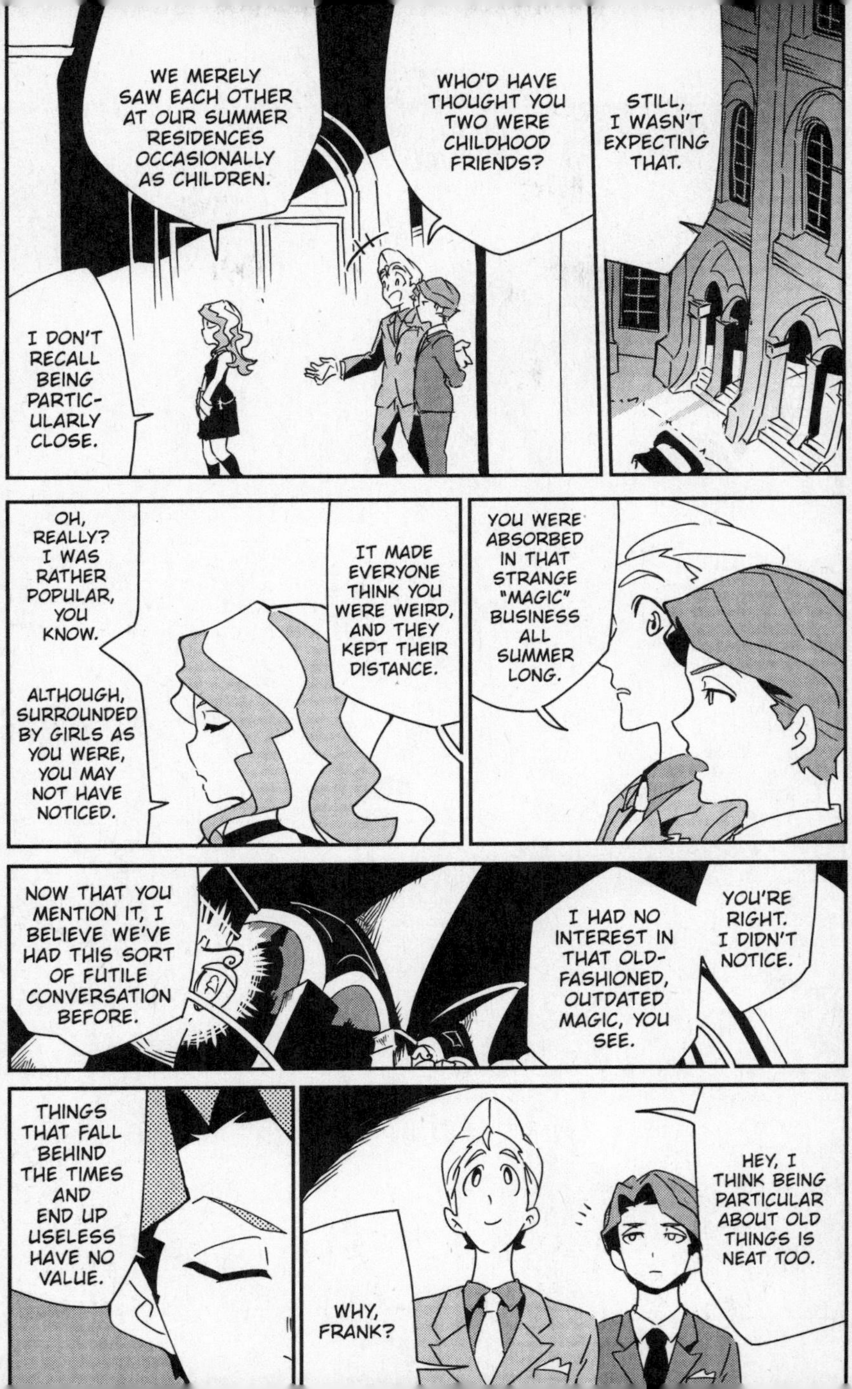
STILL, I WASN'T EXPECTING THAT.
WHO'D HAVE THOUGHT YOU TWO WERE CHILDHOOD FRIENDS?
WE MERELY SAW EACH OTHER AT OUR SUMMER RESIDENCES OCCASIONALLY AS CHILDREN.
I DON'T RECALL BEING PARTIC-ULARLY CLOSE.
YOU WERE ABSORBED IN THAT STRANGE "MAGIC" BUSINESS ALL SUMMER LONG.
IT MADE EVERYONE THINK YOU WERE WEIRD, AND THEY KEPT THEIR DISTANCE.
OH, REALLY? I WAS RATHER POPULAR, YOU KNOW.
ALTHOUGH, SURROUNDED BY GIRLS AS YOU WERE, YOU MAY NOT HAVE NOTICED.
YOU'RE RIGHT. I DIDN'T NOTICE.
I HAD NO INTEREST IN THAT OLD-FASHIONED, OUTDATED MAGIC, YOU SEE.
NOW THAT YOU MENTION IT, I BELIEVE WE'VE HAD THIS SORT OF FUTILE CONVERSATION BEFORE.
HEY, I THINK BEING PARTICULAR ABOUT OLD THINGS IS NEAT TOO.
WHY, FRANK?
THINGS THAT FALL BEHIND THE TIMES AND END UP USELESS HAVE NO VALUE.

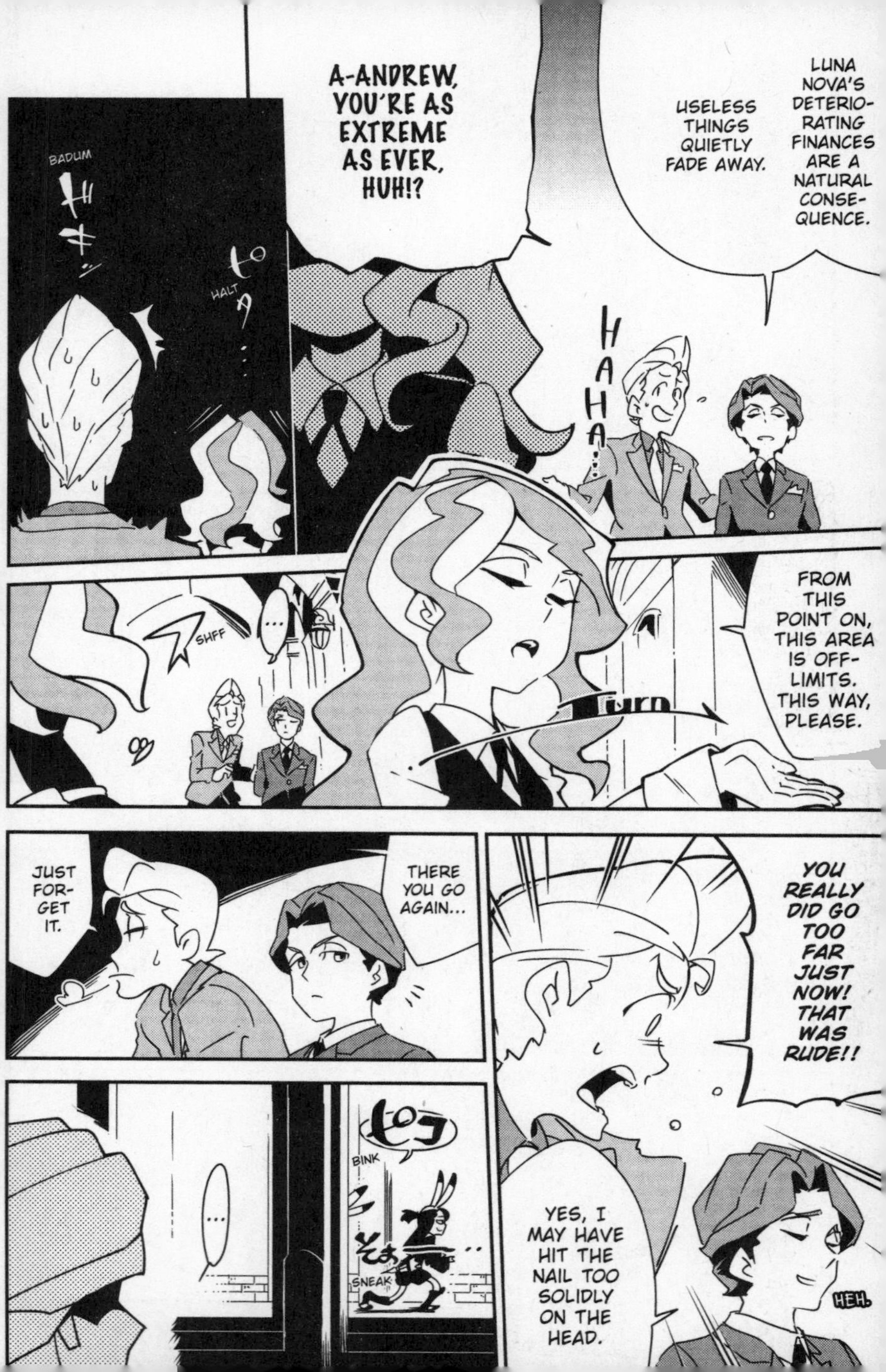
LUNA NOVA'S DETERIORATING FINANCES ARE A NATURAL CONSEQUENCE.
USELESS THINGS QUIETLY FADE AWAY.
A-ANDREW, YOU'RE AS EXTREME AS EVER, HUH!?
HAHAHA...!!
BADUM
HALT
FROM THIS POINT ON, THIS AREA IS OFF-LIMITS. THIS WAY, PLEASE.
Turn
...
SHFF
YOU REALLY DID GO TOO FAR JUST NOW! THAT WAS RUDE!!
YES, I MAY HAVE HIT THE NAIL TOO SOLIDLY ON THE HEAD.
HEH.
THERE YOU GO AGAIN...
JUST FORGET IT.
BINK
...
SNEAK

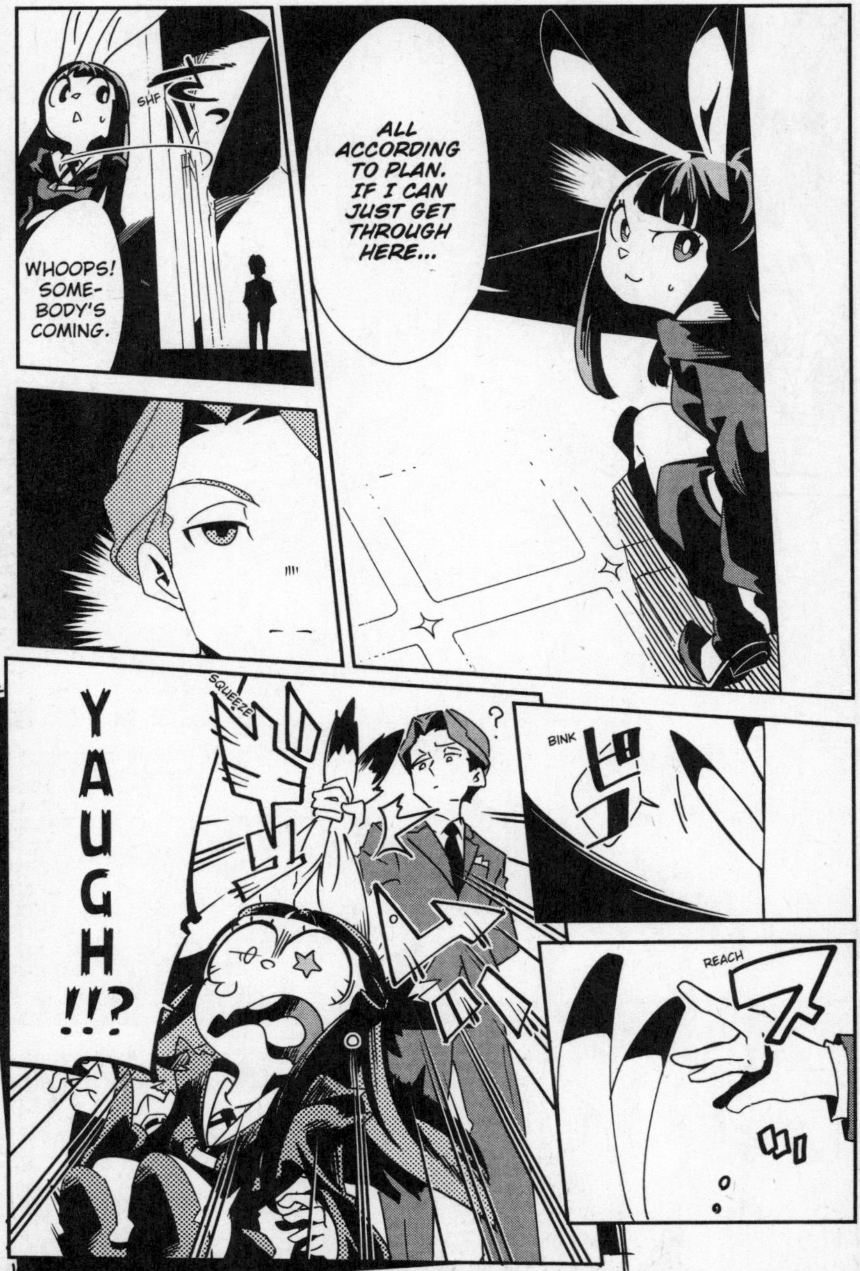
ALL ACCORDING TO PLAN. IF I CAN JUST GET THROUGH HERE...
SHF
WHOOPS! SOMEBODY'S COMING.
BINK
REACH
SQUEEZE
YAUGH!!?

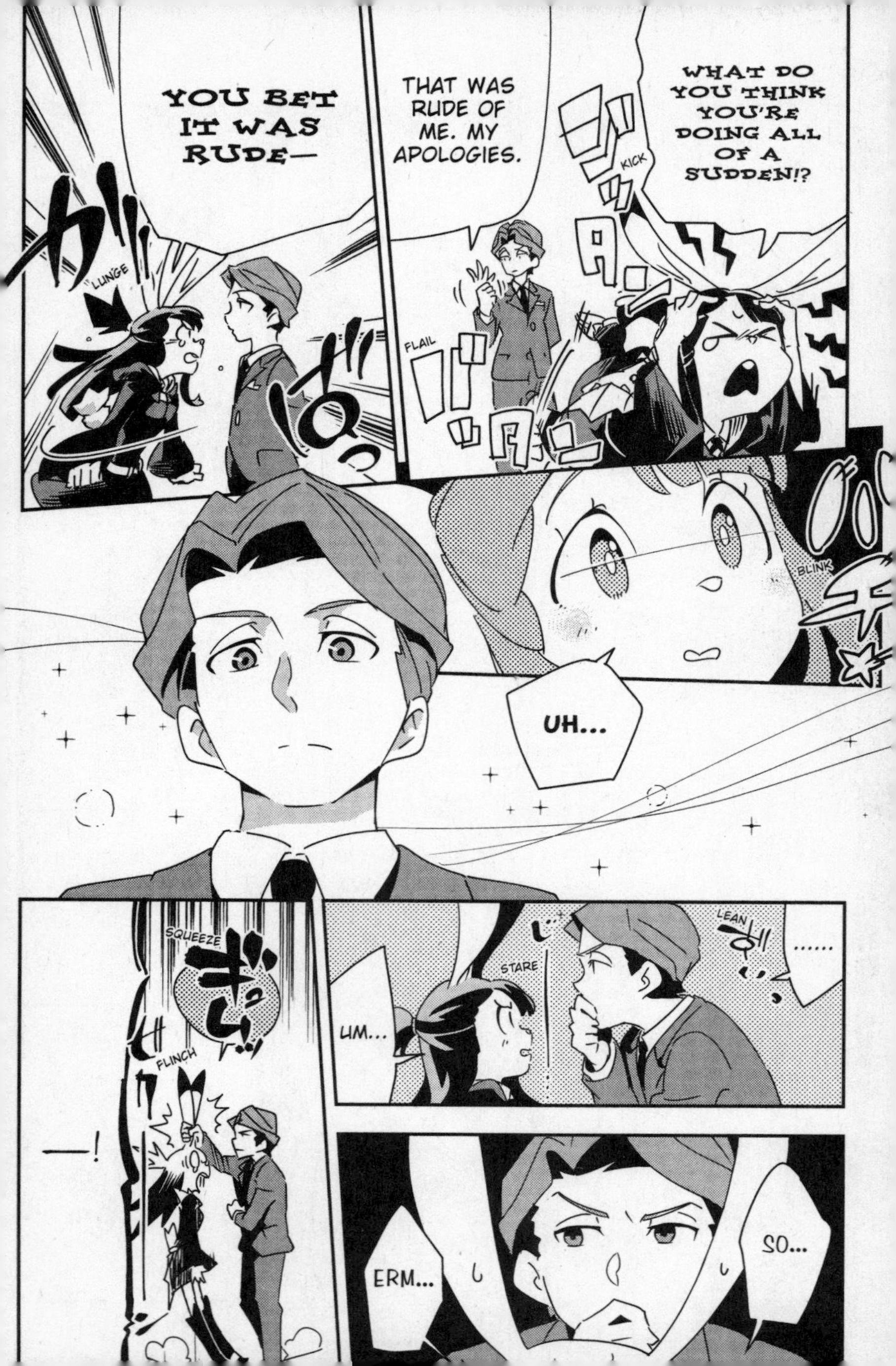
WHAT DO YOU THINK YOU'RE DOING ALL OF A SUDDEN!?
KICK
FLAIL
THAT WAS RUDE OF ME. MY APOLOGIES.
YOU BET IT WAS RUDE—
LUNGE
BLINK
UH...
LEAN
......
STARE
UM...
SO...
ERM...
SQUEEZE
FLINCH
—!

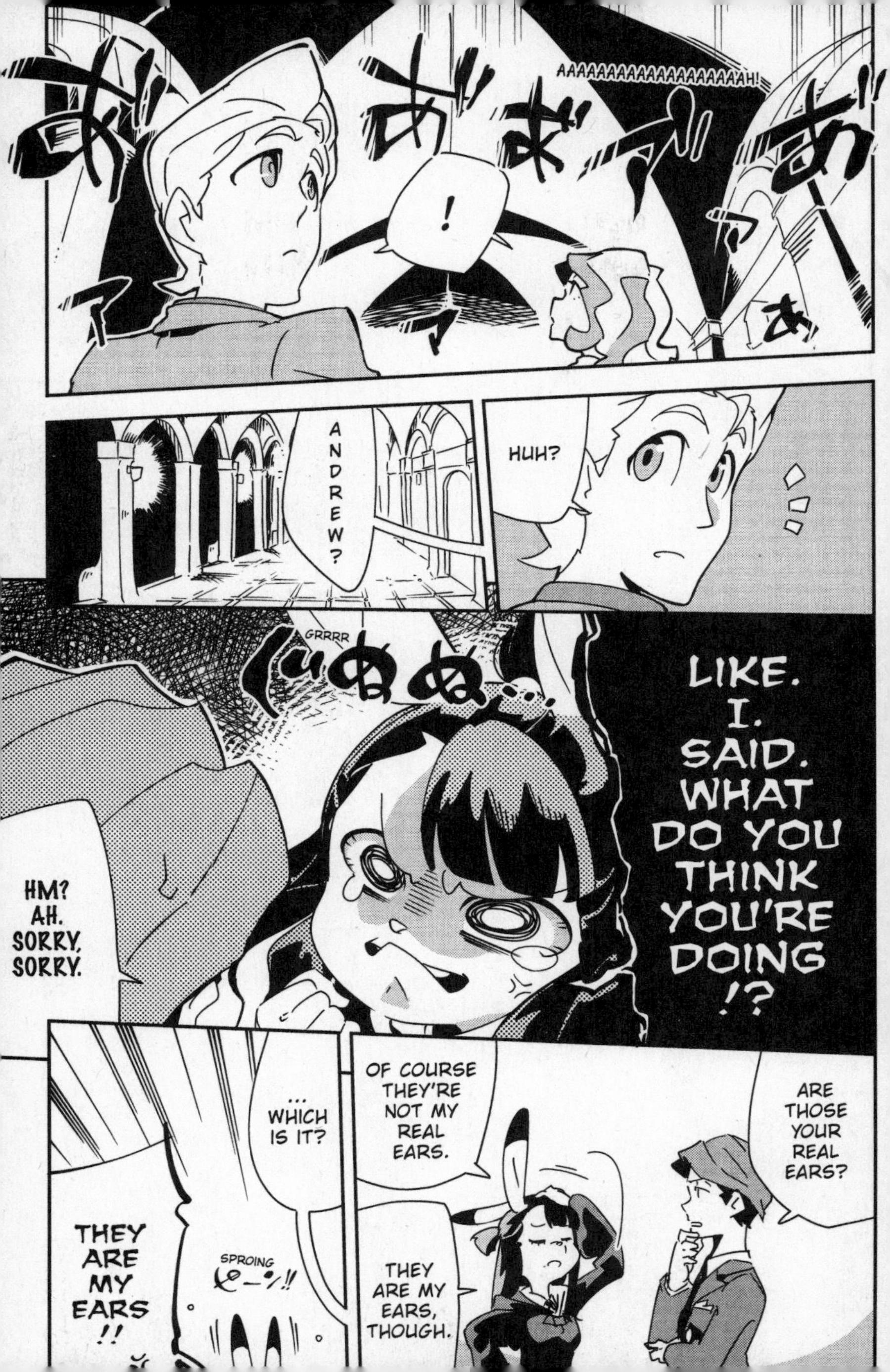
AAAAAAAAAAAAAAAAAAAAH!
!
HUH?
ANDREW?
GRRRR
LIKE. I. SAID. WHAT DO YOU THINK YOU'RE DOING!?
HM? AH. SORRY, SORRY.
ARE THOSE YOUR REAL EARS?
OF COURSE THEY'RE NOT MY REAL EARS.
THEY ARE MY EARS, THOUGH.
...WHICH IS IT?
SPROING
THEY ARE MY EARS!!

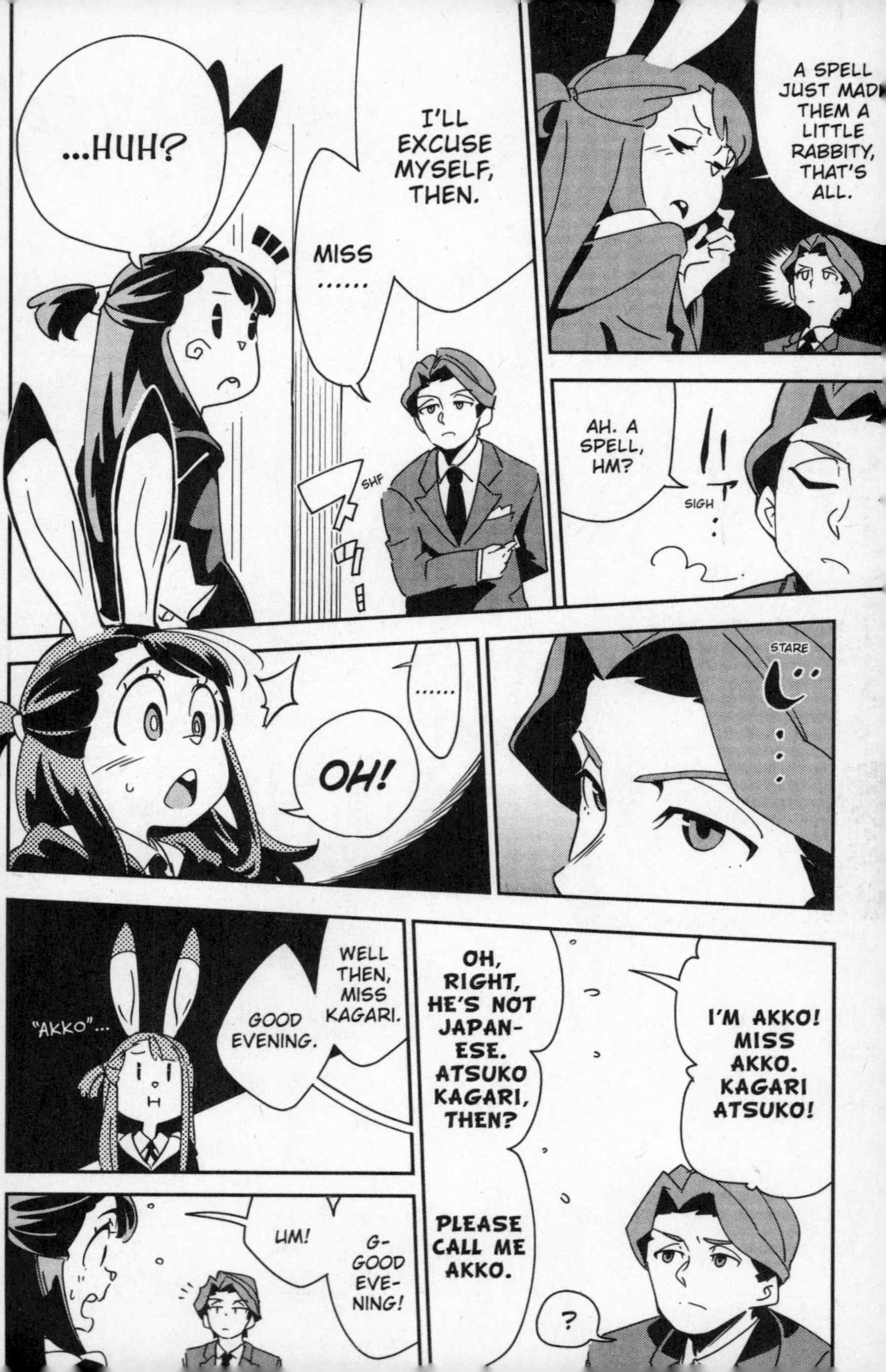
A SPELL JUST MAD THEM A LITTLE RABBITY, THAT'S ALL.
AH. A SPELL, HM?
SIGH
I'LL EXCUSE MYSELF, THEN.
MISS ......
SHF
...HUH?
STARE
......
OH!
I'M AKKO! MISS AKKO. KAGARI ATSUKO!
OH, RIGHT, HE'S NOT JAPAN-ESE. ATSUKO KAGARI, THEN?
PLEASE CALL ME AKKO.
?
WELL THEN, MISS KAGARI.
GOOD EVENING.
"AKKO"...
UM!
G-GOOD EVE-NING!

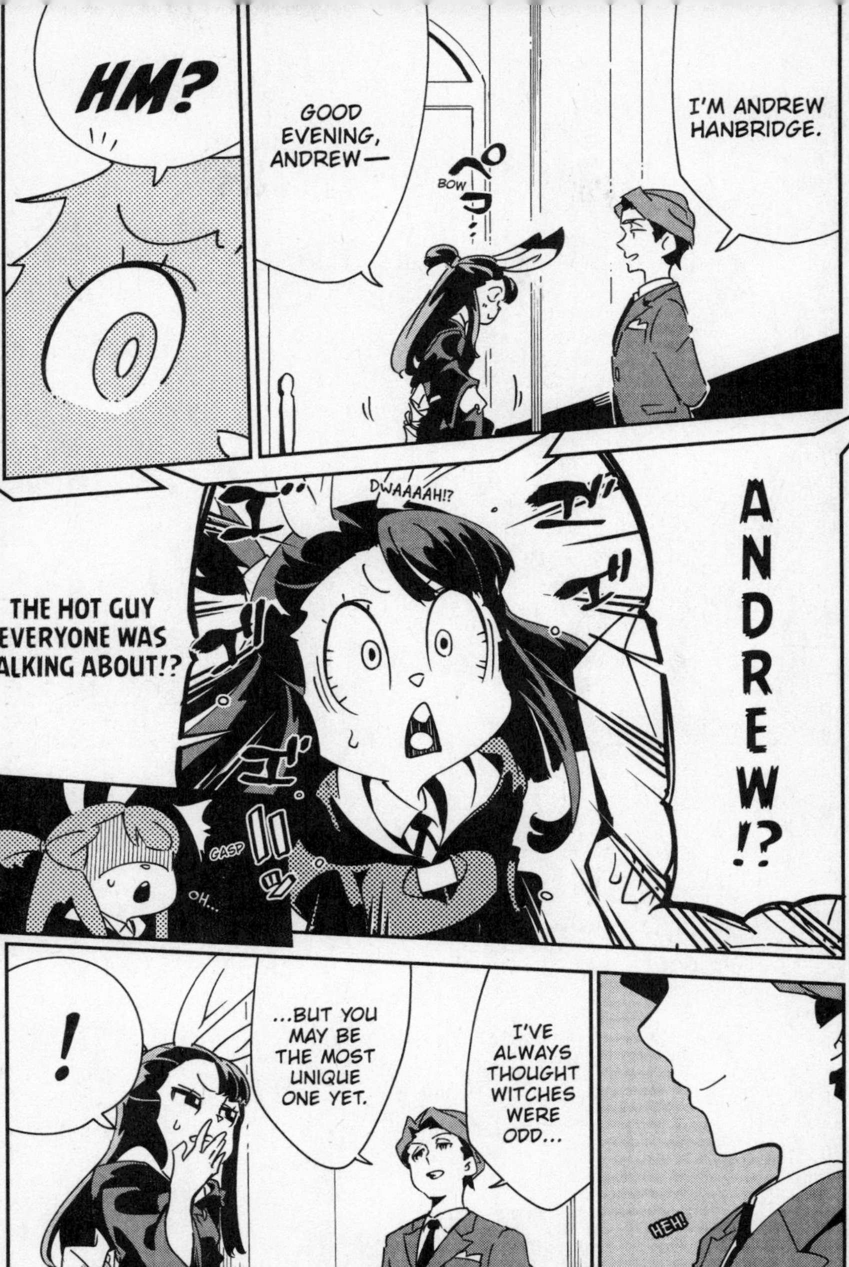
I'M ANDREW HANBRIDGE.
GOOD EVENING, ANDREW—
BOW
HM?
ANDREW!?
DWAAAAH!?
THE HOT GUY EVERYONE WAS TALKING ABOUT!?
GASP
OH...
HEH!
I'VE ALWAYS THOUGHT WITCHES WERE ODD...
...BUT YOU MAY BE THE MOST UNIQUE ONE YET.
!

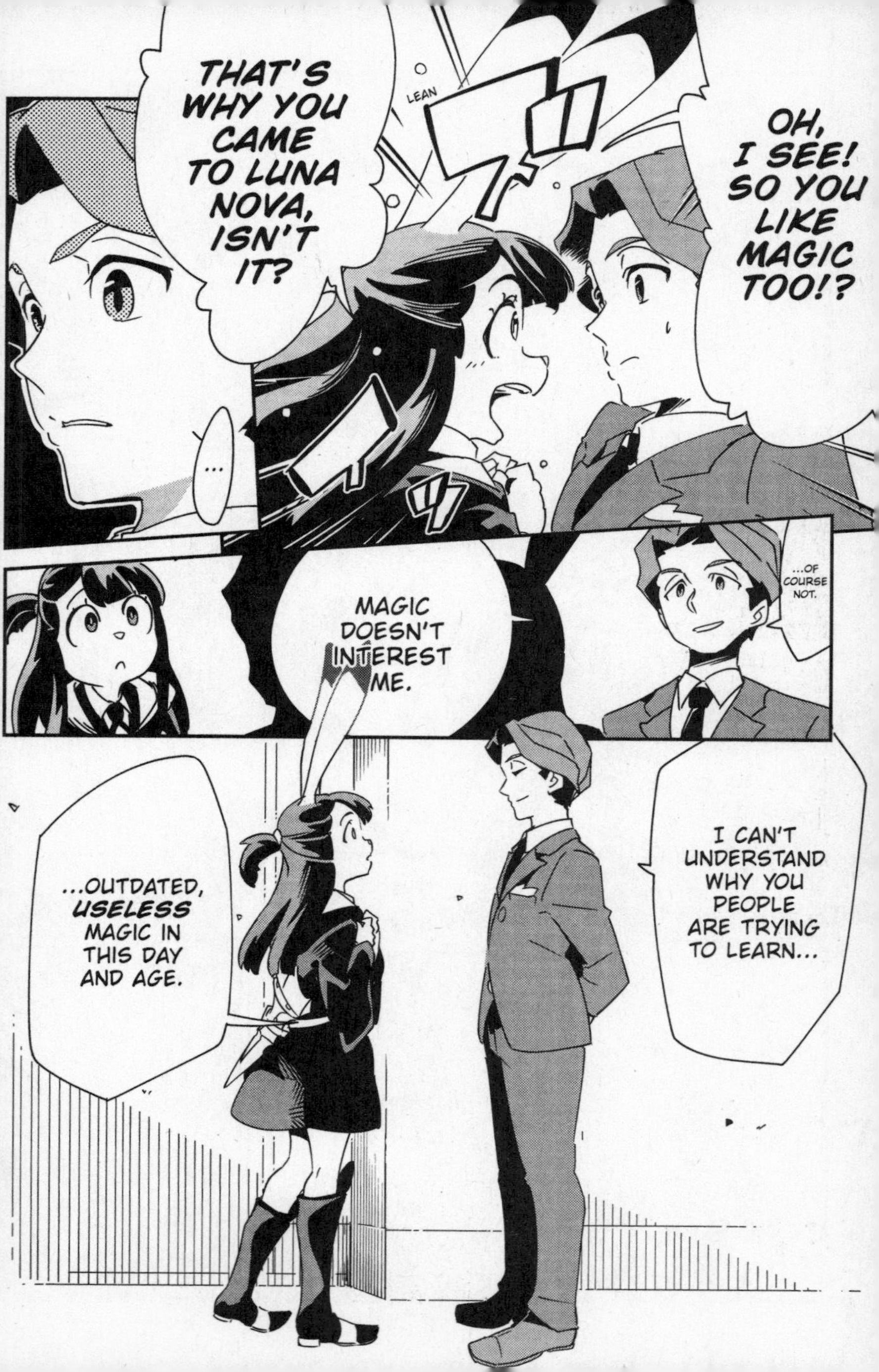
OH, I SEE! SO YOU LIKE MAGIC TOO!?
LEAN
THAT'S WHY YOU CAME TO LUNA NOVA, ISN'T IT?
...
...OF COURSE NOT.
MAGIC DOESN'T INTEREST ME.
I CAN'T UNDERSTAND WHY YOU PEOPLE ARE TRYING TO LEARN...
...OUTDATED, USELESS MAGIC IN THIS DAY AND AGE.

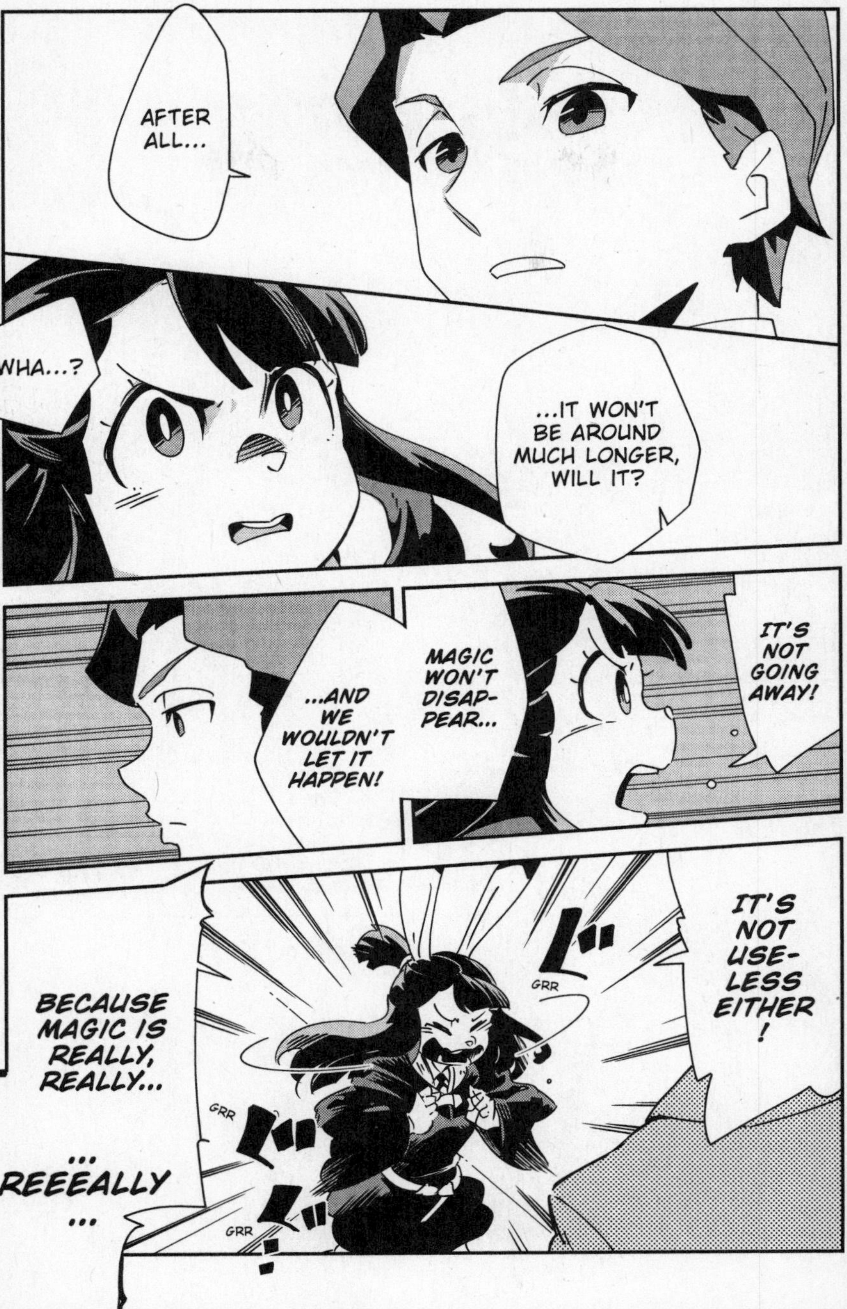
AFTER ALL...
...IT WON'T BE AROUND MUCH LONGER, WILL IT?
WHA...?
IT'S NOT GOING AWAY!
MAGIC WON'T DISAPPEAR...
...AND WE WOULDN'T LET IT HAPPEN!
IT'S NOT USELESS EITHER!
GRR
BECAUSE MAGIC IS REALLY, REALLY...
GRR
...REEEALLY...
GRR

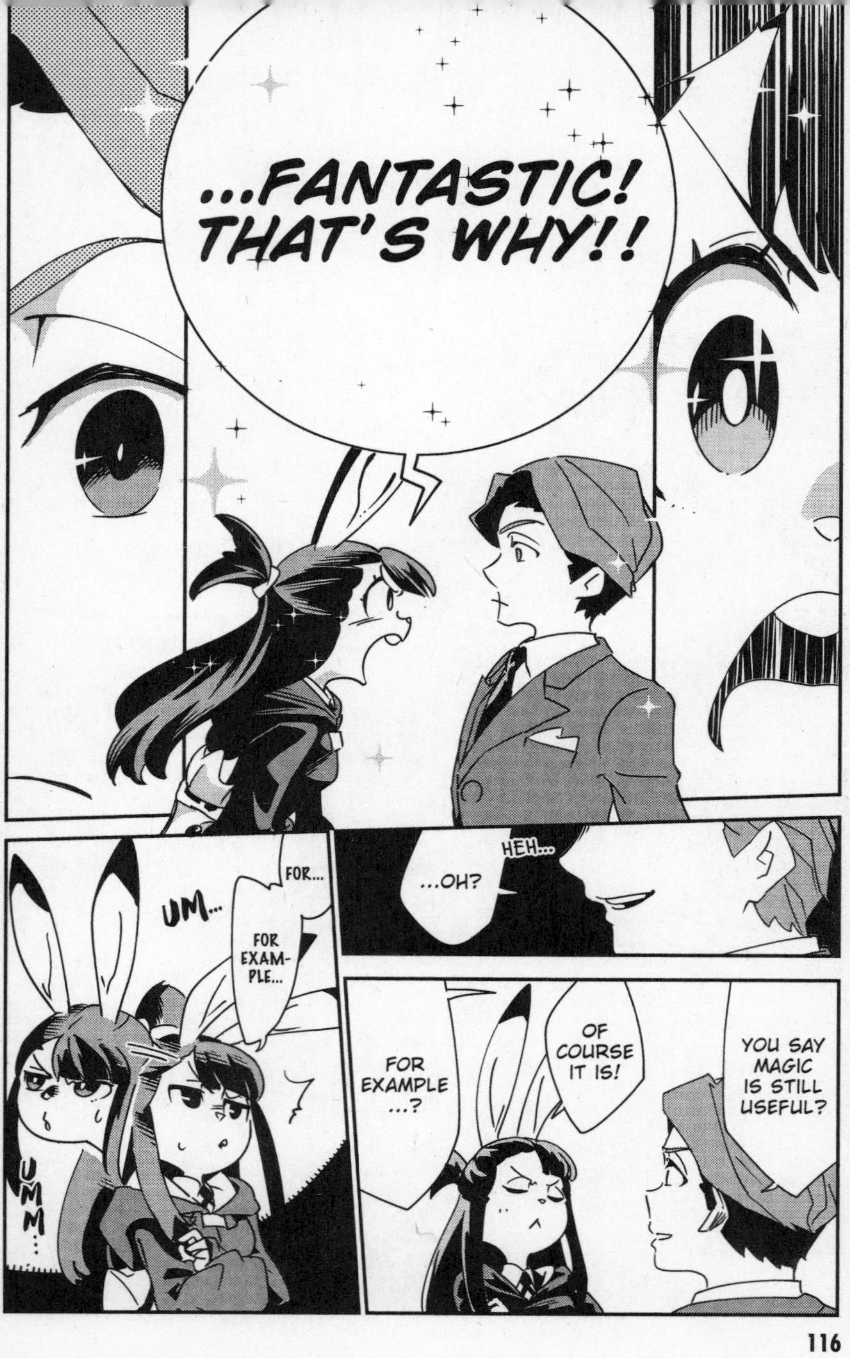
...FANTASTIC! THAT'S WHY!!
HEH...
...OH?
YOU SAY MAGIC IS STILL USEFUL?
OF COURSE IT IS!
FOR EXAMPLE ...?
FOR...
UM...
FOR EXAM-PLE...
UMM...

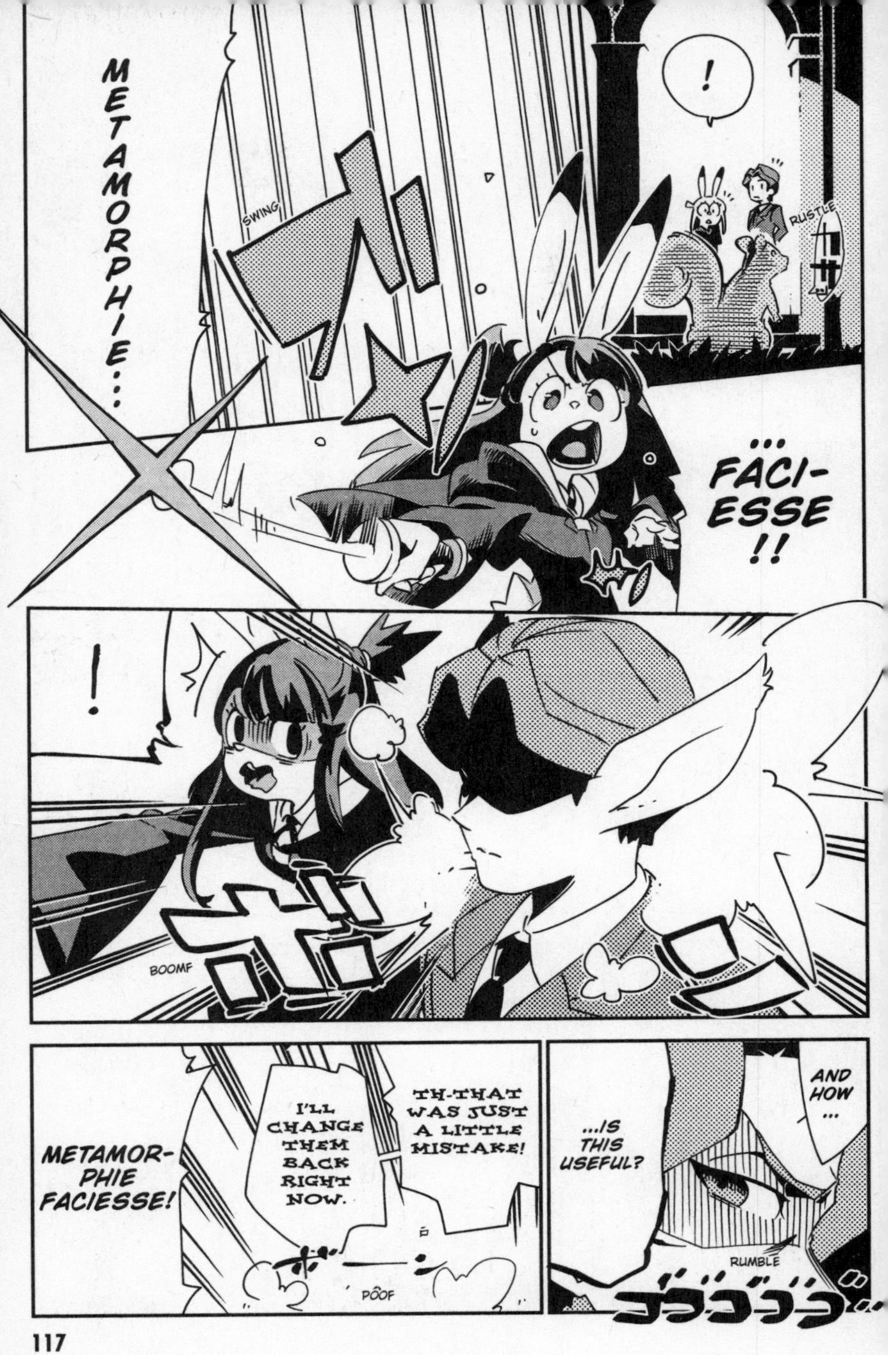
!
RUSTLE
SWING
METAMORPHIE...
...FACI-ESSE!!
!
BOOMF
AND HOW...
...IS THIS USEFUL?
RUMBLE
TH-THAT WAS JUST A LITTLE MISTAKE!
I'LL CHANGE THEM BACK RIGHT NOW.
METAMORPHIE FACIESSE!
POOF

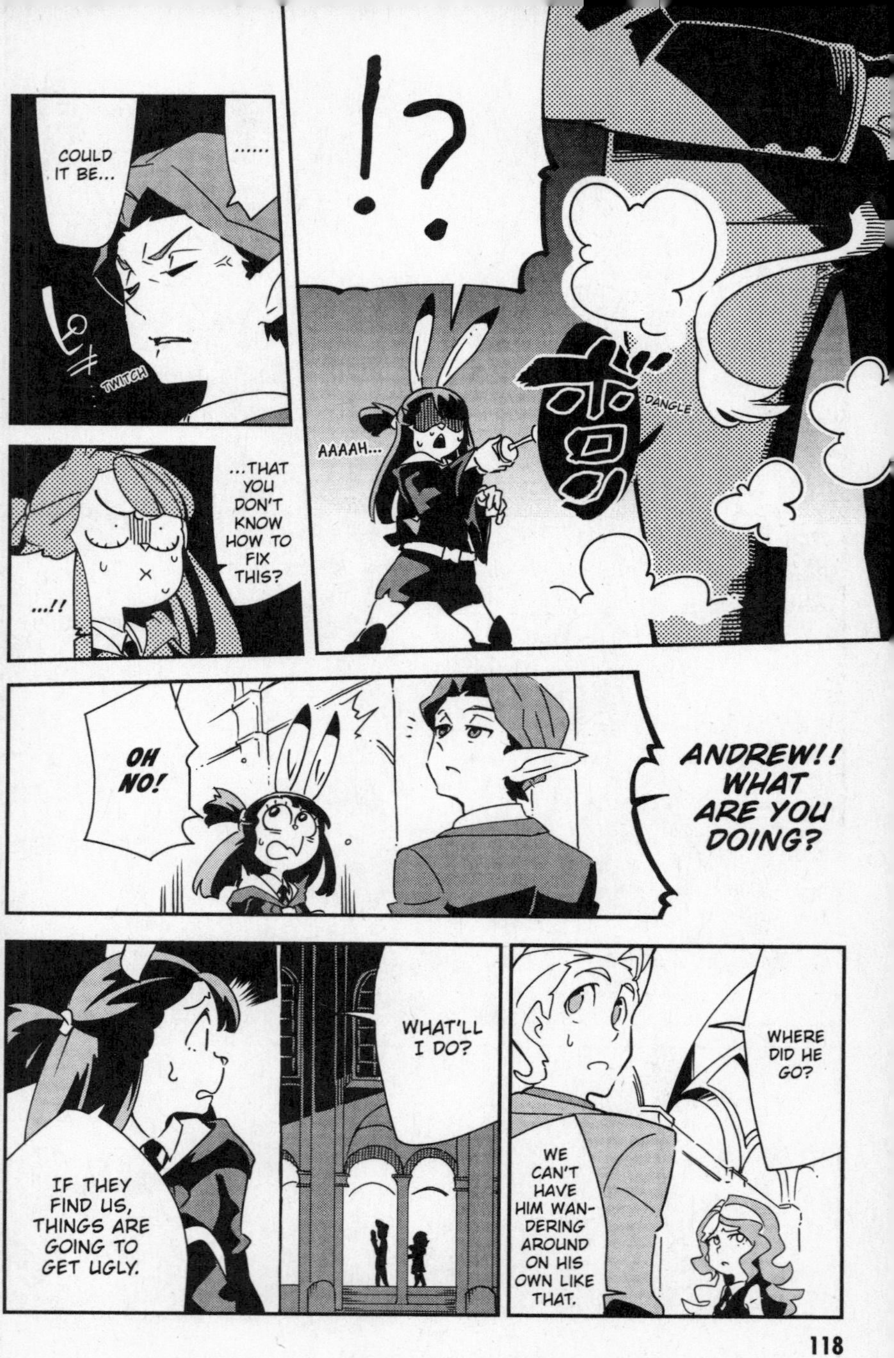
!?
AAAAH...
DANGLE
......
COULD IT BE...
TWITCH
...THAT YOU DON'T KNOW HOW TO FIX THIS?
...!!
ANDREW!! WHAT ARE YOU DOING?
OH NO!
WHERE DID HE GO?
WE CAN'T HAVE HIM WAN-DERING AROUND ON HIS OWN LIKE THAT.
WHAT'LL I DO?
IF THEY FIND US, THINGS ARE GOING TO GET UGLY.

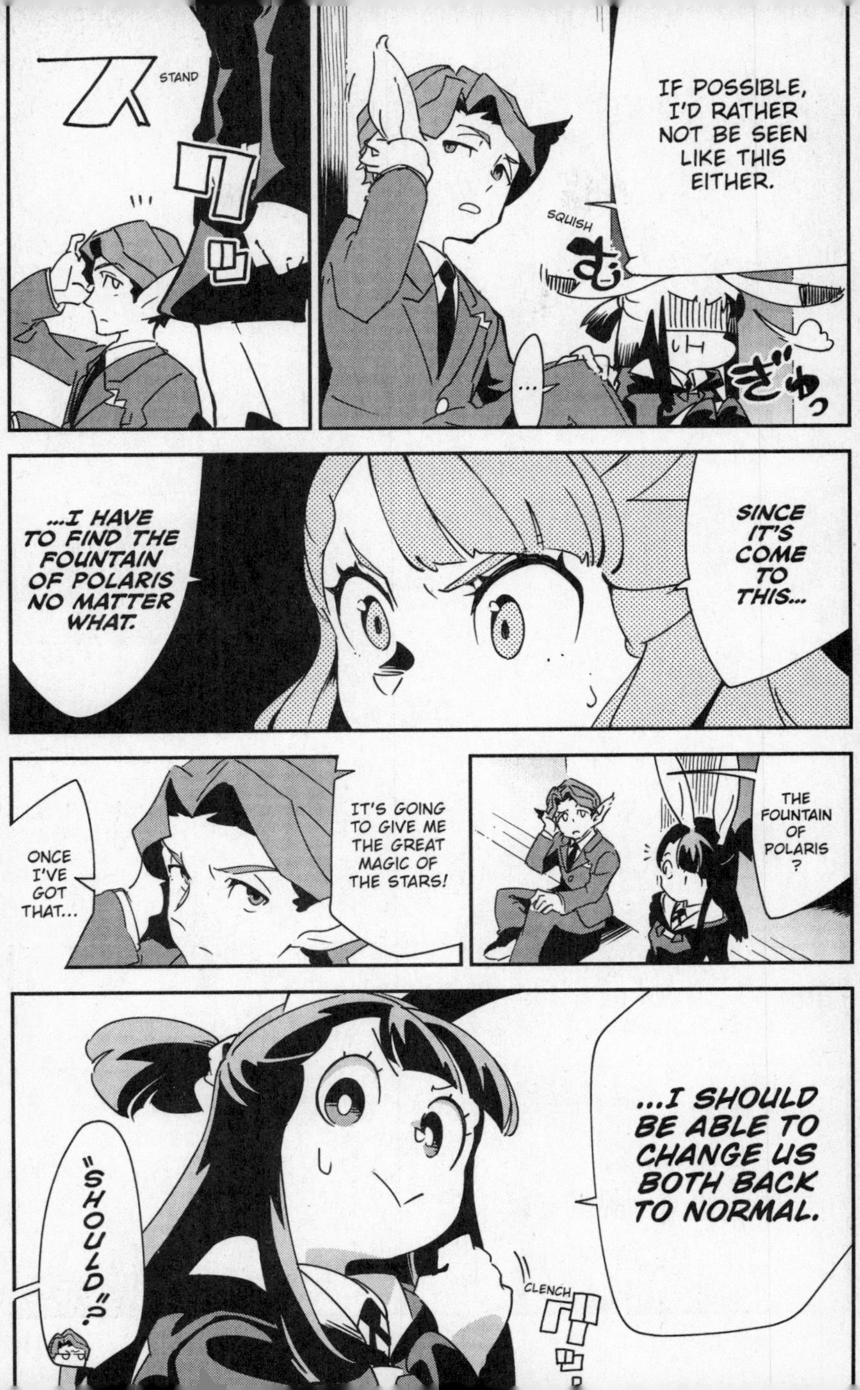
IF POSSIBLE, I'D RATHER NOT BE SEEN LIKE THIS EITHER.
SQUISH
...
STAND
SINCE IT'S COME TO THIS...
...I HAVE TO FIND THE FOUNTAIN OF POLARIS NO MATTER WHAT.
THE FOUNTAIN OF POLARIS?
IT'S GOING TO GIVE ME THE GREAT MAGIC OF THE STARS!
ONCE I'VE GOT THAT...
...I SHOULD BE ABLE TO CHANGE US BOTH BACK TO NORMAL.
CLENCH
"SHOULD"?

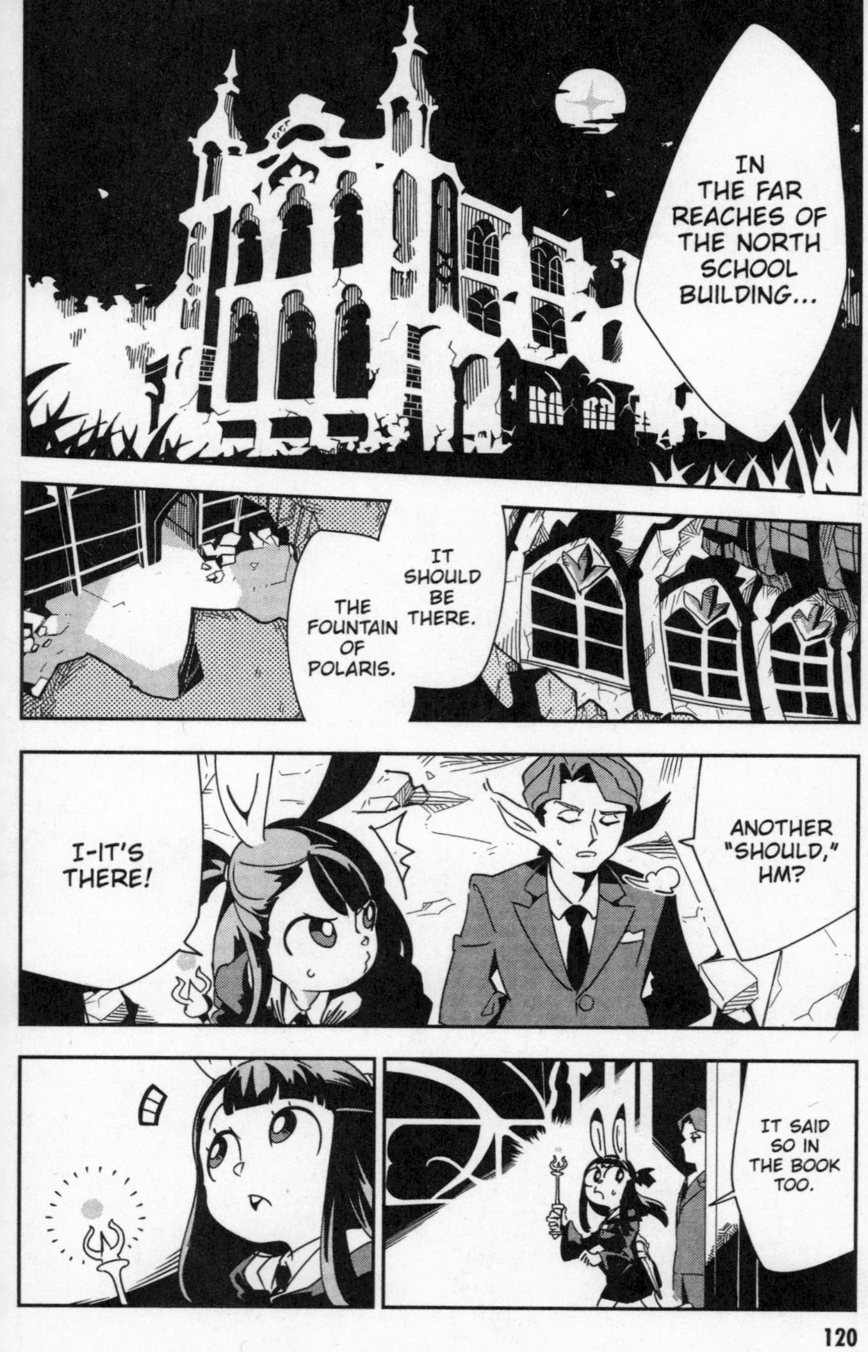
IN THE FAR REACHES OF THE NORTH SCHOOL BUILDING...
IT SHOULD BE THERE.
THE FOUNTAIN OF POLARIS.
ANOTHER "SHOULD," HM?
I-IT'S THERE!
IT SAID SO IN THE BOOK TOO.

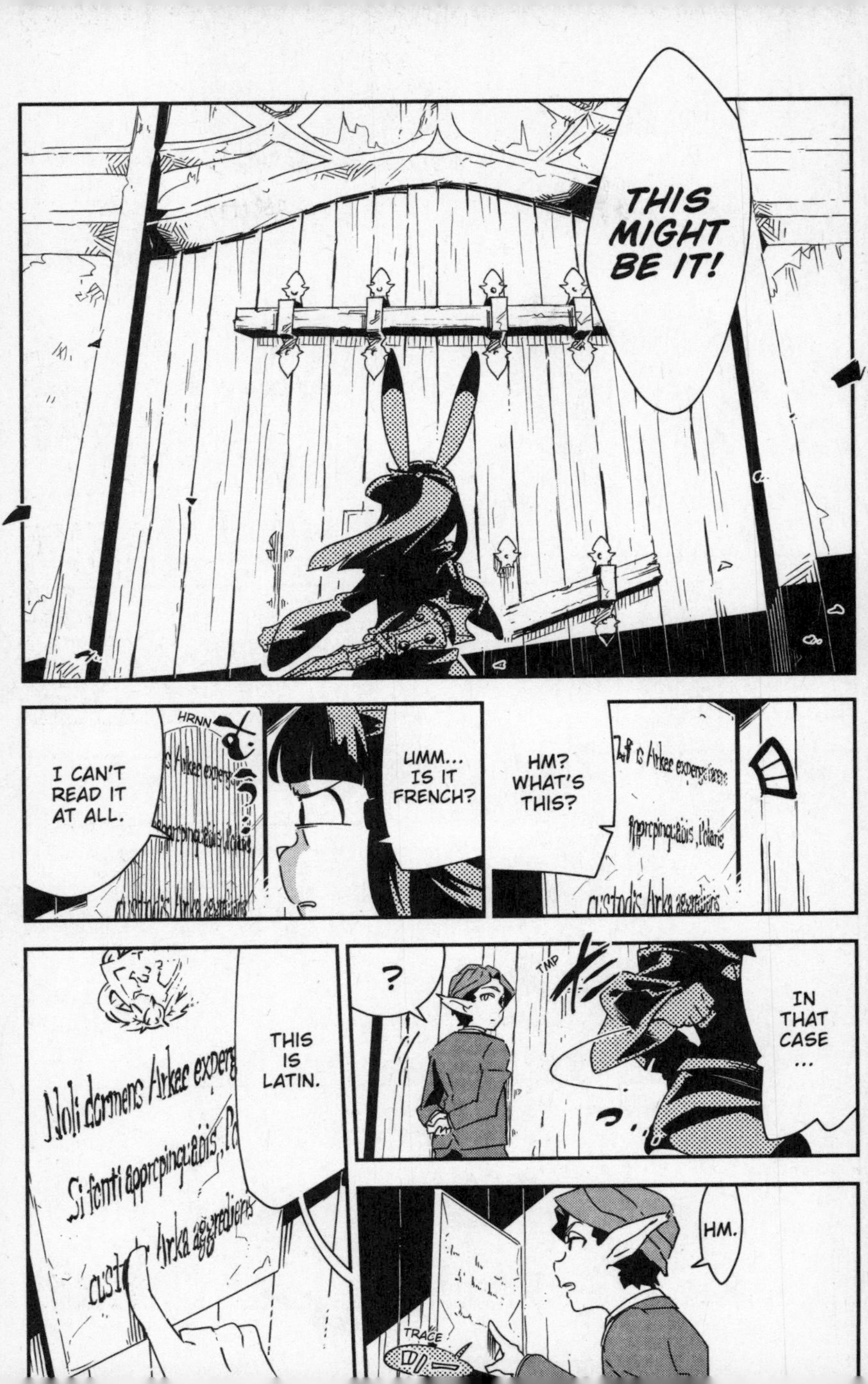
THIS MIGHT BE IT!
HM? WHAT'S THIS?
UMM... IS IT FRENCH?
HRNN
I CAN'T READ IT AT ALL.
TMP
IN THAT CASE...
?
HM.
TRACE
THIS IS LATIN.
Noli dormens Arkae experg
Si fonti appropinquabis, Po
Arka aggrediens

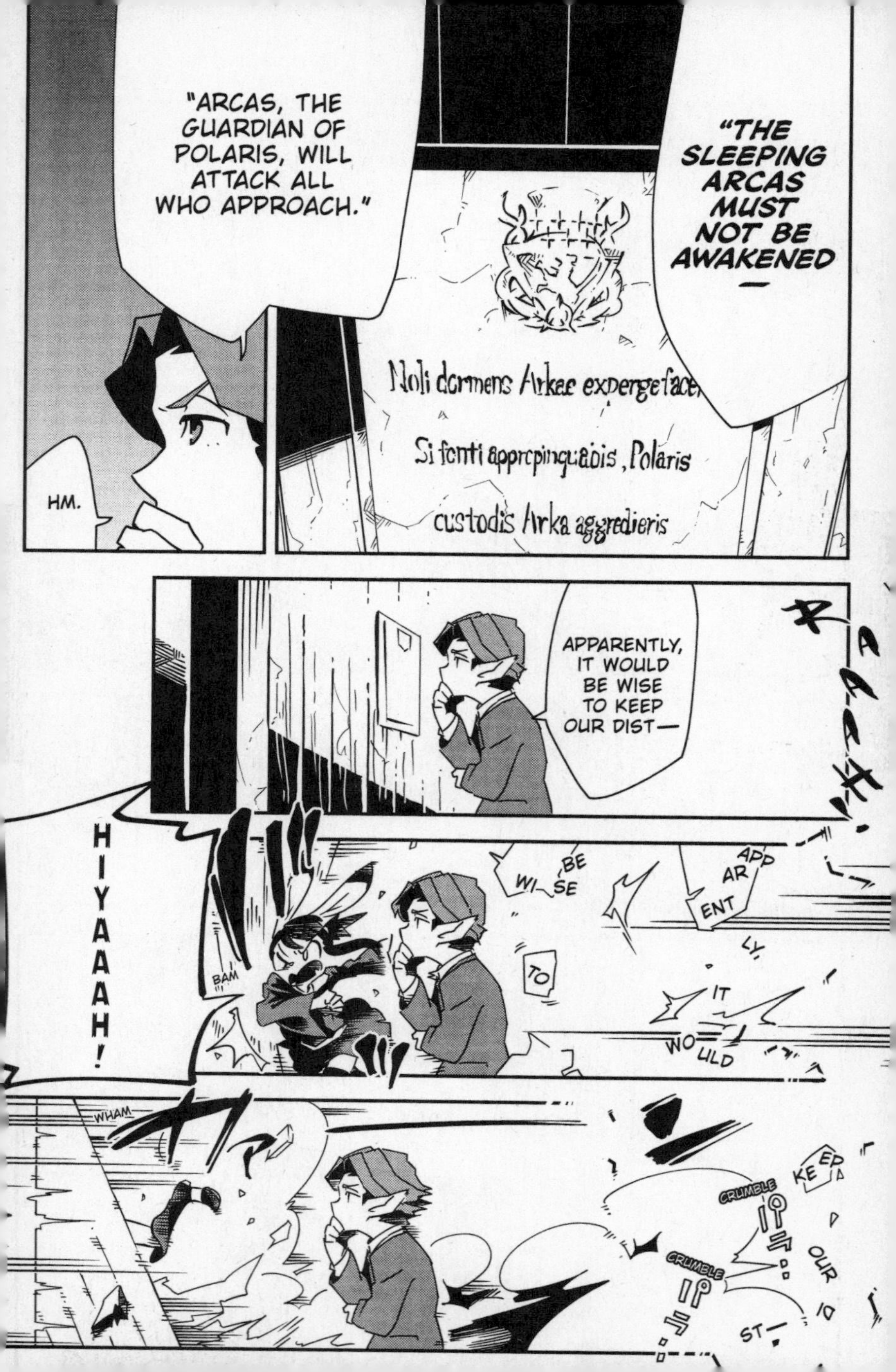
"THE SLEEPING ARCAS MUST NOT BE AWAKENED—
"ARCAS, THE GUARDIAN OF POLARIS, WILL ATTACK ALL WHO APPROACH."
Noli dormens Arkae expergefacer
Si fonti appropinquabis, Polaris
custodis Arka aggredieris
HM.
RAAAH!
APPARENTLY, IT WOULD BE WISE TO KEEP OUR DIST—
APP AR ENT LY,
BE WI SE
TO
IT WO ULD
HIYAAAAH!
BAM
WHAM
KE EP
CRUMBLE
OUR
CRUMBLE
DI ST—

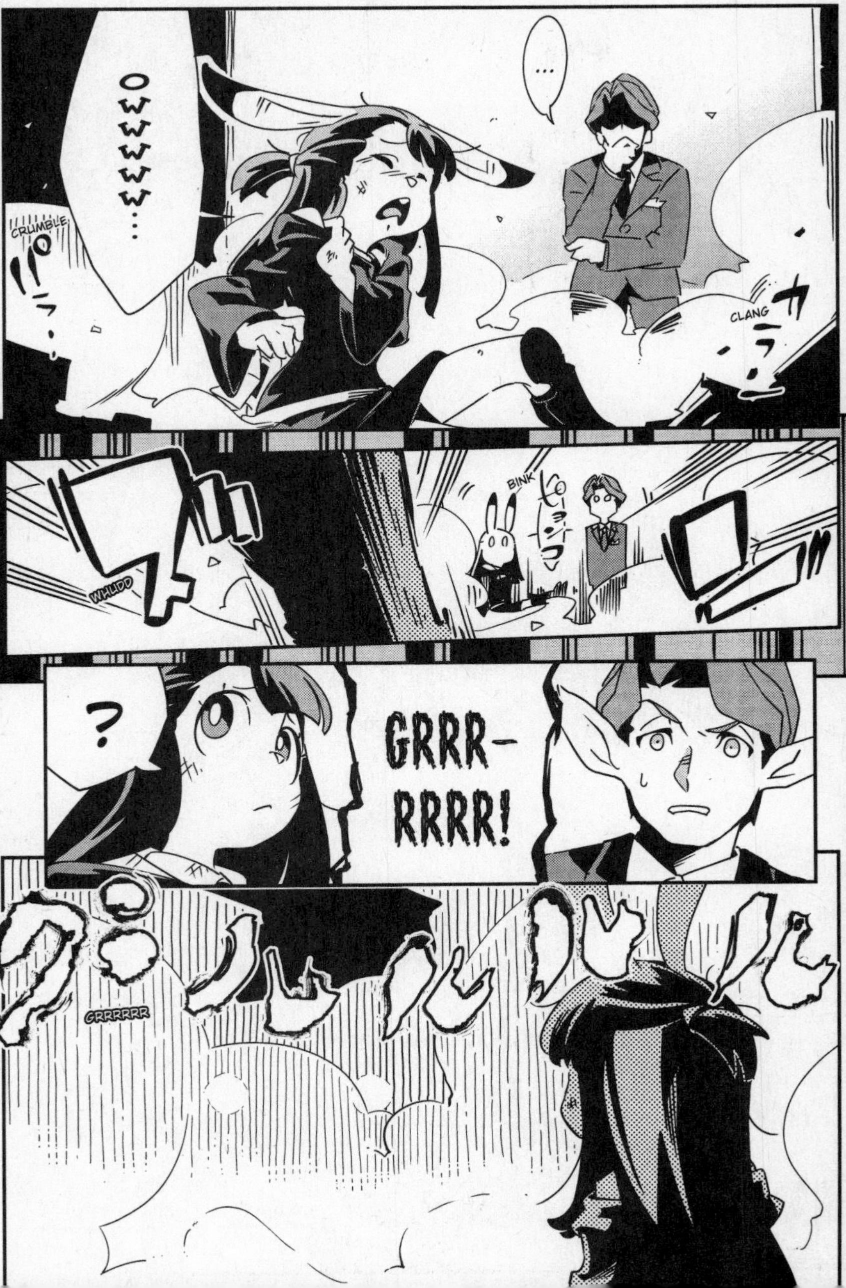
...
CLANG
OWWWWW...
CRUMBLE
BINK
WHUDD
GRRR-RRRR!
?
GRRRRRR

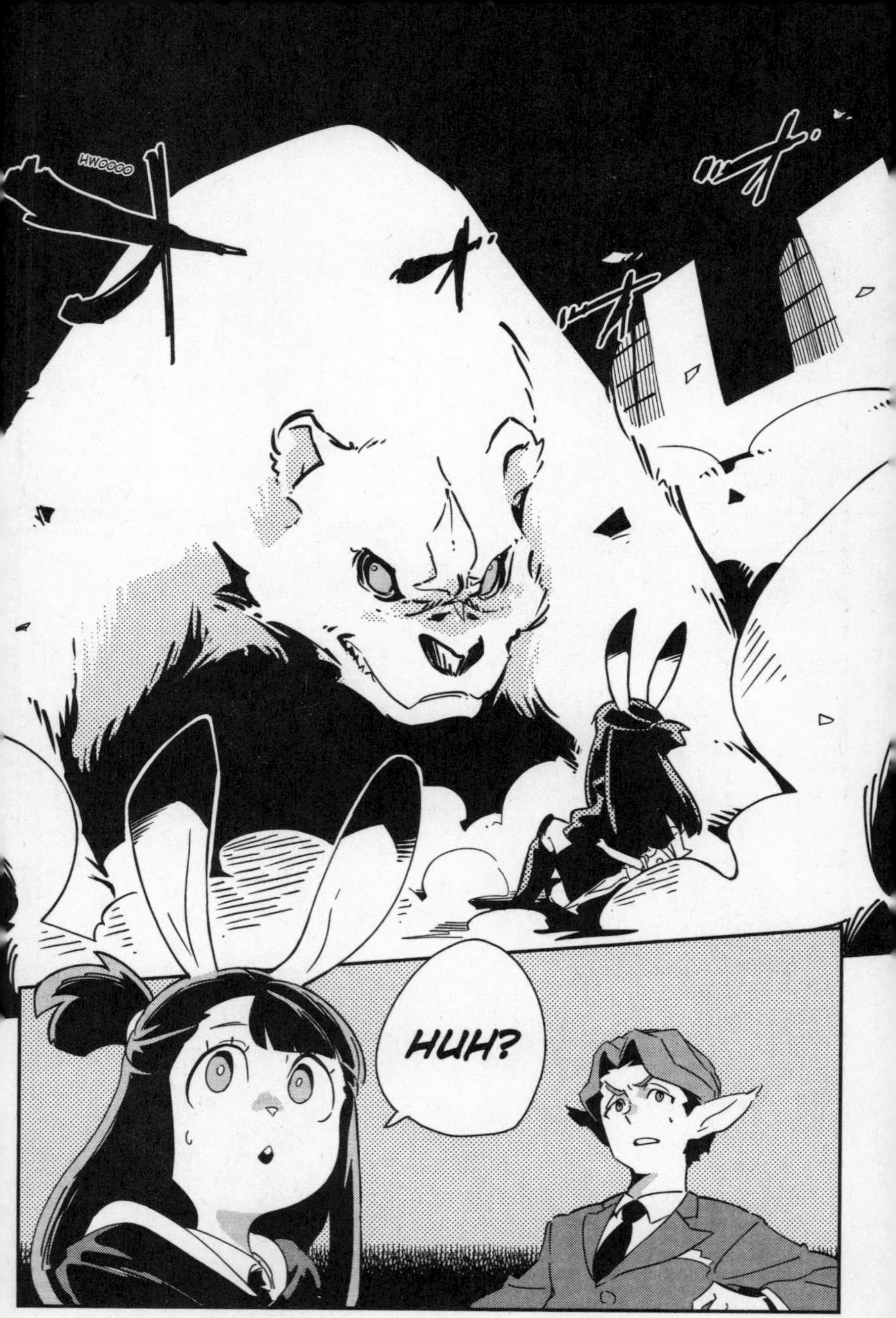
HWOOOO
HUH?

Chapter 10

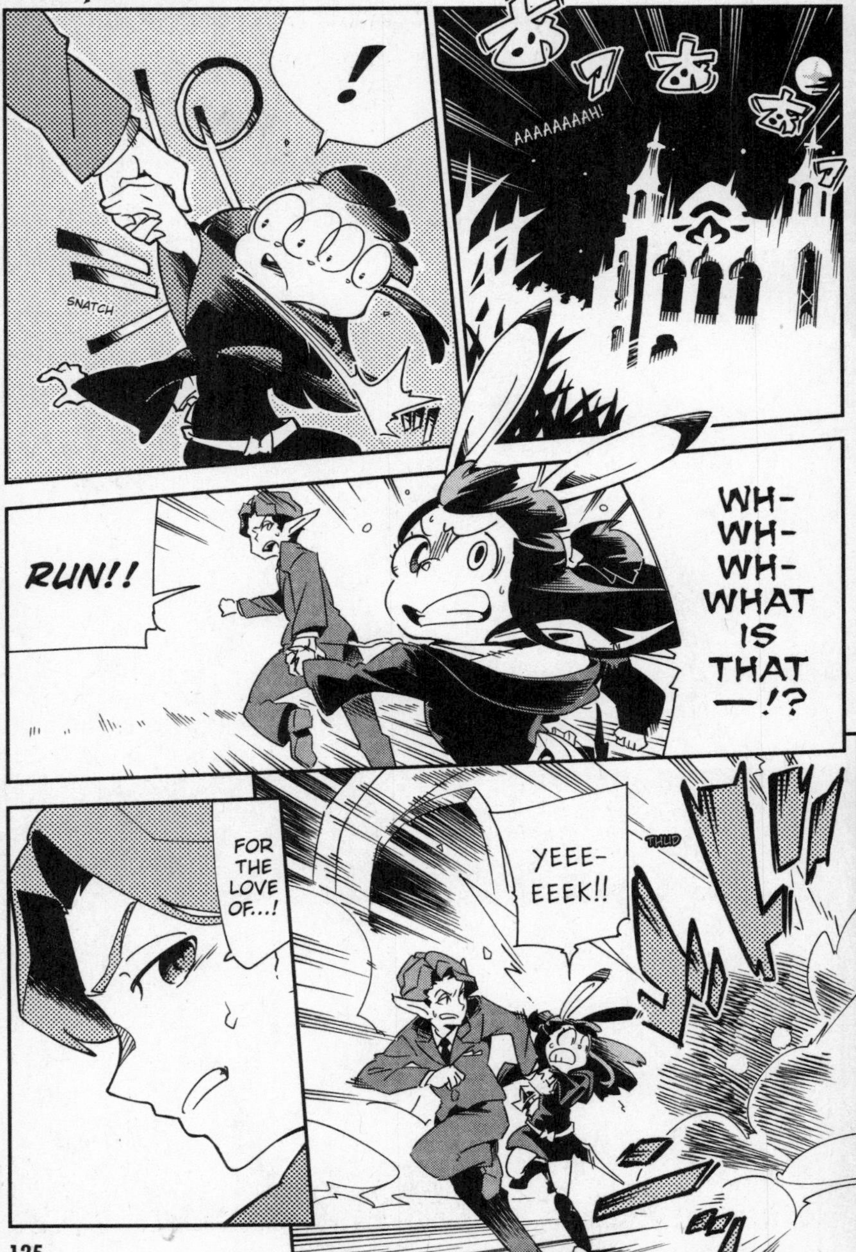
AAAAAAAAH!
!
SNATCH
WH-WH-WH-WHAT IS THAT—!?
RUN!!
THUD
YEEE-EEEK!!
FOR THE LOVE OF...!

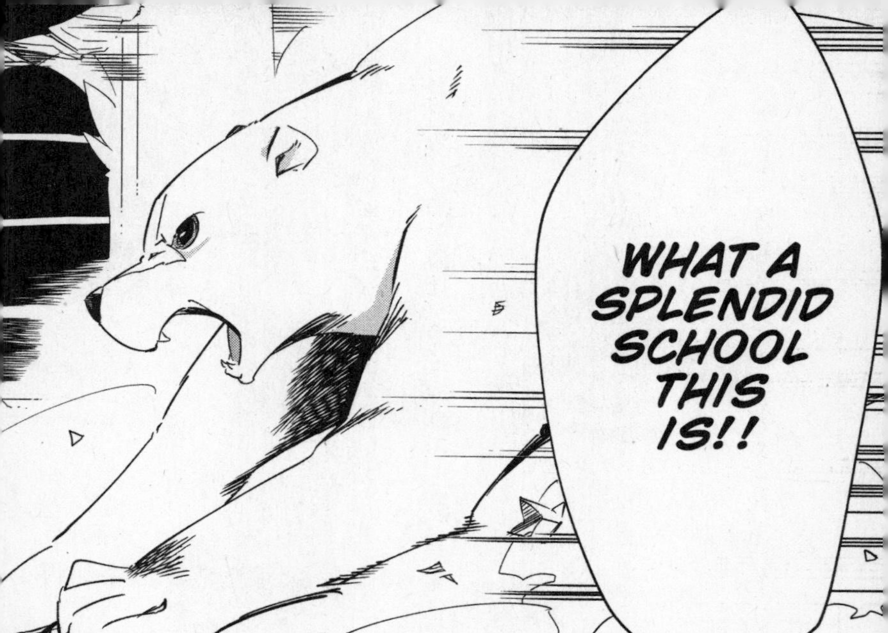
WHAT A SPLENDID SCHOOL THIS IS!!

Chapter 10 THE FOUNTAIN OF POLARIS
~THE HARDWORKING WITCH~

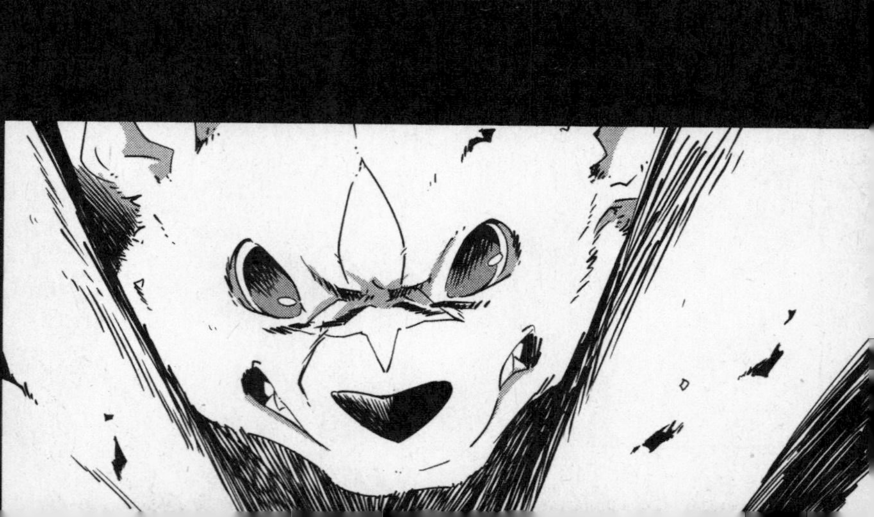

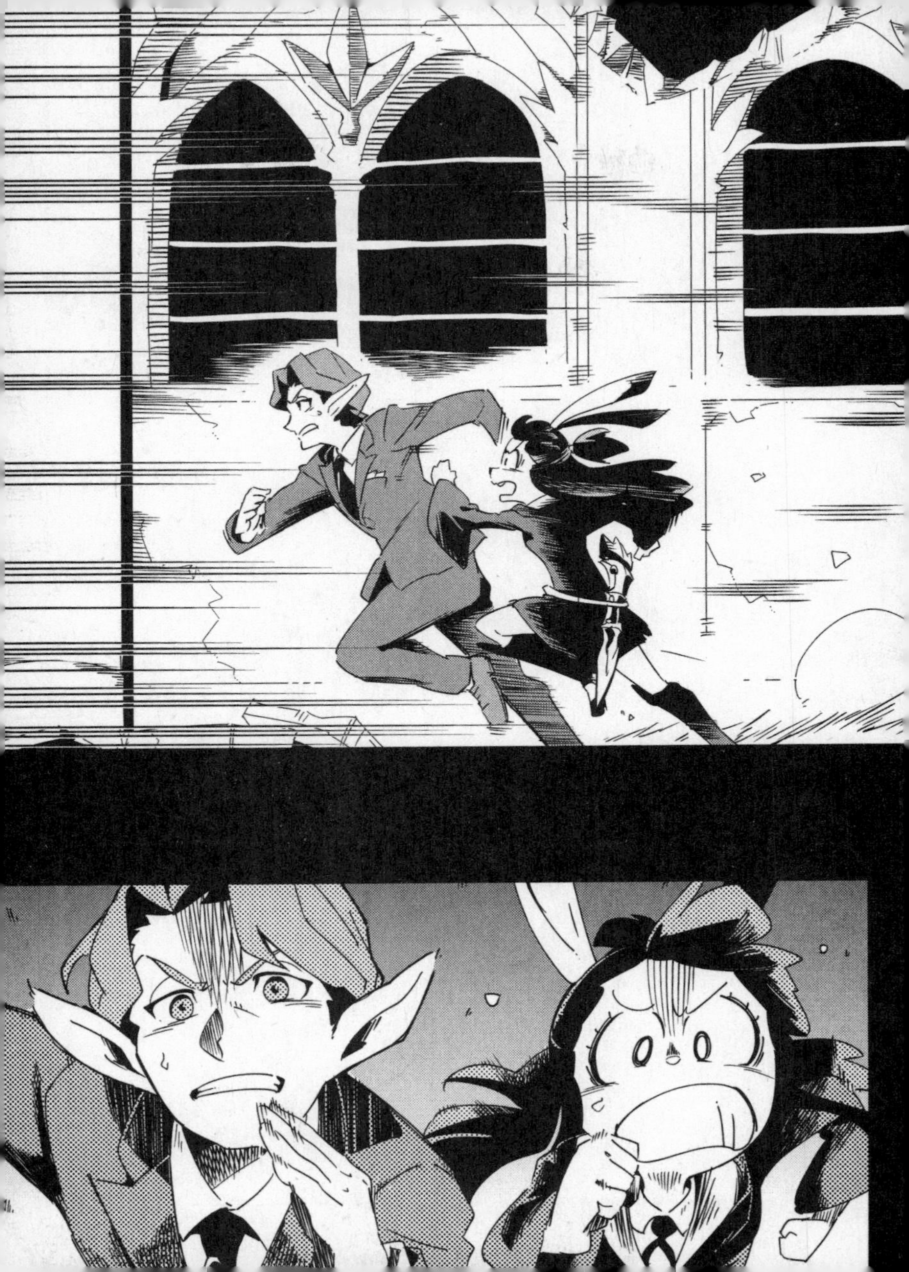

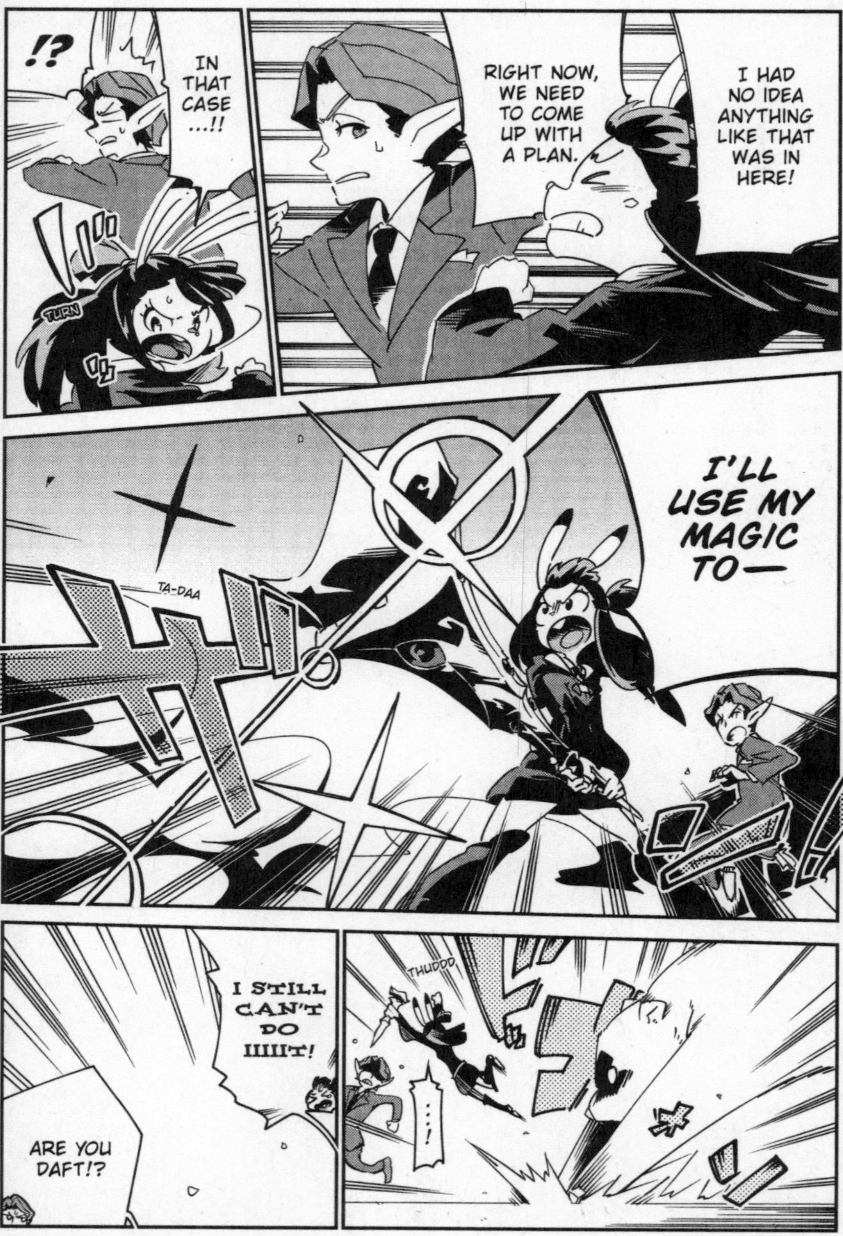
I HAD NO IDEA ANYTHING LIKE THAT WAS IN HERE!
RIGHT NOW, WE NEED TO COME UP WITH A PLAN.
IN THAT CASE ...!!
!?
TURN
I'LL USE MY MAGIC TO—
TA-DAA
THUDDD
...!
I STILL CAN'T DO IIIIIT!
ARE YOU DAFT!?

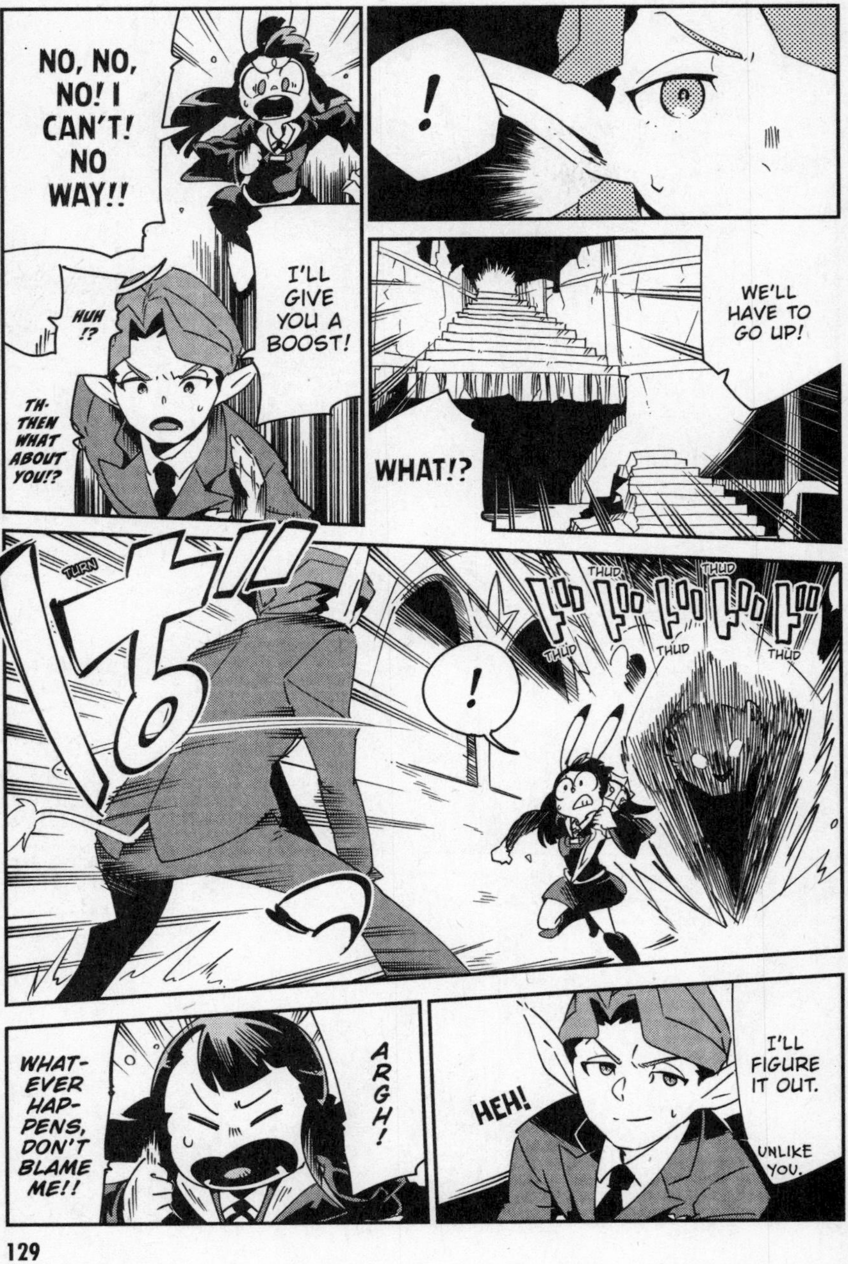
!
WE'LL HAVE TO GO UP!
WHAT!?
NO, NO, NO! I CAN'T! NO WAY!!
I'LL GIVE YOU A BOOST!
HUH !?
TH-THEN WHAT ABOUT YOU!?
THUD THUD THUD THUD THUD THUD
!
TURN
I'LL FIGURE IT OUT.
HEH!
UNLIKE YOU.
ARGH!
WHAT-EVER HAP-PENS, DON'T BLAME ME!!

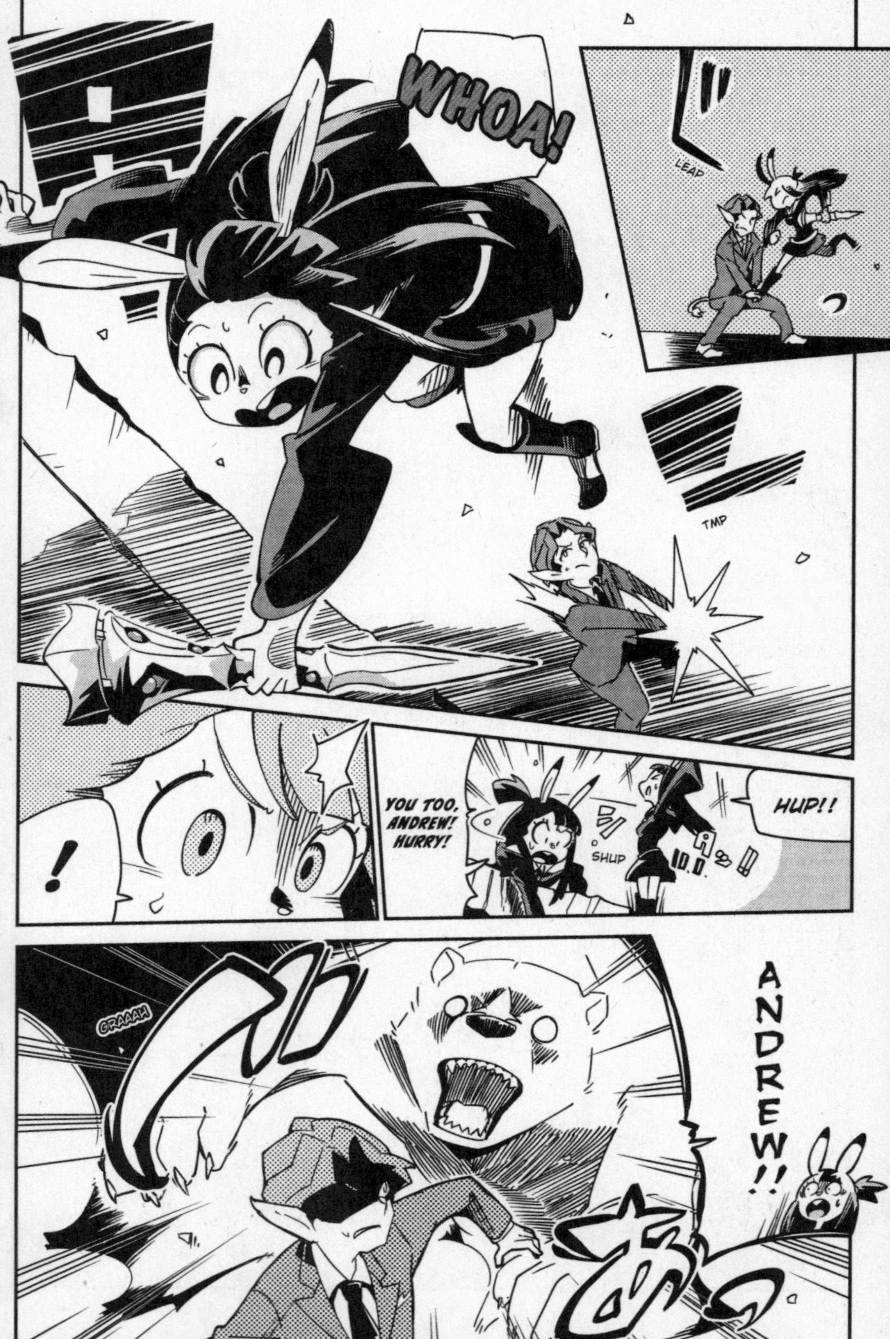
LEAP
WHOA!
TMP
HUP!!
YOU TOO, ANDREW! HURRY!
SHUP
!
ANDREW!!
GRAAAH

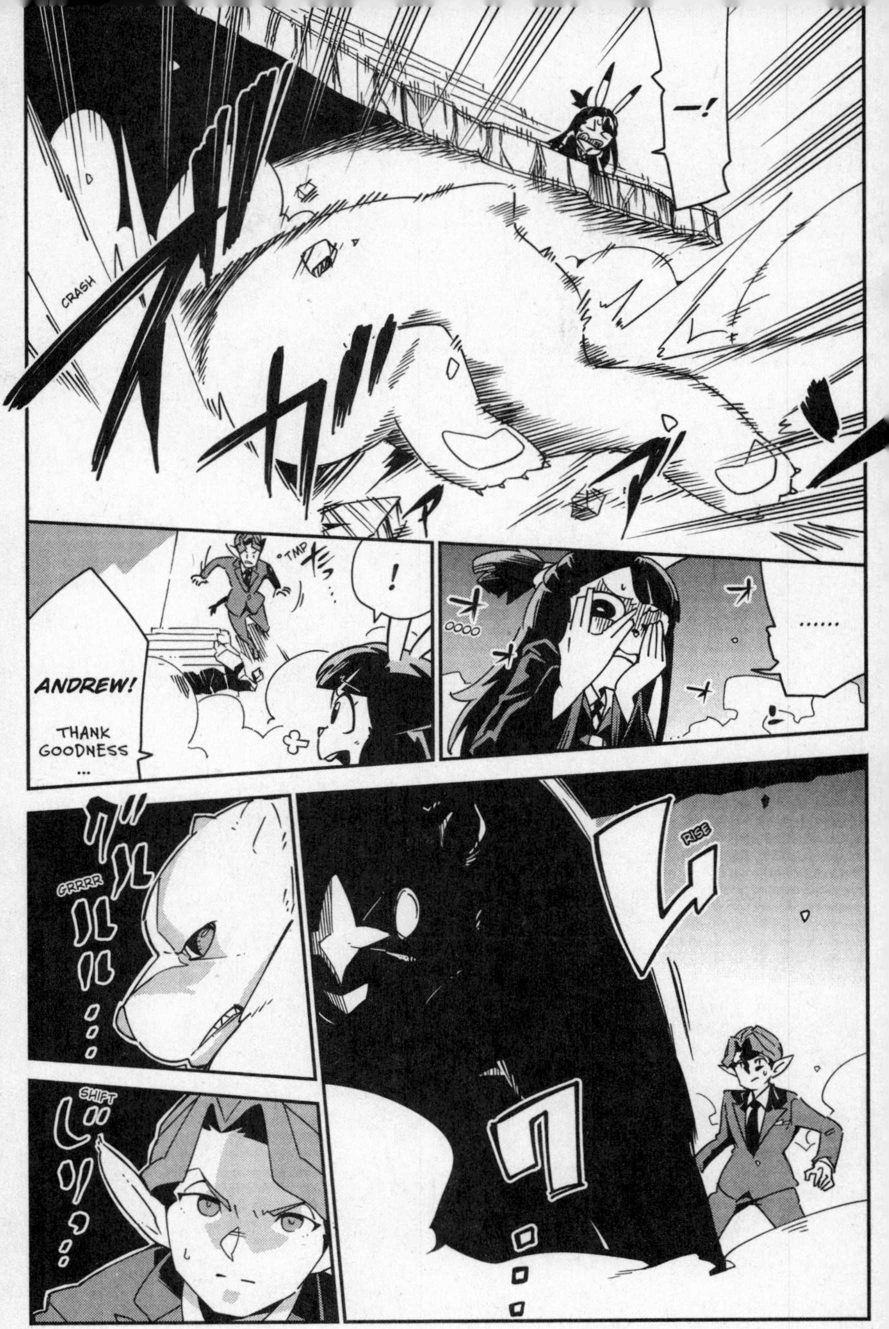
—!
CRASH
......
TMP
!
ANDREW!
THANK GOODNESS ...
RISE
GRRRR
SHIFT

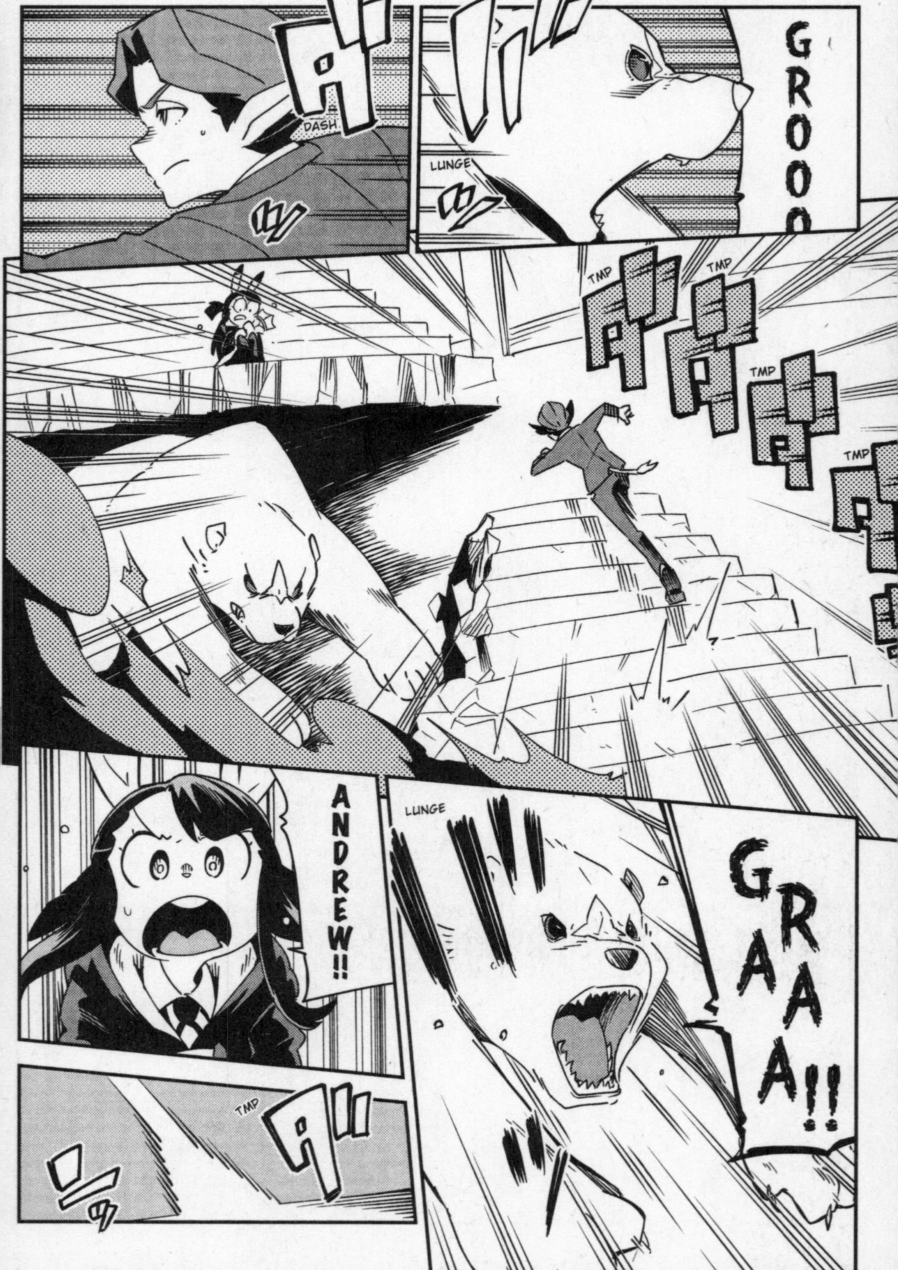
GROOO
LUNGE
DASH
TMP
TMP
TMP
TMP
LUNGE
GRAAA!!
ANDREW!!
TMP

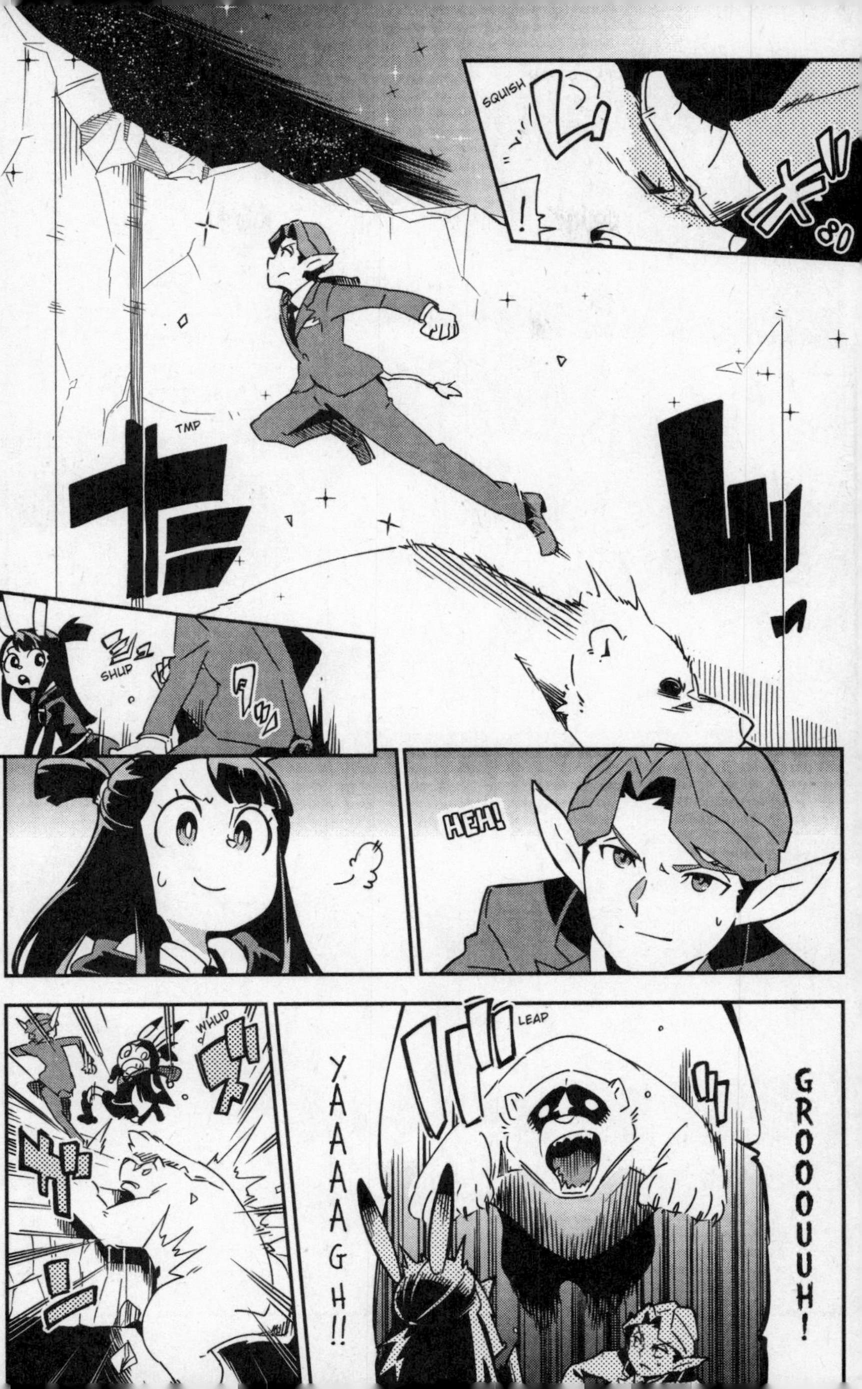
SQUISH
!
TMP
SHUP
HEH!
GROOOUUH!
LEAP
YAAAAGH!!
WHUD

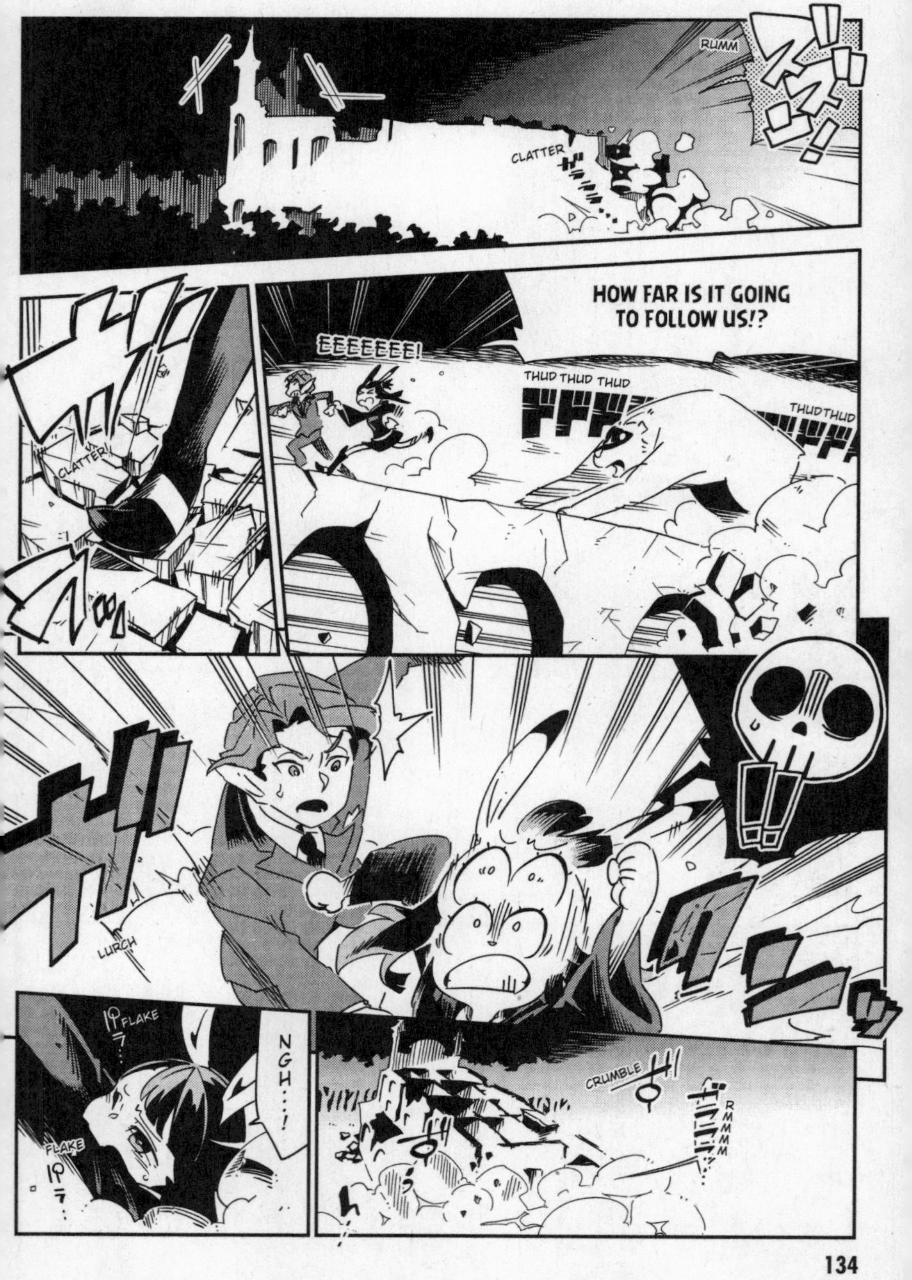
RUMM
CLATTER
HOW FAR IS IT GOING TO FOLLOW US!?
EEEEEEE!
THUD THUD THUD
THUDTHUD
CLATTER
LURCH
CRUMBLE
RMMMM
NGH...!
FLAKE
FLAKE

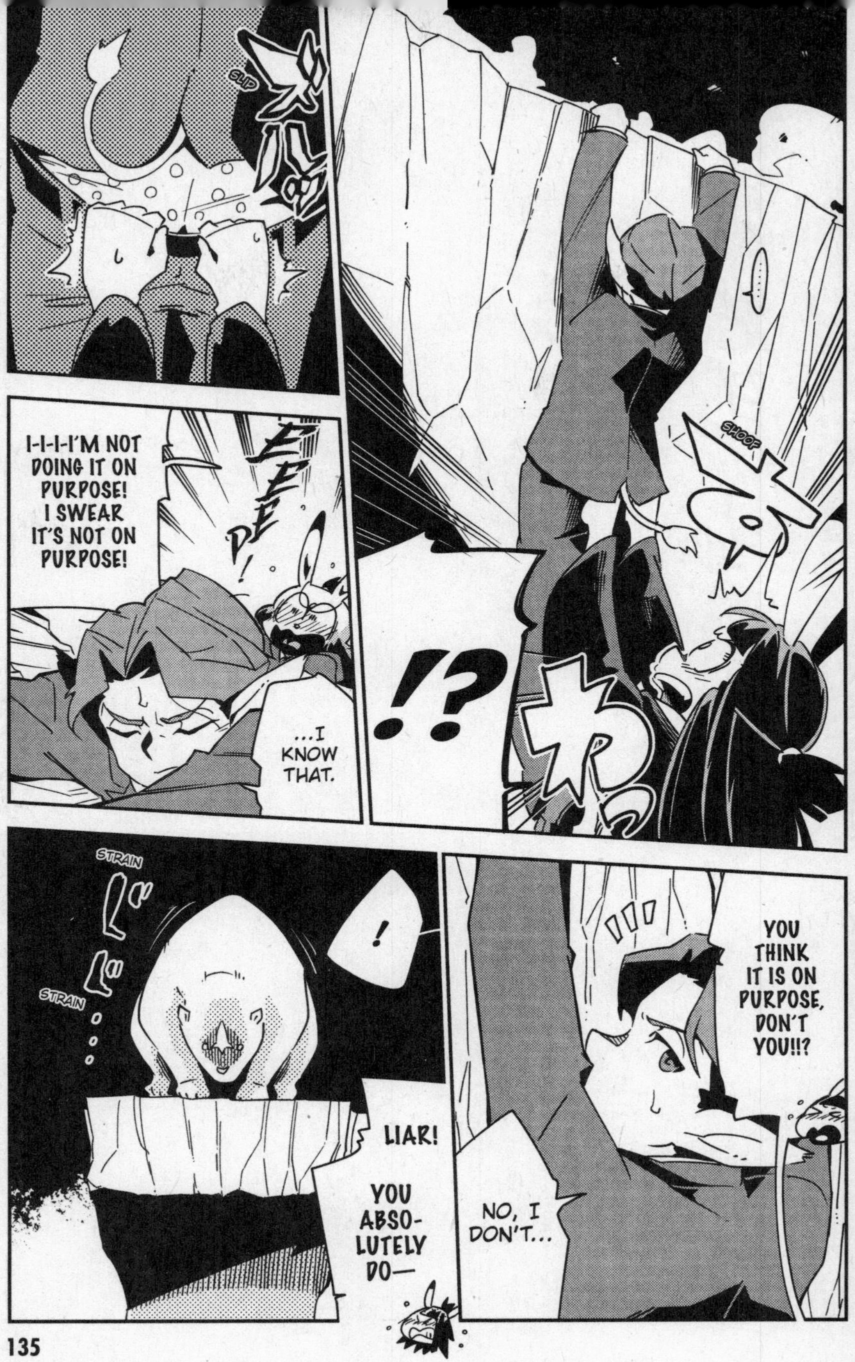

...
SHOOP
!?
SLIP
I-I-I-I'M NOT DOING IT ON PURPOSE! I SWEAR IT'S NOT ON PURPOSE!
EEEP!
...I KNOW THAT.
YOU THINK IT IS ON PURPOSE, DON'T YOU!!?
NO, I DON'T...
STRAIN
STRAIN
!
LIAR!
YOU ABSO-LUTELY DO—

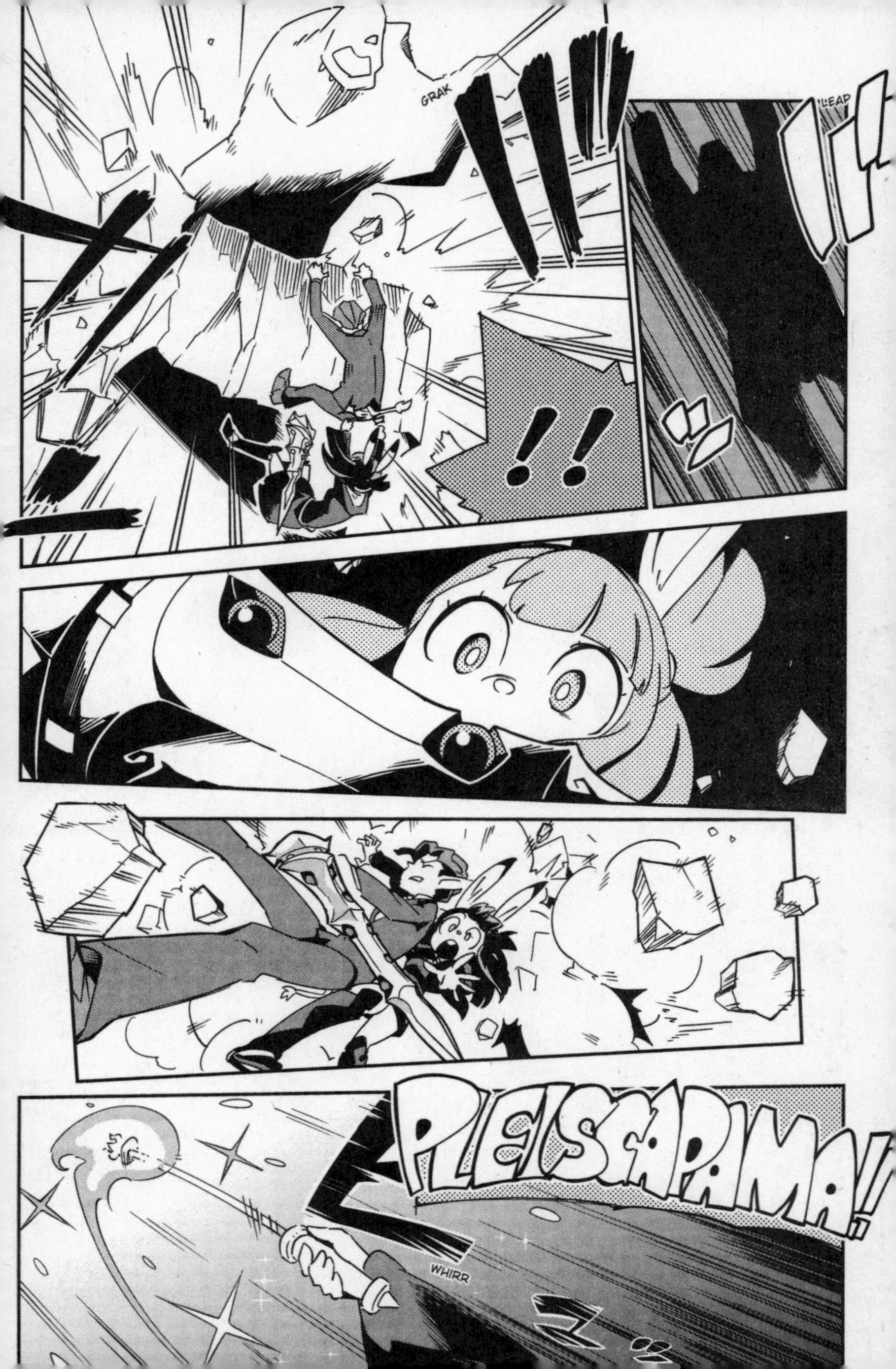
LEAP
GRAK
!!
PLEISCAPAMA!
WHIRR

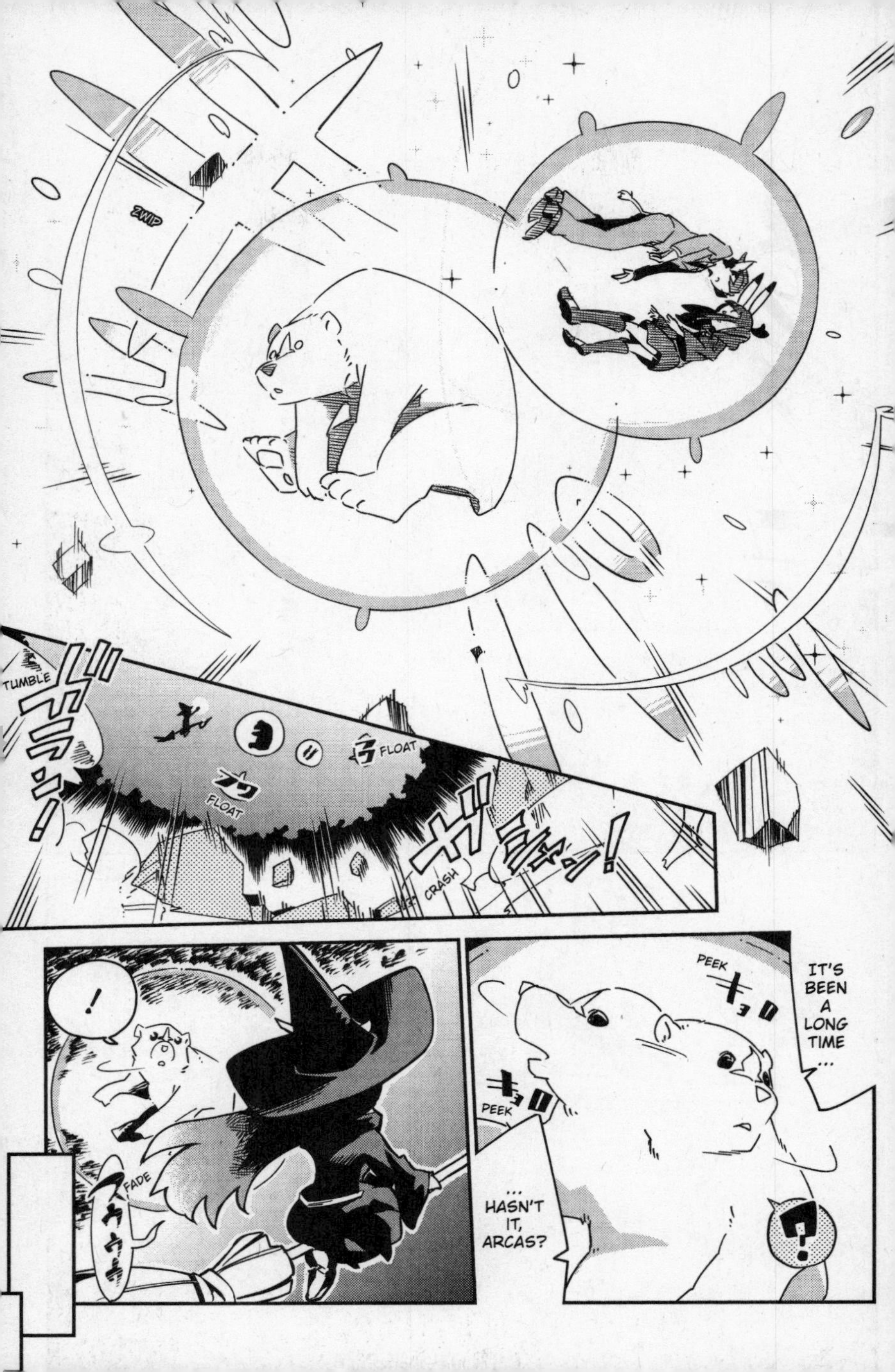
ZWIP
CRASH
FLOAT
FLOAT
TUMBLE
PEEK
IT'S BEEN A LONG TIME...
PEEK
...HASN'T IT, ARCAS?
?
!
FADE

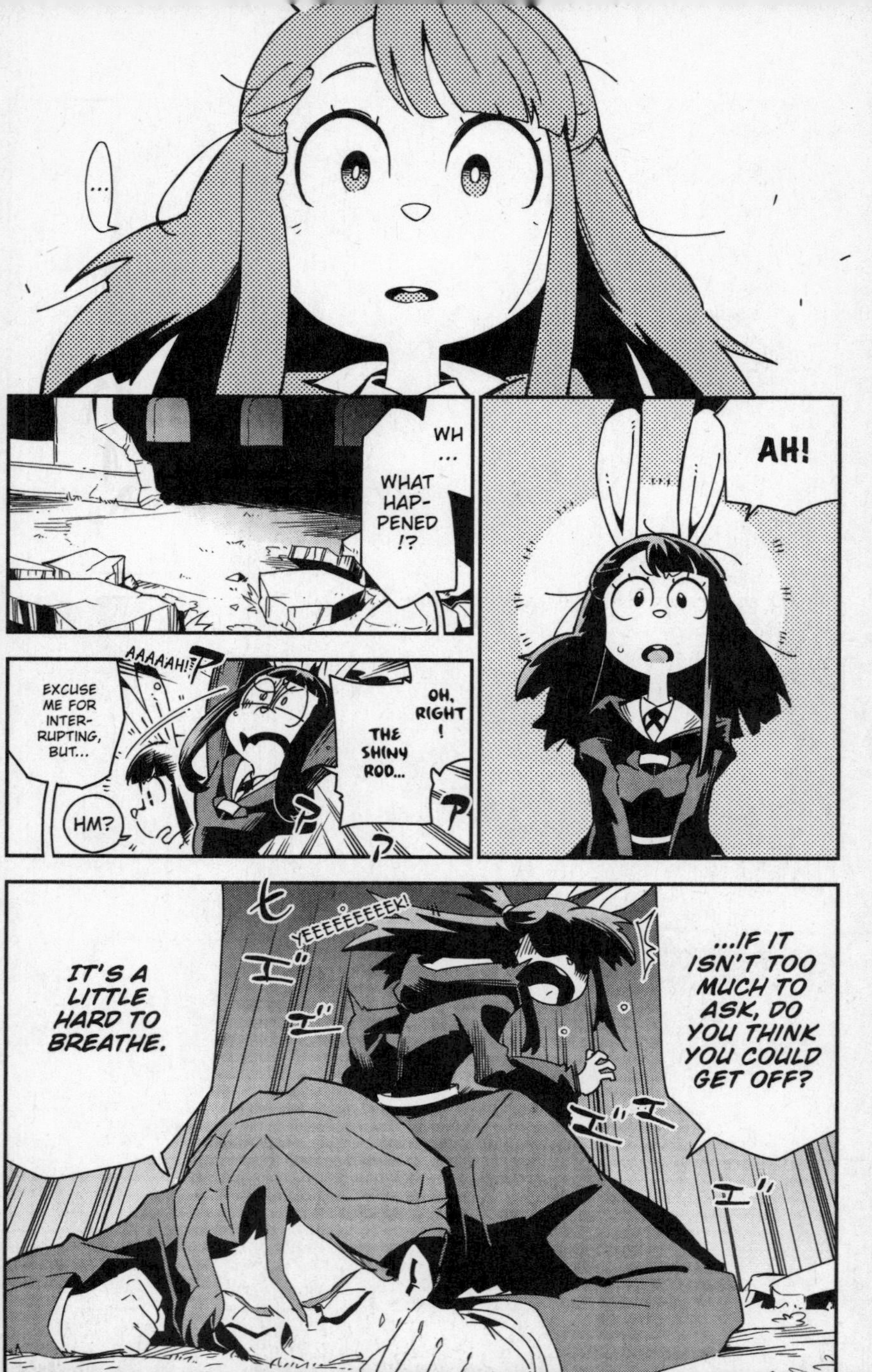
...
AH!
WH... WHAT HAPPENED!?
OH, RIGHT!
THE SHINY ROD...
AAAAAH!
EXCUSE ME FOR INTERRUPTING, BUT...
HM?
YEEEEEEEEEK!
...IF IT ISN'T TOO MUCH TO ASK, DO YOU THINK YOU COULD GET OFF?
IT'S A LITTLE HARD TO BREATHE.

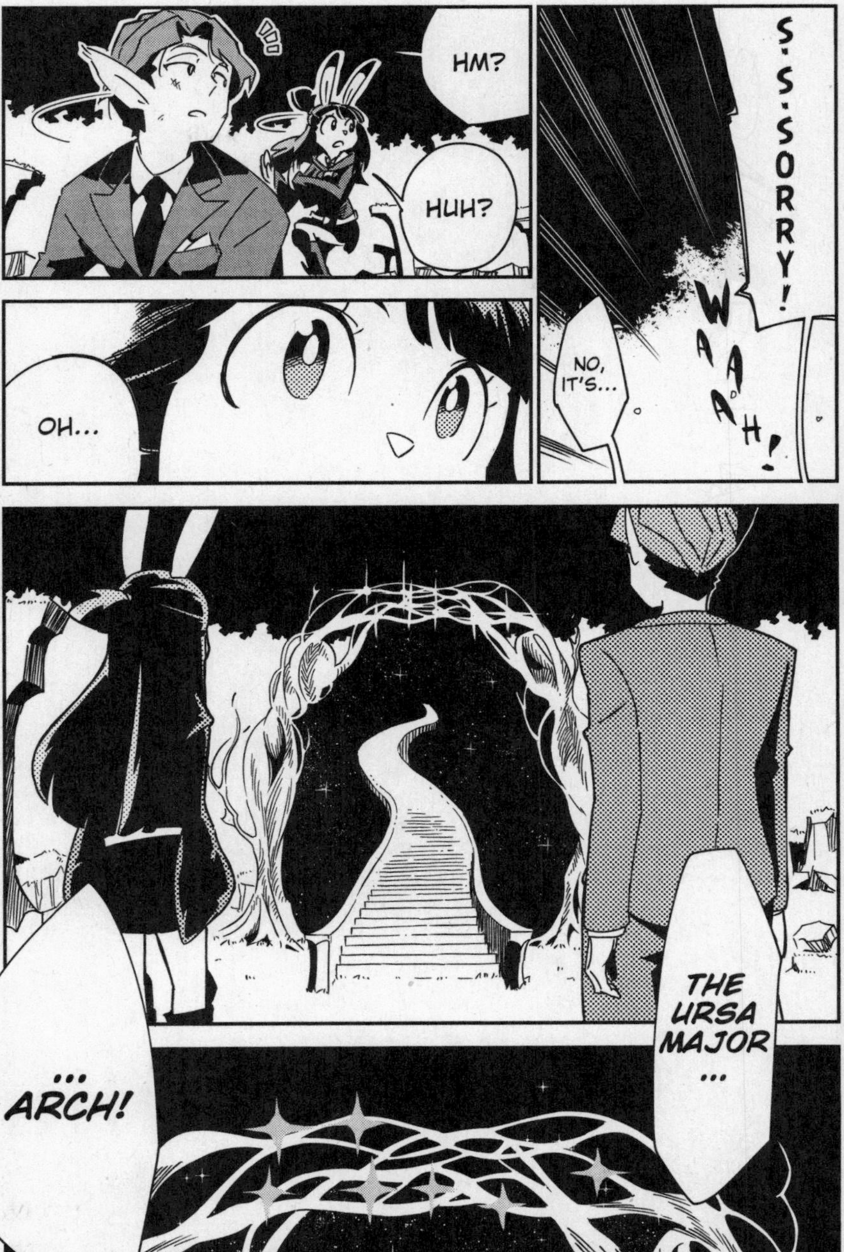
S-S-SORRY!
WAAAH!
NO, IT'S...
HM?
HUH?
OH...
THE URSA MAJOR...
...ARCH!

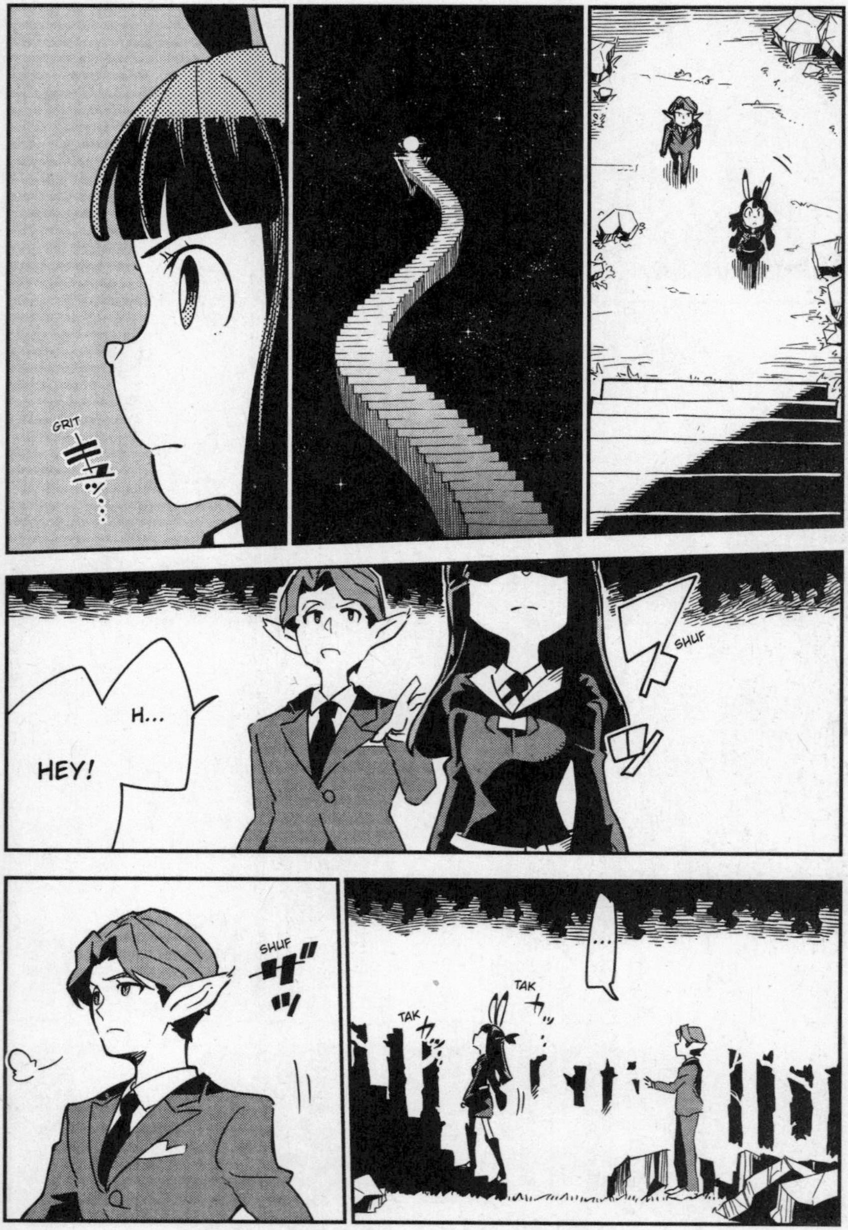
GRIT
SHUF
H...
HEY!
...
TAK
TAK
SHUF

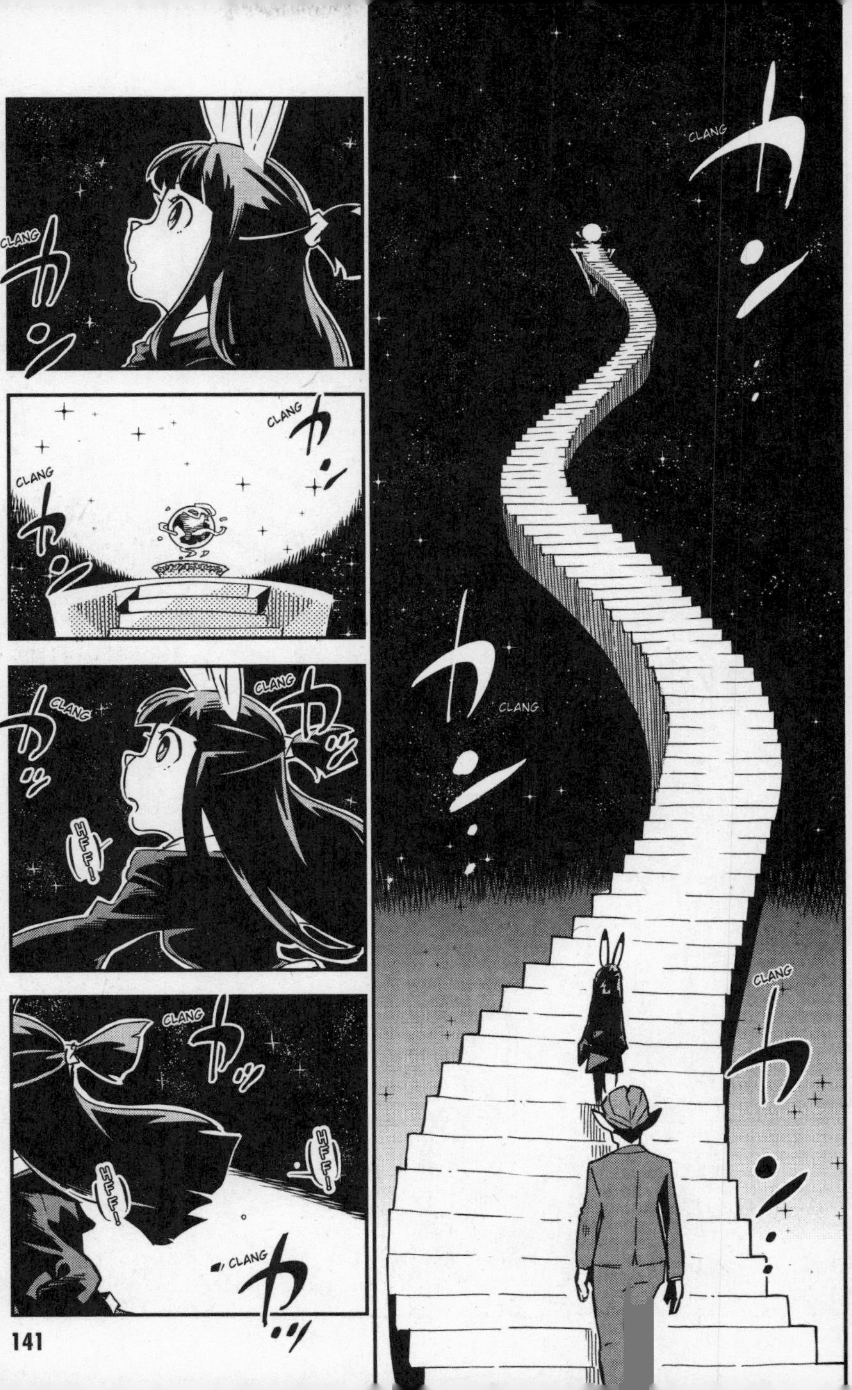
CLANG
CLANG
CLANG
CLANG
CLANG
CLANG
CLANG
CLANG
HFF!
CLANG
HFF!
HFF!
CLANG

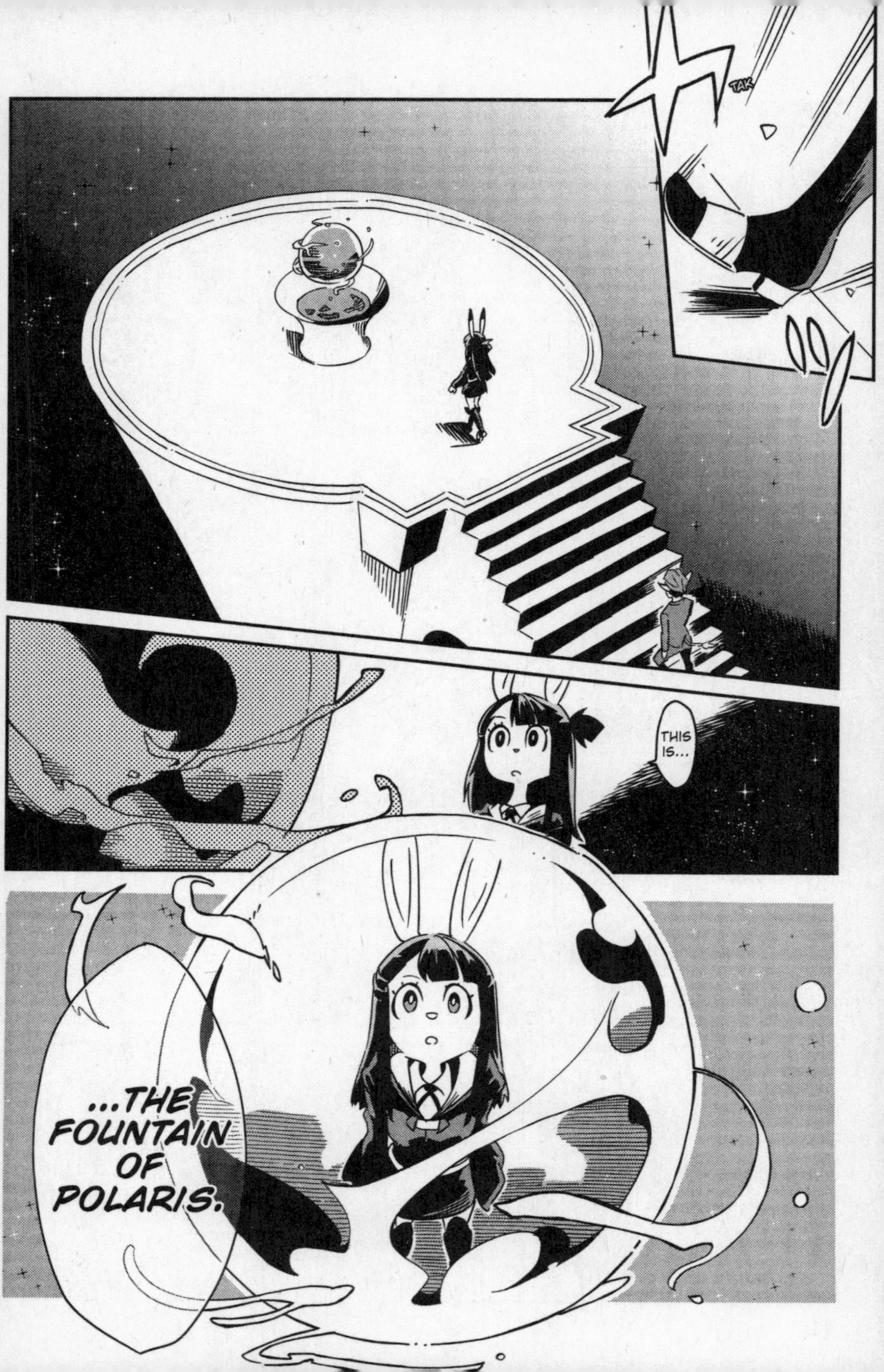
TAK
THIS IS...
...THE FOUNTAIN OF POLARIS.

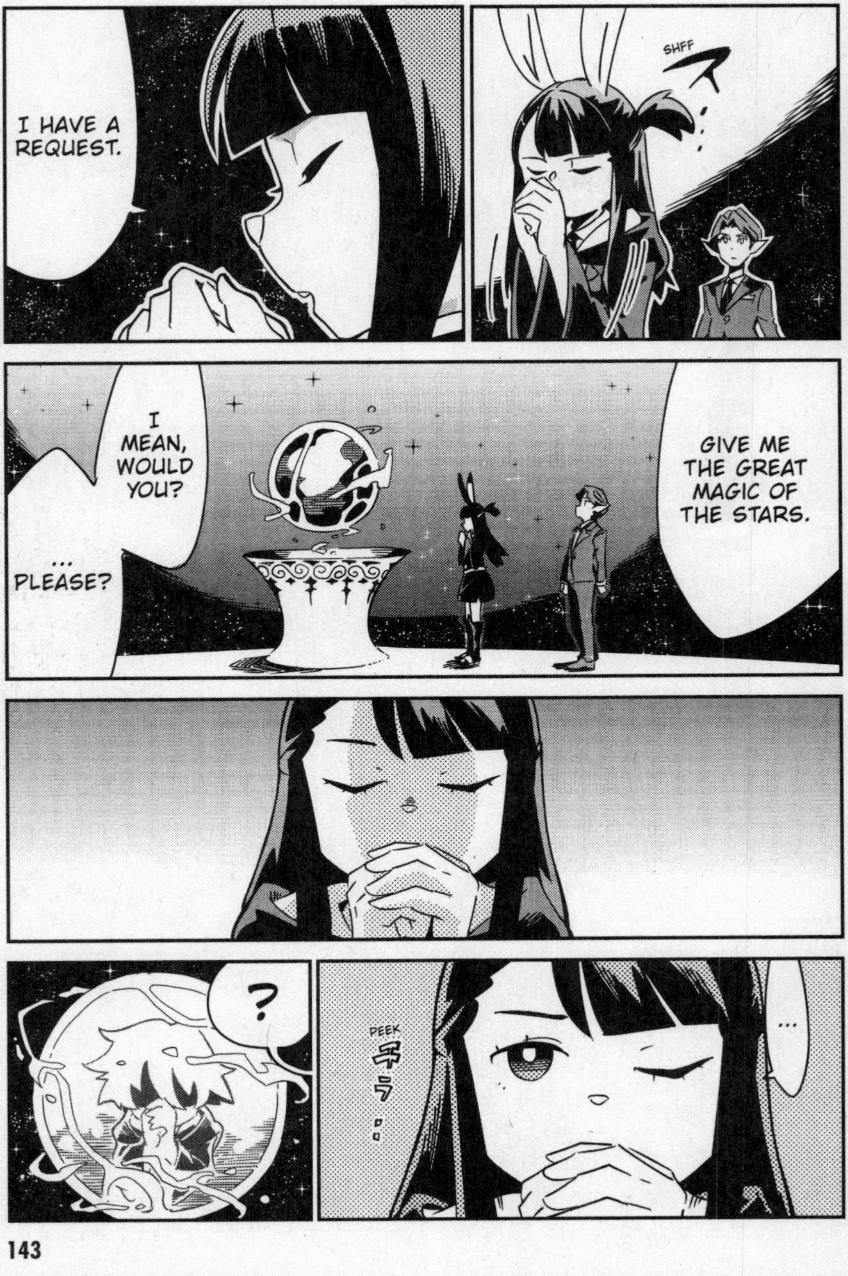
SHFF
ス
I HAVE A REQUEST.
GIVE ME THE GREAT MAGIC OF THE STARS.
I MEAN, WOULD YOU?
... PLEASE?
...
PEEK
チラ
?

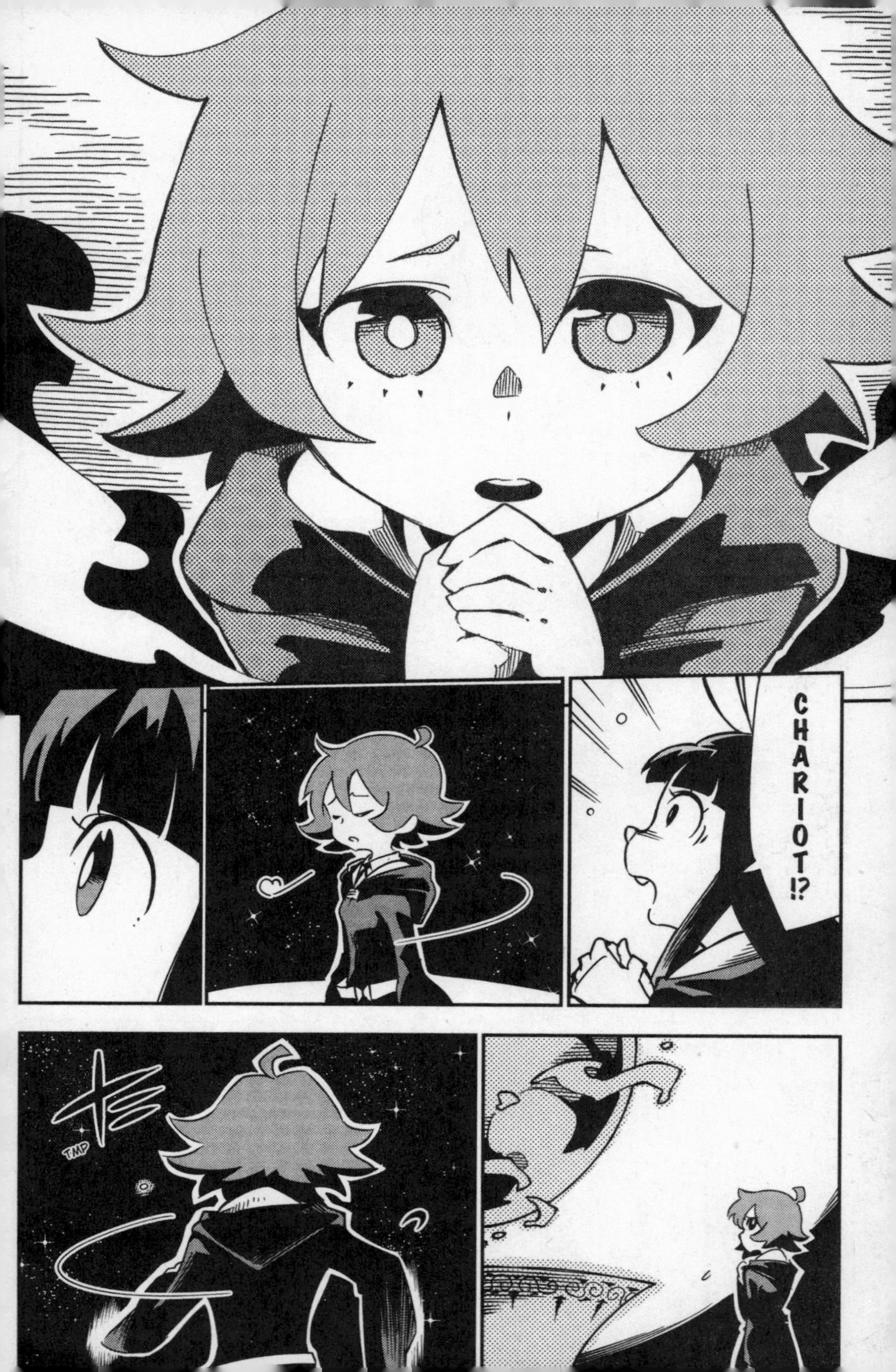
CHARIOT!?
TMP

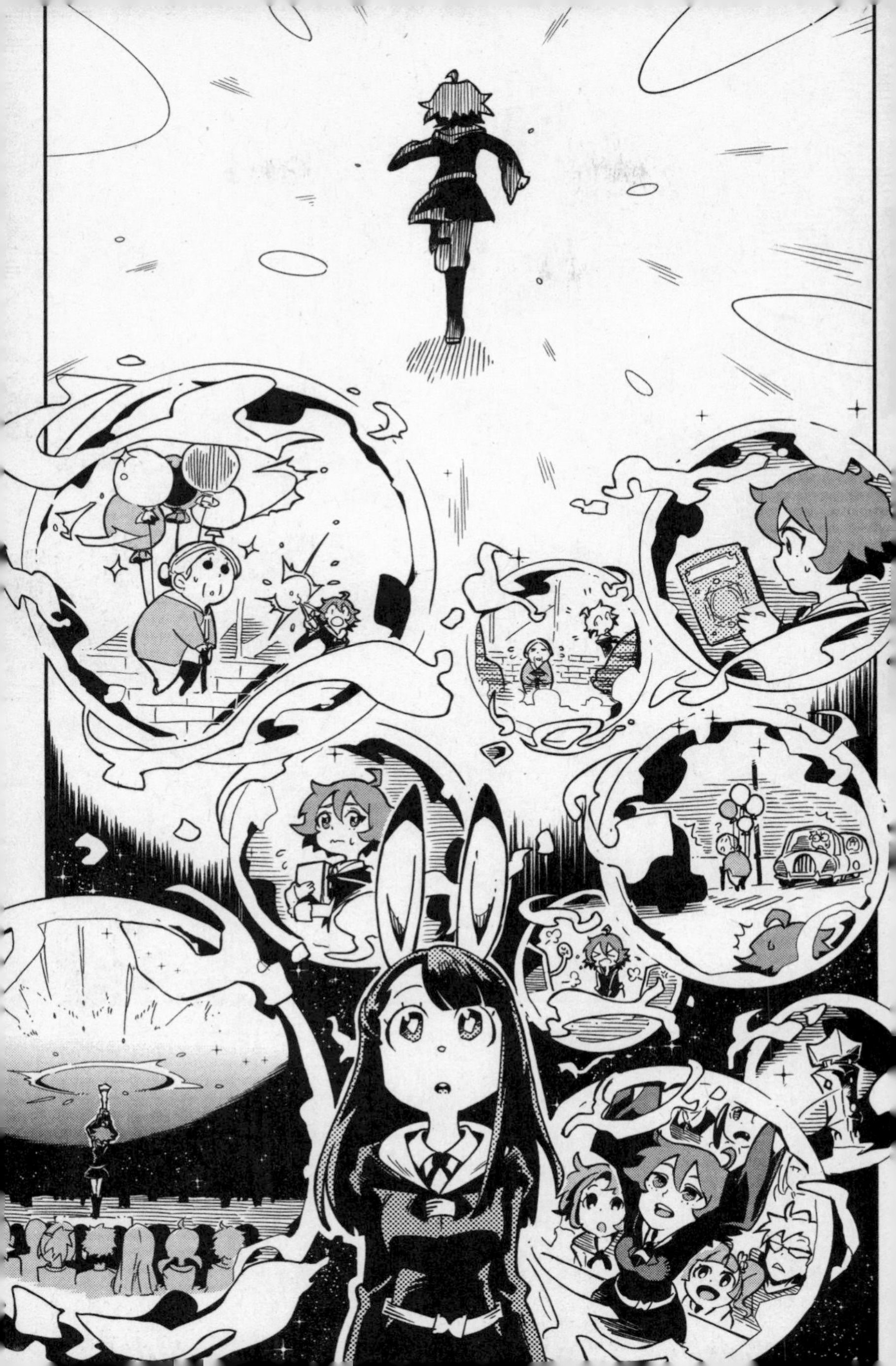

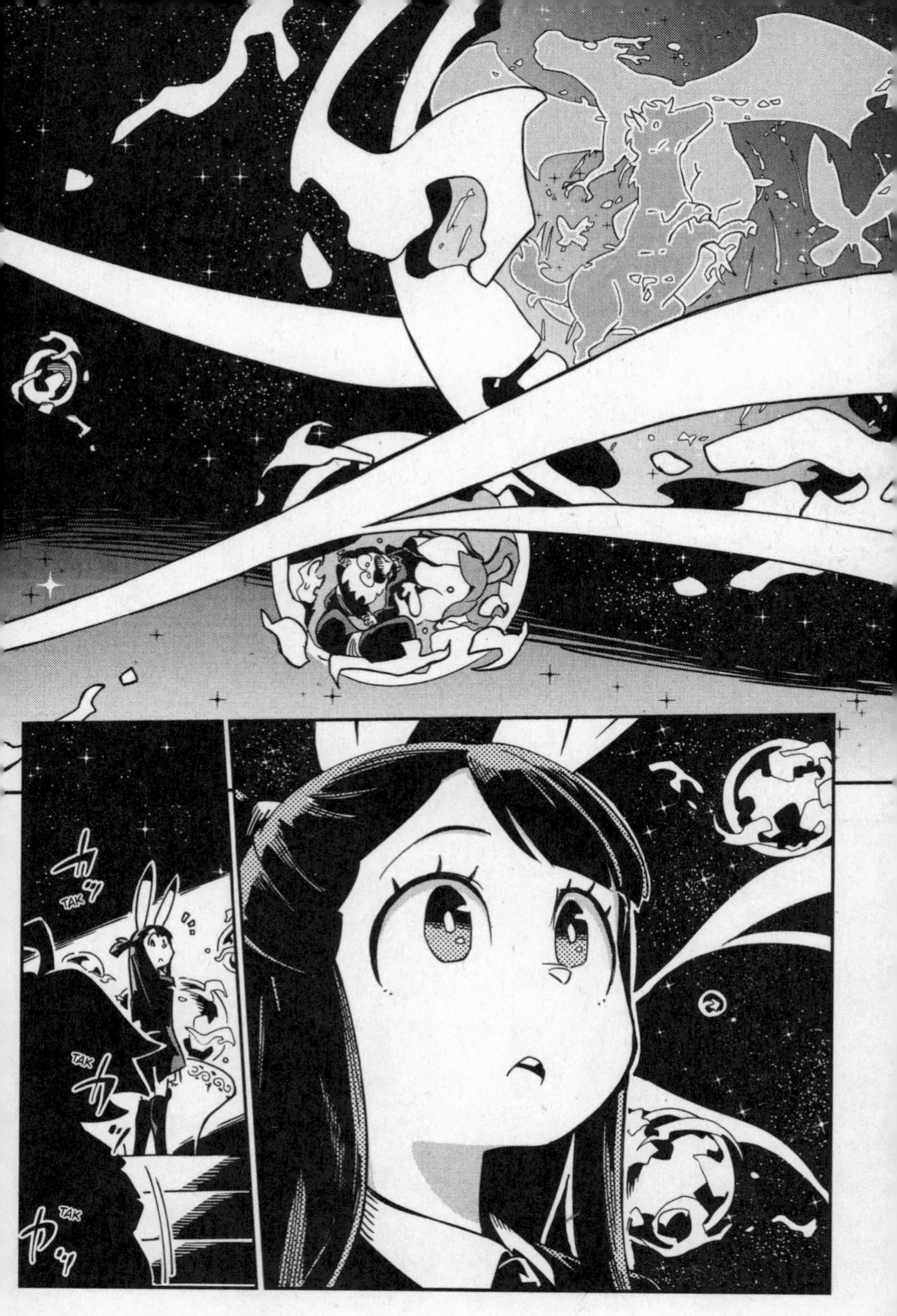

カッ
TAK
TAK
カッ
TAK
カッ

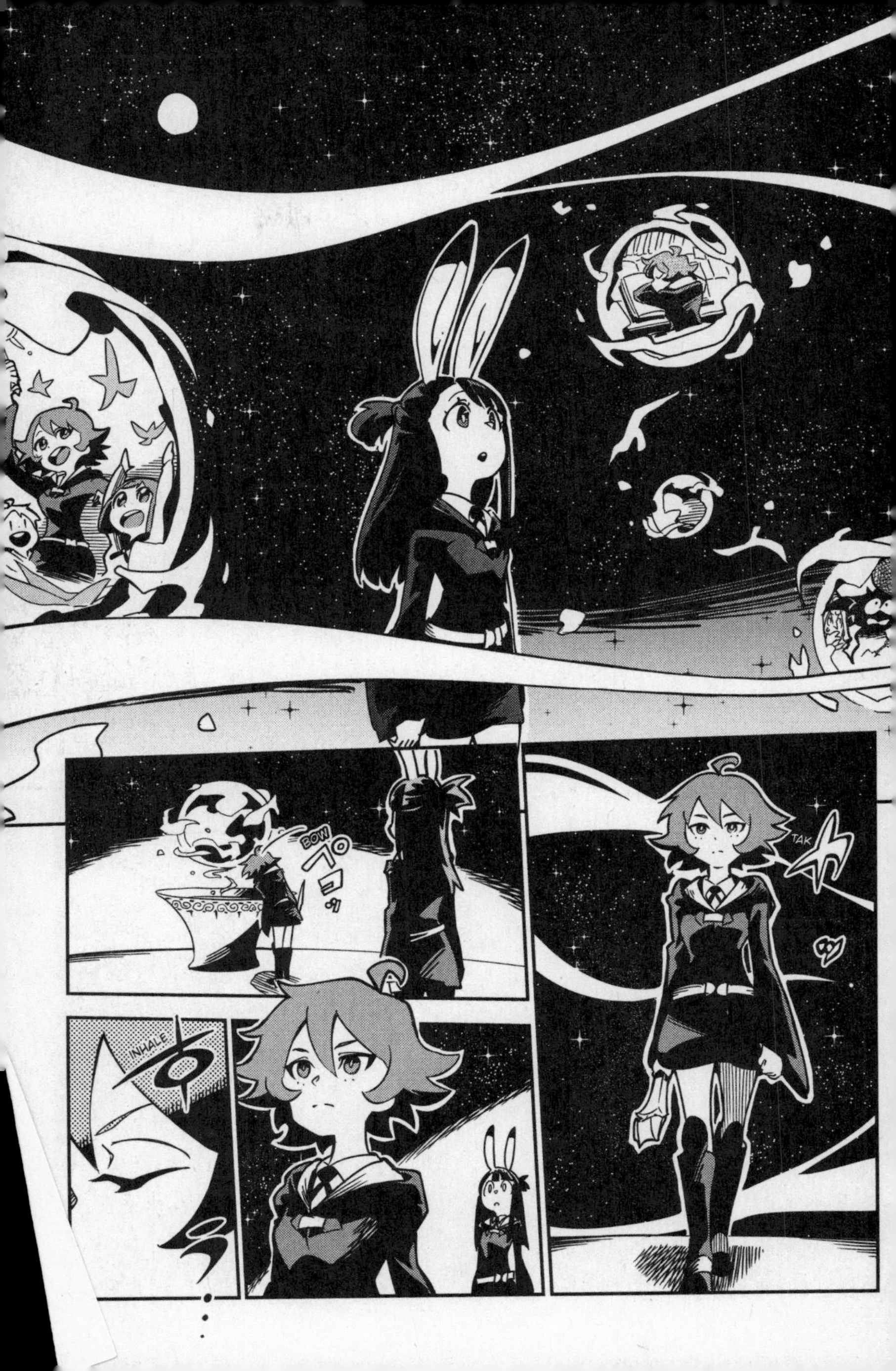
TAK
BOW
INHALE

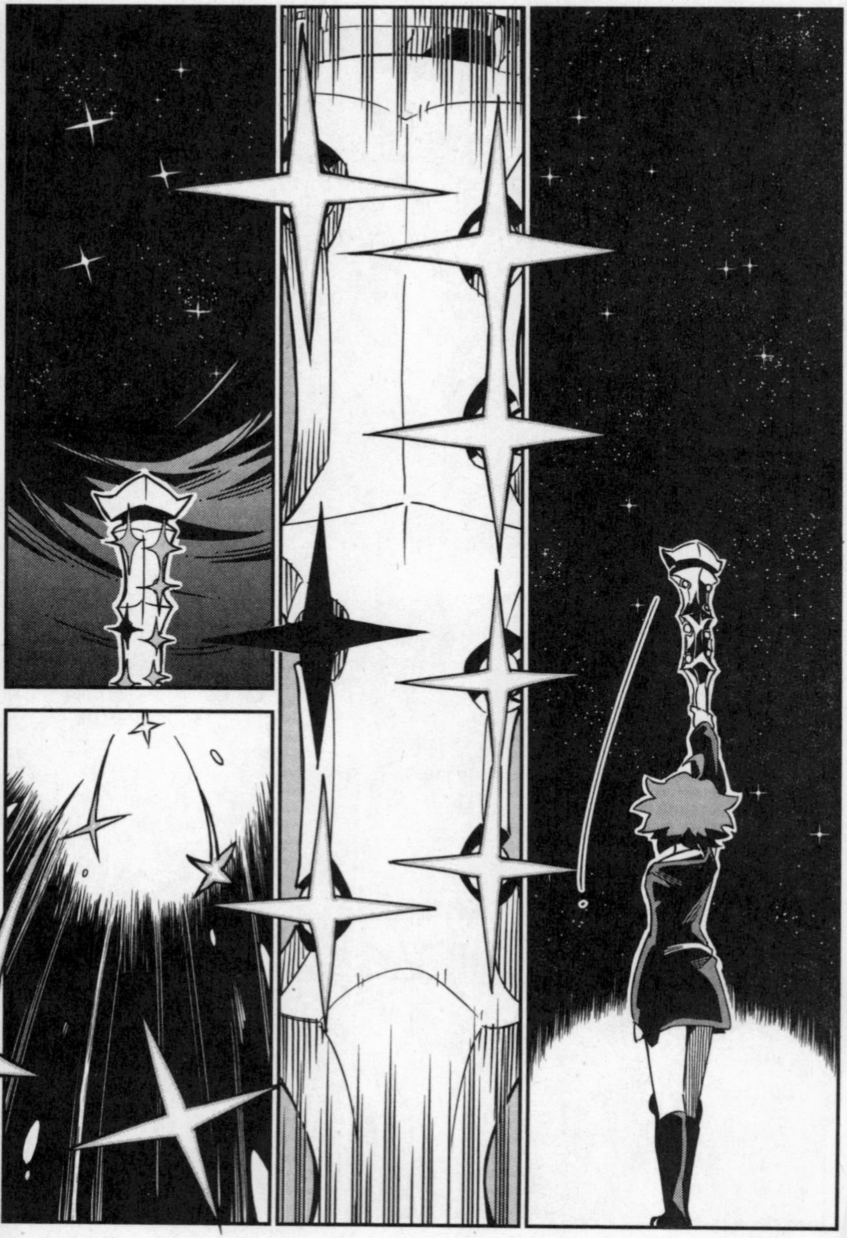

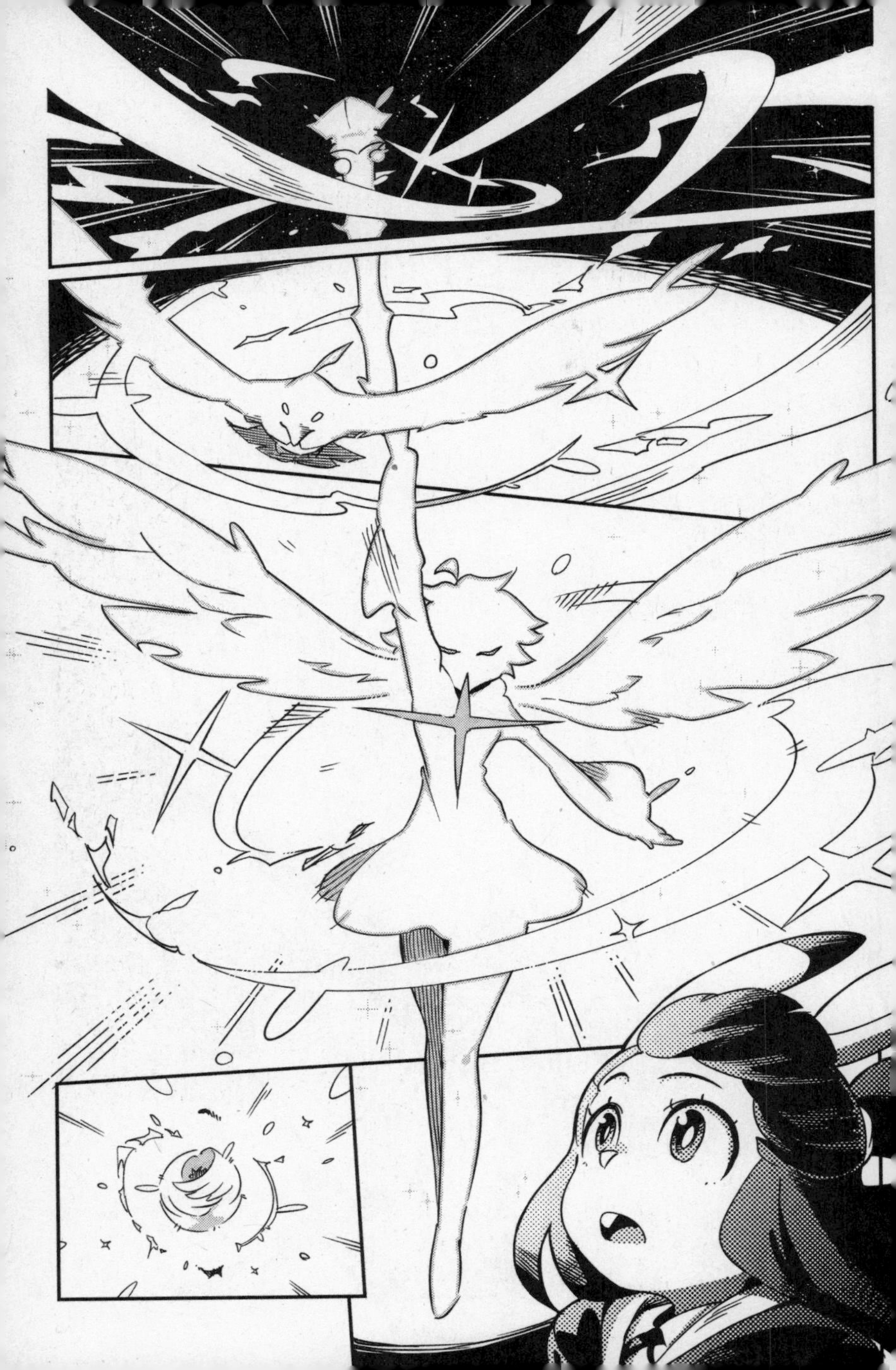

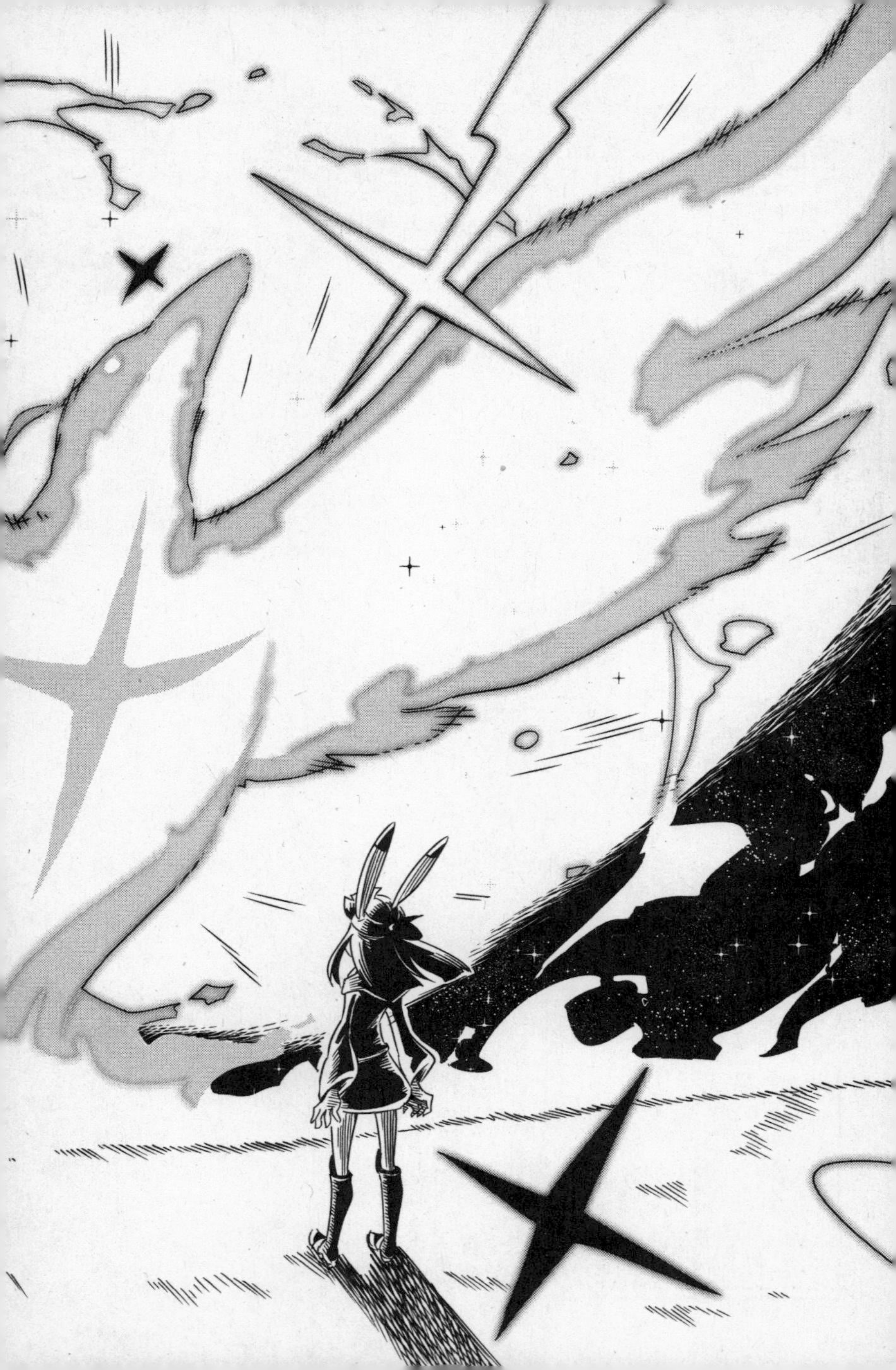

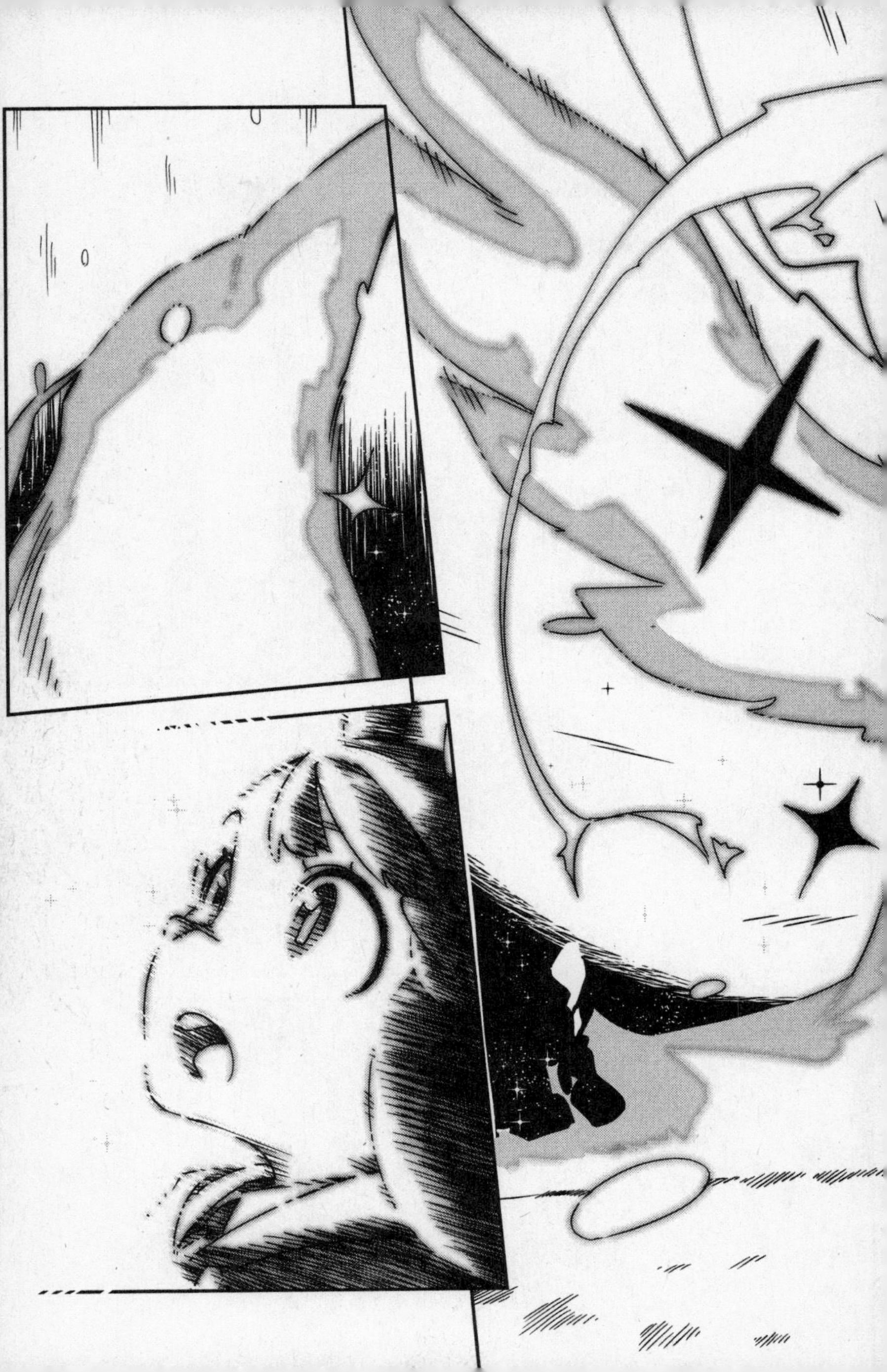

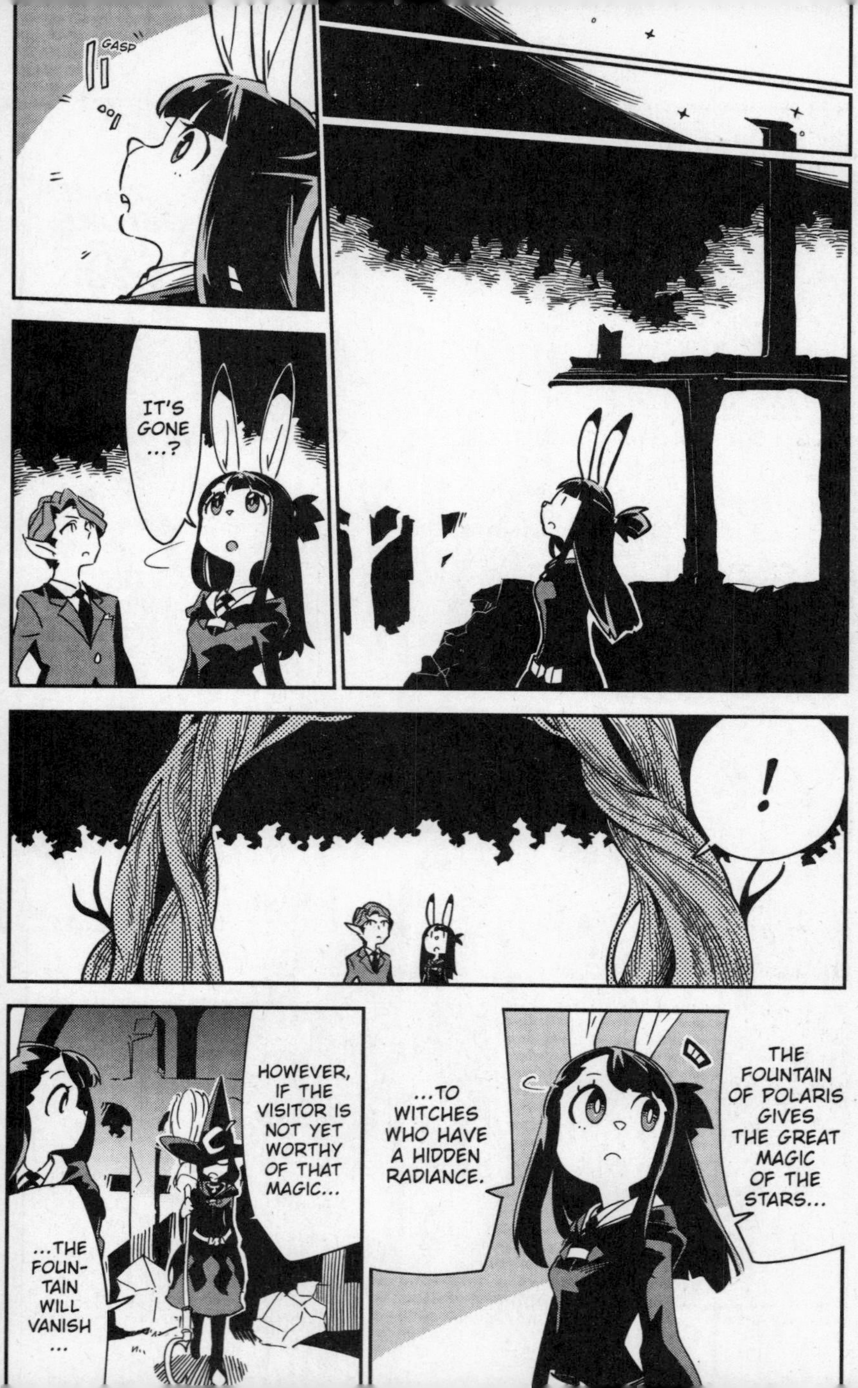
GASP
IT'S GONE ...?
!
THE FOUNTAIN OF POLARIS GIVES THE GREAT MAGIC OF THE STARS...
...TO WITCHES WHO HAVE A HIDDEN RADIANCE.
HOWEVER, IF THE VISITOR IS NOT YET WORTHY OF THAT MAGIC...
...THE FOUN-TAIN WILL VANISH ...

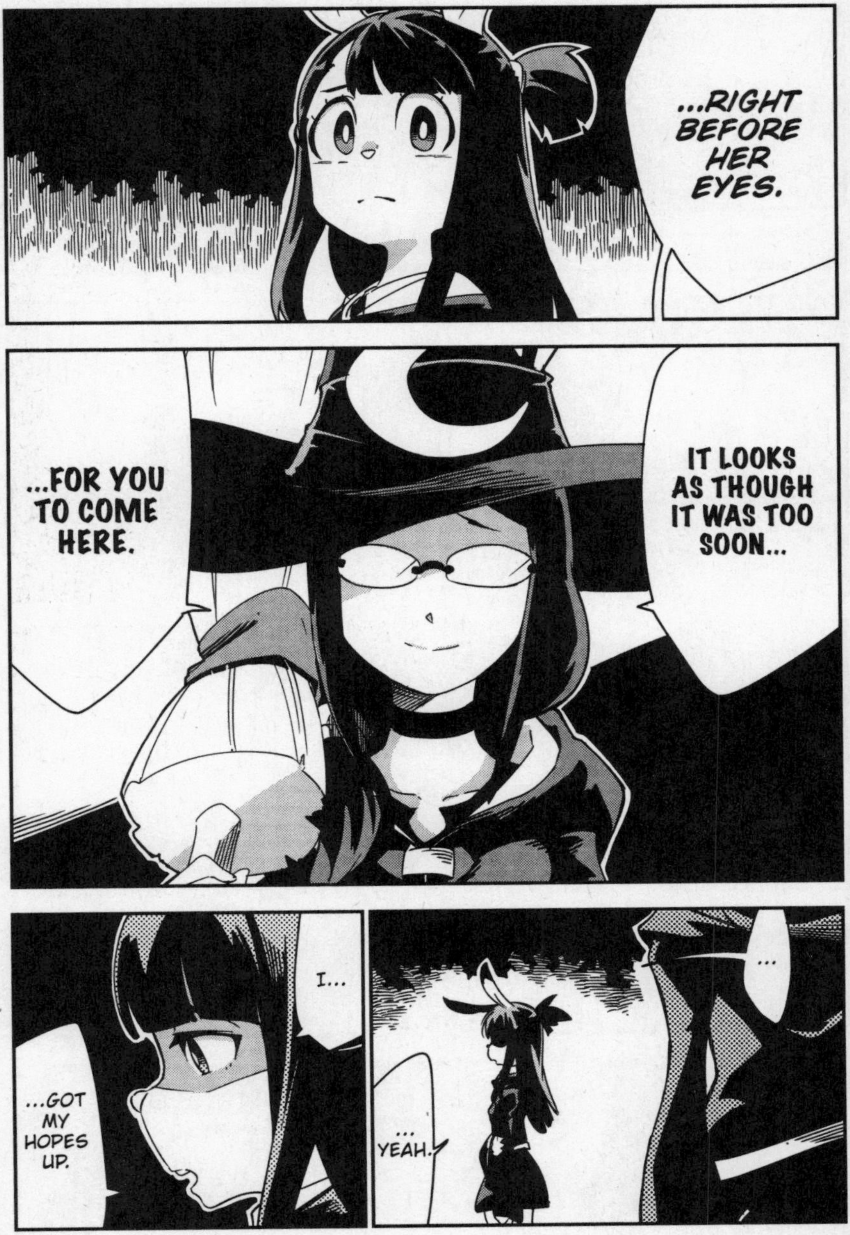
...RIGHT BEFORE HER EYES.
IT LOOKS AS THOUGH IT WAS TOO SOON...
...FOR YOU TO COME HERE.
...
... YEAH.
I...
...GOT MY HOPES UP.

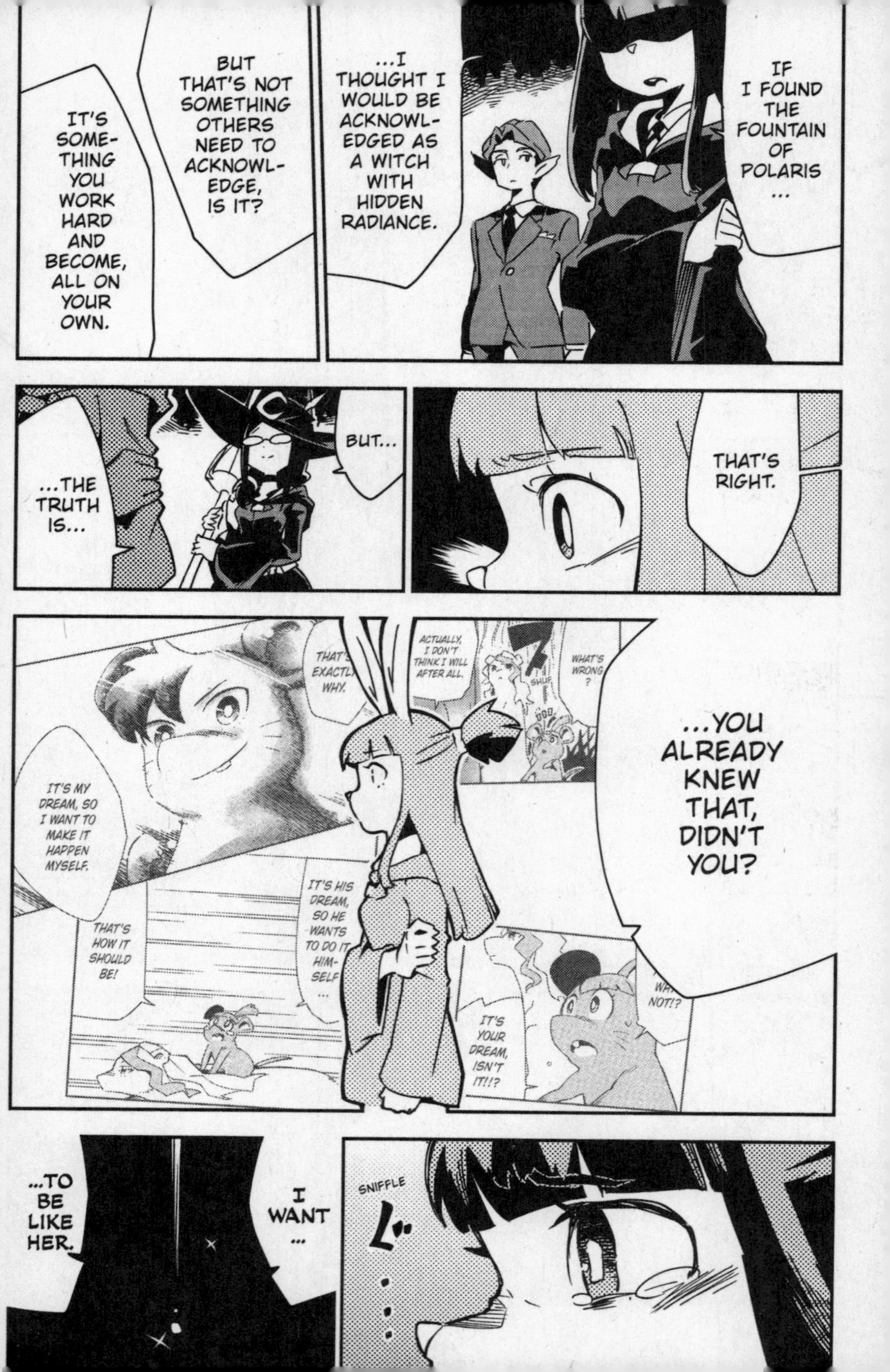
IF I FOUND THE FOUNTAIN OF POLARIS...
...I THOUGHT I WOULD BE ACKNOWLEDGED AS A WITCH WITH HIDDEN RADIANCE.
BUT THAT'S NOT SOMETHING OTHERS NEED TO ACKNOWLEDGE, IS IT?
IT'S SOMETHING YOU WORK HARD AND BECOME, ALL ON YOUR OWN.
THAT'S RIGHT.
BUT...
...THE TRUTH IS...
...YOU ALREADY KNEW THAT, DIDN'T YOU?
WHAT'S WRONG?
SHUF
ACTUALLY, I DON'T THINK I WILL AFTER ALL.
THAT'S EXACTL WHY.
IT'S MY DREAM, SO I WANT TO MAKE IT HAPPEN MYSELF.
WA NOT!?
IT'S YOUR DREAM, ISN'T IT!!?
IT'S HIS DREAM, SO HE WANTS TO DO IT HIMSELF...
THAT'S HOW IT SHOULD BE!
SNIFFLE
I WANT...
...TO BE LIKE HER.

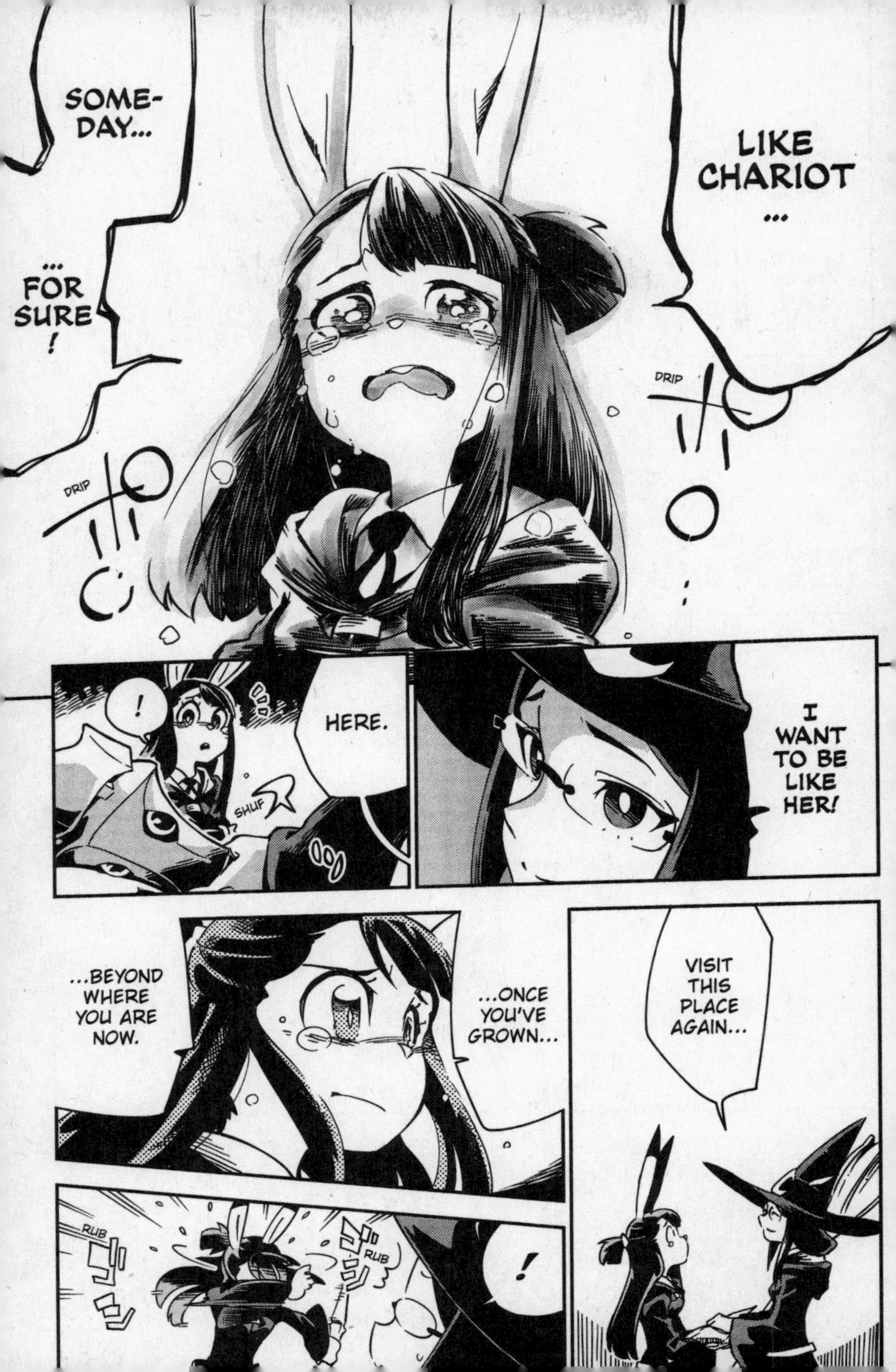
LIKE CHARIOT ...
SOME-DAY...
... FOR SURE!
DRIP
DRIP
I WANT TO BE LIKE HER!
HERE.
!
SHUF
VISIT THIS PLACE AGAIN...
...ONCE YOU'VE GROWN...
...BEYOND WHERE YOU ARE NOW.
!
RUB
RUB

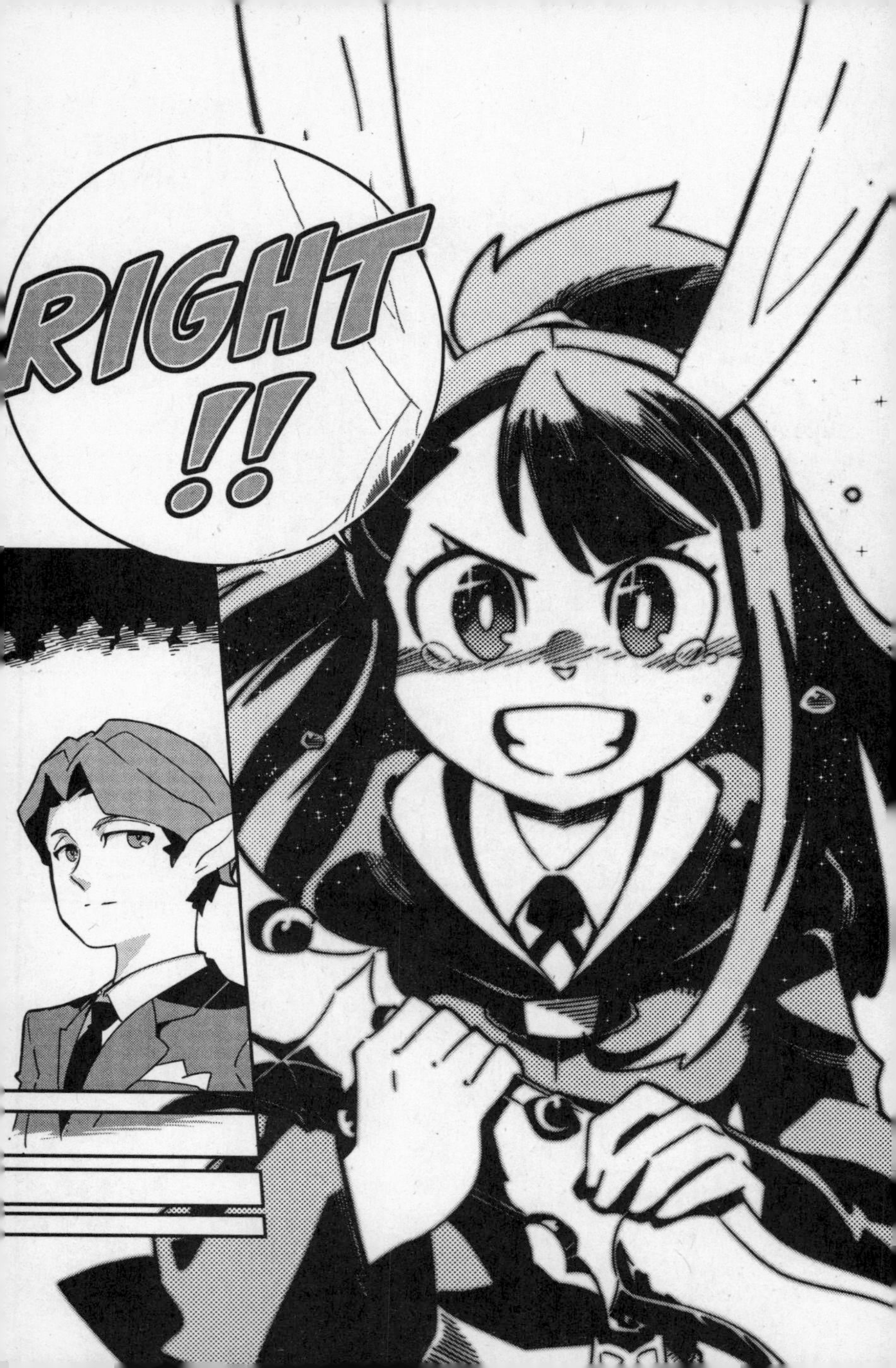
RIGHT!!

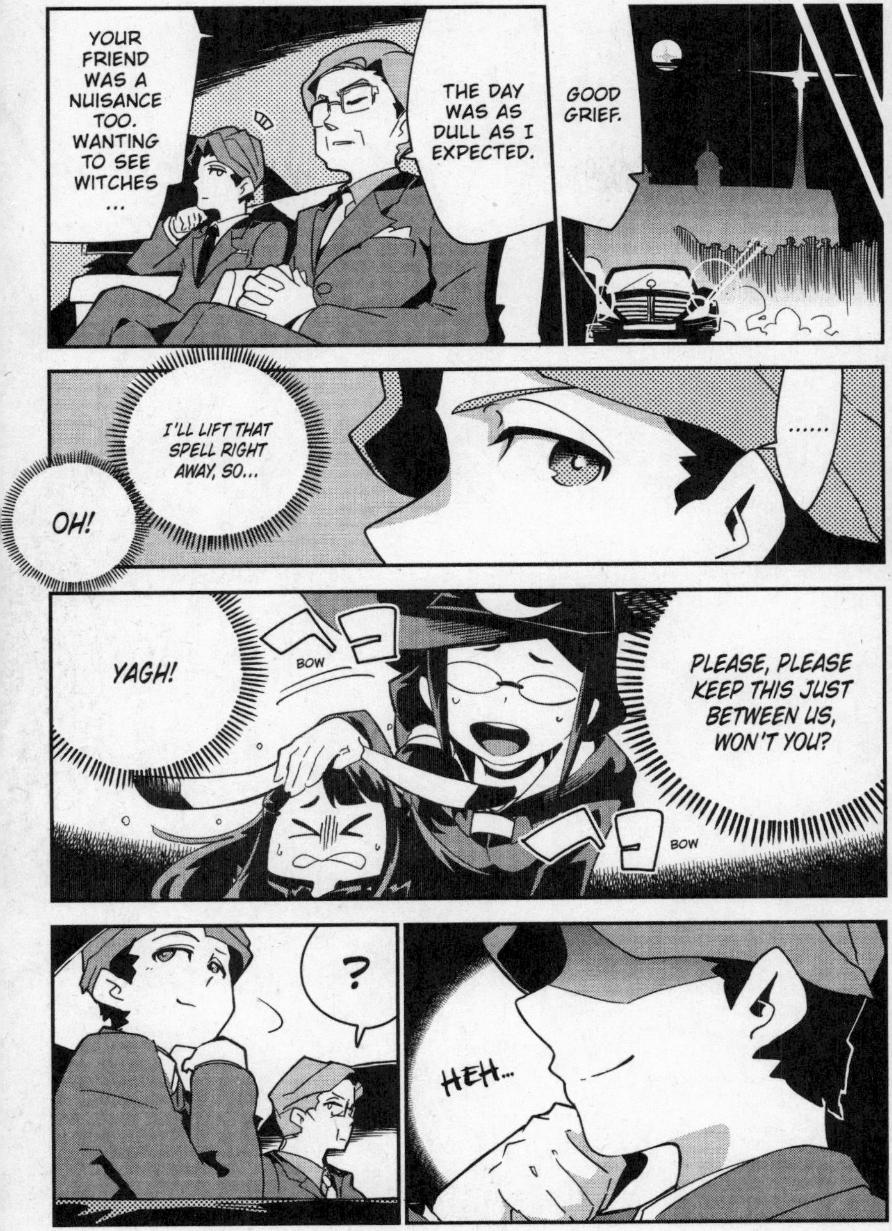
GOOD GRIEF.
THE DAY WAS AS DULL AS I EXPECTED.
YOUR FRIEND WAS A NUISANCE TOO. WANTING TO SEE WITCHES ...
......
I'LL LIFT THAT SPELL RIGHT AWAY, SO...
OH!
PLEASE, PLEASE KEEP THIS JUST BETWEEN US, WON'T YOU?
BOW
YAGH!
BOW
HEH...
?

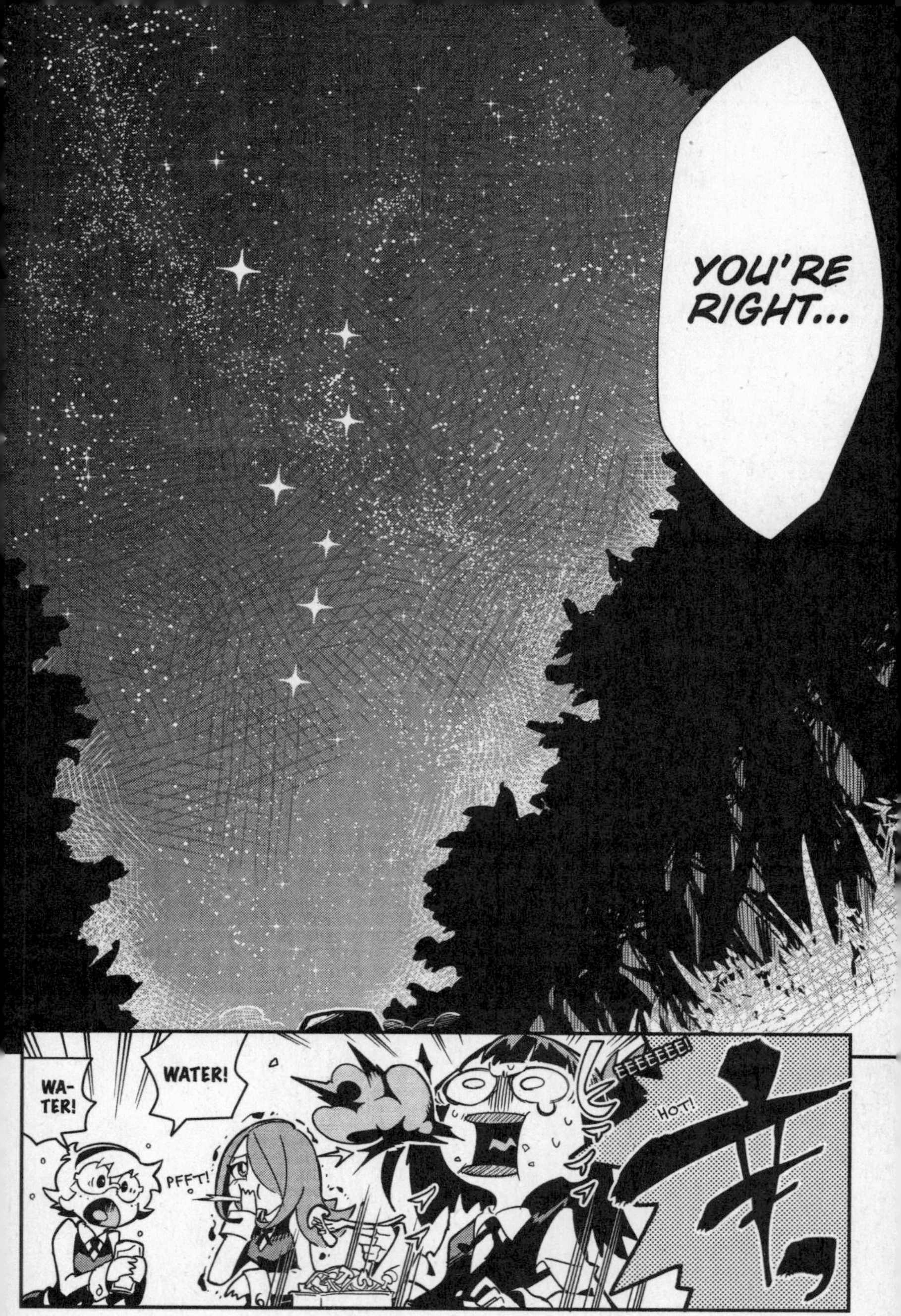

YOU'RE RIGHT...
EEEEEEE!
HOT!
WATER!
PFFT!
WA-TER!

Little
Witch
Academia

Character

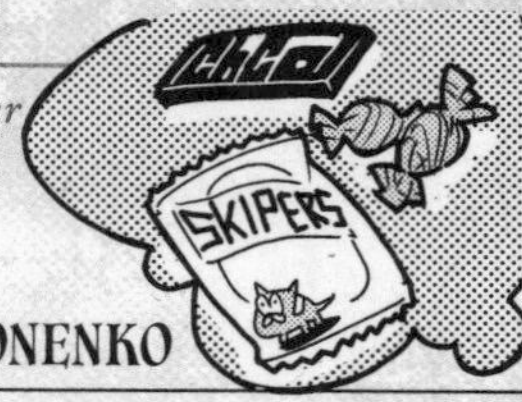
SKIPERS

JASMINKA ANTONENKO

A gourmand from Russia. She's exceedingly fond of snacks and peace. Because she eats even during class, she gets yelled at a lot.

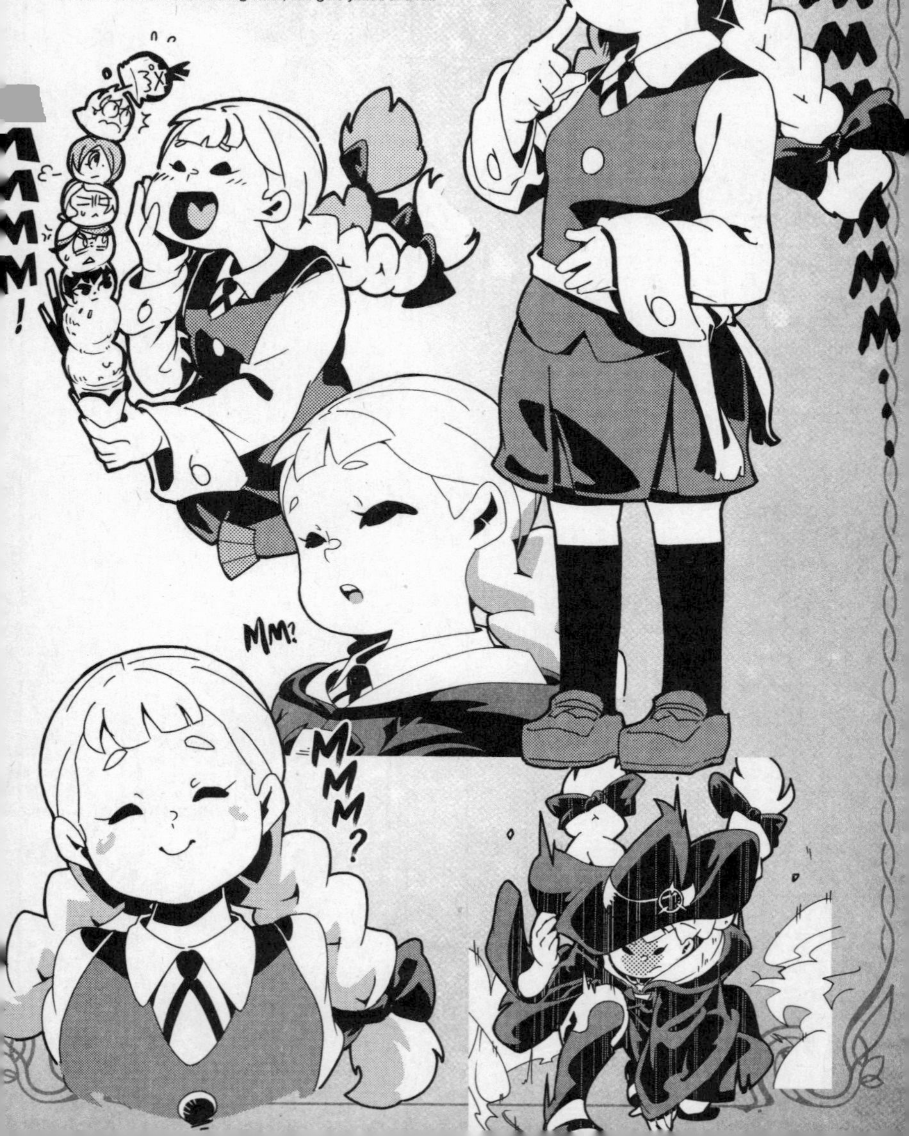
MMMMMMMM...
MMMM!
MM?
MMM?

⊰ Chapter 11 ⊱

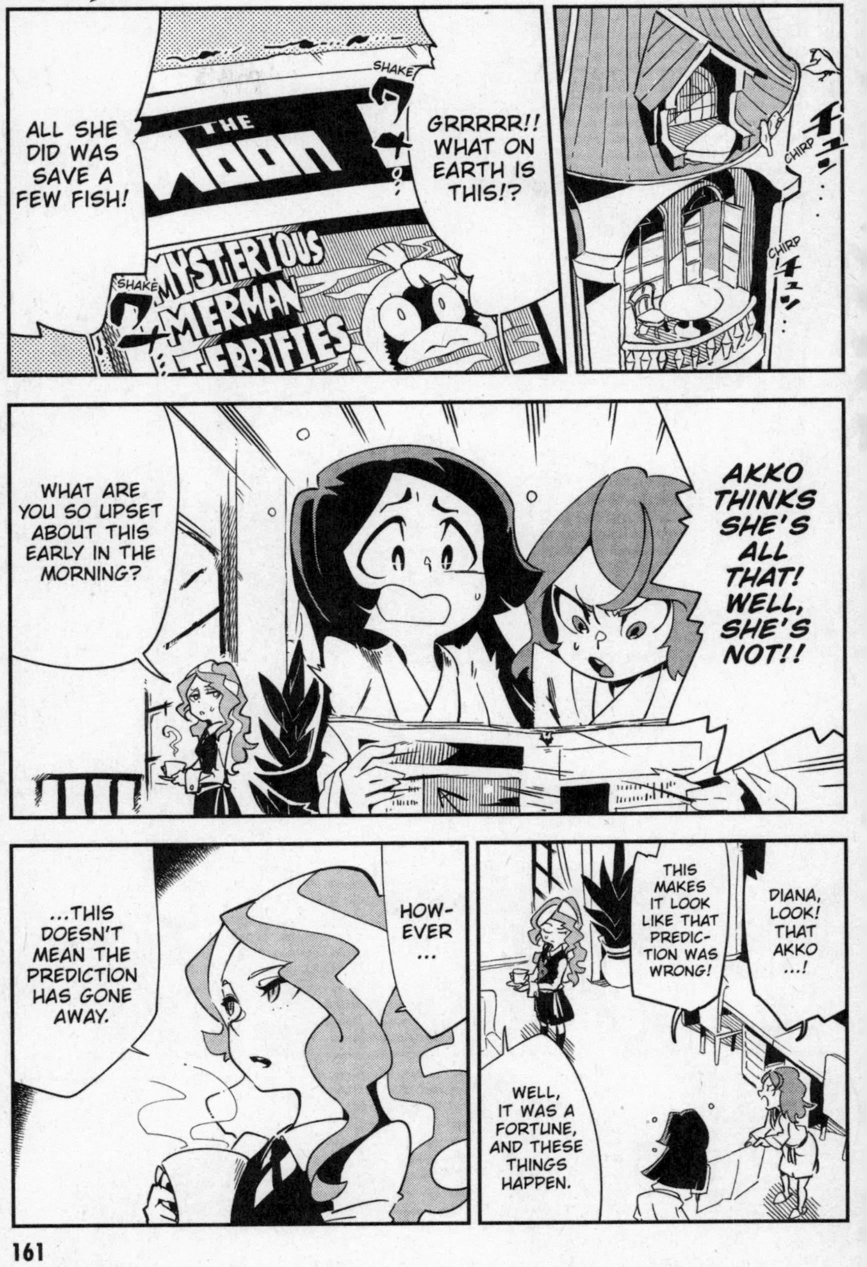
CHIRP
CHIRP
GRRRRR!! WHAT ON EARTH IS THIS!?
SHAKE
SHAKE
THE MOON
MYSTERIOUS MERMAN TERRIFIES
ALL SHE DID WAS SAVE A FEW FISH!
AKKO THINKS SHE'S ALL THAT! WELL, SHE'S NOT!!
WHAT ARE YOU SO UPSET ABOUT THIS EARLY IN THE MORNING?
DIANA, LOOK! THAT AKKO ...!
THIS MAKES IT LOOK LIKE THAT PREDICTION WAS WRONG!
WELL, IT WAS A FORTUNE, AND THESE THINGS HAPPEN.
HOW-EVER ...
...THIS DOESN'T MEAN THE PREDICTION HAS GONE AWAY.

Chapter 11 NO MORE CHEATING

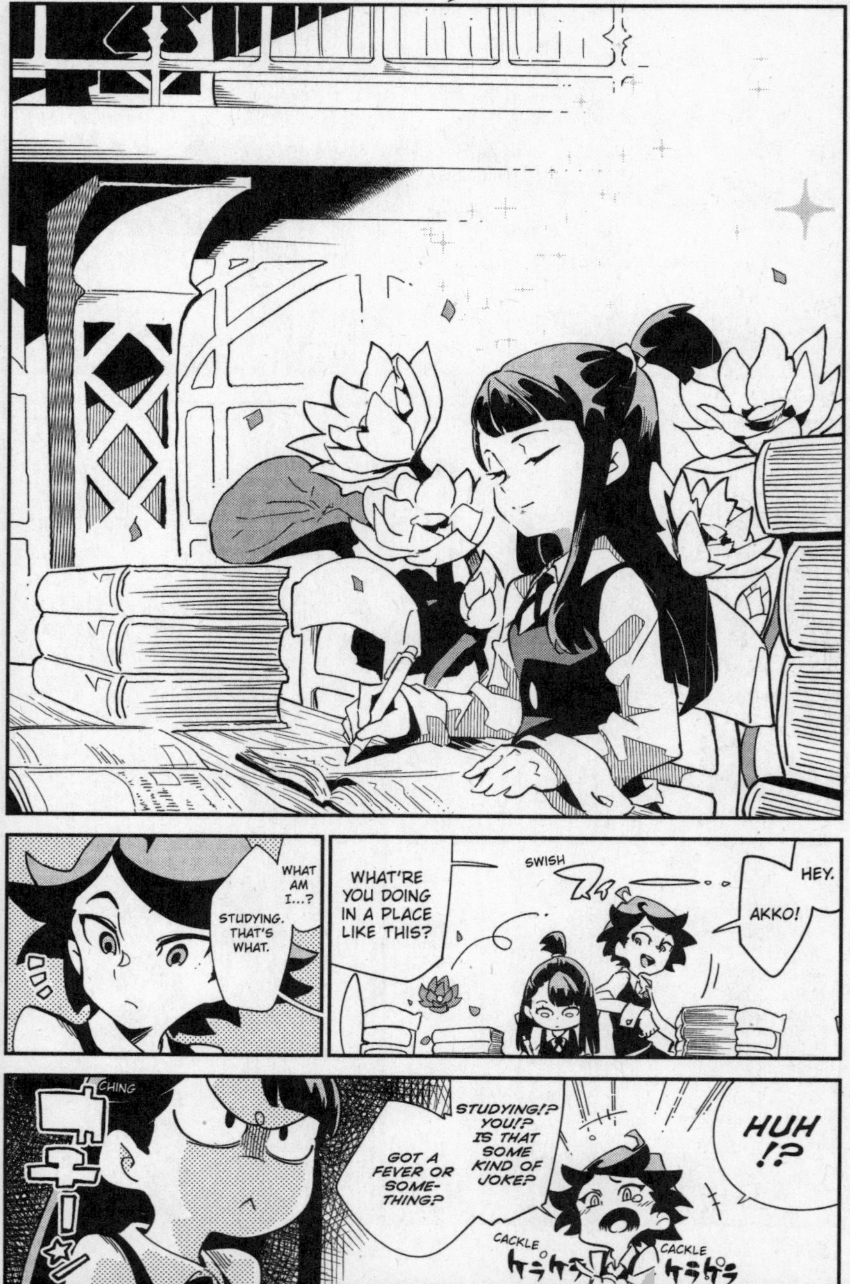

HEY.
AKKO!
SWISH
WHAT'RE YOU DOING IN A PLACE LIKE THIS?
WHAT AM I...?
STUDYING. THAT'S WHAT.
HUH!?
STUDYING!? YOU!? IS THAT SOME KIND OF JOKE?
GOT A FEVER OR SOME-THING?
CHING
CACKLE
ケラケラ
CACKLE
ケラケラ

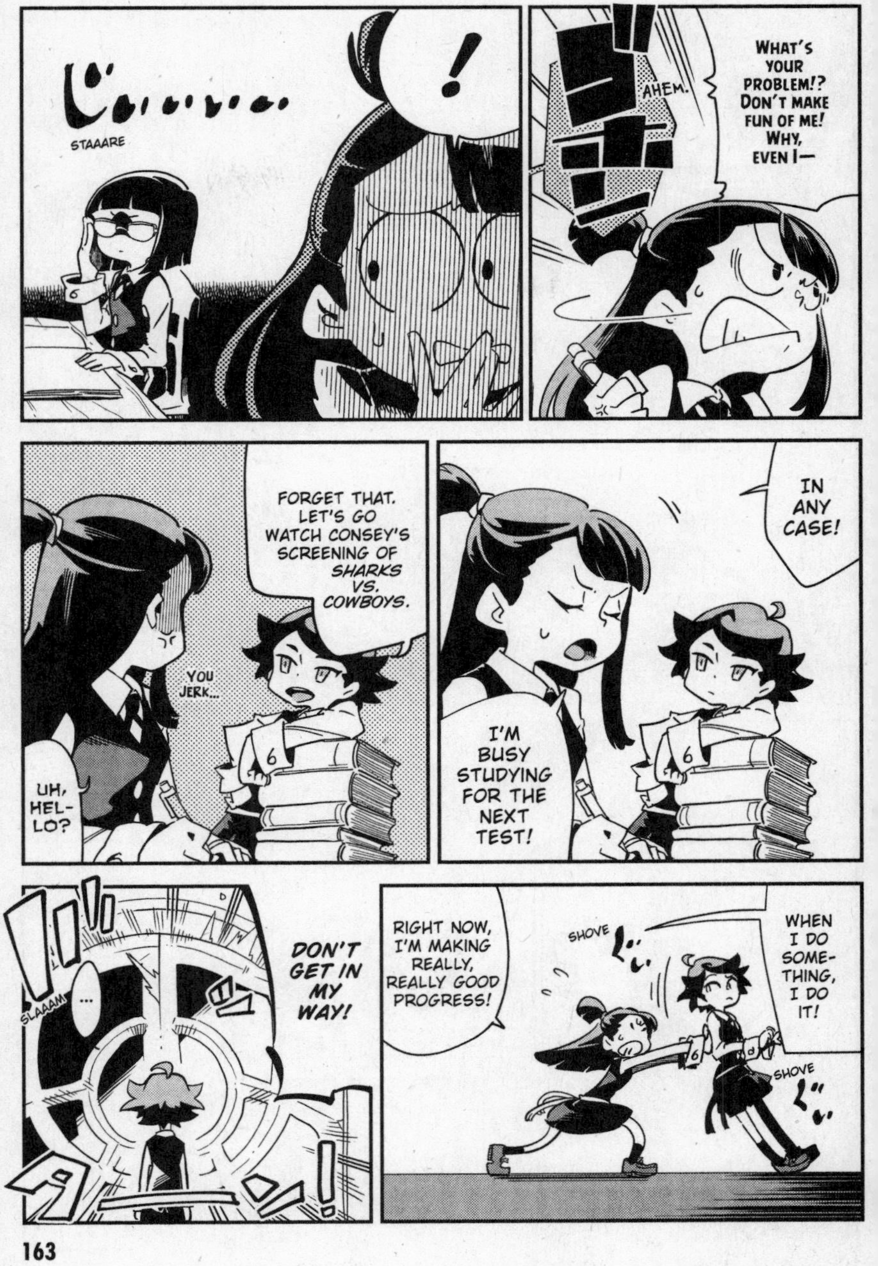
WHAT'S YOUR PROBLEM!? DON'T MAKE FUN OF ME! WHY, EVEN I—
AHEM.
!
STAAARE
IN ANY CASE!
I'M BUSY STUDYING FOR THE NEXT TEST!
FORGET THAT. LET'S GO WATCH CONSEY'S SCREENING OF *SHARKS VS. COWBOYS.*
YOU JERK...
UH, HEL-LO?
WHEN I DO SOME-THING, I DO IT!
RIGHT NOW, I'M MAKING REALLY, REALLY GOOD PROGRESS!
SHOVE
SHOVE
DON'T GET IN MY WAY!
...
SLAAAM

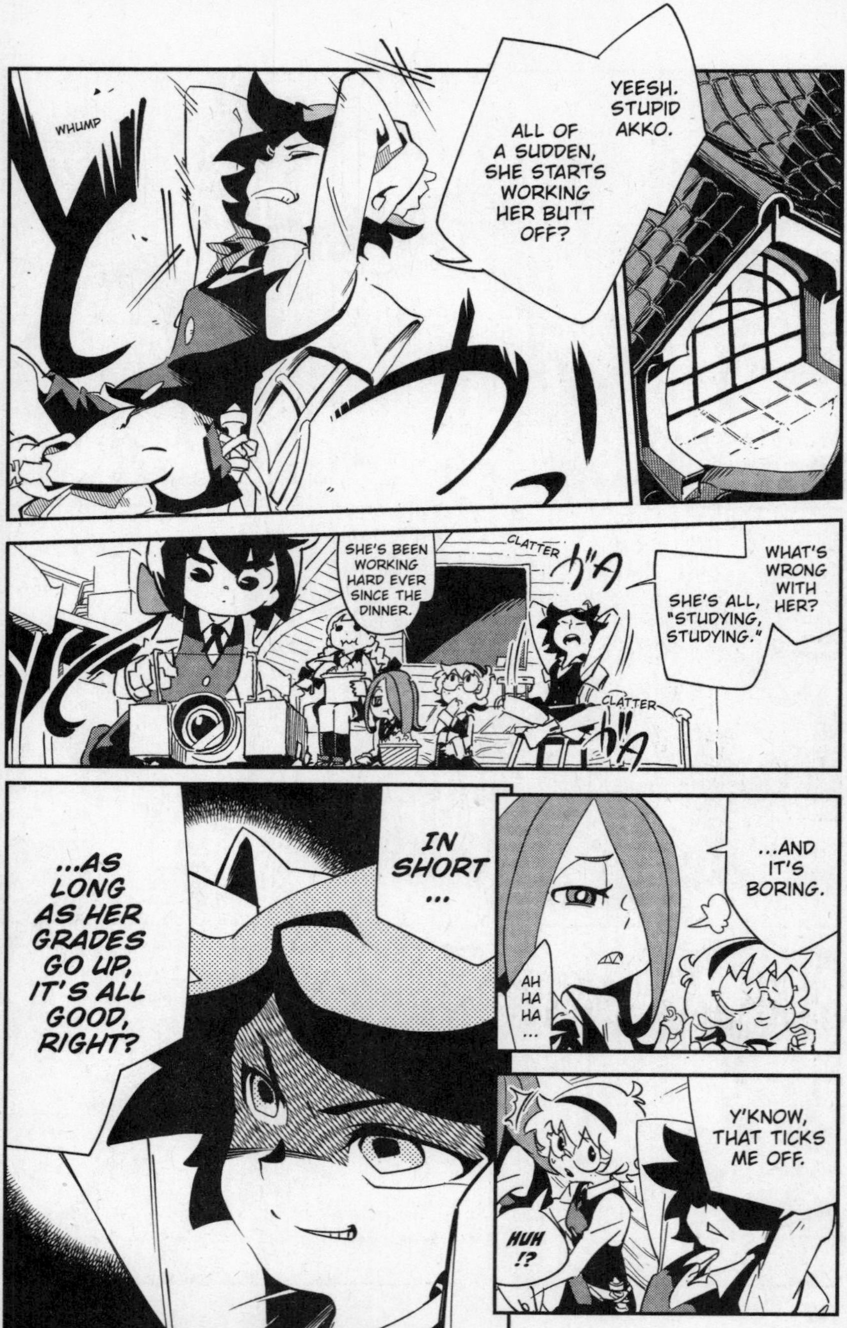
YEESH. STUPID AKKO.
ALL OF A SUDDEN, SHE STARTS WORKING HER BUTT OFF?
WHUMP
WHAT'S WRONG WITH HER?
SHE'S ALL, "STUDYING, STUDYING."
CLATTER
SHE'S BEEN WORKING HARD EVER SINCE THE DINNER.
CLATTER
...AND IT'S BORING.
AH HA HA...
Y'KNOW, THAT TICKS ME OFF.
HUH!?
IN SHORT...
...AS LONG AS HER GRADES GO UP, IT'S ALL GOOD, RIGHT?

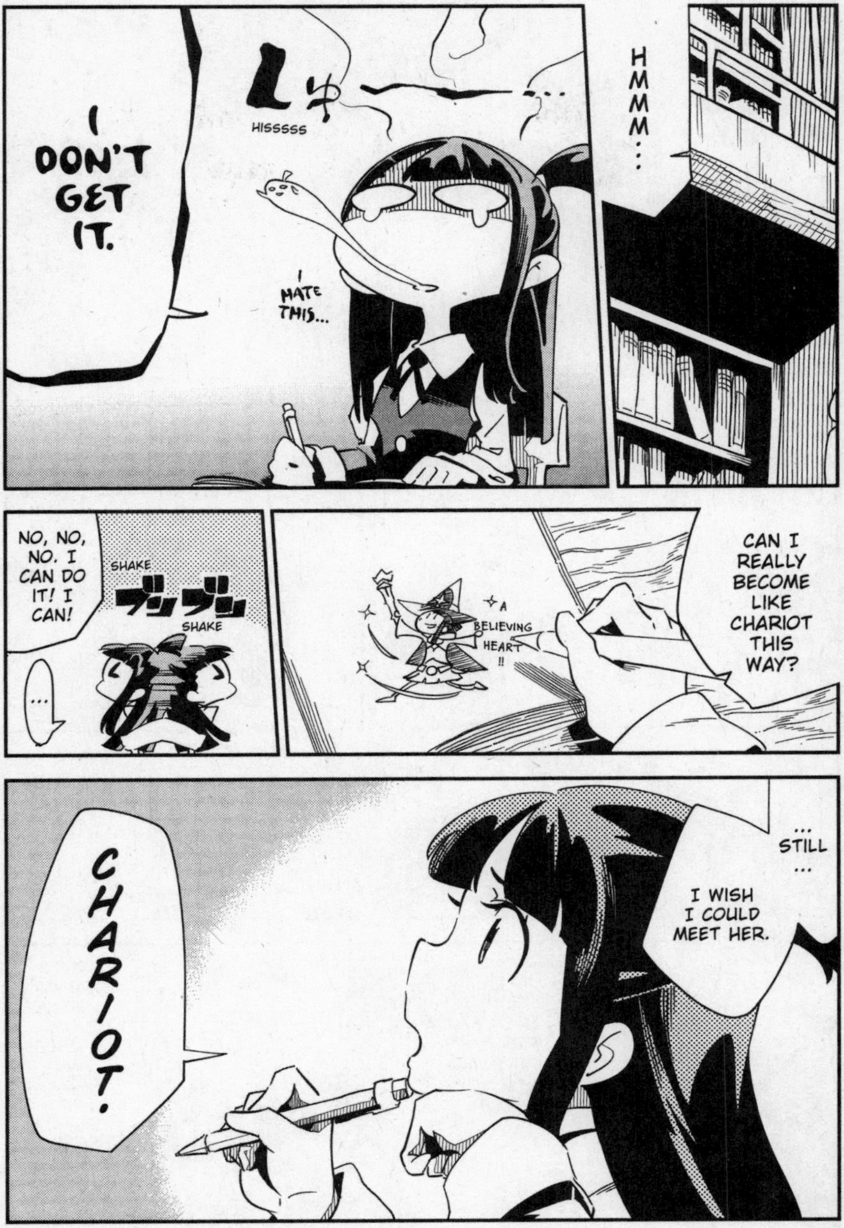
HMMM...
HISSSSS
I HATE THIS...
I DON'T GET IT.
CAN I REALLY BECOME LIKE CHARIOT THIS WAY?
A BELIEVING HEART!!
NO, NO, NO. I CAN DO IT! I CAN!
SHAKE
SHAKE
...
...STILL...
I WISH I COULD MEET HER.
CHARIOT.

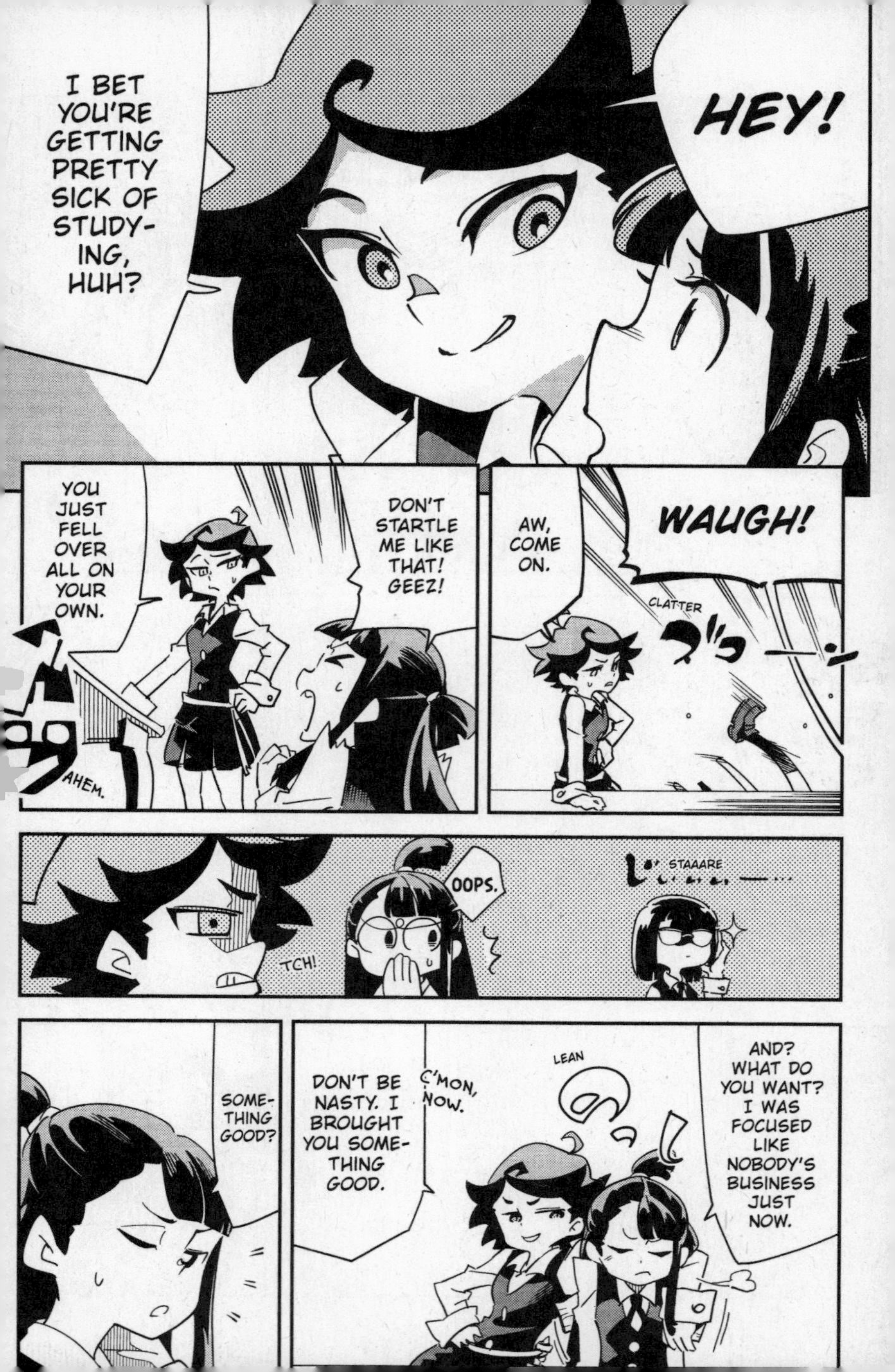
HEY!
I BET YOU'RE GETTING PRETTY SICK OF STUDYING, HUH?
WAUGH!
CLATTER
AW, COME ON.
DON'T STARTLE ME LIKE THAT! GEEZ!
YOU JUST FELL OVER ALL ON YOUR OWN.
AHEM.
STAAARE
OOPS.
TCH!
AND? WHAT DO YOU WANT? I WAS FOCUSED LIKE NOBODY'S BUSINESS JUST NOW.
LEAN
C'MON, NOW.
DON'T BE NASTY. I BROUGHT YOU SOMETHING GOOD.
SOMETHING GOOD?

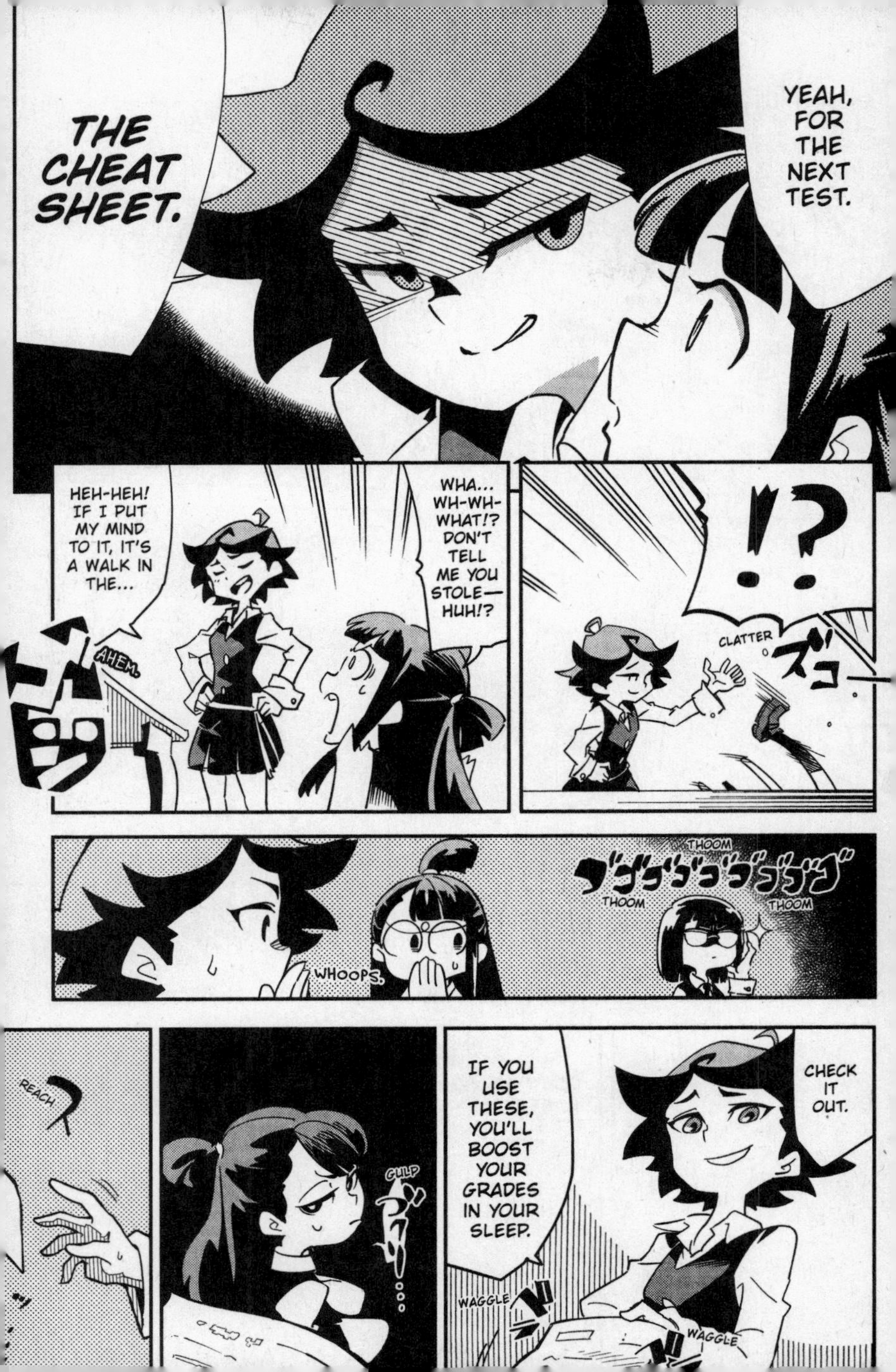
YEAH, FOR THE NEXT TEST.
THE CHEAT SHEET.
!?
CLATTER
WHA... WH-WH-WHAT!? DON'T TELL ME YOU STOLE— HUH!?
HEH-HEH! IF I PUT MY MIND TO IT, IT'S A WALK IN THE...
AHEM.
THOOM
THOOM
THOOM
WHOOPS.
CHECK IT OUT.
IF YOU USE THESE, YOU'LL BOOST YOUR GRADES IN YOUR SLEEP.
WAGGLE
WAGGLE
GULP
REACH

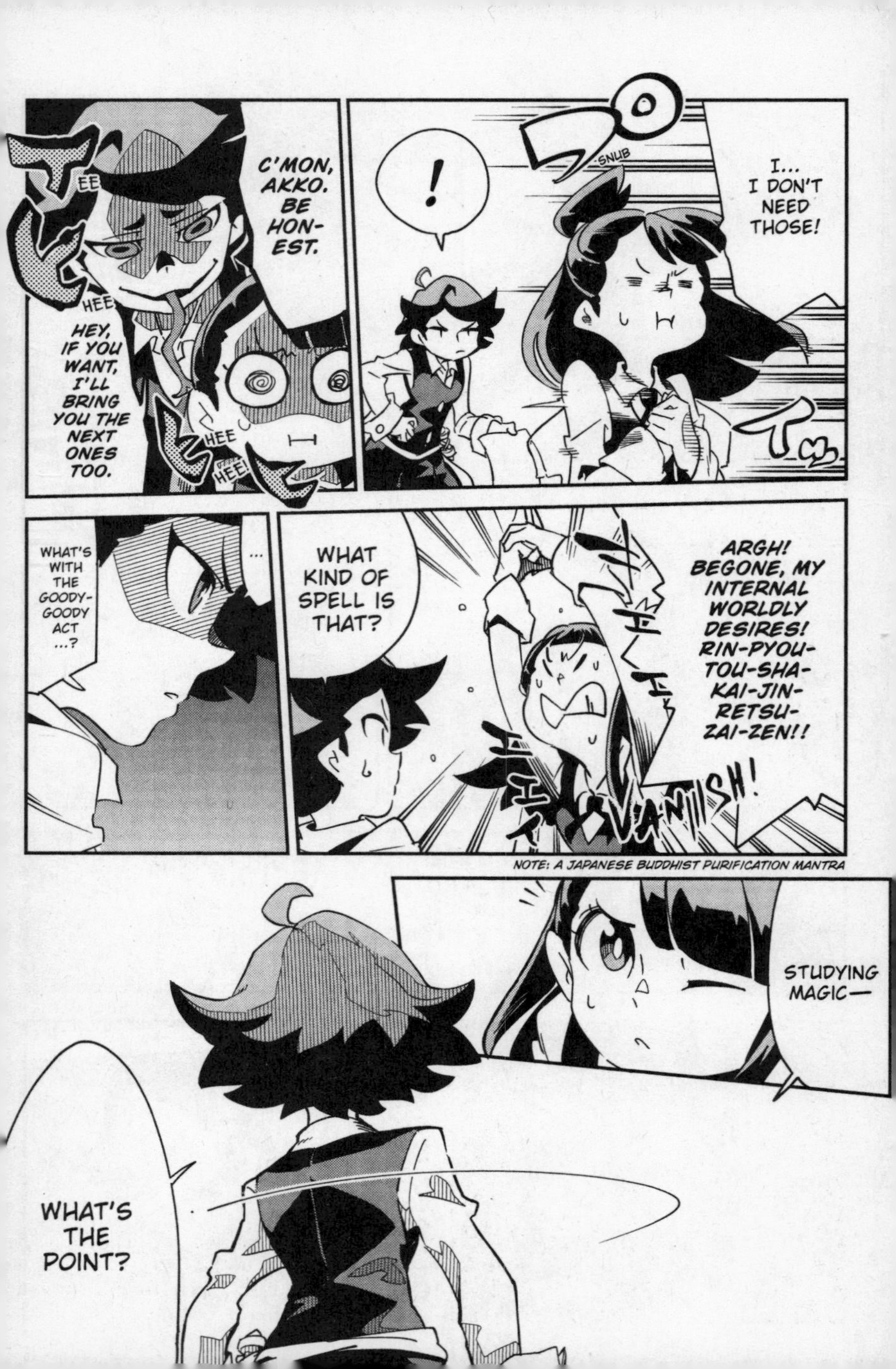
I... I DON'T NEED THOSE!
SNUB
!
C'MON, AKKO. BE HON-EST.
HEE
HEE
HEY, IF YOU WANT, I'LL BRING YOU THE NEXT ONES TOO.
HEE
HEE!
ARGH! BEGONE, MY INTERNAL WORLDLY DESIRES! RIN-PYOU-TOU-SHA-KAI-JIN-RETSU-ZAI-ZEN!!
WHAT KIND OF SPELL IS THAT?
VANISH!
...
WHAT'S WITH THE GOODY-GOODY ACT ...?
NOTE: A JAPANESE BUDDHIST PURIFICATION MANTRA
STUDYING MAGIC—
WHAT'S THE POINT?

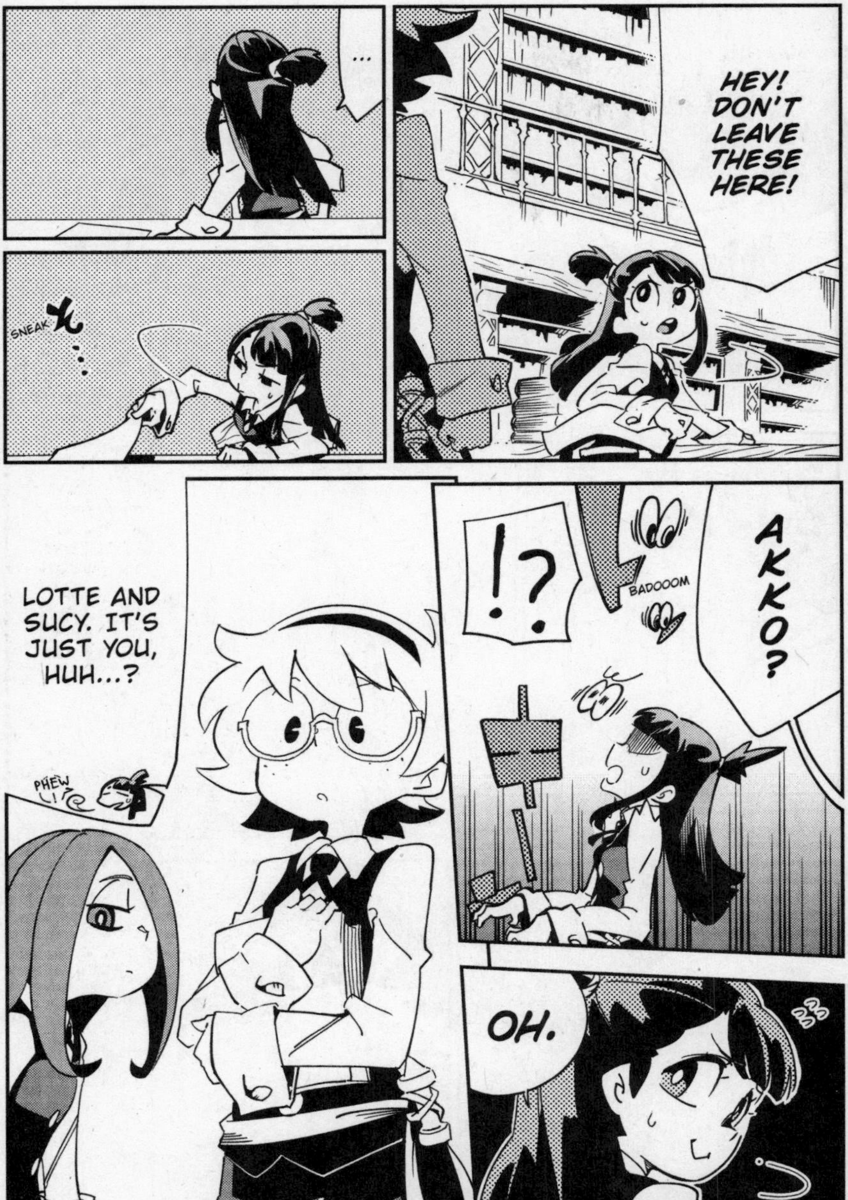
HEY! DON'T LEAVE THESE HERE!
...
SNEAK
AKKO?
!?
BADOOOM
OH.
LOTTE AND SUCY. IT'S JUST YOU, HUH...?
PHEW

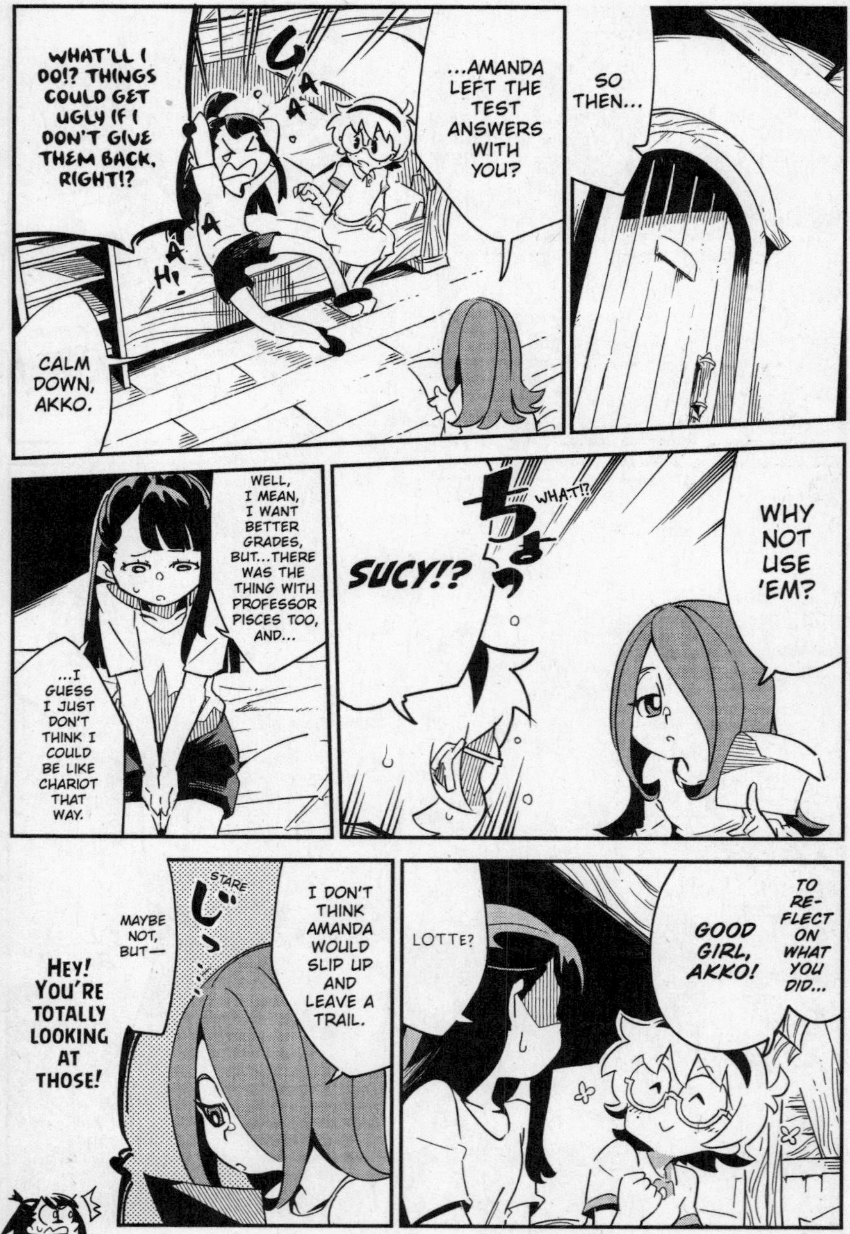
SO THEN...
...AMANDA LEFT THE TEST ANSWERS WITH YOU?
WHAT'LL I DO!? THINGS COULD GET UGLY IF I DON'T GIVE THEM BACK, RIGHT!?
CALM DOWN, AKKO.
WHY NOT USE 'EM?
WHAT!?
SUCY!?
WELL, I MEAN, I WANT BETTER GRADES, BUT...THERE WAS THE THING WITH PROFESSOR PISCES TOO, AND...
...I GUESS I JUST DON'T THINK I COULD BE LIKE CHARIOT THAT WAY.
TO RE-FLECT ON WHAT YOU DID...
GOOD GIRL, AKKO!
LOTTE?
I DON'T THINK AMANDA WOULD SLIP UP AND LEAVE A TRAIL.
STARE
MAYBE NOT, BUT—
HEY! YOU'RE TOTALLY LOOKING AT THOSE!

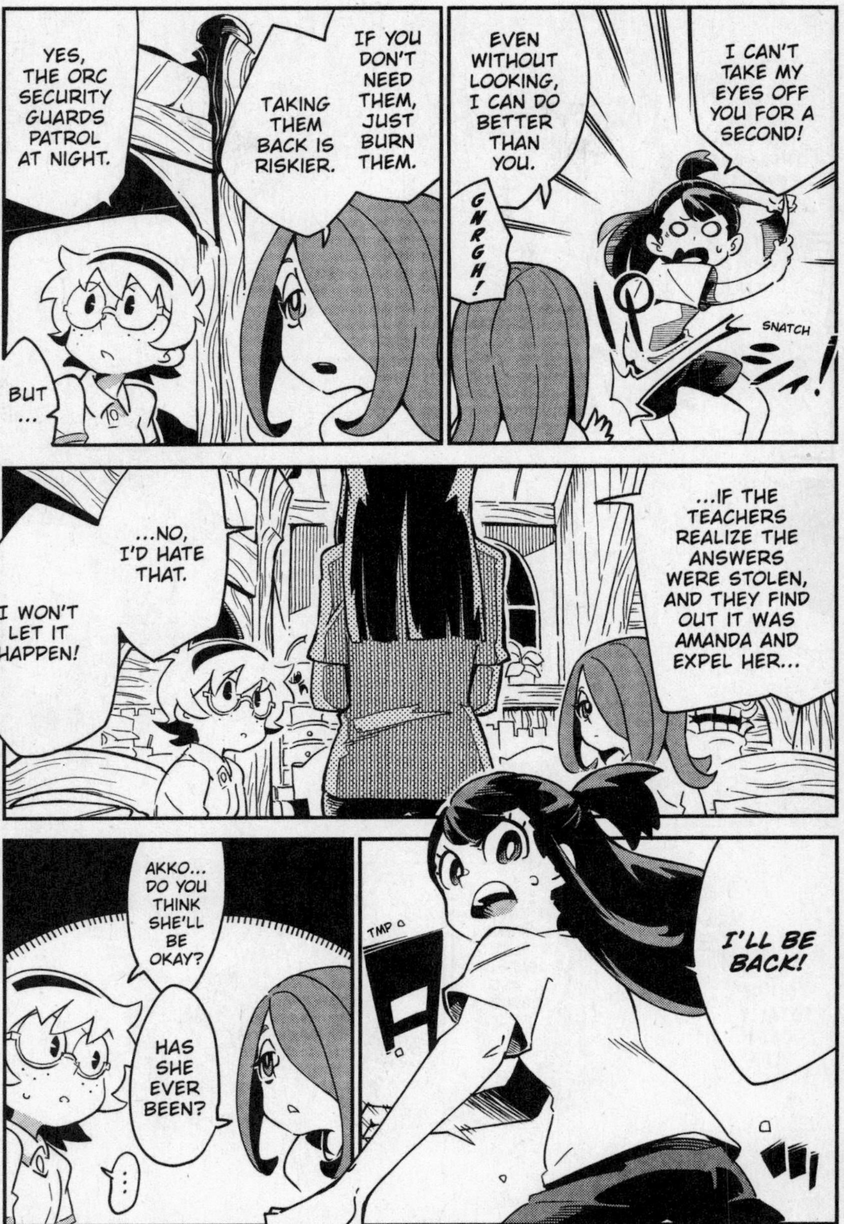
I CAN'T TAKE MY EYES OFF YOU FOR A SECOND!
EVEN WITHOUT LOOKING, I CAN DO BETTER THAN YOU.
GNRGH!
SNATCH
IF YOU DON'T NEED THEM, JUST BURN THEM.
TAKING THEM BACK IS RISKIER.
YES, THE ORC SECURITY GUARDS PATROL AT NIGHT.
BUT ...
...IF THE TEACHERS REALIZE THE ANSWERS WERE STOLEN, AND THEY FIND OUT IT WAS AMANDA AND EXPEL HER...
...NO, I'D HATE THAT.
I WON'T LET IT HAPPEN!
I'LL BE BACK!
TMP
AKKO... DO YOU THINK SHE'LL BE OKAY?
HAS SHE EVER BEEN?
...

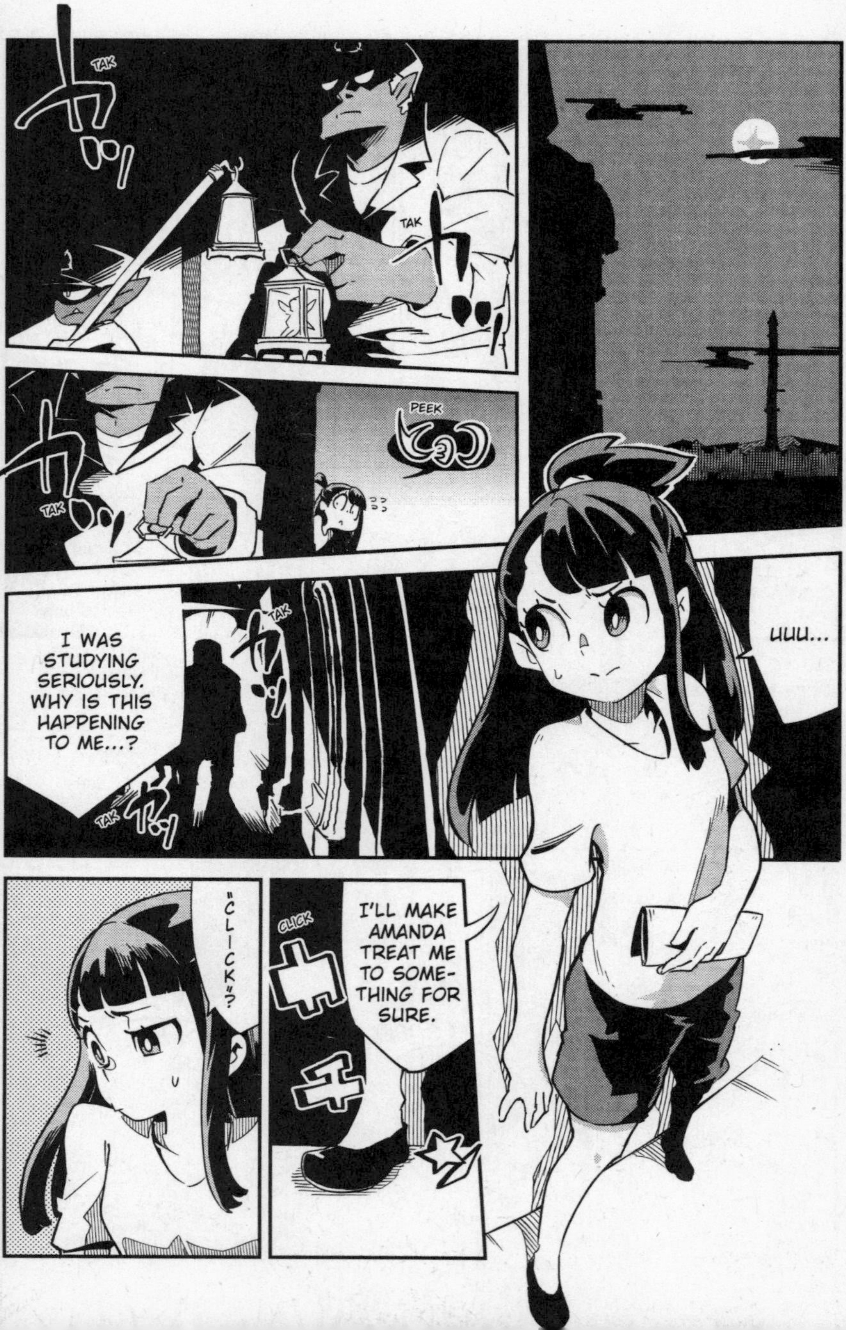
TAK
TAK
TAK
PEEK
TAK
uuu...
I WAS STUDYING SERIOUSLY. WHY IS THIS HAPPENING TO ME...?
TAK
TAK
I'LL MAKE AMANDA TREAT ME TO SOME-THING FOR SURE.
CLICK
"CLICK"?

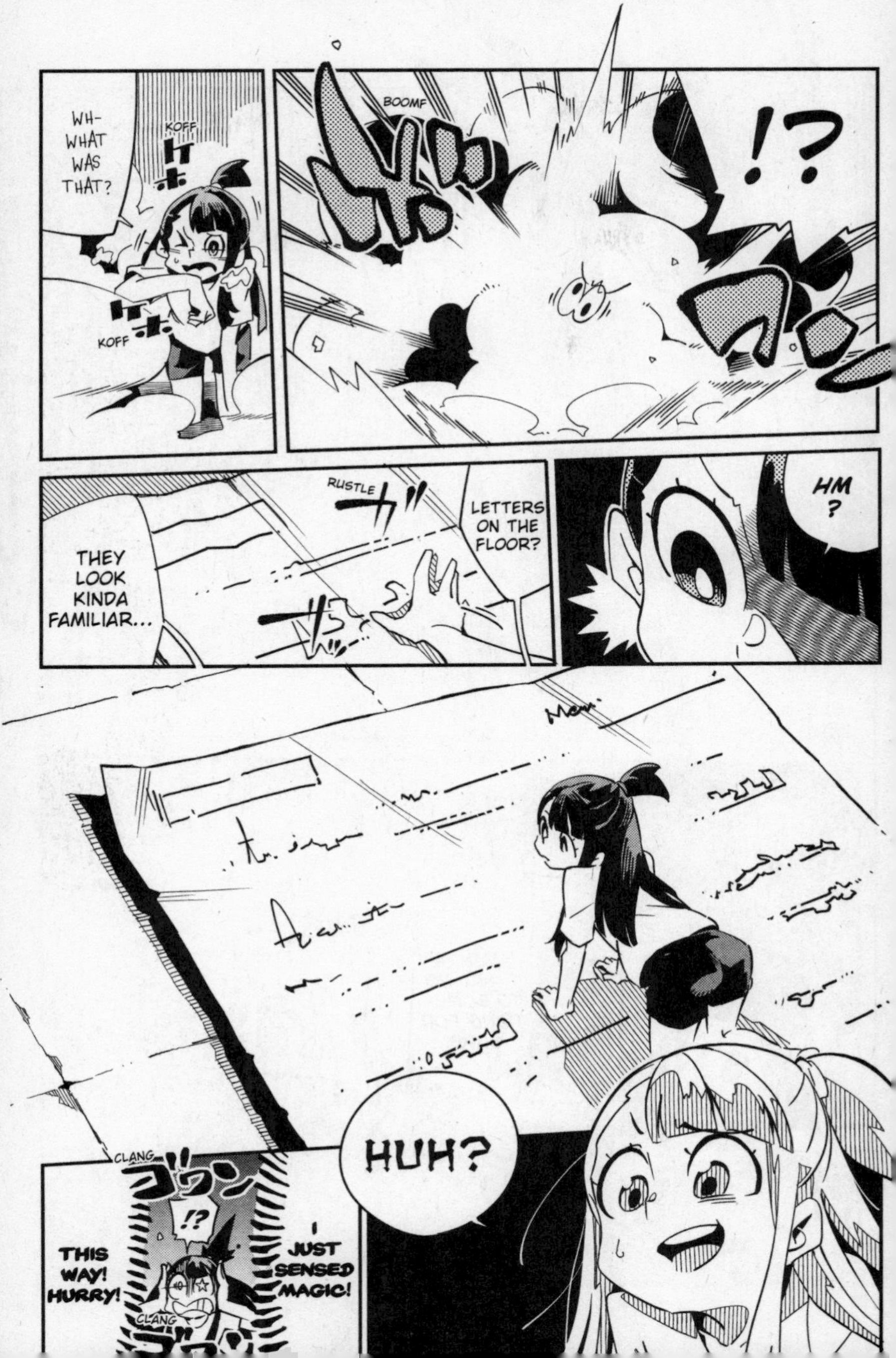
BOOMF
!?
KOFF
WH- WHAT WAS THAT?
KOFF
HM?
RUSTLE
LETTERS ON THE FLOOR?
THEY LOOK KINDA FAMILIAR...
HUH?
CLANG
!?
I JUST SENSED MAGIC!
THIS WAY! HURRY!
CLANG

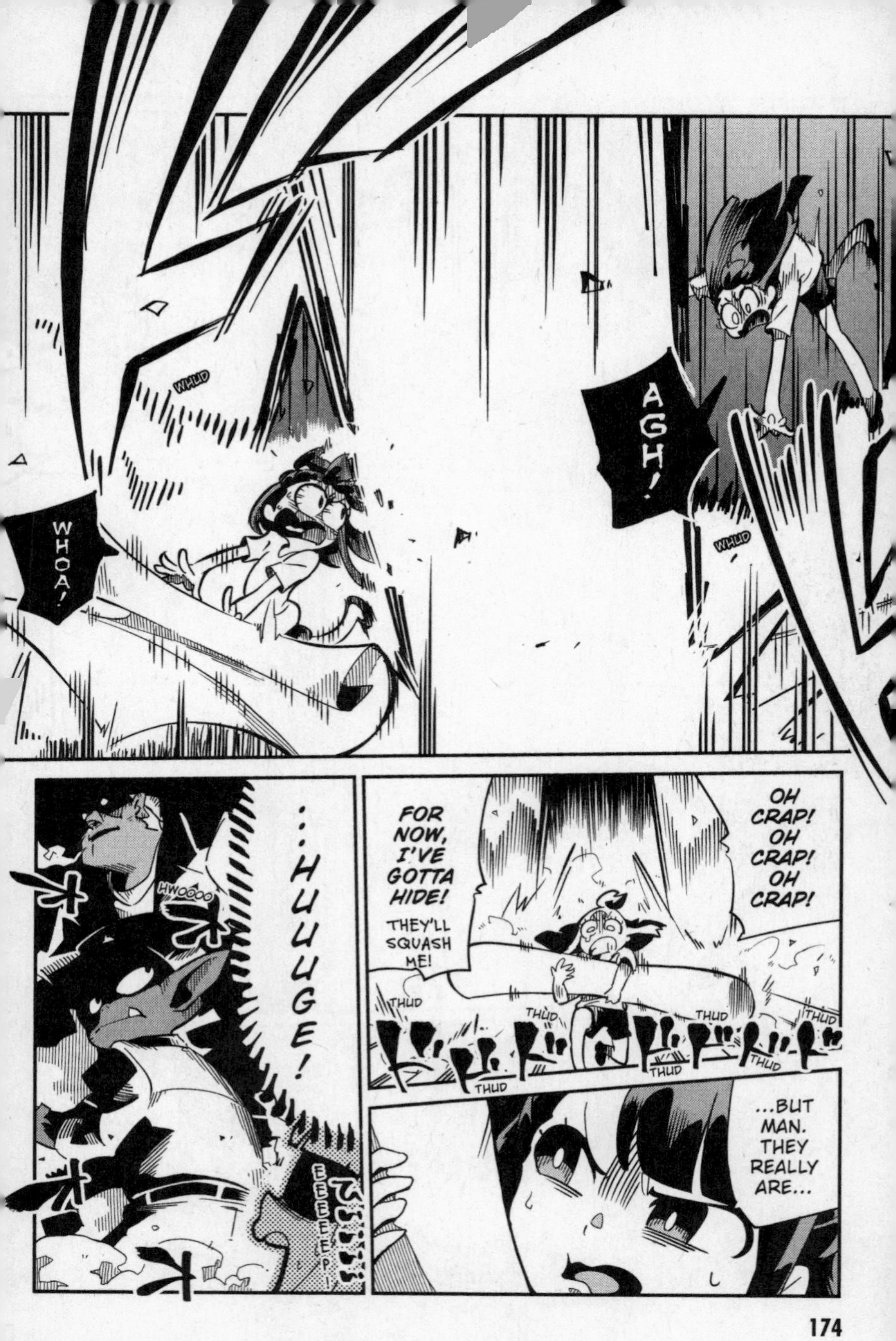
AGH!
WHUD
WHUD
WHOA!
OH CRAP! OH CRAP! OH CRAP!
FOR NOW, I'VE GOTTA HIDE!
THEY'LL SQUASH ME!
THUD
THUD
THUD
THUD
THUD
THUD
THUD
THUD
...BUT MAN. THEY REALLY ARE...
...HUUUGE!
HWOOOO
EEEEEEP!

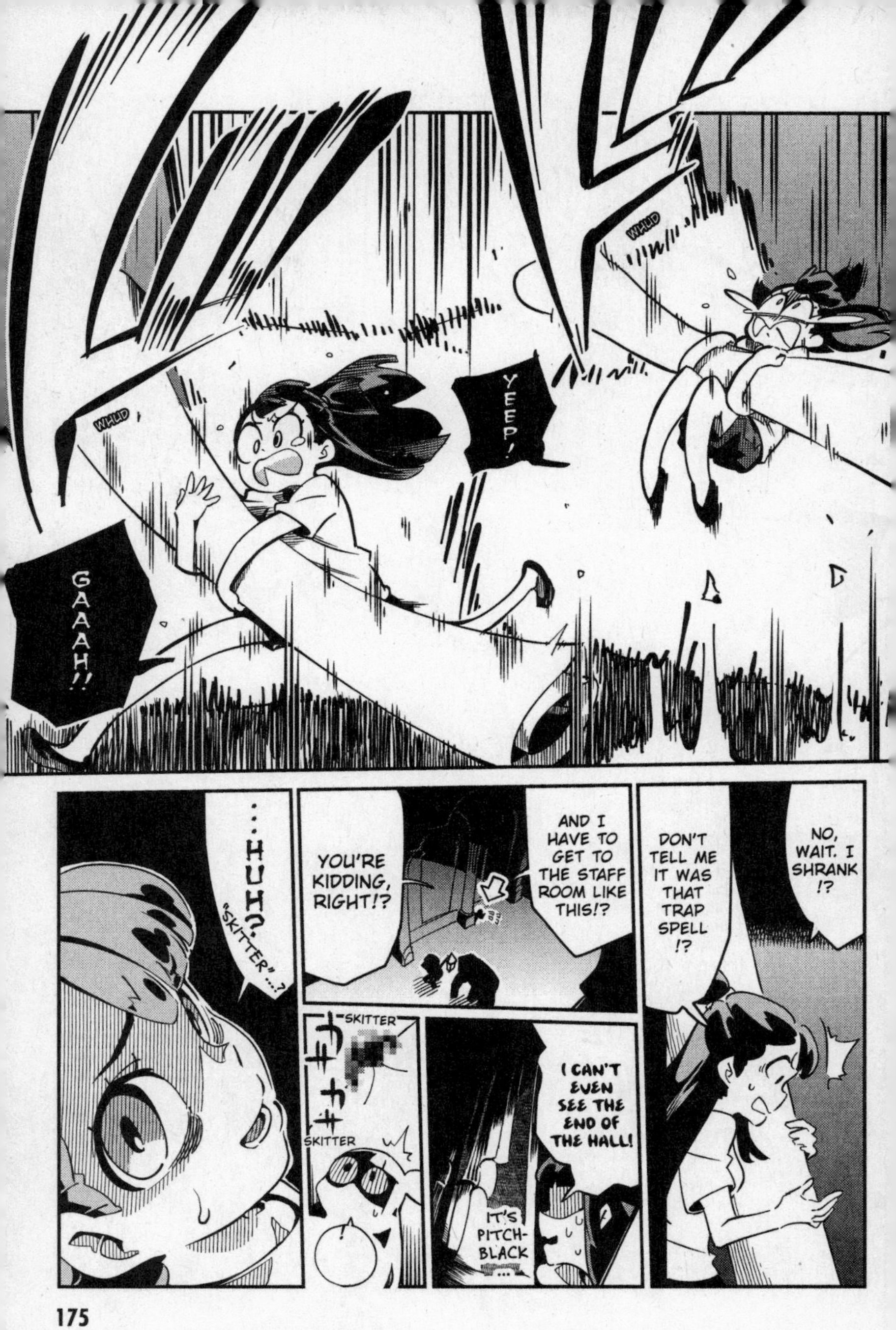
WHUD
YEEP!
WHUD
GAAAH!!
NO, WAIT. I SHRANK!?
DON'T TELL ME IT WAS THAT TRAP SPELL!?
AND I HAVE TO GET TO THE STAFF ROOM LIKE THIS!?
YOU'RE KIDDING, RIGHT!?
I CAN'T EVEN SEE THE END OF THE HALL!
IT'S PITCH-BLACK...
SKITTER
SKITTER
...HUH? "SKITTER"...?

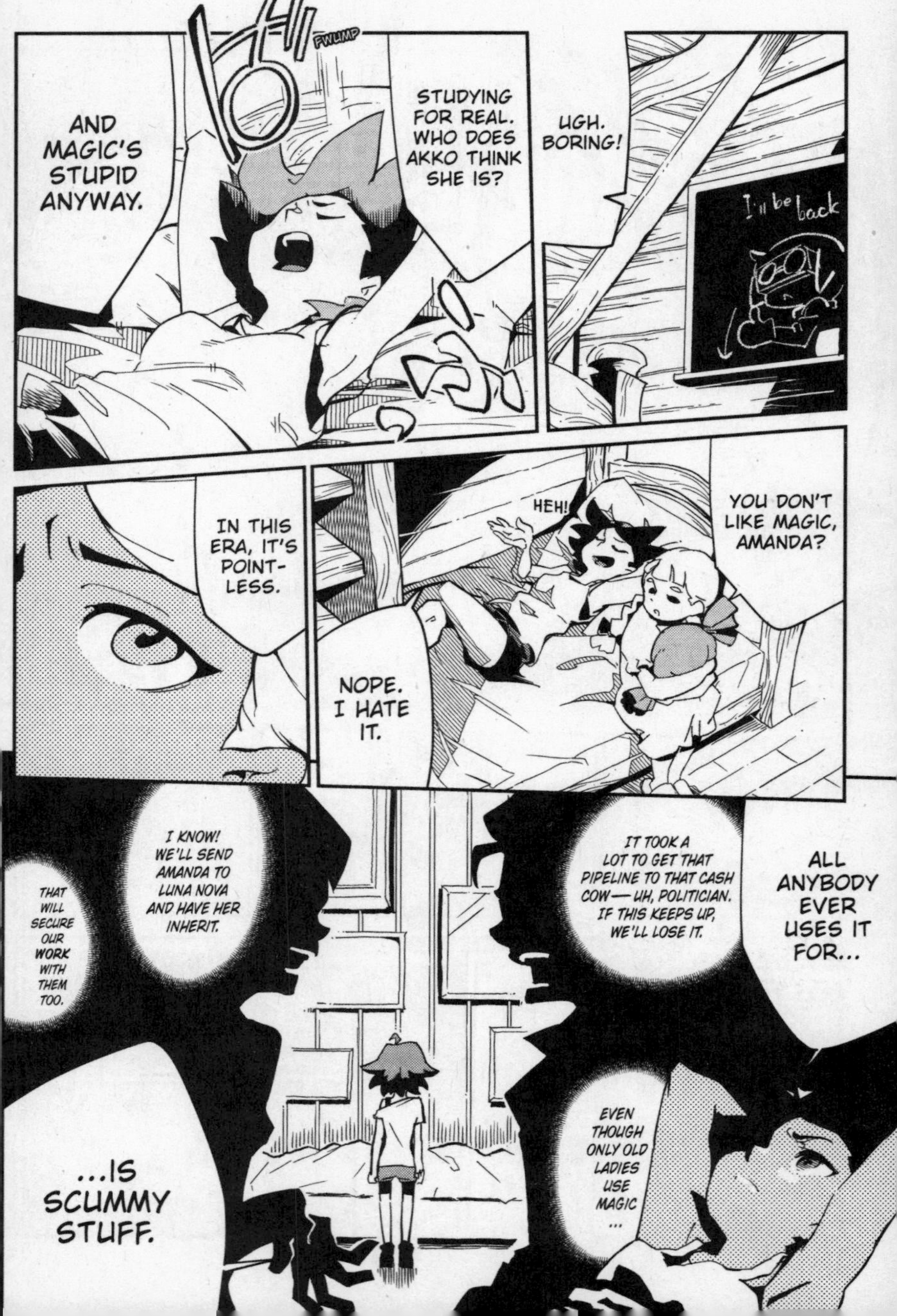
I'll be back
UGH. BORING!
FWUMP
STUDYING FOR REAL. WHO DOES AKKO THINK SHE IS?
AND MAGIC'S STUPID ANYWAY.
YOU DON'T LIKE MAGIC, AMANDA?
HEH!
NOPE. I HATE IT.
IN THIS ERA, IT'S POINT-LESS.
ALL ANYBODY EVER USES IT FOR...
IT TOOK A LOT TO GET THAT PIPELINE TO THAT CASH COW— UH, POLITICIAN. IF THIS KEEPS UP, WE'LL LOSE IT.
EVEN THOUGH ONLY OLD LADIES USE MAGIC ...
I KNOW! WE'LL SEND AMANDA TO LUNA NOVA AND HAVE HER INHERIT.
THAT WILL SECURE OUR WORK WITH THEM TOO.
...IS SCUMMY STUFF.

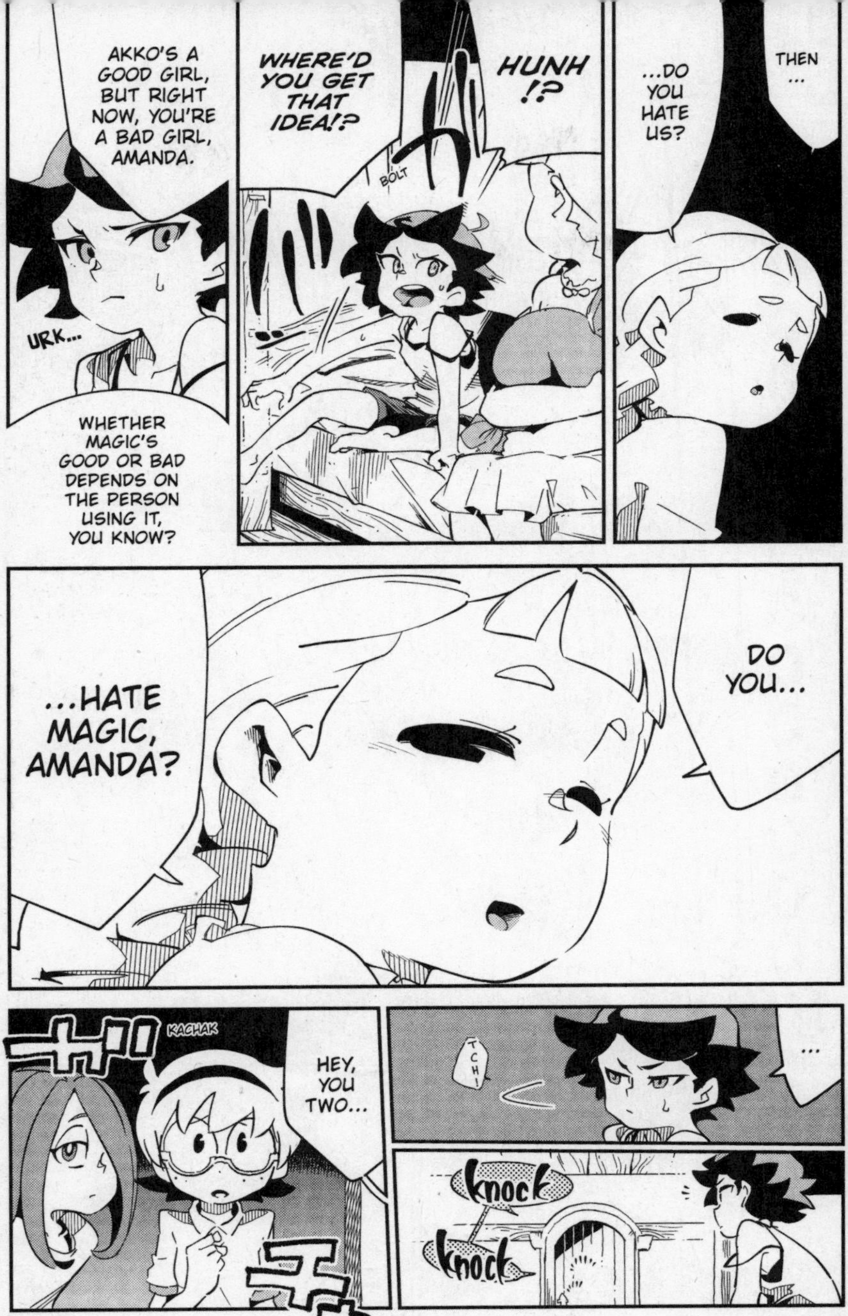
THEN...
...DO YOU HATE US?
HUNH!?
WHERE'D YOU GET THAT IDEA!?
BOLT
AKKO'S A GOOD GIRL, BUT RIGHT NOW, YOU'RE A BAD GIRL, AMANDA.
URK...
WHETHER MAGIC'S GOOD OR BAD DEPENDS ON THE PERSON USING IT, YOU KNOW?
DO YOU...
...HATE MAGIC, AMANDA?
...
TCH!
knock
knock
KACHAK
HEY, YOU TWO...

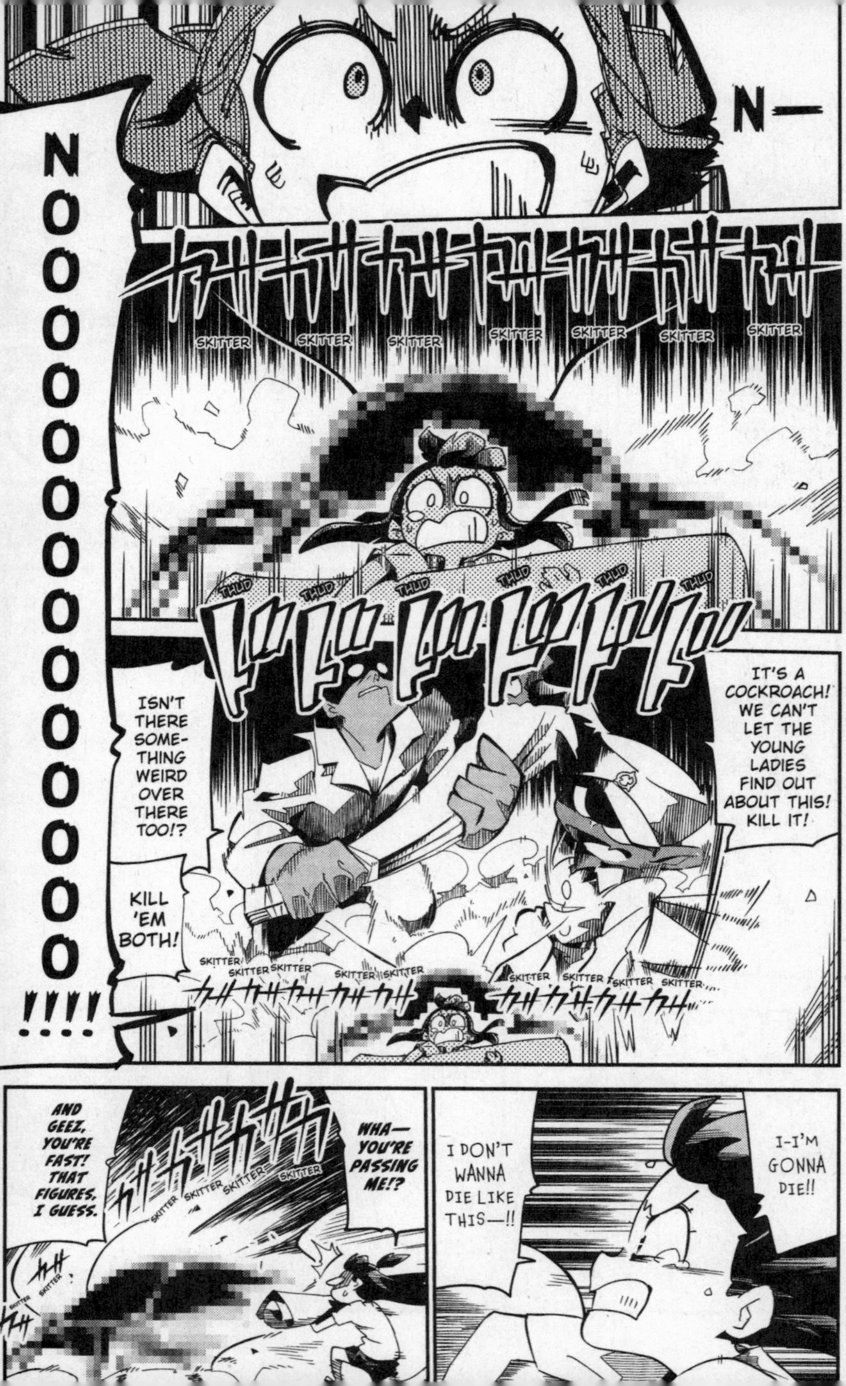
N—
NOOOOOOOOOOOOOOO!!!!
SKITTER SKITTER SKITTER SKITTER SKITTER SKITTER SKITTER
THUD THUD THUD THUD THUD THUD
IT'S A COCKROACH! WE CAN'T LET THE YOUNG LADIES FIND OUT ABOUT THIS! KILL IT!
ISN'T THERE SOME-THING WEIRD OVER THERE TOO!?
KILL 'EM BOTH!
SKITTER SKITTER SKITTER SKITTER SKITTER SKITTER SKITTER SKITTER SKITTER
I-I'M GONNA DIE!!
I DON'T WANNA DIE LIKE THIS—!!
WHA— YOU'RE PASSING ME!?
AND GEEZ, YOU'RE FAST! THAT FIGURES, I GUESS.
SKITTER SKITTER SKITTER SKITTER
SKITTER SKITTER

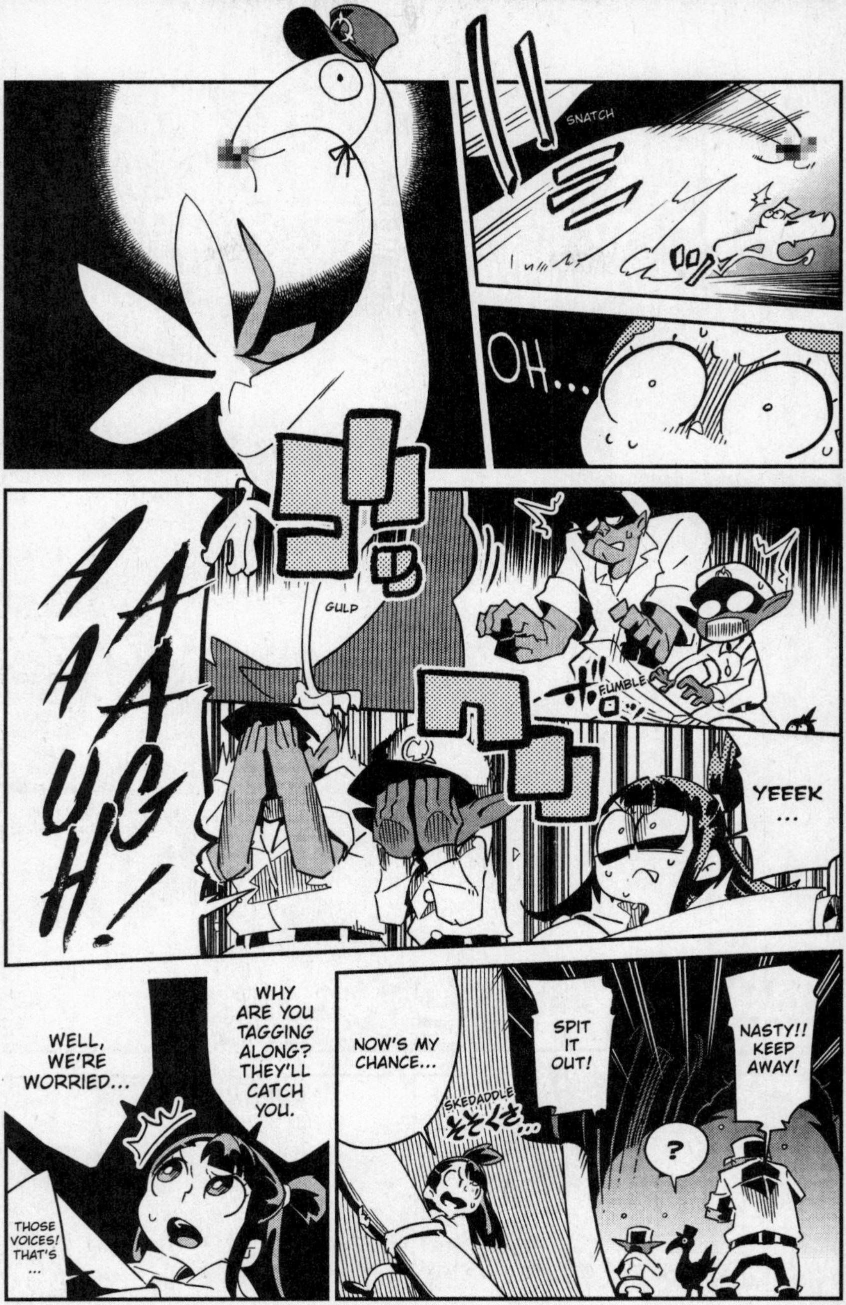
SNATCH
OH...
FUMBLE
GULP
YEEEK ...
AAAAUGH!
NASTY!! KEEP AWAY!
SPIT IT OUT!
?
NOW'S MY CHANCE...
SKEDADDLE
WHY ARE YOU TAGGING ALONG? THEY'LL CATCH YOU.
WELL, WE'RE WORRIED...
THOSE VOICES! THAT'S ...

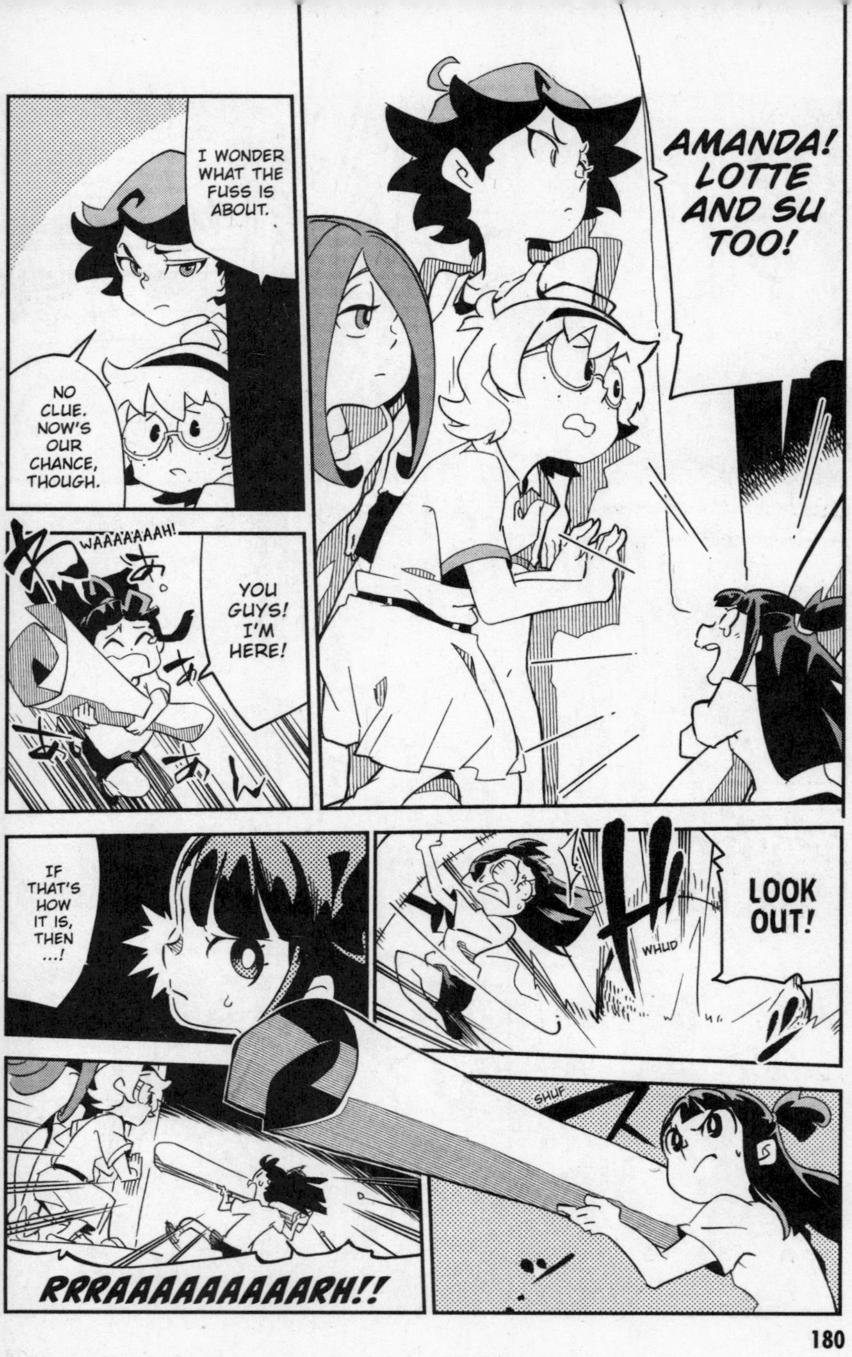
AMANDA! LOTTE AND SU TOO!
I WONDER WHAT THE FUSS IS ABOUT.
NO CLUE. NOW'S OUR CHANCE, THOUGH.
WAAAAAAAH!
YOU GUYS! I'M HERE!
LOOK OUT!
WHUD
IF THAT'S HOW IT IS, THEN ...!
SHUF
RRRAAAAAAAAAARH!!

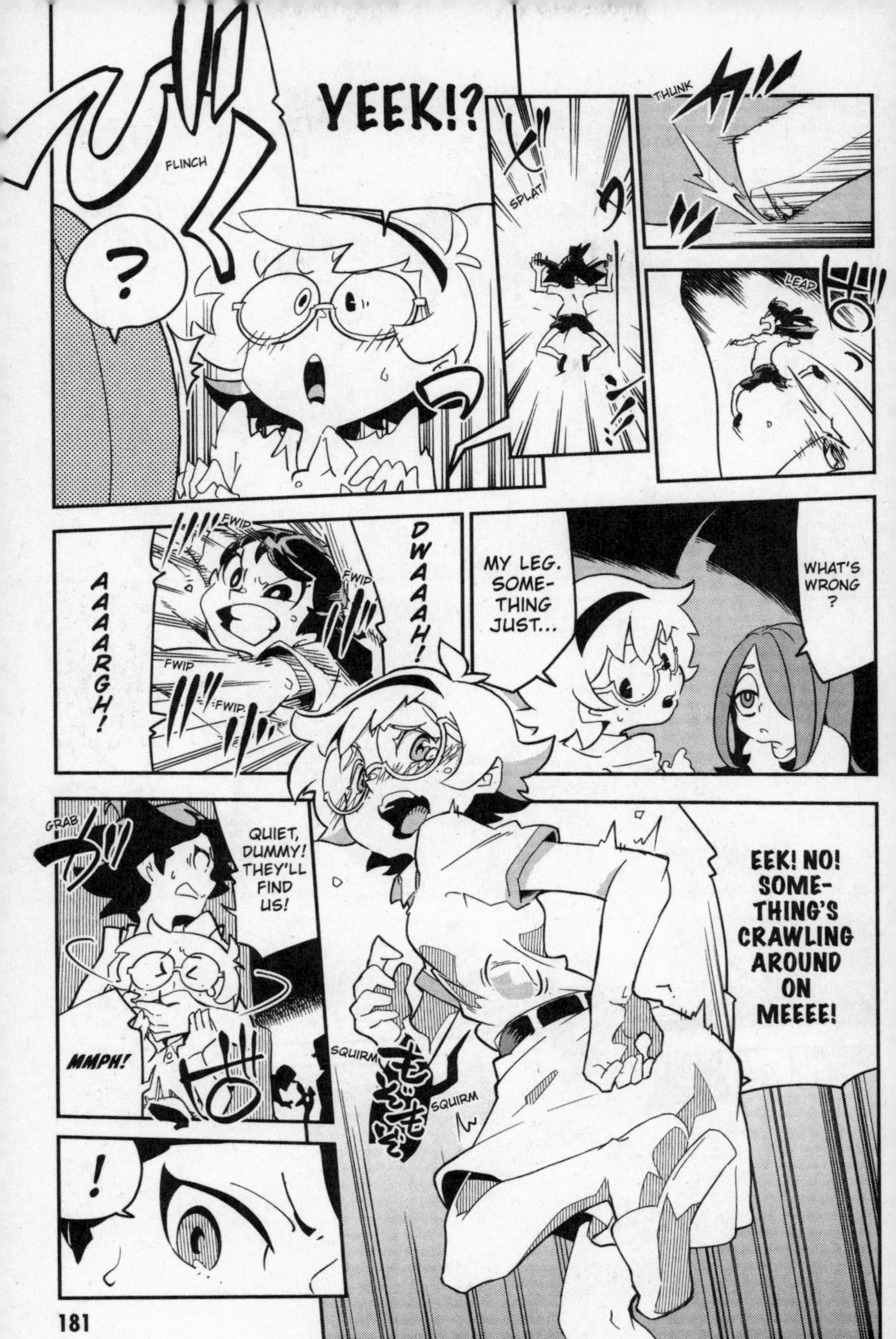
THUNK
LEAP
SPLAT
YEEK!?
FLINCH
?
WHAT'S WRONG?
MY LEG. SOME-THING JUST...
DWAAAAH!
FWIP
FWIP
AAAAARGH!
FWIP
FWIP
EEK! NO! SOME-THING'S CRAWLING AROUND ON MEEEE!
SQUIRM
SQUIRM
GRAB
QUIET, DUMMY! THEY'LL FIND US!
MMPH!
!

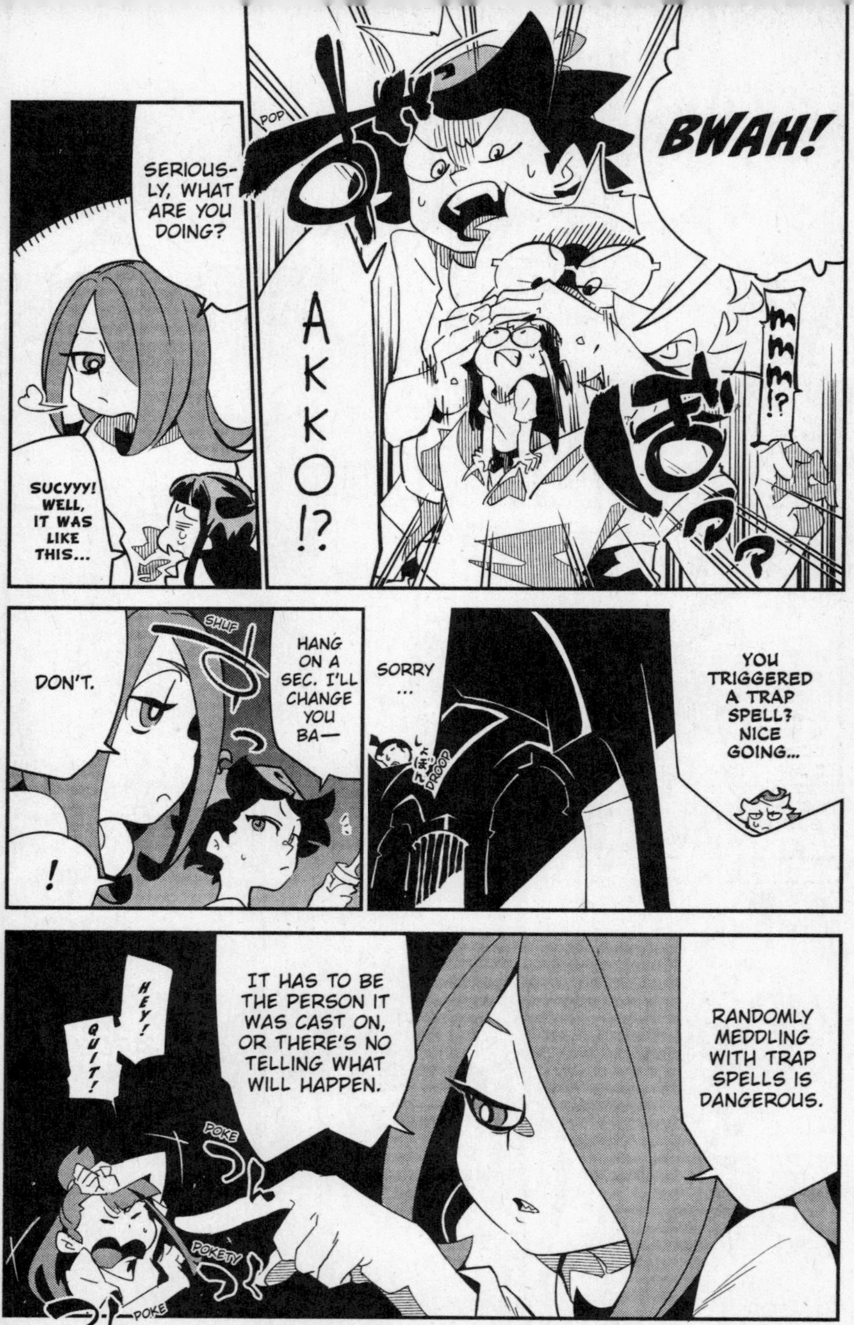
BWAH!
POP
MMMM!?
AKKO!?
SERIOUS-LY, WHAT ARE YOU DOING?
SUCYYY! WELL, IT WAS LIKE THIS...
YOU TRIGGERED A TRAP SPELL? NICE GOING...
SORRY...
DROOP
HANG ON A SEC. I'LL CHANGE YOU BA—
SHUF
DON'T.
!
RANDOMLY MEDDLING WITH TRAP SPELLS IS DANGEROUS.
IT HAS TO BE THE PERSON IT WAS CAST ON, OR THERE'S NO TELLING WHAT WILL HAPPEN.
HEY!
QUIT!
POKE
POKETY
POKE

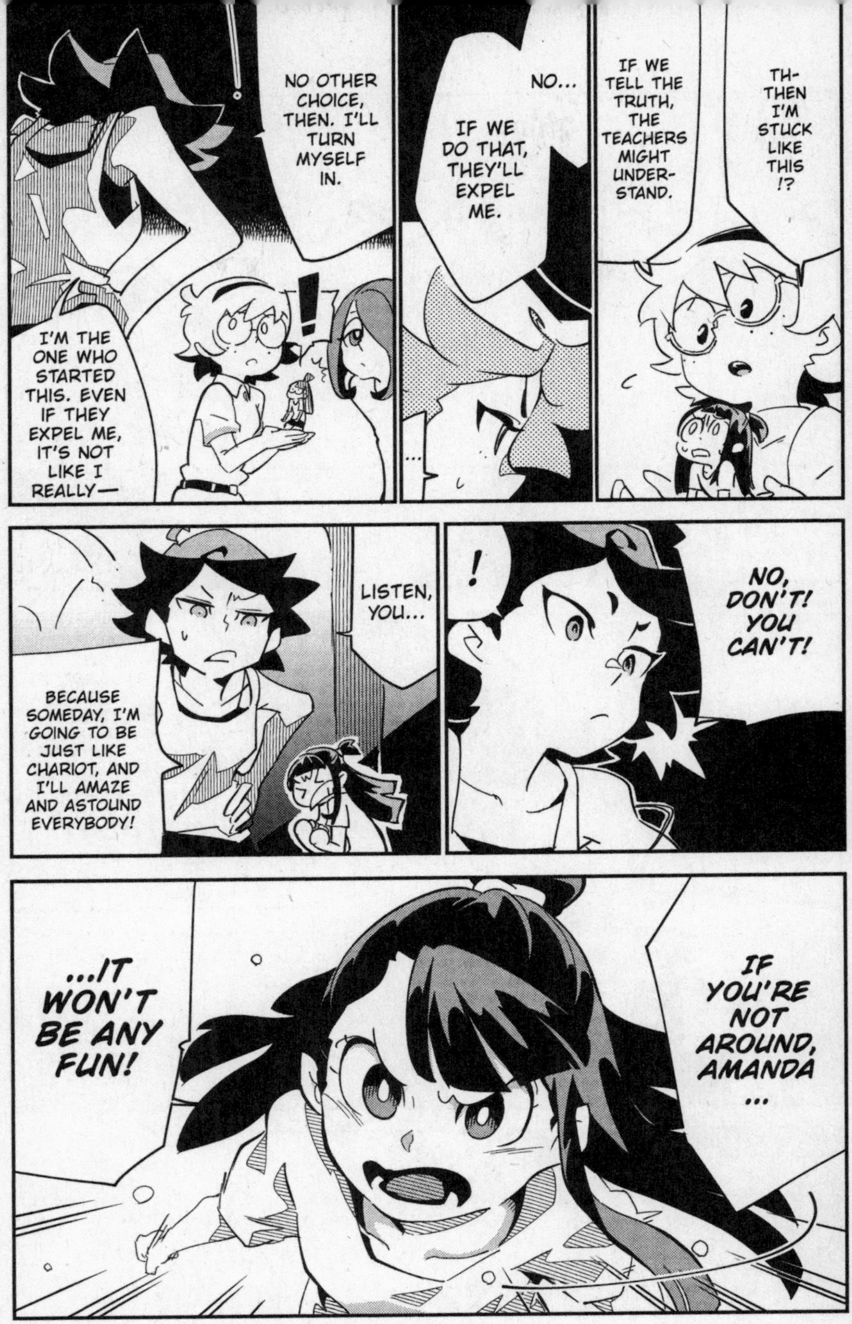
TH-THEN I'M STUCK LIKE THIS!?
IF WE TELL THE TRUTH, THE TEACHERS MIGHT UNDER-STAND.
NO...
IF WE DO THAT, THEY'LL EXPEL ME.
...
!
NO OTHER CHOICE, THEN. I'LL TURN MYSELF IN.
!
I'M THE ONE WHO STARTED THIS. EVEN IF THEY EXPEL ME, IT'S NOT LIKE I REALLY—
NO, DON'T! YOU CAN'T!
!
LISTEN, YOU...
BECAUSE SOMEDAY, I'M GOING TO BE JUST LIKE CHARIOT, AND I'LL AMAZE AND ASTOUND EVERYBODY!
IF YOU'RE NOT AROUND, AMANDA...
...IT WON'T BE ANY FUN!

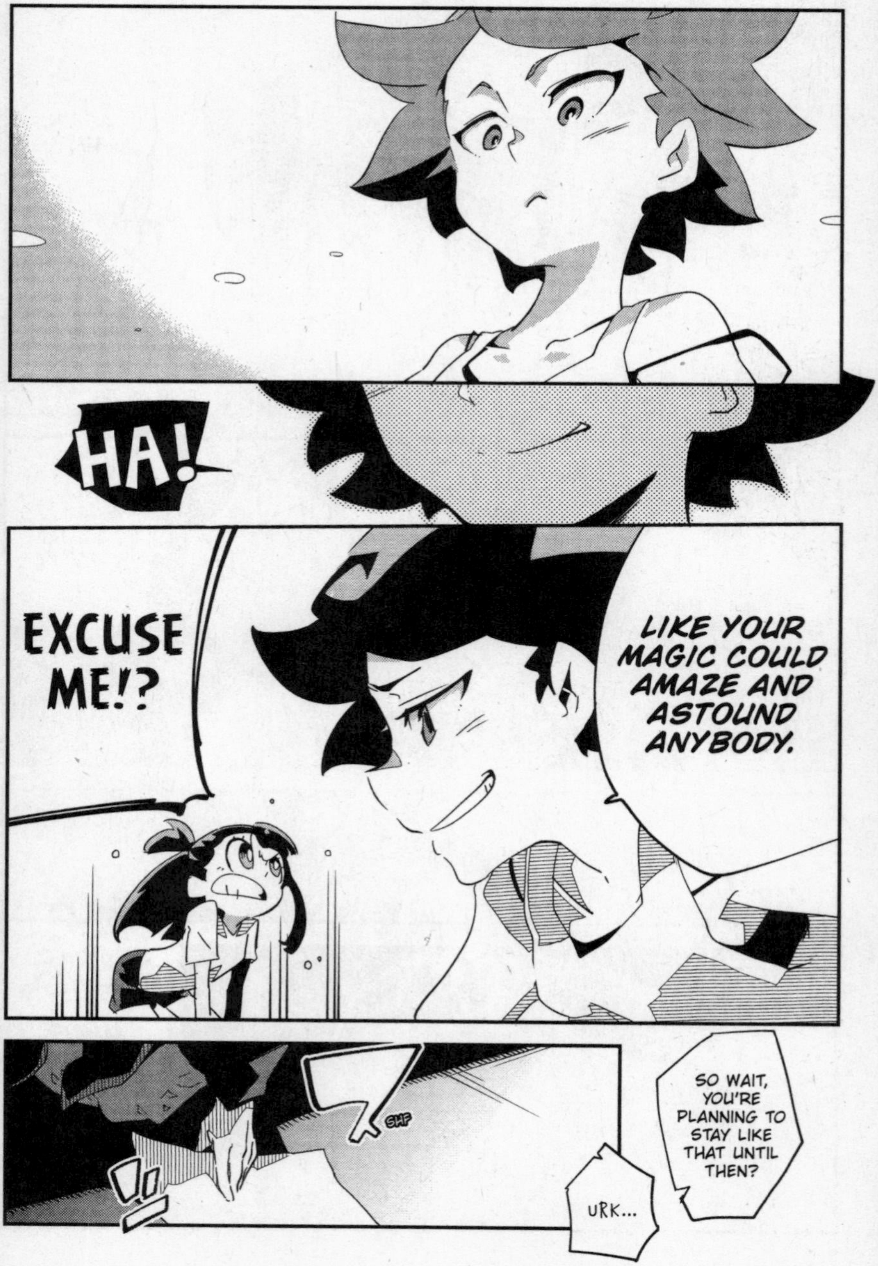
HA!
LIKE YOUR MAGIC COULD AMAZE AND ASTOUND ANYBODY.
EXCUSE ME!?
SO WAIT, YOU'RE PLANNING TO STAY LIKE THAT UNTIL THEN?
SHF
URK...
!!

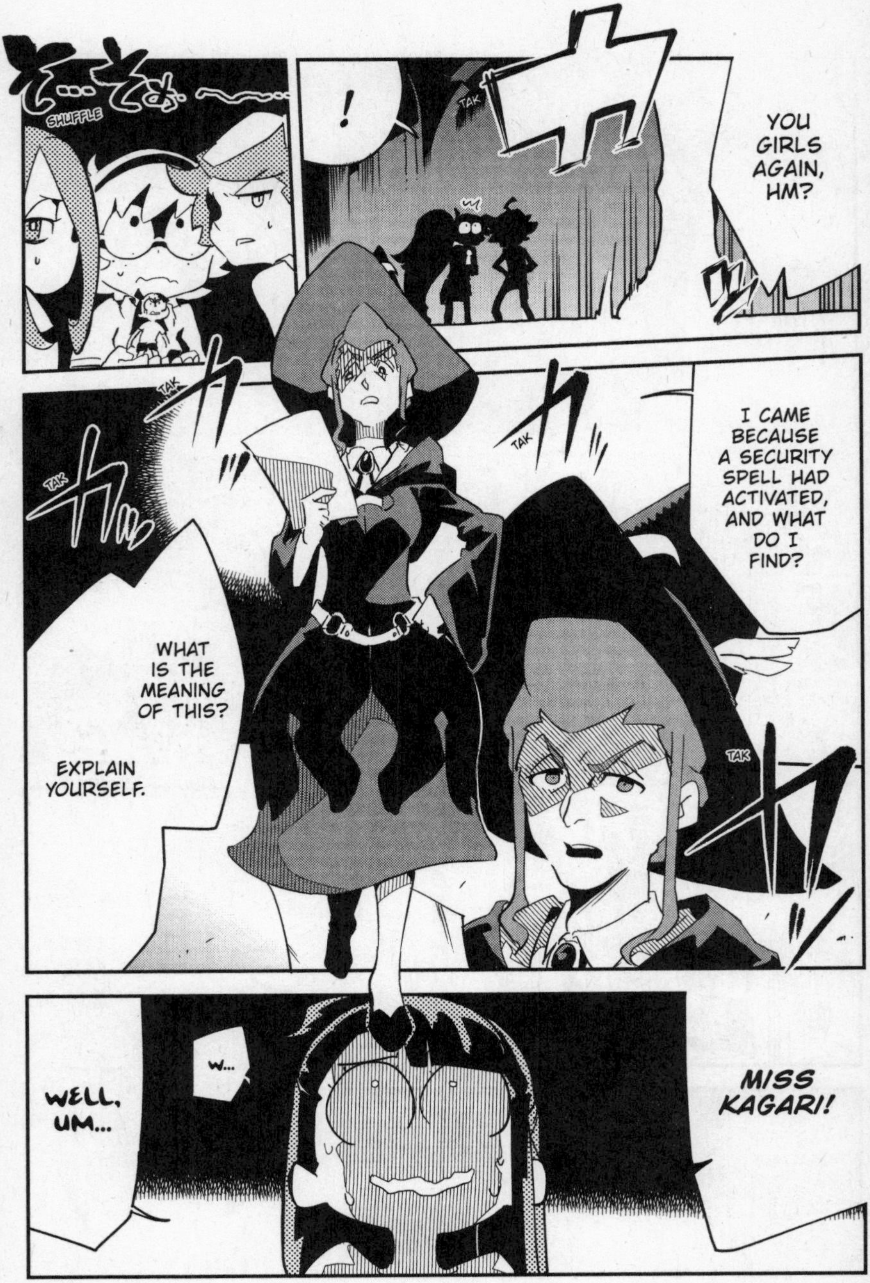
!
TAK
YOU GIRLS AGAIN, HM?
SHUFFLE
TAK
TAK
I CAME BECAUSE A SECURITY SPELL HAD ACTIVATED, AND WHAT DO I FIND?
TAK
TAK
WHAT IS THE MEANING OF THIS?
EXPLAIN YOURSELF.
MISS KAGARI!
W...
WELL, UM...

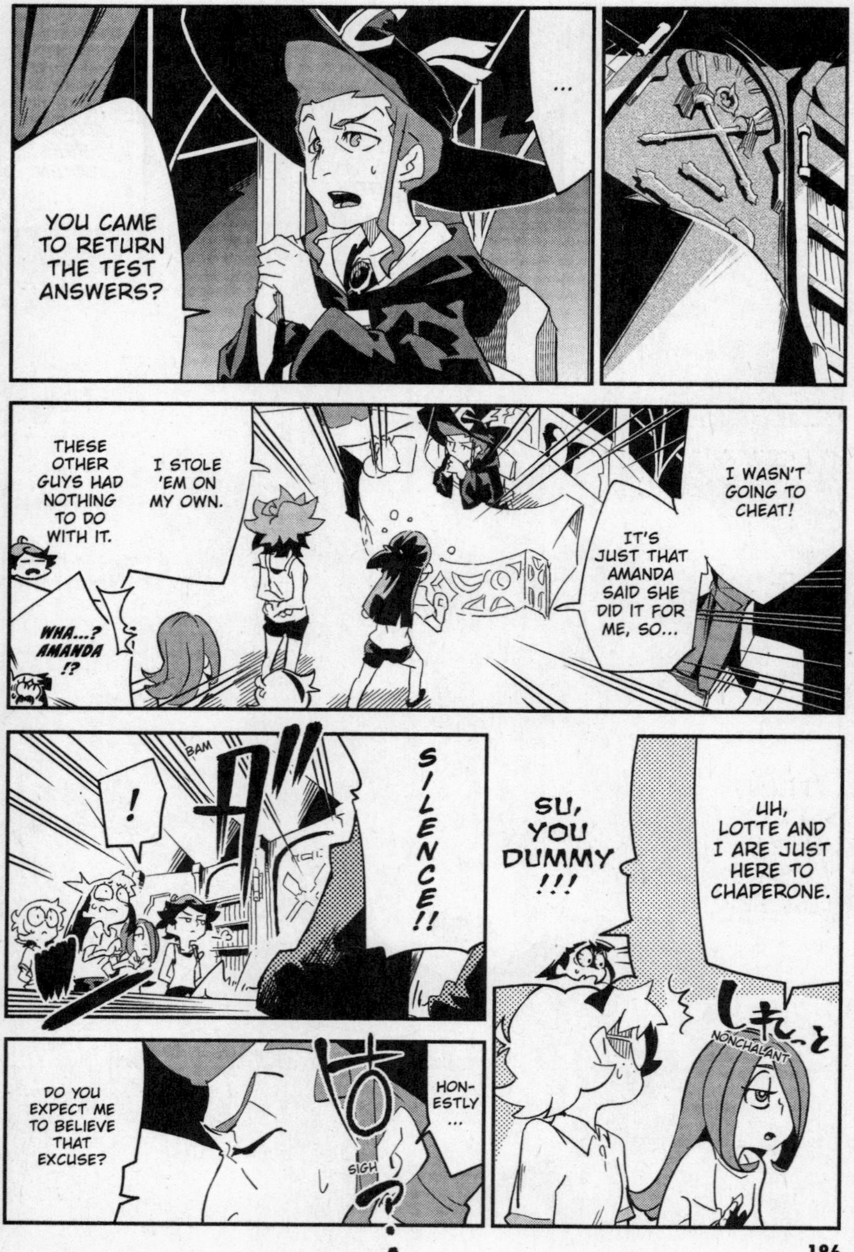
...
YOU CAME TO RETURN THE TEST ANSWERS?
I WASN'T GOING TO CHEAT!
IT'S JUST THAT AMANDA SAID SHE DID IT FOR ME, SO...
I STOLE 'EM ON MY OWN.
THESE OTHER GUYS HAD NOTHING TO DO WITH IT.
WHA...? AMANDA!?
UH, LOTTE AND I ARE JUST HERE TO CHAPERONE.
SU, YOU DUMMY!!!
NONCHALANT
SILENCE!!
BAM
!
HON-ESTLY...
SIGH
DO YOU EXPECT ME TO BELIEVE THAT EXCUSE?

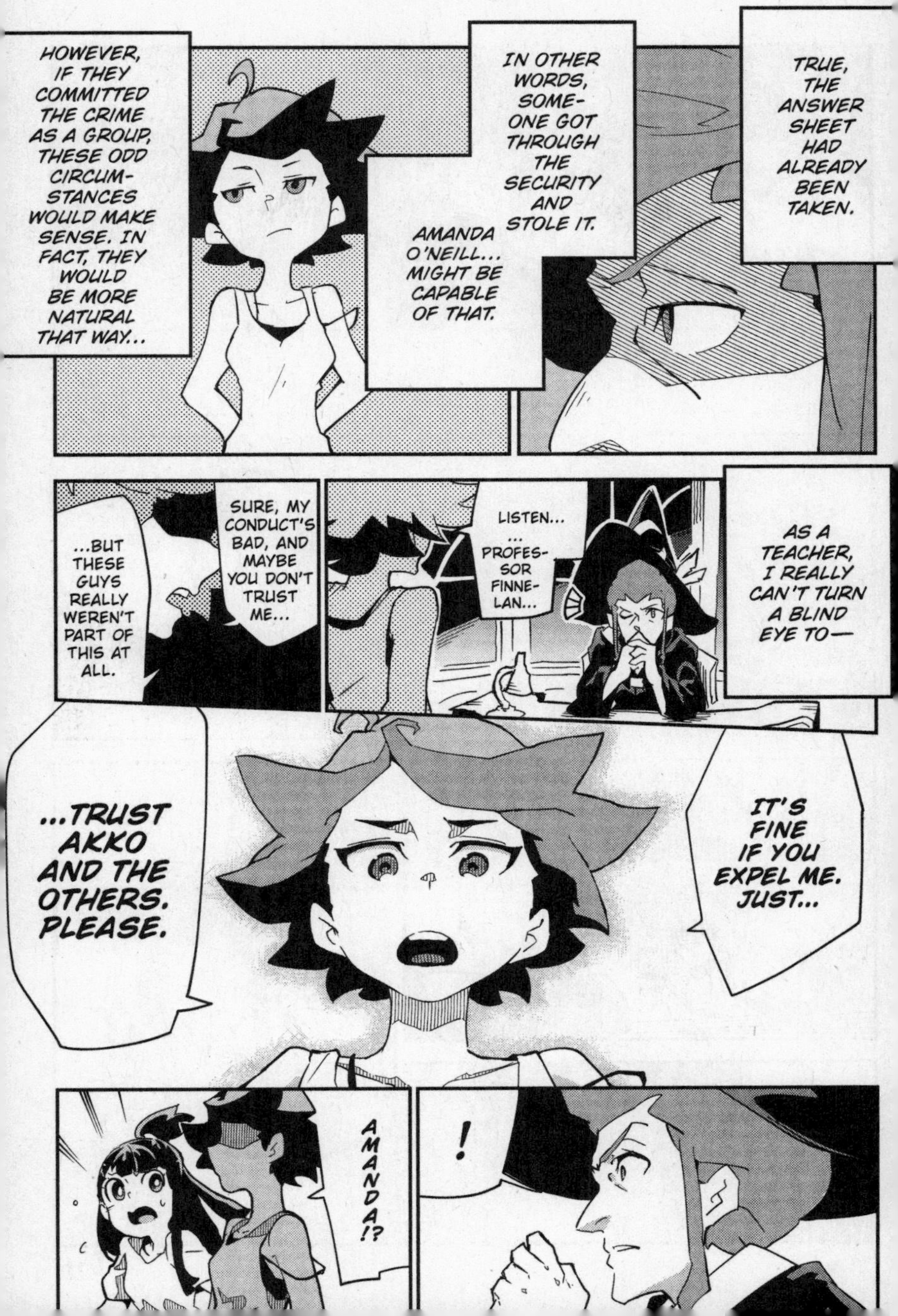
TRUE, THE ANSWER SHEET HAD ALREADY BEEN TAKEN.
IN OTHER WORDS, SOMEONE GOT THROUGH THE SECURITY AND STOLE IT.
AMANDA O'NEILL... MIGHT BE CAPABLE OF THAT.
HOWEVER, IF THEY COMMITTED THE CRIME AS A GROUP, THESE ODD CIRCUMSTANCES WOULD MAKE SENSE. IN FACT, THEY WOULD BE MORE NATURAL THAT WAY...
AS A TEACHER, I REALLY CAN'T TURN A BLIND EYE TO—
LISTEN... ... PROFESSOR FINNELAN...
SURE, MY CONDUCT'S BAD, AND MAYBE YOU DON'T TRUST ME...
...BUT THESE GUYS REALLY WEREN'T PART OF THIS AT ALL.
IT'S FINE IF YOU EXPEL ME. JUST...
...TRUST AKKO AND THE OTHERS. PLEASE.
!
AMANDA!?

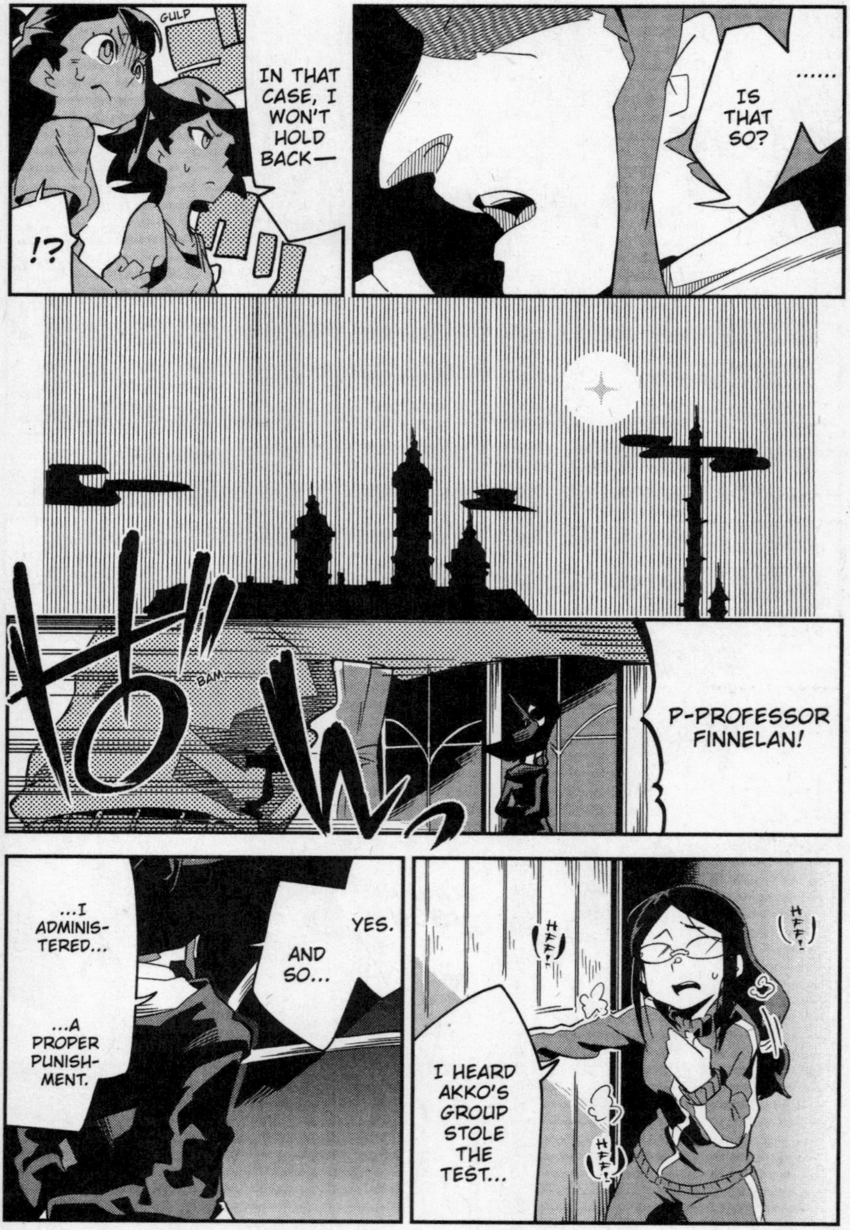
......
IS THAT SO?
IN THAT CASE, I WON'T HOLD BACK—
GULP
!?
P-PROFESSOR FINNELAN!
BAM
HFF!
HFF!
I HEARD AKKO'S GROUP STOLE THE TEST...
HFF!
YES.
AND SO...
...I ADMINISTERED...
...A PROPER PUNISHMENT.

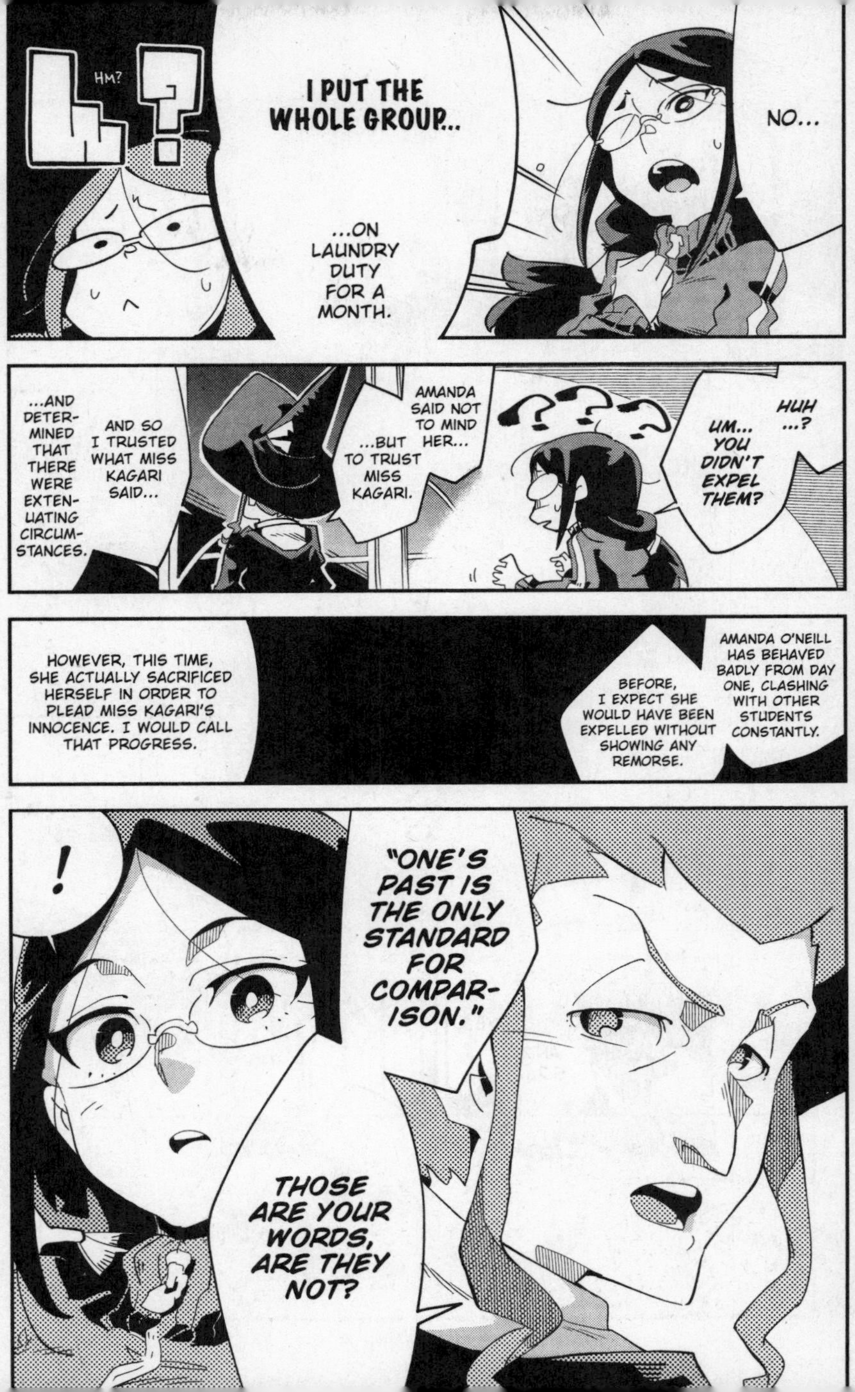

NO...
I PUT THE WHOLE GROUP...
...ON LAUNDRY DUTY FOR A MONTH.
HM?
HUH ...?
UM... YOU DIDN'T EXPEL THEM?
AMANDA SAID NOT TO MIND HER...
...BUT TO TRUST MISS KAGARI.
AND SO I TRUSTED WHAT MISS KAGARI SAID...
...AND DETERMINED THAT THERE WERE EXTENUATING CIRCUMSTANCES.
AMANDA O'NEILL HAS BEHAVED BADLY FROM DAY ONE, CLASHING WITH OTHER STUDENTS CONSTANTLY.
BEFORE, I EXPECT SHE WOULD HAVE BEEN EXPELLED WITHOUT SHOWING ANY REMORSE.
HOWEVER, THIS TIME, SHE ACTUALLY SACRIFICED HERSELF IN ORDER TO PLEAD MISS KAGARI'S INNOCENCE. I WOULD CALL THAT PROGRESS.
"ONE'S PAST IS THE ONLY STANDARD FOR COMPARISON."
THOSE ARE YOUR WORDS, ARE THEY NOT?
!

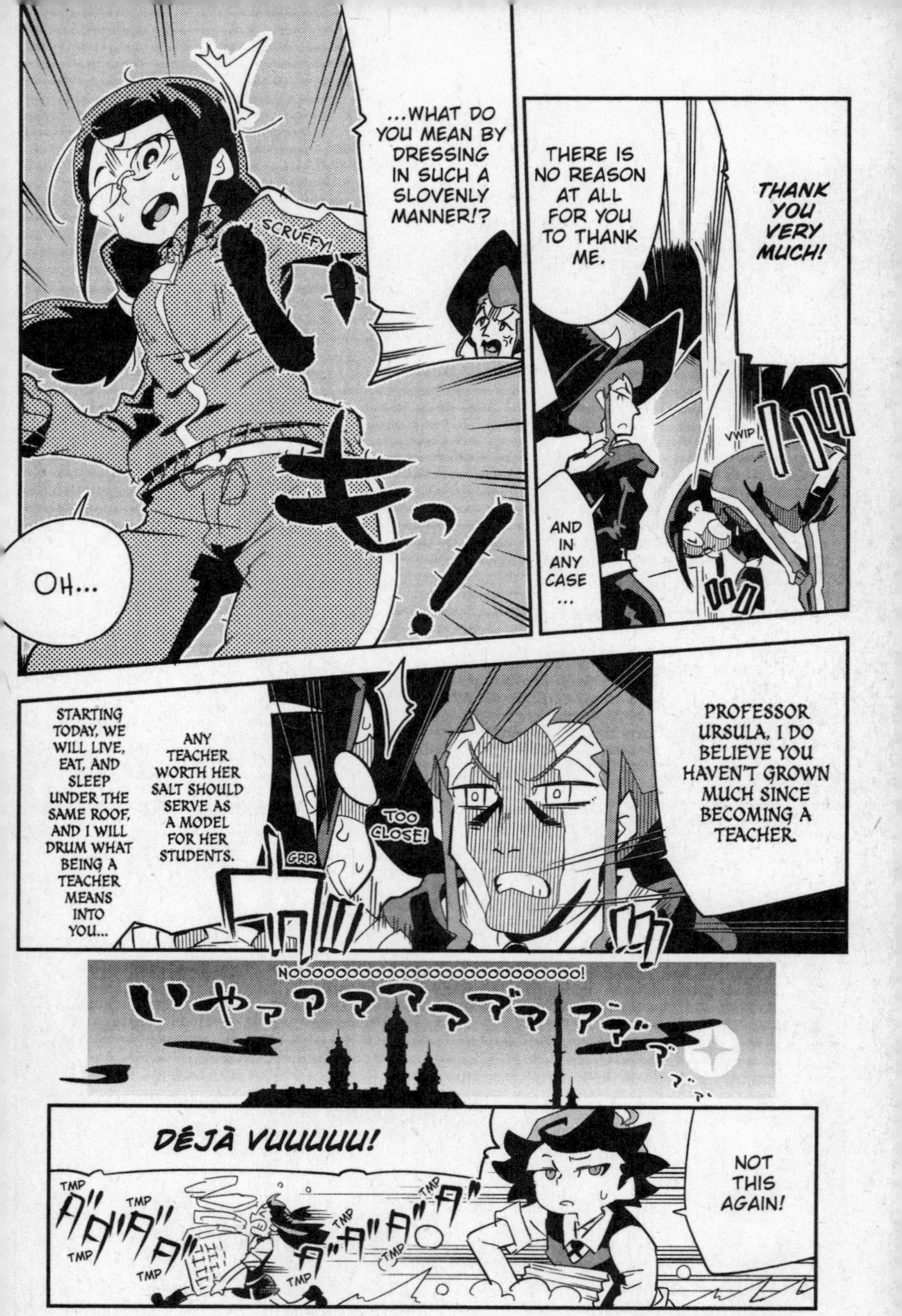
THANK YOU VERY MUCH!
THERE IS NO REASON AT ALL FOR YOU TO THANK ME.
VWIP
AND IN ANY CASE ...
...WHAT DO YOU MEAN BY DRESSING IN SUCH A SLOVENLY MANNER!?
SCRUFFY!
もっ!
OH...
PROFESSOR URSULA, I DO BELIEVE YOU HAVEN'T GROWN MUCH SINCE BECOMING A TEACHER.
TOO CLOSE!
GRR
ANY TEACHER WORTH HER SALT SHOULD SERVE AS A MODEL FOR HER STUDENTS.
STARTING TODAY, WE WILL LIVE, EAT, AND SLEEP UNDER THE SAME ROOF, AND I WILL DRUM WHAT BEING A TEACHER MEANS INTO YOU...
NOOOOOOOOOOOOOOOOOOOOOOOOOOO!
NOT THIS AGAIN!
DÉJÀ VUUUUUU!
TMP
TMP
TMP
TMP
TMP
TMP
TMP
TMP

LITTLE WITCH ACADEMIA ② ......THE END

Little
Witch
Academia

BONUS MANGA

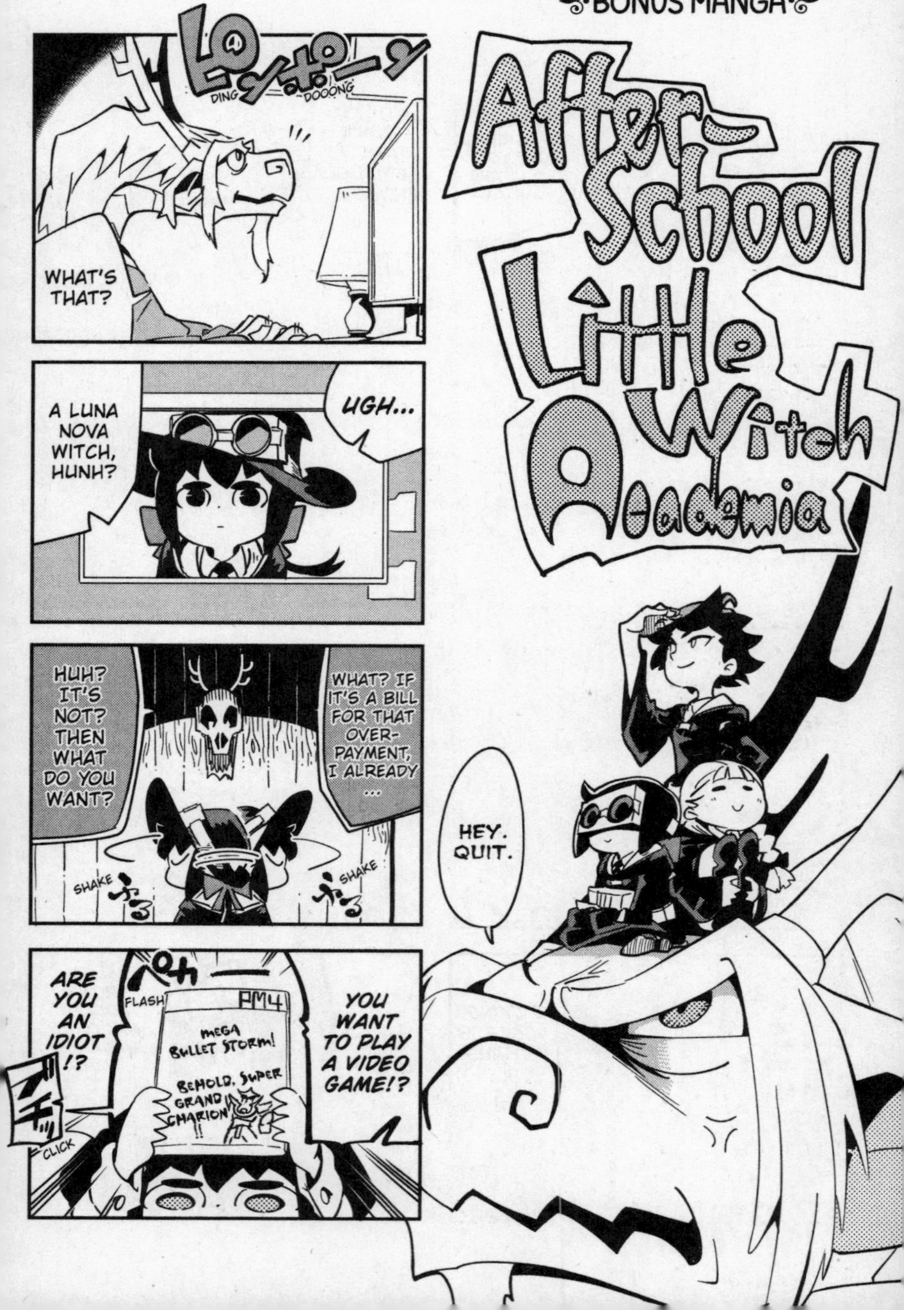
After School Little Witch Academia
HEY. QUIT.
DING DOOONG
WHAT'S THAT?
UGH...
A LUNA NOVA WITCH, HUNH?
WHAT? IF IT'S A BILL FOR THAT OVER-PAYMENT, I ALREADY...
HUH? IT'S NOT? THEN WHAT DO YOU WANT?
SHAKE
SHAKE
YOU WANT TO PLAY A VIDEO GAME!?
PM4
MEGA BULLET STORM!
BEHOLD, SUPER GRAND CHARION!!
FLASH
ARE YOU AN IDIOT!?
CLICK

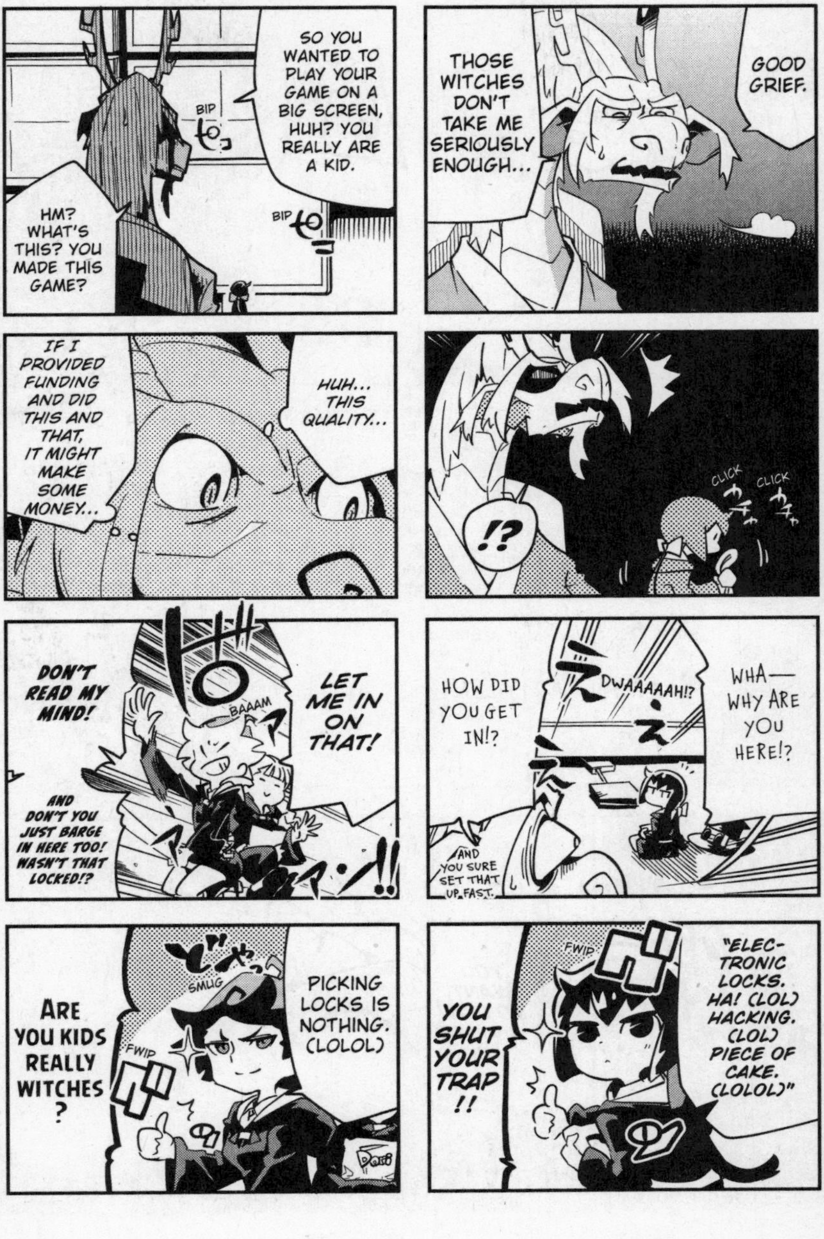
GOOD GRIEF.
THOSE WITCHES DON'T TAKE ME SERIOUSLY ENOUGH...
SO YOU WANTED TO PLAY YOUR GAME ON A BIG SCREEN, HUH? YOU REALLY ARE A KID.
BIP
BIP
HM? WHAT'S THIS? YOU MADE THIS GAME?
!?
CLICK
CLICK
HUH... THIS QUALITY...
IF I PROVIDED FUNDING AND DID THIS AND THAT, IT MIGHT MAKE SOME MONEY...
WHA— WHY ARE YOU HERE!?
DWAAAAAH!?
HOW DID YOU GET IN!?
AND YOU SURE SET THAT UP FAST.
LET ME IN ON THAT!
BAAAM
DON'T READ MY MIND!
AND DON'T YOU JUST BARGE IN HERE TOO! WASN'T THAT LOCKED!?
"ELEC-TRONIC LOCKS. HA! (LOL) HACKING. (LOL) PIECE OF CAKE. (LOLOL)"
FWIP
YOU SHUT YOUR TRAP!!
PICKING LOCKS IS NOTHING. (LOLOL)
SMUG
ARE YOU KIDS REALLY WITCHES?
FWIP

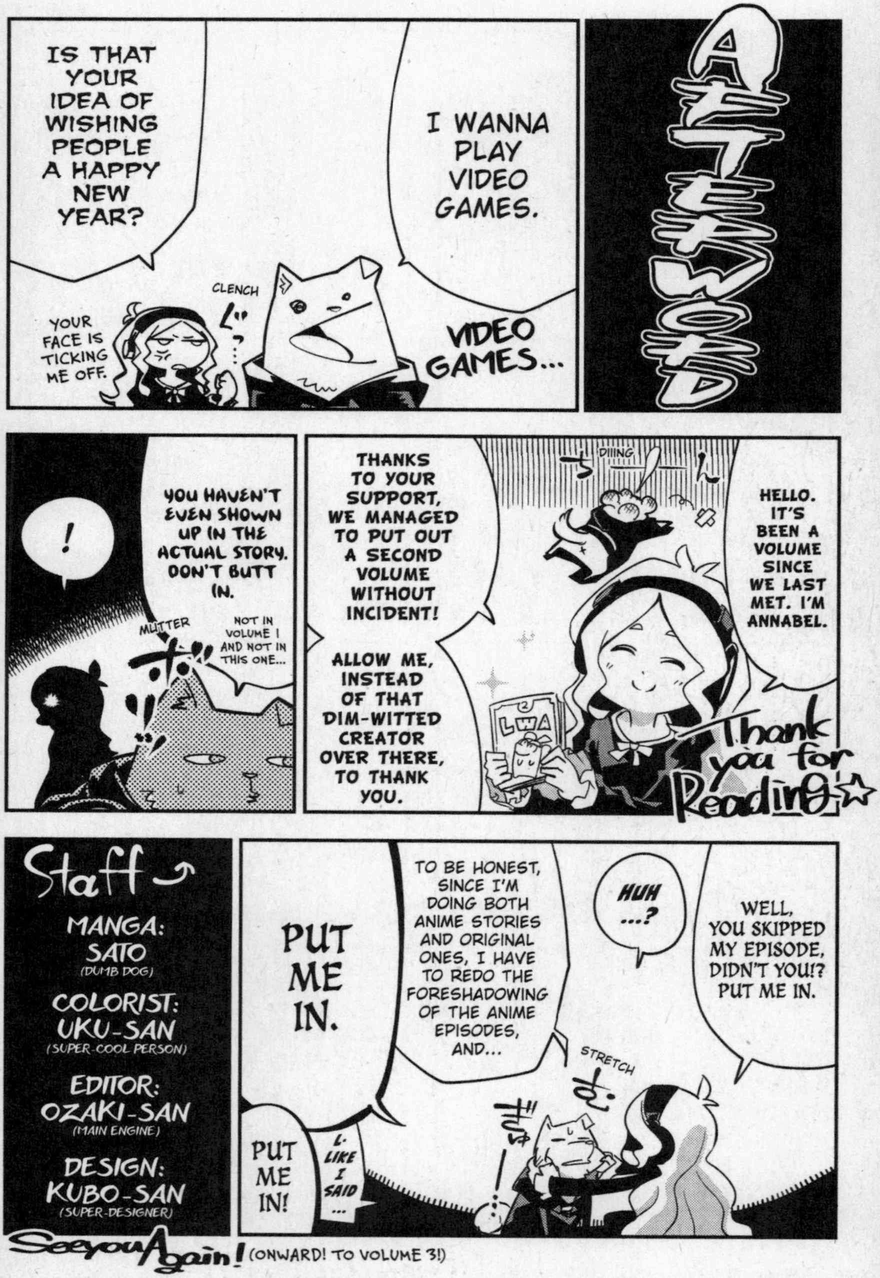
AFTERWORD
I WANNA PLAY VIDEO GAMES.
IS THAT YOUR IDEA OF WISHING PEOPLE A HAPPY NEW YEAR?
CLENCH
VIDEO GAMES...
YOUR FACE IS TICKING ME OFF.
Thank you for Reading☆
DIIING
HELLO. IT'S BEEN A VOLUME SINCE WE LAST MET. I'M ANNABEL.
THANKS TO YOUR SUPPORT, WE MANAGED TO PUT OUT A SECOND VOLUME WITHOUT INCIDENT!
ALLOW ME, INSTEAD OF THAT DIM-WITTED CREATOR OVER THERE, TO THANK YOU.
LWA
YOU HAVEN'T EVEN SHOWN UP IN THE ACTUAL STORY. DON'T BUTT IN.
!
NOT IN VOLUME 1 AND NOT IN THIS ONE...
MUTTER
WELL, YOU SKIPPED MY EPISODE, DIDN'T YOU!? PUT ME IN.
HUH ...?
TO BE HONEST, SINCE I'M DOING BOTH ANIME STORIES AND ORIGINAL ONES, I HAVE TO REDO THE FORESHADOWING OF THE ANIME EPISODES, AND...
PUT ME IN.
STRETCH
L-LIKE I SAID...
PUT ME IN!
Staff
MANGA: SATO (DUMB DOG)
COLORIST: UKU-SAN (SUPER-COOL PERSON)
EDITOR: OZAKI-SAN (MAIN ENGINE)
DESIGN: KUBO-SAN (SUPER-DESIGNER)
See you Again! (ONWARD! TO VOLUME 3!)

Little
Witch
Academia

Little Witch Academia

2

Original Story: TRIGGER / YOH YOSHINARI
Art: KEISUKE SATO

Translation: TAYLOR ENGEL ✦ Lettering: TAKESHI KAMURA

Little Witch Academia Volume 2
©2018 TRIGGER / Yoh Yoshinari / "Little Witch Academia" Committee
©Keisuke SATO 2018
First published in Japan in 2018 by KADOKAWA CORPORATION, Tokyo.
English translation rights arranged with KADOKAWA CORPORATION, Tokyo through TUTTLE-MORI AGENCY, INC., Tokyo.

English translation © 2018 by Yen Press, LLC

JY
1290 Avenue of the Americas
New York, NY 10104

Visit us at yenpress.com ✦ facebook.com/yenpress ✦ twitter.com/yenpress ✦ yenpress.tumblr.com ✦ instagram.com/yenpress

First JY Edition: November 2018

JY is an imprint of Yen Press, LLC.
The JY name and logo are trademarks of Yen Press, LLC.

Library of Congress Control Number: 2018935620

ISBNs: 978-1-9753-2810-8 (paperback)
978-1-9753-2853-5 (ebook)

10 9 8 7 6 5 4 3 2 1

WOR

Printed in the United States of America